Nina Milne has always d... Mills & Boon—ever sinc... her mother's stacks of Mills & Boon romances ... a child. On her way to this dream Nina acquired an English degree, a hero of her own, three gorgeous children and—somehow!—an accountancy qualification. She lives in Brighton and has filled her house with books—her very own *real* library.

Rachael Stewart adores conjuring up stories, from heartwarmingly romantic to wildly erotic. She's been writing since she could put pen to paper—as the stacks of scrawled-on pages in her loft will attest to. A Welsh lass at heart, she now lives in Yorkshire, with her very own hero and three awesome kids—and if she's not tapping out a story she's wrapped up in one or enjoying the great outdoors. Reach her on Facebook, Twitter @rach_b52, or at rachaelstewartauthor.com.

SNOWBOUND REUNION IN JAPAN

NINA MILNE

MY UNEXPECTED CHRISTMAS WEDDING

RACHAEL STEWART

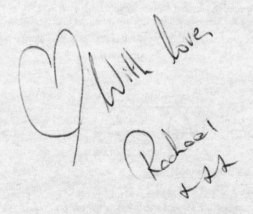

With love,

Rachael x x

MILLS & BOON

First published in Great Britain 2023
by Mills & Boon, an imprint of HarperCollins*Publishers* Ltd,
1 London Bridge Street, London, SE1 9GF

www.harpercollins.co.uk

HarperCollins*Publishers*, Macken House, 39/40 Mayor Street Upper, Dublin 1, D01 C9W8, Ireland

Snowbound Reunion in Japan © 2023 Harlequin Enterprises ULC

Special thanks and acknowledgement are given to
Nina Milne for her contribution to The Christmas Pact miniseries.

My Unexpected Christmas Wedding © 2023 Rachael Stewart

ISBN: 978-0-263-30656-9

11/23

This book is produced from independently certified FSC™ paper to ensure responsible forest management.
For more information visit: www.harpercollins.co.uk/green.

Printed and Bound in the UK using 100% Renewable Electricity at CPI Group (UK) Ltd, Croydon, CR0 4YY

SNOWBOUND REUNION IN JAPAN

NINA MILNE

MILLS & BOON

To Kenneth Milne, my father-in-law.

PROLOGUE

THEA GLANCED AT her watch and quickened her foot-steps; she didn't want to be late, especially as her family would ask why, and Thea really didn't want to tell them she'd been in the office. On a Sunday morning. Again.

She knew her mum, her dad and both her sisters, older sister Sienna and younger sister Eliza, all worried about how hard Thea worked.

She sighed. She wished they would get it—she *wanted* to work, *needed* to work, because the prospect of partnership was so tantalisingly close. Her jaw clenched in determination; she would achieve her ambition, and once she'd attained partnership she'd be off on to the next rung, climbing higher and higher. And if she smashed through a few glass ceilings on the way all the better.

She approached the Chiswick pub overlooking the Thames where they were meeting for Sunday lunch, a traditional venue for family get-togethers, usually for some occasion, a birthday or a celebration. But today her mum had called and suggested an impromptu meal.

Thea felt a welcome sense of familiarity as she entered the pub, with its polished wooden tables, the staff carrying loaded plates, the tantalising smell of food and its view of the river with boats moored by the side.

Tradition was important to the Kendalls. It bonded them together. Thea wondered if it was too early to bring up the subject of Christmas. Not that any planning was necessary; Christmas was the most cherished Kendall tradition of all.

She spotted her family and waved, heading over with a broad smile.

'Good day at the office?' Eliza greeted her with a cheeky grin.

'No comment,' Thea quipped back, as she blew everyone a kiss and sat down.

'Excellent. Now you're here, let's order,' her mum said, and Thea glanced at her in surprise.

Lila Kendall was usually happy to have a catch-up and linger over her food and drink choices. Even at a Sunday lunch there would normally be some discussion over which roast to go for, whether to try the vegetarian option, whether to have a glass of wine or a soft drink.

But clearly not today.

In record time the family were sitting with their plates in front of them and Thea was sure her mum was avoiding everyone's eye, her gaze fixed on her food or occasionally flickering to her unusually quiet father.

Thea helped herself to extra gravy and decided to offer a cheerful conversational topic. 'This is lovely. It's making me think about Christmas dinner, even if it's only October.'

She gave a small happy sigh as she pictured the turkey with all the trimmings, the crackers, the massive box of chocolates Sienna always brought, and the amicable bickering over the last favourite, sitting in their Christmas pyjamas watching Christmas movies on the massive overstuffed sofa in her parents' living room.

'Actually…' her mum said.

The word fell heavy as a stone and Thea felt a sudden sense of foreboding.

Lila trailed off and looked at her husband, then resumed again.

'There's something we want to tell you.'

The sense of foreboding deepened.

'We want to do something different this Christmas.'

There was a beat of confused silence before Eliza summed up what they were all thinking as she stuttered, 'Wh…what?'

'Like your mum said,' her dad started, 'we've decided to do something different for Christmas. We've booked a month-long cruise!'

The words came out in a rush and he looked at his wife. They exchanged a quick smile that spoke of relief that they'd got the words out, imparted their news.

The statement seemed to reverberate around the table as Thea struggled to actually absorb its meaning, aware of a childish urge to cover her ears. Now silence stretched, and she was aware of how they must look, a frozen tableau of shock, with her sisters clearly as stunned as she was as they stared at their parents.

Until finally Sienna pushed her chair backwards, almost as if she were going to leave, flee the scene. 'I should have known there was an ulterior motive for this spontaneous lunch,' she muttered.

But Thea couldn't see how anyone could have predicted this.

Her mum took a deep breath. 'It's our fortieth wedding anniversary this year. We wanted to do something just for ourselves.' Her voice held a near plea. 'You have your own lives, your own circles of friends. I thought you might appreciate the chance to do something different.'

Thea had absolutely no idea why her mum would think anything of the sort. This was *Christmas*. She could see a similar sense of disbelief and bewilderment on her siblings' faces, knew that for all three of them Christmas was all about coming home, being together. It offered comfort and certainty and happiness. Her parents must know that.

'Next you're going to tell us you've sold the family house,' she said. She knew she sounded sulky but she couldn't help it. It might be ridiculous, but she felt betrayed and bereft. She loved their traditional Kendall Christmas and she'd thought her parents did too.

Her dad sighed, exchanged a glance with his wife. 'Why would we do that?'

Sienna leant forward. 'Well, why would you do *this*?'

It was a question that held all the outrage that Thea felt too, and yet it was a good question—one that stopped Thea in her tracks.

Why *would* her parents do this? Her parents were the most amazing people Thea knew, especially her mother. All evidence showed that her mum put her family first, she always had, and Thea felt a familiar sense of admiration when she recalled exactly how true that was.

When Eliza had been diagnosed with acute myeloid leukaemia aged six it had, of course, impacted on all of them. Thea could still feel the fear, the terror, that had gripped her eleven-year-old self. But it had been their mum who had completely changed her life from thereon in, had given up her career plans and ambitions and centred her life around her youngest daughter.

Because although Eliza had gone into remission, the illness had returned when she was a teenager and there had been other illnesses in between. And always, always, the overhanging shadow of worry.

Yet thanks to her parents the Kendalls had always been a happy family—a family who pulled together, a family who loved spending time together, especially at Christmas. And so much of that was down to her mum. Again, Thea felt admiration, but as always it was tinged with a sense of her own inadequacy.

Because she knew she could never be like her mum, could never sacrifice so much and never show even a smidgeon of resentment. Still be calm and loving and the rock they all depended on, despite her whole life being upended by Eliza's illness. Thea knew she could never be that selfless, could never risk not being a good enough parent.

For a second sadness touched her, even though she knew her decision to be the right one—she *knew* it wasn't possible to have it all. So motherhood was not for her. Her career was too important and she'd invested too much in it.

But her mother wasn't like Thea, and she would know how important Christmas was to her daughters. So what was going on?

Thea blinked, realising she'd been so caught up in her thoughts she'd missed the ensuing conversation.

She caught the tail end of her mother's words to Eliza. 'It's like a ton weight from all of our shoulders.'

She knew her mother was reminding them of their massive relief that Eliza had had the all-clear, had been given her final discharge from the hospital.

Thea saw emotion skitter across Eliza's face and then, 'It sounds wonderful,' Eliza said.

'Really?' their mum asked.

Thea could hear the mixture of disbelief and hope in her voice and the penny dropped. Her parents were free—free from anxiety and worry—and they wanted to celebrate forty years of marriage alone.

She nodded, and knew her sisters had got it too as Sienna chipped in, 'Of course I understand.'

Eliza launched into all the reasons why of course their parents must go. Then they turned to looked at Thea, and gamely she did her bit, because her parents deserved this.

'Absolutely you must go,' she said firmly, as Eliza rose to her feet and went to hug her parents before turning to her sisters.

'Sienna, Thea, come and help me get another round of drinks.'

Thea glanced at her little sister, heard the underlying quaver in her voice and got to her feet, waiting as Sienna followed suit and headed after Eliza. Then she flashed her best, most reassuring smile at her parents. 'Truly,' she said. 'We all get it. I think the cruise is a wonderful idea too.'

Once the sisters were out of their parents' sight, Eliza pulled them down onto some chairs at another table, Sienna on one side of her, Thea the other. Thea felt a rush of love for her little sister, and could only imagine how she must be feeling.

'You OK?' she asked her.

In an almost synchronised movement she and Sienna both reached out to cover their sister's hand, and Thea knew Sienna felt the same protective urge she did. She suspected it would take more than an all-clear to remove that instinct. But right now they were all in the same boat, adrift on an unfamiliar sea where Christmas was no longer a given.

'I can't believe this,' she said.

'We have to let them go,' Eliza said, her voice full of determination.

Sienna sighed. 'I just don't understand… This seems to have come out of nowhere.'

And in that instant Thea knew that this was even worse for Sienna than it was for her—Sienna was coming to terms with so much this year, and needed the security blanket of a traditional Christmas.

Eliza removed her hands in a gentle movement. 'It's time. They've spent years worrying about me. You all have. They deserve this break, a chance to concentrate on themselves again.'

Thea knew Eliza was completely right.

Sienna nodded. 'Agreed. But is it wrong that I'm an adult but still love going to our parents' house for Christmas to spend time with my family?'

'Me too,' said Thea.

'We all do,' said Eliza. 'But this year it has to be different.'

Thea gave a small groan as different scenarios chased through her mind. Should the three of them still get together in the Kendall family home? Or go and have a meal in a restaurant? Perhaps they could book a hotel somewhere? Every idea felt wrong.

'What will we do instead?'

She saw Eliza's eyes light up. 'We should do something different too,' she said. 'Let's make a pact.'

Sienna's brow furrowed. 'A pact? We haven't done that since we were teenagers.'

Thea laughed, relieved to have a memory to look back on. 'And that leave-the-windows-open pact so that we could sneak in and out didn't exactly work.' She pushed up the sleeve of her jumper and looked ruefully at the small scar on her elbow. 'I have the scar to prove it.'

Eliza grinned, but wasn't to be distracted. 'This will be our Christmas pact. To have a Christmas adventure of our own. I think we should all step outside our comfort zones and each go away for Christmas.'

'By ourselves?' Sienna choked out. 'Even you?'

'Yes, even you, Eliza?' Thea asked, and then wished the words back as she saw the stubborn tilt to Eliza's chin.

Sympathy touched her. How must it feel to always

be cossetted and protected? At Eliza's age Thea had already finished uni and had been on the first rung of her career ladder. She had been on her way to success and her first promotion, a big step on her way to the partnership that she craved…that she was now so close to. If she stayed focused, with her eye on the prize, as she knew so well how to do, she knew it was within reach.

'Especially me,' Eliza said. 'Our Christmas pact will be that we each go away for two weeks—one before and one during Christmas. We will choose for each other, and do it in secret. Each destination will be a complete surprise. We'll pack each other's cases, and only find out our destination when we arrive at the airport.'

Eliza sounded very sure of her plan, although Thea was pretty sure it could only just have occurred to her.

'She's lost it,' said Thea, shaking her head and smiling at Sienna, sure that her sister would agree it was a terrible idea. Christmas alone? Plus, it was completely impractical—no way could Thea take a two-week holiday from work. The idea was preposterous.

'She has,' agreed Sienna. 'But it's not the worst idea I've heard.'

'Huh?' Thea gazed open-mouthed at her older sister.

'I like the idea that we will challenge ourselves,' Sienna said.

'It could be brilliant,' Eliza said.

And, seeing how vital, how excited Eliza looked, Thea swallowed her protests. She understood that her baby sister wanted to stretch her fledgling wings.

Then, her sister's face fell. 'Oh, but how will I pay?'

Thea glanced at Sienna. That was an easy fix—both

of them earned more than enough to cover this idea, however hare-brained it was.

'We can cover it,' she said.

'But that's not fair.'

Thea could see the frustration on Eliza's face.

'It's just how it is. No argument. This is a brilliant idea and it's happening.'

Eliza hesitated, and then gave a massive smile and a small nod that conveyed more than words could.

'I like it that we get to pick for each other,' said Thea.

At least she could find something positive to say. Because she and Sienna could make sure that their sister went somewhere safe. In fact, Thea already had an idea. And she and Eliza could pick somewhere amazing for Sienna to go, somewhere her sister could truly relax and escape from the year she'd had.

'So we're really going to do this?' asked Eliza.

Sienna nodded. 'We're doing it,' she said confidently. 'Right, Thea?'

Thea nodded too, and laughed, hoping it didn't sound too fake. 'What have I just let myself in for?' she asked.

She hoped she sounded light-hearted even as she wondered exactly that. But surely there would be loopholes. At least the pact didn't mean she had to promise not to work at all. Maybe her sisters would pick somewhere in Europe, somewhere from where she could pop across to London in an emergency, or for a sneaky meeting.

Sienna held out one fist, her knuckles facing her sisters. 'To the Christmas pact.'

'To the Christmas pact!' Thea and Eliza replied, bumping their fists against Sienna's.

CHAPTER ONE

THEA OPENED HER EYES and blinked, her dream dissipating into the unfamiliar surroundings.

The image of a massive Christmas tree faded, along with the scent of pine and the vision of her mother looking down from atop the ladder after positioning the Christmas star so that it nestled among the top branches to her satisfaction.

Thea's sleep-fogged brain tried to work out where on earth she was.

The ceiling was the wrong shade…and surely too far away. The mattress underneath her spine was firmer than she was used to. Clearly she wasn't in her king-sized bed in her London flat.

Then memory started to unfurl. She was sleeping on a futon, unrolled onto *tatami* mats, in a *ryokan*—a hotel at a ski resort in Japan.

Because of the Christmas pact.

Her sisters had not chosen Europe. They had chosen Japan. A twelve-hour flight from London, so there would be no chance of any sneaky work meetings. The only saving grace was the fact that she was able to work remotely, and could still attend meetings via video conference. Something she was sure her sisters wouldn't be surprised by.

She did make sure that she spent part of each day doing something 'holiday-like', and so far, a week into her adventure, she was loving the whole experience. But she couldn't afford to let up. She needed to go the extra mile and put in the work.

Standing, she stretched, and as she had every morning she looked round the room in appreciation at its functionality and the beauty of the understated.

Fifteen minutes later she'd rolled up the futon and put it into a wardrobe with pretty painted sliding doors called *fusuma*, and was seated on the floor cross-legged in front of the low table, laptop open in front of her.

She was ready for her morning routine: check her emails, deal with everything urgent, make changes to her work diary, catch up on the news, make sure she knew what was happening in the world.

Because, in order to continue her climb up the professional ladder, she needed to offer more than just one of the sharpest legal minds in the business. Clients and bosses liked people who could impress with legal expertise *and* a whole lot of social flair and savvy. So Thea made sure she researched, prepared, kept up to date and up to the mark.

Thea Kendall was going to fly high. She'd known that from the moment she'd been accepted at Cambridge University to study law.

The moment was etched on her mind, with the words of the acceptance jumping off the page, the sense of a new beginning, a move away from home—somewhere she would be Thea Kendall, not Sienna's younger sister or Eliza's older one. Of course she'd always be there for her family, would come back to help as needed, and of course she'd still be supportive of Eliza. But she'd also be on the first step towards the career ladder she was determined to climb.

And not just her.

Sitting in the cool, minimalist room she let an image come into her head. Zayne Wood, the boy next door, a part of her childhood as familiar as the massive over-stuffed sofa in her parents' lounge, the boy who'd been her friend, who she'd climbed trees with, built dens with, learnt to ride a bike with, walked to school with.

And the boy she'd shared that awkward first kiss with. Her decision.

'I think we should kiss. A real one. That way we'll know what we're doing when it counts.'

'Gee, thanks,' he'd said, an irrepressible grin on his face.

Thea blinked, closed the memory down. After all, with hindsight the kiss had been a mistake—had changed their dynamic, changed everything. Or maybe change would have come anyway, with puberty and age and their separate ambitions.

Either way, there was little point thinking of Zayne now. Because at the same time she'd got her acceptance for Cambridge, he'd got his for MIT, and they'd gone their separate ways. Now Zayne was a multi-millionaire IT wizard. And Thea was on her way to a partnership in a top five London law firm. One of the so-called 'magic circle'.

She scrolled through her emails, saw a message from her boss.

Hey, Thea,
Riika Itawa is thinking of moving law firms for Itawa's London HQ. She's in Tokyo on business and she loves to ski. Could you take her out on the slopes, talk to her, pitch for her business? If you win it she's your client. Competition is circling.

She can meet December twenty-fourth. Please confirm direct with her. Details below.

Riika Itawa. Be still her heart. If she could win Itawa's business, the kudos she would gain would be substantial—would boost her chances of making partner tenfold.

So what did she need to do?

First up she'd get herself onto the slopes, make sure she could manage the intermediate runs. So far, she'd only tried out the beginners' slopes. Breakfast would have to wait. She'd grab an energy bar en route.

And then she'd need to research, research, research. Get her pitch honed and sharp and ready.

An hour later she alighted from the ski lift and felt a sudden momentary qualm, one she quelled as irrational. She'd mastered the easier slopes in the last couple of days, completing a few runs every morning. Her confidence was returning, the techniques she'd learnt and practised in previous years coming back to her with an exhilarating adrenalin as she'd twisted and turned.

So there was no reason why the more difficult slopes should present any problem. She'd mastered this level years ago, when she and Ian had gone skiing twice a year. Two brief breaks...holidays taken with other like-minded professional couples. Only gradually those couples had fallen by the wayside as more of their circle had settled down, had children and...

And nothing. Ian was over—lesson learnt. Now it was time for her to manoeuvre down a harder slope, so that in a few days she could ski with ease and grace down these runs with Riika Itawa, in a demonstration of competence and flair to mirror what she would promise professionally.

As she glided and swooped down the powdered snow, with the crisp mountain breeze on her face, Thea let her mind dwell on the idea of winning the business not simply for the prestige, but for the interest, the new things she would learn, the experience she would gain. Because for Thea it wasn't only about ambition. She did love her job. The law fascinated her. She found its twists and turns as exhilarating as those she executed on the ski slopes.

Still caught up in thoughts of the Itawa business empire, she saw a fraction of a second too late that the person who had been way in front of her the whole way down had slowed dramatically. She was aware that she had perhaps let herself get too close, and now would need to swerve out of the way. But there was

someone coming down to her right…a small figure—
a child, in fact.

So now what?

Her choices seemed limited. If she had to crash
into someone, an adult was preferable to a child, so
she veered towards the figure, frantically executing
an emergency hockey stop, but still unable to prevent
the collision.

She felt the *oomph* as she crashed into the other
skier.

She realised that he'd braced himself for impact,
and was aware of an impression of solidity as he back-
stepped but remained upright, taking her weight and
somehow steadying her. And then they stood facing
each other.

'Are you OK?'

They both spoke at once.

Thea thought for a second, making sure that nothing hurt. Then, 'I'm good. You?'

'Yup. All in one piece. We'd better get out of the
way of anyone else.'

Thea nodded, even as the potential legal implications
of the collision ran through her brain. It was unlikely
to be a problem, as neither was hurt, but what if this
stranger developed an injury? Liability, fault… She was
the uphill skier—but had he been standing in a way
that obstructed the path? Had he even been in her view.

Time to get to the bottom of the run safely and then
assess.

She checked for safety and pushed off, focused completely on making sure that she demonstrated how good

she actually was. She came to a stop at the bottom of the run and her fellow skier came to a skilful stop beside her, before pulling off his mask and goggles.

Thea stared in complete shock, her mouth opening and closing as she hurriedly pulled off her own.

'Zayne?' she said.

He stared at her in equal shock.

'Thea?'

CHAPTER TWO

FOR THE FIRST TIME in a very long time Zayne was bereft of speech, even as his brain analysed the probability of this happening. The chances were infinitesimal, and for a daft moment the word *fate* crossed his mind.

God. He'd been listening to his mother too much.

'Ay, Zayne. You need to stop running around with all these different women. You'll find the right one—it will be fate. Just like your father and me.'

Problem was, Zayne wasn't sure he wanted what his parents had had. Arjun and Samira Wood had been happy, truly happy but a price had been paid. Arjun Wood had collapsed with a heart attack when Zayne was twenty, in his second year at MIT, and Samira had been devastated, torn apart by grief and loss…a grief she had taken years to recover from.

Her husband had been her world. Zayne wasn't sure if that was what he wanted—the idea of being that important to someone, of letting anyone be that important to him. It didn't make sense.

And then there had been his parents' love for him, their child. They had both sacrificed so much for him, worked every possible hour, scrimped and saved so he could have everything in life. If his dad had worked less hard, been less stressed, wanted less for Zayne, would he have lived longer? Had a better life?

Questions Zayne had asked himself repeatedly over the years, wishing that he'd called a halt, could have seen what fate had in store for his dad.

Not that fate should even be a factor. After all Zayne was a tech whiz, a man who had made his fortune from coding and programming formulae and rules.

Anyhow, right now, whatever had brought him and Thea together, here they were.

'Thea?' he repeated. 'Is that really you?' Then, 'Of all the mountains, in all the ski resorts, in all the countries, in all the world...'

It was an impression to be proud of, and as he launched into the famous paraphrase he was transported back to fifteen years ago. To the big, overstuffed cushion-strewn sofa in the Kendalls' house. Himself, Thea, Eliza and Lila Kendall sat watching old black and white movies.

Eliza had been complaining of tiredness and being under the weather. He'd seen the worry in her mum's face as Lila had tucked a blanket around her, been aware of that ever-present worry that Eliza's illness would return. But Eliza had never been one for self-pity or despair—none of the Kendalls had. When he'd done his best Humphrey Bogart impression it had made Eliza giggle, as Thea had teased him and Lila had appeared with a bowl of freshly buttered popcorn. He could almost taste it now, as Thea's face creased into a smile.

'You've improved,' she said, and there was an echo of that same teasing note.

And as he looked at her, his breath caught in his throat; shafts of sunlight glinted on the glossy chestnut hair visible under the woolly hat. Her eyes were the same. Perhaps a few more lines around them, but still that amazing colour that fluctuated from amber to green, depending on the light and her mood. There was the straight nose, the classic cheekbones, and then her lips, generous and soft.

And now another memory whammed out of nowhere. Of exactly how soft those lips were. His first kiss. Her first kiss. The nerves jangling inside him. The anticipation. The worry that he'd do something wrong, and then the reassurance that it didn't matter because this was Thea. Followed by the knowledge that, actually, it mattered all the more, because he wanted her first kiss to be memorable. The reminder that it was OK—this was a practice run. For both of them. Her idea. Her decision.

He could hear her teenage voice.

'I think we should kiss. A real one. That way we'll know what we're doing when it counts.'

'Gee thanks,' he'd said, *'Who are you getting the practice in for? Ben? Toby? They both really like you. Keep trying to bribe me to use my influence with you.'*

He'd refused, of course. Neither of them had been good enough for Thea.

She'd screwed her face up as she shook her head. *'Not interested. I don't have anyone in mind. I...'* She'd shrugged. *'I just like to be prepared.'*

Her voice had been serious.

'Fair enough. I get that.'

And he had. Like Thea, he'd been ambitious, focused and determined, and they'd both understood the importance of preparation.

'But,' he'd continued, *'this is a big deal. A first kiss. You sure you don't want to wait? For the right guy?'*

'You are the right guy.'

She'd seen his expression and laughed.

'I don't mean Mr Right. I mean you're who I want to share my first kiss with. Because I trust you.'

'Then...whenever you're ready,' he'd said.

'But only if you're sure. I mean, maybe you want to wait...want your first kiss to be with...someone special.'

'You are special,' he'd said, and his heart had gone pitter-pat in acknowledgement of the truth of his words. Until he'd reminded herself that this was Thea, his best friend, and this kiss was a practical idea, born of logic.

All those thoughts had jostled, and in an effort to drown them out he'd decided to get on with it.

They'd been in his room, his parents both at work. He'd leant forward and pressed his lips against hers, tasted mint, felt the firm yet soft texture of her lips. And in that instant he'd known they'd made a mistake, miscalculated. Because it hadn't about logic—it had been about something way more than that. Something he didn't understand, evoking feelings he hadn't been prepared for. Feelings that had churned inside and dizzied him as they'd kissed.

He'd known this would change things, and he hadn't wanted things to change. Not with Thea. But as they'd pulled away, stared at each wide-eyed, awkwardness had loomed, and he'd known something *had* changed. Because he'd wanted to kiss her again...wanted to do it better, do it right, kiss her without doubts, kiss her because she wanted him to for different reasons.

They'd stared at each and he'd seen flecks of green in her eyes, seen a spark, seen something that he hadn't known how to identify. He'd seen the pink flush on her cheeks and shock morph into wariness, and then she'd exhaled on a small sigh.

'Thank you, Zayne. That will take the pressure off both of us.'

In what way? he'd wanted to ask. *Because I set the bar so low anything will be an improvement? Was it OK? Did you feel as I felt?*

But he hadn't asked. He'd told himself that for Thea this was likely something she could tick off her list of things to achieve before she was sixteen. Milestone done.

But he'd been right—something had changed between them after that. There had been an underlay of awkwardness that had meant their old, easy camaraderie had seemed fake. And gradually, almost without them realising it, they'd seen less of each other, found excuses to study separately, not to walk to college together any more.

But that was then and this was now—that first kiss should be long forgotten. Or if not forgotten certainly not at the forefront of his brain, so vivid and real he was almost tempted to ask her if she remembered it too?

Really, Zayne? What had happened to the poised,

charming Zayne who had dated the most beautiful women in the world? Graced the red carpet with an award-winning actor? Clearly he'd been left behind in LA. And now, whilst he was revisiting memory lane, silence loomed.

A silence she broke. 'Zayne Wood. I really cannot believe it's you. In the flesh.'

She gulped slightly on the last word, and he'd have sworn that her gaze lingered on him, cast him a swift, assessing gaze. God, he hoped so, hoped this odd, unexpected reaction was a two-way street.

'It's definitely me. For real.' He held out a hand, pulled of his glove and prodded his palm with his finger. 'In the flesh.'

'I can't believe it. I mean, what are you doing here?'

If he were to be dramatic, he would tell her he was here to find himself. If he were to be truthful, he'd tell her he wasn't sure. That he was having some sort of existential crisis where his 'work hard, play hard' lifestyle no longer fitted.

But as he had no intention of being either dramatic or fully honest, he settled for, 'I was working in Tokyo and decided to take a bit of a break. A week turned into a few weeks and I'm still here.' He glanced around. 'Have you got time to go somewhere and catch up? It's been way too long.'

'Twelve years,' she said, and he wondered if he imagined the soupçon of hurt in her voice.

But that wasn't fair. He hadn't got in touch, but neither had she. When they'd said their goodbyes he'd sensed they'd both wanted a clean break—no ties other than familial. Their friendship had already been cooling off, and when he'd gone to MIT his parents had decided to move to the US with him.

'Then a coffee is long overdue. Plus, I'm starving, so how about some food as well?'

She hesitated, and then nodded. 'Sure. I'd like that. But I do need to get myself back on the slopes at some point today.'

'Is it your last day?' he asked.

'No. But I've got a work meeting here in a few days. I'm taking a prospective client out, so I need to make sure I'm familiar with the intermediate slopes. Imagine if I collide with someone when I'm with her. Though hopefully no one will be obstructing my path.'

He raised his eyebrows. 'Best if you make sure you keep an eye on where you're going.'

'I *was* keeping an eye and you know it. You were the one who—'

'Slowed down gradually when I became aware of a group of kids careening down, out of control.'

'A group? I saw *one* child.'

'Then you weren't looking,' he said.

'I—'

Zayne raised a hand and gave a sudden smile. 'OK. We're reverting to childhood. This sounds like an argument over who ate the last biscuit left in our den. How about we don't decide to prove who's right or wrong and just be pleased no one got hurt?'

She exhaled. 'You're right. I'm sorry, Zayne, and I'd love to catch up over coffee and some food. I'm tetchy because all I've had is an energy bar, and all I keep thinking of now is the breakfast I missed.'

'Then I know the perfect place to take you.'

'Great.' She glanced up at him. 'And, for the record, I did not eat that biscuit.'

'Neither did I.'

'I reckon we should blame Sienna. Eliza was probably too young.'

'Agreed.'

'Then lead the way.'

As they walked, for once Thea was oblivious to the picturesque scenery around her—the traditional architecture of the buildings, with their curved gable roofs topped with snow, the narrow cobbled streets lined with a hodgepodge of restaurants, souvenir shops and *onsens*, the public hot spring baths the village was renowned for.

Instead, with each step she tried to figure out how she was feeling. She wanted to bring her mind and her emotions to order. Right now, disbelief at the surrealness of the situation was uppermost.

She'd been tempted to actually prod his proffered hand to check that he was really real. But something had stopped her, and she knew what it was. In that first instant before her brain had fully recognised his identity she'd felt something—a shock, a jolt of...*awareness*. Her brain and her body had registered him as an attractive man.

Zayne.

The idea made her edgy as she stole a sideways

glance at him. Tried to be objective. Zayne *was* an attractive man. The whole world acknowledged that. And the years certainly hadn't done him any harm. The dark hair, courtesy of his Indian heritage, was shorter than it had been in his teens, but still held a hint of unruly curl. His features were leaner, the jut of his nose stronger, but the deep brown eyes were the same: intense, with an irrepressible glint of humour in them.

But there was something else too—a wariness that hadn't been present in the young Zayne. A slightly hooded guard that indicated the years had maybe brought some downs as well as ups.

Her gaze lingered on his mouth, those firm lips that looked made for…

For what, Thea?

Self-irritation sparked. Was she really so shallow that she now found Zayne attractive because he was a success, a billionaire, a man who had dated a succession of the world's most beautiful, most successful women? Or had she always found him attractive?

Of course not. She'd grown up with him. He was the boy next door, her friend, her partner in crime. He had been 'just Zayne'. Until…until that kiss. That ill-fated kiss that had seemed such a good, sensible idea but had changed everything. Yes, it had been clunky and awkward, but it had also been a revelation. Had sent a tremor through her tummy and a shiver down her spine. And when she'd opened her eyes she'd seen Zayne differently.

Because when his lips had touched hers something had happened—something her fifteen-year-old self hadn't been able to or wanted to explain, understand or even acknowledge. Not only because it had been Zayne who had evoked those feelings, but because Thea hadn't wanted to feel them, hadn't wanted to let control slip away. And she'd known that if Zayne kissed her again there was a risk that she'd enter uncharted territory where she couldn't control everything.

Another sideways glance, and it occurred to her that that was exactly how she felt now. Which was ridiculous. Zayne hadn't even sent her a postcard in the past twelve years. Now she'd bumped into him by accident, they'd have a cup of coffee and go their separate ways. No big deal and she would be one hundred percent in control.

'You OK, Thea?'

'Huh? Yes. Sorry.'

She realised that as she'd been thinking she'd slowed her steps and now had almost stopped.

He moved over to a small recess next to a shop selling bamboo arts and crafts and turned to face her.

'Feel free to finish your assessment. You've been casting furtive looks at me the whole way.'

'I was not being furtive. I was trying to be discreet.'

'Whilst checking me out?'

There was a teasing glint in the brown eyes now, and to her own annoyance she felt heat touch her cheeks.

'I am not checking you out. It's natural to have some curiosity, and it's *interesting* to see how you've changed. Feel free to assess me right back.'

The words dropped from her lips without thought, and she wasn't prepared for the result.

He stilled, hands loose by his sides, and looked at her, really looked at her. And what she saw in his eyes made her heart race, even as she reminded herself that this was what Zayne was good at. She had seen countless photographs of that smouldering look being aimed at whichever model, actress, celebrity was the subject of his attention. His short-lived attention. Those women never lasted long, although there had been no acrimonious splits or public spats. Zayne seemed to manage his episodic love-life with respect and without drama.

She forced himself to meet his gaze, to keep her body still and relaxed, her weight evenly balanced. After all, she was used to being on display in her job, used to presenting a calm, professional front under scrutiny. It would take more than Zayne Wood to ruffle Thea Kendall's composure. Plus, she'd invited this assessment.

Now he smiled, and it sent a tingle down her spine. The slightly crooked tilt to his lips, the dimple in his left cheek, the lines that creased the skin around his eyes and spoke of the laughter and experience of twelve years…

'Something funny?' she asked.

'Nope. I was just thinking that it's good to see you. And how you look the same, but different.'

'I think you'll find that's what twelve years does,' she said, her voice tarter than she'd meant it to be, aware that she still harboured a touch of perhaps hypocritical resentment that he'd walked away from their friendship so easily.

'You're still beautiful,' he said now, and then he blinked, as if the words had surprised him.

They'd surprised her too, and also warmed her—a warmth she instantly banished. 'I'm sure you say that to all the girls nowadays. You certainly never said it to me all those years ago.'

'Well, maybe I should have.'

He took a step forward and Thea found herself doing the same, even as a warning bell clanged loud and furious in her brain. What on earth was she doing? Falling for Zayne's charms like all those other women? No way!

She stepped back. 'You definitely shouldn't have. That would have been downright strange.'

Her words broke the spell, if indeed there had been a spell. Maybe this was all a figment of her overheated imagination, or the light-headedness brought about by hunger.

'Anyway, let's find this café.'

And now, as she walked, she made sure to focus on the picturesque charm of their surroundings. The bright blue of the sky, the tang of snow mixed with the now familiar slightly eggy smell of the *onsen*.

'I love it here,' she said. 'It's the feeling of history... the fact that the hot springs have been here for centuries. Even though tourists come here, it doesn't feel touristy.'

'Maybe it's because the tourists have only been here for the blink of an eye, whilst the traditions and legends of this place have been here for ever,' he said, and she glanced up at him, felt an affinity. He got what she meant.

'Do you know any of the legends?' she asked.

'There's one that says the village was discovered when one day long ago a hunter was tracking a bear. He shot the bear with an arrow in the forest, and was following the wounded creature up the mountain—Mount Kenashi. When he found it, the bear was in one of the hot springs, healing itself. And so the village was founded around that *onsen*, which is still here.'

'I love that. And I hope the hunter let the bear go. I'll make sure I go and try out that *onsen*.' She gave a small laugh. 'Unless you think that makes me a real tourist?'

'No. I think it makes you someone who wants to be a part of this place's traditions and history. Plus, that's what the *onsens* are for. Enjoying.'

'I do enjoy them. It's become part of my morning routine.'

And once she'd got used to the idea that you had to bathe naked, she'd grown to love the incredible warmth of the hot springs, marvelling at the idea that nature provided the steaming, cleansing water. Now she wouldn't wear a bathing suit even if she was allowed to, because that would somehow feel wrong.

'The *ryokan* I'm staying in has its own *onsen*. I use it every morning before breakfast, and sometimes after skiing as well. It's an incredible experience.'

'The outdoor ones are a pretty amazing experience too, especially if it's snowing. You sit there in the steaming water whilst cold snowflakes float down and land on your face.'

Just like that, an image invaded her brain. Zayne sitting gloriously naked in a swirl of opaque steaming water, with flakes of snow coming down in a flurry, touching the sweeping contours of his face...

She made a sudden small choking sound, saw him glance down at her, and knew her face was tinged pink. Again.

'You OK?' His gaze held hers with seeming concern, but she'd swear they also held a knowing glint of amusement.

'I'm good. I'll make sure I try out an outdoor pool. Just picturing it is awesome,' she added, with a touch of defiance.

Now something else sparked in those deep brown eyes. 'It is, isn't it?' he said, and now his voice deepened, seemed to shiver over her skin. 'The heat of the water on your body...the sharp, crisp cold of the air outside...the tang of snow...the sense of nature...'

'Yup. I'll definitely give it a go.'

Was that really her voice? Slightly breathless? She needed to get a grip.

'Here's the café,' he said, and she gave a sigh of relief as she saw a small, unpretentious building, with the two now familiar wooden statues outside the door, statues that were everywhere in the village.

She smiled. 'I think I may get a couple of these to take home with me,' she said. 'It sounds silly, but I'll miss them.'

'It's not silly.' He grinned back. 'Or if it is, I'm silly

too. I actually find myself wishing this particular pair good morning. They're *dosojin*—guardians and protectors. These particular ones were said to be happily married, with a child, so they are said to be the gods of healthy marriage and healthy children.'

'Oh…' Thea regarded the statues again. 'Then I'm happy for them.'

A sudden touch of wistfulness touched her as she realised that she wouldn't be bringing them home with her now. What was the point? Children were definitely not in her future, and neither was marriage—happy or otherwise. She'd definitely learnt that from her disastrous relationship with Ian.

She'd already known she wasn't mum material, that she didn't make the grade. After Ian, she'd known she wasn't destined to be a wife either. She was fine with that, and yet her gaze lingered on the statues one last time as they entered the café.

Zayne pushed the door open and Thea welcomed the blast of warmth, the smell of coffee and the sizzle of eggs cooking. The chatter of tourists and locals was a mix of language and cadence that somehow grounded her, gave her context. She and Zayne were just chance-met tourists, and soon enough she would get back to work and put this surprisingly unsettling encounter out of her mind.

'This looks great.' She glanced around, assessed the locals to tourists ratio. 'And not too touristy.'

'No,' he agreed. 'I found it about a month ago, and I've been a regular ever since. Not many cafés do traditional Japanese breakfasts, but the *onigiri* here are fantastic.'

'Those are the steamed rice balls, aren't they?' Thea said.

'Yup. They do the best ones around here, with a variety of fillings.'

'Sounds good to me. I'm famished.'

They made their way to an empty table and he waited until she'd sat down, then seated himself at the small table, his knee inadvertently bumping hers as he did so.

Thea bit back a small gasp at the casual contact. Eyes wide at the effect it had had on her, she hurriedly looked down at the menu, hoping he hadn't noticed her reaction.

'So, what do you recommend?' she asked, hopeful that her face had lost its flush, and relieved that he had shifted so they were no longer touching. Though her relief was tempered by the temptation to shift and reconnect...see if she'd imagined the reaction.

Had Zayne felt it too? Of course not. This man had dated the most beautiful women in the world. Bumping Thea's knee was hardly going to rate any notice.

'Why don't I get a selection? That way you can sample them all. And coffee?'

'Sounds good. Strong and black, please.'

She watched as he went over and engaged in conversation with the man behind the counter, saw them both smile, and had little doubt Zayne had already befriended half the neighbourhood.

He returned holding two steaming mugs of coffee,

and she waited whilst he sat down, this time taking care to avoid knee contact.

'So,' he said. 'Tell me about the last twelve years.'

'I'm a lawyer.'

'No surprises there. I'd have put money on that, and I'm guessing you're a highly successful one.'

'Yes,' Thea said simply. 'I am.'

He grinned at her. 'Good for you, Thea. I know how much you wanted that.'

'I did. I still do. If everything goes to plan—*my* plan—I'll make partner in the next year or so. I was headhunted by a firm from Cambridge, but I've moved once since then. I work for one of the "magic circle" firms now, and I'm climbing the ladder. I'm nearly there. I can almost taste it.'

Thea heard the pride in her voice. She *was* proud of her achievements, but she was also very aware that Zayne looked as though he was waiting for more. But what was she to say? List her clients? Recount her hours in the office, the late nights, the work she took home with her? Her life was her work and she was happy with that—wanted that, had chosen that.

It was with relief that she greeted the arrival of the food. 'Wow. These look great. And taste even better!'

She revelled in the tang of salt, the sharpness of the plum pickle, which was the perfect foil for the sticky texture of the rice and the crisp seaweed wrapping.

For a while they ate in a comfortable, appreciative silence, but once the edge of her appetite was sated she looked at him.

'Your past twelve years have been well documented.

High-flying MIT graduate, going on to found one of the fastest-growing, most successful tech companies ever. Then you sold that for an undisclosed number of millions, created a number of start-ups, and now you're described as a billionaire entrepreneur…top one hundred.'

She smiled at him.

'You did it, Zayne. You made it. Just like you always said you would. I can almost see you now, aged fifteen, sat in front of your computer, making it do things the rest of us did not understand. Do you remember that time you tried to explain it, and your parents and I stood there utterly baffled?'

He grinned. 'It was the first and last time. My mum was convinced I'd broken it and was trying to cover it up, and my dad was trying to pretend he was following along. He enrolled in a computer course the next day.'

'Your parents must be so proud of your success.'

It had been the wrong thing to say. Those last words had changed the dynamic, and the smile was erased from his face.

'Actually, my dad died.' The words were jerky. 'I thought you might know.'

Shock froze her as an image of Arjun Wood as she had last seen him came to her mind. Not a tall man, but a man with presence and a booming laugh, a man who had meant something to her.

'No. I didn't. I mean, I do read articles about you, but I don't think I've seen any mention of your parents apart from to mention your ethnicity sometimes.'

The words came as if automatically as she tried to absorb what he had said. The enormity of it.

Zayne's dad had been a larger-than-life figure—a man who, however tired he was, had always found a smile. He'd been special to Thea. And she'd been special to him. In Zayne's house she had been an individual, not just one of the Kendall sisters, and that had meant more to her than she'd ever admitted. To Zayne or perhaps even to herself. Because she'd known she was being unfair.

She had known that her parents loved all their children equally. But once Eliza had fallen ill, of course the focus had been on her, and Thea had got that. She and Sienna had both stepped up, wanting to be there, and had understood Eliza had to be put first. But Zayne's parents had been there for *her*...for Thea.

'I didn't know,' she repeated. 'I've always imagined your parents living a happy, contented life in the States, watching your success and—' She broke off, reached out to cover his hand. 'Your mum...she must be devastated. When did it happen? Was it recent?'

He looked down at her hand over his. 'Actually, it happened a while ago.'

'How long?'

'Over ten years.'

She stared at him, her mind doing the maths. 'So, whilst you were at MIT?'

'Yes.'

Emotions struggled inside her—grief, hurt and anger—as she pulled her hand away. 'Then why didn't you tell me?' she asked. 'They'd only just moved to the States. I'd just seen them. I must have seen your dad just months before he died.'

Seen him for the last time, when Arjun had returned to London to finalise the sale of the house.

She pushed her plate away, tried to gather perspective, felt the incipient prickle of tears and rose to her feet. She wouldn't cry, not in front of Zayne. Wouldn't create a drama. After all, this was his grief and his loss, even if it was one he had had time to process. He was the important one here. Yet it still hurt.

'Sorry. It doesn't matter.' She forced herself to meet his gaze. 'I think we're all caught up. There's nothing more to say. Please give my love to your mum.'

Turning, she headed to the door.

CHAPTER THREE

HELL AND DAMNATION.

'Thea! Wait.'

But he knew she wouldn't. And he couldn't blame her. He'd seen genuine grief and hurt in her green eyes.

He should have explained better...shouldn't have assumed she already knew.

He knew that most articles about him simply said things like *Born in England to parents of Indian ethnicity, Zayne Wood moved to the US to study at MIT...*

And when his mum had remarried, just over a year ago, it had been a small family-only affair, with absolutely no publicity whatsoever.

Zayne closed his eyes. He should have told Thea years ago, when his dad had died. But he hadn't, and now he owed her an explanation. More than that, he wanted to give her comfort. He had seen the tears she'd tried so hard to hold back. For Thea, the grief would be new.

He looked towards the counter and the owner waved at him, indicating that he should follow Thea, could return and pay later.

Exiting the café, he looked around, saw her striding away, and headed after her.

'Thea. Wait. Let me explain.'

She didn't so much as slow down.

'You don't need to explain anything, Zayne. He was your father, and at the time I know you would have had so much to think about—your own grief, your mum… There would have been no reason for you to contact me. I was shocked. That's all. So really, it's fine. It was good to see you again.'

For a shameful moment he was tempted to take her at her word, let her go. He didn't want to revisit his own grief, didn't want to expose it to Thea's all-seeing amber gaze. But the moment passed. There was no way he could let Thea walk away.

'It's not fine, and I don't want to end this here. Like this. I messed up.Please give me a chance to try and put it right. We had so much once. I'd hate for it to end like this.'

She stopped and turned, wiped a hand over her eyes. His chest twisted as he realised she was crying for his dad, and his own grief panged, along with the searing of guilt and the might-have-beens and what-ifs that he had replayed in his mind so many times.

Then she nodded—a small nod, but an agreement—and he exhaled in relief.

'OK,' she said.

'We can't talk here. Have you been to any of the local shrines?'

She shook her head.

'There's one near here. Would you like to go there? It's beautiful and peaceful.'

'That sounds good.'

'Thank you.'

'There's no need to thank me. Unless you've changed fundamentally, I know you probably don't want to talk at all.'

Her voice was tight, but he sensed her hostility had lessened, and that their conversation wouldn't be dominated by anger. That had never been Thea's way. Injustice made her angry, but she was always willing to try to resolve an argument through discussion.

That was something she'd gained from being part of a family with siblings—she'd learnt all about resolving arguments, talking things through. None of which Zayne was good at. He wondered what his life would have been like if he'd had siblings. He knew his dad, in particular, would have liked a large family, knew, too, that his parents had decided against it because they'd realised that Zayne was 'something different... someone special' early on, and they'd wanted to give him every opportunity. So that was another thing his dad had sacrificed.

Instead, his parents had fostered children for a time, something his father had loved doing. But even that had come to an end...another decision Zayne felt responsible for.

They walked in a silence that was neither companionable nor hostile. Thea's expression was closed, contemplative, but he had no clue as to what she was thinking.

'It's this way,' he said, and indicated the approach to a long flight of cedar-lined stone steps stairs that led up to the shrine.

Snow edged each stair, gleaming pristine white in neat layers, providing an unsullied path upwards to the edifice. The effect was impressive, and he could see why some people felt that this shrine guarded the village.

'It's beautiful,' she breathed into the quiet, cold air as they started the climb, their feet crunching in the powdered snow. 'Is there anything we should do? To show respect?'

'Every shrine has a gate, called a *torii* gate. It's the line between the outside world and the holy ground of the shrine. To acknowledge that you should bow before entering. Also—and I am not sure why this is—you're not supposed to enter centrally. You have to veer a little left or right.'

'Thank you.'

Once they were standing outside the shrine, Zayne watched Thea's reaction.

'It's beautiful,' she said.

'It's one of my favourite places to come and think.'

After all, that was why he was here, in Japan, holidaying alone. Because he needed to think, consider his future, where he wanted to go next. And here was a good place to think. Peaceful, with the giant beauty of the cedar trees. He admired the skill and care that had gone into the building of the shrine out of cedarwood, the fluid curve of the roofs, the intricate wooden carvings of mythical creatures along with the everyday people found in this small village. It gave him a sense of peace…completion.

'Thank you for bringing me here.'

She stepped away from him and he gave her some space, watched as she studied the carvings, saw the interest and the wonder on her face, sensed she too recognised that this was a place that was special.

'It's so...*complete*.' She gave a half-laugh. 'I'm not sure if that's the right word.'

'I don't know either, but it works for me.'

It did: he knew exactly what Thea meant.

The realisation sent a small shock through him, a sense of a connection reignited. Because after all this time apart he still got her. He suspected, too, that she would still get him, in a way no other woman ever had. How many of the women he'd dated had looked at him with incomprehension, uttering the words, *'I don't understand what you mean, darling?'* Or *'Was that a joke? I don't get it.'*

'Are you OK to talk now?' she asked. 'I know it will be painful for you, but...'

'It's OK,' he said quickly.

'Do you think it's all right to sit on the steps?' she asked. 'We can move if anyone else comes.'

He nodded, and they sat on the wooden steps outside the shrine.

'Would you mind telling me what happened?' she asked.

Steeling himself, he tried to make his words as brief and gentle as possible. 'It was a heart attack. He wouldn't have known anything. It happened when he was out jogging. There was nothing anyone could have done.'

She was quiet for a moment. Then, 'I'm glad it was

painless. But the shock must have been devastating. For your mum and for you.'

'It was. Mum was just cooking lunch for the two of them. I was at a lecture...'

That was all he ever let himself remember. He'd pushed down the horror of it all, the disbelief, the wondering if he should have noticed something, could have somehow prevented the whole unfair tragedy of it all. If he'd been different, not 'special', would his dad still be alive?

All too aware that Thea's gaze was on him, he met her eyes, confident that years of keeping the guilt buried, only allowing it to surface in the privacy of his thoughts, would keep it safely hidden.

'I'm sorry.' She shifted closer to him. 'I wish I'd known. Why didn't you tell me?'

It was the same question she'd asked earlier, but uttered now without anger.

Then she shook her head. 'Actually... It's OK. You don't have to explain. Of course you didn't think of me. Why should you have? You'd just lost your father. There was no reason for you to.'

'It wasn't like that. I did think about you. So did Mum. You were important to Dad.'

'He was important to me.'

'We decided it was better not to tell you.' Though really the decision had been his. 'I knew you would be midway through your degree, studying for exams. I didn't want you to feel that you had to jump on a plane. I didn't want to impact on your studies.'

All valid reasons, and exactly what he'd told his

mum, perhaps what he'd told himself. But now as he looked at her, with the wintry rays of the sun dappling her face, her amber eyes full of compassion and comfort, he knew it had been more than that.

He hadn't wanted Thea's compassion or comfort. Not then and not now.

Back then he had needed to stay strong, to be there for his mother, to make up for a loss that he knew was somehow down to him. So he'd vowed to provide for her, to be the son his father had wanted, to achieve the success that his father had sacrificed so much for. And to do that he'd known he'd need to be strong, not allow himself the luxury of grief or the indulgence of compassion. His guilt would serve to motivate him, to drive him, so he'd need to keep it close.

Thea would have made him weak, maybe he'd always known that.

Even that day after they'd received their offers—hers from Cambridge, his from MIT—when they'd met to say goodbye, hadn't he been tempted to stay? Stay in England. See if he could get into Cambridge too, or study elsewhere in the UK. But of course he hadn't. He couldn't have done that to his parents, or to himself. He'd always known MIT was the best place for him, an opportunity to study he'd be a fool to pass up. And for what?

Another question he hadn't known the answer to.

'Zayne?' Her voice was small. 'It's OK. I understand those reasons. Really, I do. I don't agree, but I understand. But I wish I'd known. He was important to me. I know he wasn't there that often, but I knew him—

he was part of my life. An important part. He used to ruffle my hair or tug on my plaits whenever he saw me, and I remember how he said my name, with a lilt to it. And he'd always buy me *gulab jamun.*'

'I remember.'

He did remember; could see his dad rising to his feet from the armchair he'd found in a second-hand furniture store. *'Wait here, Thea. I have it for you. In the special tin.'* Then he'd present the tin to her with a flourish. Zayne could see the young Thea eating the round orange sticky Indian sweets, and his dad beaming at her, happy that someone else shared his fondness for the sweet treat.

'He always remembered to get me some, always from the same shop at the local Indian market. Just for me. He always remembered me. However busy he was. That meant a lot to me.'

'He liked you a lot, you know.'

'And I liked him.' She glanced at him. 'At least you have happy memories to look back on, you know he loved you.'

'Yes.'

But the agreement sounded hollow. Because for Zayne the happy memories were overlaid with the grief that they'd been cut short, that there would be no more to make. That his dad had missed out on seeing Zayne's success, missed out on a life of relaxation and peace with his wife. Payback for all those years of hard work and graft, the late hours at a job he hadn't really wanted to do, the time not spent with his family, the decision to have an only child… All of it.

Instead his mum was enjoying retirement with a new husband and Zayne knew he wasn't handling that well either, which added a new layer to his guilt. Because of course he wanted his mum to be happy.

The knowledge made him edgy, urged him to get on. To run, walk, set up a new business, go on a date, engage his brain and his body so he didn't dwell on the past.

As the thoughts raced through his mind they set his leg jiggling on the step below. Thea slipped her hand into his, her fingers warm around his, offering comfort.

He looked down at their clasped hands and the mood shifted again. He could almost see the connection fire up the synapses, imbue the simple clasp with something else. Warmth and a frisson of bubbling desire. All he wanted to do now was kiss her. But of course he wouldn't. This was Thea. And there were way too many emotions flying all over the place. And the one thing Zayne did not do was mix emotions and kisses.

Instead, he said, 'Thank you for listening. And for understanding.'

'Thank you for following me out of the café.' She looked at her watch. 'And now...'

'You need to get back to work,' he said.

And he needed to let her go. But as he looked into her face he knew he didn't want to. Not yet.

A warning bell clanged at the back of his head and he shut it down. Of course he wasn't ready yet.

'I get that, but how about we have dinner later? I mean, there's still a lot to catch up on. I want to know how your family are doing, and we've hardly got started on your past twelve years.'

Hesitation danced over her features and he tried to work out how to sweeten the pot.

'Come on. You need to eat. I know a place in Nagano I think you'd love, and if we go there the temple is a must-see—especially at night when its illuminated. What do you think?'

CHAPTER FOUR

IT WAS A good question. What did she think? Right now she couldn't even rely on instinct, because different instincts tugged her in different directions. A part of her wanted to have dinner with him, but she wasn't sure why. To finish catching up with an old friend? If that was the case she'd accept without hesitation. After all Zayne was right—she had to eat.

But Thea had a panicky feeling that she wanted to have dinner with Zayne because she wanted to explore this strange zing of attraction, see if it was reciprocated. But even if it was, what then? The idea of she and Zayne was ludicrous. Or it should be.

But it wasn't.

Or was it?

For Pete's sake. She was behaving like an adolescent. Great. Maybe she was regressing, or looking back and wondering what would have happened if the aftermath of that first kiss had gone differently.

She had to get a grip. That kiss had been over half her lifetime ago. And this attraction, mutual or not, was a non-starter. Thea Kendall had no intention of becoming another notch on Zayne's bedpost. Falling for the famed Zayne Wood charm. But as she looked at him, saw the muscular frame, the jut of his jaw, the thick dark hair, the brown eyes that surveyed her with a question in his eyes, she could feel herself doing exactly that, actually leaning towards him.

So obviously she should end this here, politely refuse his offer and go on her merry way back to work, followed by a solitary dinner. Which didn't sound so merry now she came to think of it. Plus, she'd love to see Nagano. Sure, she could go on her own, but it would be nicer with Zayne. That was it. *Nicer.* A gentle word, a friendly word. Thea had this under control.

'I'd like that,' she said, and was rewarded with that crooked smile.

'You're sure? It took you a long time to answer.'

'Just figuring out the angles,' she said. 'Weighing up the pros and cons.'

He raised his eyebrows. 'Fascinating,' he said. 'That's pretty much how you used to decide which chocolate biscuit to choose—it used to drive me nuts. So, tell me the pros.'

'I get to see the temple with someone who knows what he's talking about, so it saves me booking a guided tour, and I get to have dinner somewhere without researching the best place to go. Both those things give me some excellent topics of conversation for my potential client meeting.'

She stopped and he looked at her, an exaggerated expression of hurt on his face as he put a hand to his heart.

'I'm wounded, Thea. Wounded. Where in your pro

list is the chance to spend time with Zayne, the handsome, charismatic man from your past?'

'Wrong list,' she said. 'That was on my con list.'

Now he laughed, a deep chuckle that brought an answering laugh to her lips.

'Seriously, though. Catching up some more sounds great. As for handsome and charismatic... I hadn't noticed.'

The lie dropped from her lips with a touch too much defiance and he raised his eyebrows, the amusement in his eyes replaced by a spark, a lingering look that held so much promise she almost gasped.

'You sure about that?' he asked.

'Yes.' The syllable was so high-pitched, so squeaky, she couldn't believe it was her voice. She took a breath and rose to her feet. 'I'm sure.'

And if she wasn't now then she would be by the time they got to dinner.

'So what was on your con list?' he asked, his voice silky-smooth. 'If it wasn't worrying about succumbing to my charms?'

Her eyes narrowed as she tapped her cheek in supposed thought. 'There is no "if" about it. I can't succumb to something I haven't noticed.'

There was that toe-curling smile. 'Touché.'

'And my con list is simple—I can't take too much time away from work. If it would impact badly on my workload I wouldn't go with you. As it doesn't, I will.'

'Got it,' he said, his tone serious. Too serious, surely. 'Perhaps I should find a fast food place instead, to minimise the time it takes us to eat. Or we could get a takeaway and eat whilst you look at the temple.' He snapped his fingers. 'Or I could hire a helicopter to lessen the travel time. Or...'

It took Thea until the helicopter to realise he was teasing her, and now she put her hands on her hips as she looked at him, saw the smile on his face.

'Ha-ha-ha! That won't be necessary. I have factored in time to eat and time to enjoy the temple.'

But she knew her chagrin wasn't real. It was nice to be teased, to have someone not take her seriously. *Nice.* That was all it was. Her new favourite word.

'Thank you for asking,' she added. 'But please don't book anywhere fancy, just somewhere simple with good food.'

'Like I said, I've got the perfect place in mind. I promise you won't be disappointed.'

There it was again; that smile, that look in his eye, that damned charm that he seemed able to turn on at will.

The charm she was not going to fall for.

'I'll pick you up at five.'

Zayne surveyed his reflection, realised to his own irritation that he was nervous. Which made no sense. There was nothing to be nervous about. There was also no need for this equally unfamiliar sense of anticipation. He hadn't seen Thea for over a decade and he'd survived just fine, thank you very much.

Grabbing his car keys, he exited the cabin he'd rented and, as always, took a moment to look at the surroundings. The wooden edifice surrounded by trees, their boughs and branches loaded with snow, the air fresh and the silence broken only by the sound of an occasional bird or the soft scurry of an animal.

Zayne inhaled deeply and felt the peace of the place bringing a sense of calm.

However, it was short-lived, as his car bumped its way down the rutted track that meandered towards the village.

And Thea.

He pulled up in the *ryokan* car park, saw her walk towards him and there it was again, that twist in his gut as he climbed out of the car to greet her. She looked beautiful—simply dressed, in skinny jeans that accentuated the length and shape of her legs, a bright red woollen coat belted at the waist, knee-high boots. Her brown hair fell in loose waves to her shoulders, and as she came closer he could smell the light floral scent of her perfume.

'Hi,' he said, and fell silent, oddly tongue-tied.

'Hi.' She looked at the car. 'I wasn't sure if we would go by train or car.'

'Car. I rented it once I decided to stay on in Japan.'

More silence. His mind was a blank, her store of small-talk clearly used up.

'Um…' She took a step forward holding up her phone. 'Would you mind if we took a picture? I want to send it to my sisters. I told them earlier I'd seen a familiar face, but I haven't told them who as yet.'

'Sure. Do you want to take it here? Or wait until we get to the city?'

'Here will be fine.'

He caught a definite sense of *let's just get it over with* and he understood why, as they walked round the car towards each other. He braced himself, preparing for the effect of her proximity, and kept his breathing even with an effort.

She turned so her back was to him and held her phone up. She was so close that now he could identify the jasmine of her perfume…so close that her hair nearly tickled his chin…so close that if he took one step forward her back would touch his chest.

'Smile,' she said, and he caught the breathless note in her voice as he forced his lips upwards.

He was good at this; had perfected an easy grin for the camera, ensuring his press photographs and any random snaps from journalists left him looking good.

She stepped away, with a thank-you.

'No problem. Could you send it to me and I'll send it to my mum?'

'Sure,' she said as she climbed into the car. 'Speaking of whom, how *is* your mum?'

He focused on starting the car, kept his gaze on the road, not wanting Thea to clock his expression. Being with someone who had once been able to read his every mood, who'd known him pre his days of success, was disconcerting. Zayne wasn't at all sure he liked it.

'Mum is doing great. She's settled in California. The first few years after Dad died were really tough for her, but she threw herself into helping me. Mostly by making sure I could focus completely on work. She looked after me. Even when I moved out she'd come round and stock my freezer, or I'd get home and the house would have been cleaned from top to bottom. She's set up her own business as well. There is a small but thriving Indian community in Silicon Valley, and she has set up a grocery store-cum-café which is a massive success. She never, ever tells anyone that she's my mum, though, and when I visit she calls me by my middle name.'

'Why?'

'She says she wants people to come and eat her food because it is the best there is, not because she has a famous son.'

'Her food *is* the best. I loved her *pakoras*. I think half the neighbourhood used to walk past your house at certain times just to smell your mum's food.'

'I don't know how she did it,' Zayne said. 'Looking back, I took it for granted. She worked so hard as well. So many hours in the pharmacy.'

Thea shook her head. 'I have no idea how she did it either. I rely on takeaways and some very, very simple meals that I can make in ten minutes flat. My *spaghetti al olio* is incredible, and I do a mean omelette. And a *miso* soup that I randomly throw things in. But your mum—she made complicated food. From scratch.' She glanced across at him. 'What about you? How do the super-rich eat? Do you cook? Does someone cook for you? Do you eat off plates of gold?'

He grinned at her. 'Yes, yes and no. I do cook and I do enjoy it. But it's a recent hobby. Until recently my mum has cooked for me. I know how terrible that sounds, but I couldn't stop her. She'd just come round with food.'

'That sounds wonderful, not terrible. How did you

convince her to stop?' She shook her head. 'More to
the point, *why* did you convince her?'

It was an opportunity to casually explain that his
mum had remarried. But the words wouldn't come. He
told himself there was no need for detail. Thea knew his
mum was happy. There was no need for more…no need
to expose himself to Thea's scrutiny. After all, he didn't
understand his own irrational, mixed emotions, so he'd
already figured that the best thing to do with them was
bury them, down deep, where no one could see them.

'I guess me turning thirty finally got Mum to realise
it was time I learned to cook for myself. And so far so
good. I'm enjoying my efforts, anyway. I haven't tried
them out on anyone else.'

'Huh? You must have cooked for someone at some
point in the past year.'

'Actually, I haven't.' He shrugged. 'Why would I?
I live alone.'

'That doesn't mean you can't ask someone round for
dinner,' Thea pointed out.

It was a fair point, but… 'That's not something I do.
If I eat with someone we eat out.'

When he dated women he took them to the best
restaurants in the world, partied with them on yachts,
flew them to private islands. He certainly didn't offer
to dish up a meal at home. If he did he knew his date
would either laugh in his face or take it as a signal that
he was actually contemplating a serious relationship.
Which would be even worse.

'I mean, when was the last time *you* cooked dinner
for someone? Assuming you live alone, that is?'

He realised he'd pressed down a little harder on the accelerator as he waited for her answer.

'I do live alone. I bought my flat a couple of years ago and I love it, love the space and the freedom to eat when I want, what I want, and work as late as I want. But I do ask people round for a meal sometimes.'

He watched as she thought for a moment.

'The last time it was Sienna, back in October, and I made her a cheese toastie. That counts as a meal, right? I put olives in it, and chillies, so I bet I covered a lot of the food groups,' she added.

'That sounds pretty good to me,' he said as they pulled into a car park. 'I thought we'd park here, at the station, and walk to the temple.'

'Sounds perfect.'

CHAPTER FIVE

AS THEY WALKED Thea gave a small gasp as she saw the sweep of the paved street festooned with twinkling lights, providing a magical background to the shops and stalls that were all open, all enticing and busy, with a happy buzz of chatter and laughter adding to the ambience.

'This is amazing.'

'It is, isn't it? Definitely worth seeing.'

'It's so much bigger than the village.' She shook her head at the absurdity of her statement. 'Obviously because it's an actual city, isn't it?'

'Biggest one in the region,' he replied. 'Population of over three hundred and fifty thousand people.'

'I love it.' Thea looked down the illuminated street. 'It's like an avenue of light leading to the temple.'

'I've been here in the day as well, and I'd love to come back to this region in the spring or summer, see the trees in bloom and compare how different it is.'

'You really do love it here.' She glanced up at him. 'I didn't think this would be a typical Zayne Wood holiday.'

'Why's that?'

'Well, according to the magazines I read in the dentist's waiting room, your usual vacation is on a sunny private island or a yacht, and you always have a beautiful woman in tow. There are parties and expensive restaurants. Right now there are no yachts or beautiful women in sight.'

'I wouldn't say that,' he said, and suddenly his voice had deepened to a near caress as he looked down at her, and she gave an almost audible gulp.

'Well, I would,' she managed tartly. 'You're here on your own, and it looks to me as though you're living life under the radar. No glamour or parties.'

'It was a whim, an unplanned solo break. I am quite capable of spending time alone.'

She raised her eyebrows. 'No need to sound so defensive. I know you are. You spent most of your teen years holed up in your room. But that was a long time ago.'

He shrugged. 'I still spend time holed up in my office, but I figure it's important to have fun as well. There is more to life than work, and it's important to kick back and have fun.'

'Work *is* fun,' Thea said.

'Sure. But there's more than one kind of fun. And it's important to explore that. What do you do for fun in general? *Apart* from work, I mean.'

'I… I see my family. I try to get back there every couple of weeks for a day.'

OK, she always took her laptop or a work file with her, but she wasn't going to share that.

'I see friends…go to the cinema…'

Only she didn't, not really. Not in the past two years.

Not since the break-up with Ian. Since then her drive, her ambition, had intensified. And there was nothing wrong with that.

'Though right now not so much. I don't want to miss out on a partnership for the sake of a dinner with friends or a night out. There will be time enough for that later. I mean, that's how it was for you, right? Whilst you were setting up ZW Systems, I bet you didn't go in for a whole lot of fun.'

'Well, I wouldn't say that. Fun was still a part of my life, though I didn't prioritise it, no. When I graduated from MIT I already had an idea in my head, but I needed time to make sure it was right, time to work out how to finance it. So I got a graduate job on the West Coast, well paid and enjoyable, but I'd go to work all day and then I'd work on my idea most evenings. But even then I'd take a night off, go out with friends. Or spend a day on the beach, go for bike rides, help my mum out with her business. Once I had my company up and running, and I'd seen turnover hit a certain level, then I did start to have a lot more fun.'

'Well, I'm not sure I'll ever manage fun by your standards, but once I'm partner I'm sure I'll find more time to relax.'

'Really? Surely when you get to be partner your workload will increase and then you'll set your sights on climbing higher.'

'And if I do? Is there anything wrong with that?'

'Of course not. But you don't want to burn out. Life shouldn't be all about work.'

'Why not?' Her stride increased along with her irritation. 'If that's what drives me, makes me happy, then what is wrong with that? Why shouldn't it be?'

'Because it will make you one-dimensional. And you'll miss out.'

'One-dimensional?' Thea tried not to let her steps falter. 'Don't you think that is a tad judgemental?'

A memory came of Ian's words, the judgement in his tone and the almost pitying look of assessment on his face as he'd judged her and found her wanting.

'You're not a real woman, Thea. I deserve someone better.'

'As for missing out—what would I be missing out on, exactly?'

Children? A family? Was that what he would say? And why would it upset her so much if he did? She'd made her choices and she knew they were right. It wouldn't be fair, or morally right, to bring a child into this world if she wouldn't be able to put that child first, no matter what. Like her mother had. So it didn't matter whether she wanted children or not. It mattered what sort of parent she could be.

Zayne came to a stop, raised a hand in apology. 'You're right. I've overstepped. I haven't seen you in over a decade and I had no right to say what I said. I'm sorry. You know what makes you happy. And right now I don't want you to miss out on the beauty of this place because I'm being overbearing. I'm truly sorry, Thea.'

She could see that he meant it, could read sincerity and concern in his brown eyes, and she nodded. 'It's OK. I should be used to it by now. My family is also giving me a hard time, telling me all work and no play makes Thea a dull girl. If I had a penny for every time one of them says that I'd have a fortune. So, apology accepted.'

Then her thoughts halted, along with her feet, as they approached the gateway to the temple and she blinked in sheer bedazzlement as she took in the gigantic lit-up statues that flanked the walkthrough, bathed now in a magical purple light.

'They're magnificent,' she breathed. 'They give me goosebumps.' She stood still, trying to absorb the sheer aura of them. 'Are they guardian statues too? That is exactly how they feel—as though they will stand in defence of this place for ever.'

Zayne nodded. 'They are called Agyo and Ungyo. Agyo symbolises the beginning of everything and Ungyo the end of it all. That's why they are placed where they are. Agyo will be the first to be lit up by the winter solstice sunrise and the setting sun's last rays will shine on Ungyo. It's all about the circle of life and balance.'

They stood and stared at the figures and she thought about what they represented. She glanced up at Zayne and felt suddenly at peace, all the earlier rancour of their conversation dissipated.

'Shall we move on?' he asked after a while, and she nodded a farewell to the guardian statues.

They walked on into the hustle and bustle of a shopping area, lined with stalls and shacks all open in honour of the illuminations, and Thea's stomach gave a sudden growl at the waft of appetising scents that filled the air.

He grinned. 'Why don't we stop for a minute for a snack, before we head on to the temple?'

'A snack sounds good. Any recommendations?'

'Try the *oyaki*. They are dumplings, filled with seasonal wild greens. Or you can get a pumpkin filling, or…'

'We could get both. I'll still be able to eat dinner. Honestly I will.'

'OK. I'll be back in a minute.'

He entered the shop and returned a few minutes later, handed her a steaming, round flattish dumpling.

'The green vegetable is called *nozawana*—I think they are turnip leaves—and then there are pickles inside as well.'

'It's lovely.'

For a moment she sat and savoured the tart taste of the pickle, complementing the firm, chewy layers of the bun that encased it. She looked around at the grey pavement speckled with snow, at the light from the illuminations so bright and festive and beautiful, and yet so very different from the Christmas lights she was used to. And as she sat there she appreciated that difference, and the fact that she was in a new and different place that could be something exciting.

'I'm glad you're enjoying it,' said Zayne.

'I am. Not just the food, but all of it. The atmosphere…the whole experience.'

'Better than working?' His voice was tentative. 'I'm not trying to reopen the discussion, but I sense what I said upset you earlier and I wanted to try and explain. I didn't mean to be judgemental, though I get that I sounded it. Work is important, but so is this—experiencing a new country, a new culture. If you spend your whole time in your room working, you're missing out.'

'I am not spending my whole time in my room.'

How had this become personal?

'No need to sound so defensive.' His words echoed her own earlier. 'But what have you done since you got here? Apart from work?'

'Plenty. I've been skiing every day, and I've gone to the *onsen*. I've eaten lots of food and I've walked to the village a couple of times.'

But she hadn't been to the village shrine, hadn't ventured to Nagano, hadn't done so many things.

'Right now I have to prioritise work.'

'I do get that. You always did, even when you were six years old and we had a spelling contest at school. And all the way through to your exams, when you knew what you needed to get a place at Cambridge. But throughout all of it we did other things. Climbed trees, rode our bikes, built dens, sneaked out with a couple of bottles of cider and—'

He broke off, and Thea knew he was remembering that kiss. For a moment she too was transported back in time, could see a kaleidoscope of memories. She and Zayne playing in the garden, learning how to ride their bikes together, hiding out with biscuits, growing up, trying that first forbidden sip of cider. And then that kiss…

And somehow teenage Zayne morphed into the Zayne now sitting by her side, and she was looking at his lips, remembering their taste, their texture, the feel of his hand in hers. She wondered how different it would be now, remembering the awkward sweetness of their kiss, the awakening of something that had made her feel edgy, wound up tight.

Back then she'd sensed it was something new and powerful, but she'd told herself that the edginess was due to awkwardness. Now she knew better, and she recognised in a moment of clarity that that first kiss had awoken something she hadn't been ready to acknowledge.

'Thea?'

His voice was gruff, raspy, almost as if he could feel some kind of pull.

Thea blinked hard, dispersed the images, the memories of the past, and also the fantasy present she'd conjured up.

Kissing Zayne had been a mistake back then and it would be a mistake now. She was sure of it. Even if she couldn't quite answer the little voice in the back of her mind that was asking her why. Back then it had changed their friendship, triggered their growing apart. Now... Now what harm could it do?

One kiss. To satisfy her curiosity.

Perhaps she should ask him, like she had all those years ago? Sell the idea to him as an exercise in curiosity?

Thea sighed to herself. Nope. She'd trust her instinct. The one that told her that this time a kiss might unleash more than she wanted to handle. Might lead to complications, a distraction from what she needed to focus on most. Her meeting with Riika Itawa.

Which reminded her—she had an argument to win. But somehow the best she could do was say, 'That was then. This is now. Now I am happy with my work-life balance and that's what matters. So, please, can we just go and enjoy this beautiful place?'

'Agreed.' His smile rueful. 'And I won't bring it up again.'

'Good.'

A few more minutes' walk and they reached the temple area itself. Again Thea came to a stop at the sight of the two-storey wooded edifice. She knew from her reading that it was the *hondo*, or main hall.

'I read that it's built from sixty thousand lengths of wood. I can't imagine what that even means. And the roof is made solely from cypress bark. I mean…how?'

Zayne shook his head. 'It's pretty impressive and pretty old.'

'It's incredible that it was originally built in the seventh century. So many hundreds of years ago; there's something about it that engenders awe. As in "awesome" in the real sense of the word.'

'Many people would say that comes from the fact this temple houses what is said to be the first Buddha statue ever brought to Japan. It's hidden away, and it is decreed that no one should ever see it—not even the temple's chief priest. And that is a serious commandment that has been adhered to for centuries. There is a replica, and that is only shown to the public every six years.'

Thea thought about that, thought about a statue so precious, so revered, that no eye could see it. Thought about the strength of character it must take not to look and for a moment it was wonderful to simply stand there, next to the warm, solid bulk of Zayne, before they moved on and she took in more of the illuminations.

She watched the incredible dance and play of colour, and the magical way that images danced and flickered across the roofs and walls. The statues and the golden carvings lit up. Birds, flowers and animals moved through the spectrum in bursts of colour, and the glitter of golden statues flickered and sparkled in the moving pictures.

'When it was built, all those years ago, when battles were fought, the people couldn't have imagined how it would be today, with these illuminations, this slide-show of images,' she said. 'Would they feel that what we're doing is wrong? Coming here to watch as tourists, not worshippers, being allowed to visit the temple, attend prayers?'

'I'd like to think they would be pleased that what they built has endured, and that there are people who still come to worship and pray, people who still stand by the commandments laid down all those years ago,' he said. 'Maybe they'd appreciate that there are people here who respect their beliefs and come here out of genuine interest and enjoyment.'

'Hopefully they would see this for what it is—a way of celebrating their beautiful creation and their beliefs. A tribute.'

'But we can't really know, can we?' he asked, and she caught a sadness in his voice. 'We can't ever really know what the people who are gone think or would think if they were still here. Their thoughts, opinions, are lost to us.'

Her heartstrings tugged; there was no bitterness in his voice, only that sadness as they stood in front of this history-steeped place.

'You must miss your dad a lot,' she said softly. 'I truly can't imagine what it must be like.'

The idea of not having her parents in her life was hard to fathom. And in addition to that Zayne was an only child.

'But I am sorry.'

'Thank you. I think about him a lot when I come to places like this. I remember him and I try to imagine what he would tell me, advise me. What he would think of my life and my achievements. But I can't know, because in the end he doesn't know me, not the Zayne I am now.'

'No, he doesn't. But I know that he would be proud of what you have achieved. This is what he wanted for you—to be a success, to fulfil your potential.'

'I hope so,' Zayne said.

But she could hear the doubt in his voice and she turned to face him, took both his hands in hers.

'I know so. I remember how proud your dad was when you won that science prize, and the time the local newspaper interviewed you. And when you got into MIT I thought he'd burst, he was so proud. He wasn't just proud, he was happy for you, happy that you'd achieved what you'd worked so hard for.'

She saw a shadow cross his face and wondered why.

'He loved you, Zayne,' she told him. 'And in the end he would have been proud of you no matter what. Loved you no matter what. His love for you was unconditional. He wanted the best for you and I know he would be so very proud of you now.'

'Because I've made millions?'

'Yes. But not just for that. Because you've achieved what you wanted to achieve, attained your goals. You've helped and supported your mum. You've made a good life for yourself.'

He smiled, but she sensed that she hadn't assuaged the doubt that still clouded his brown eyes. She wished she could do something to help.

'Like I said, I can't imagine how hard it must be to lose a parent. I'm sorry, Zayne.'

'It's OK.'

His voice was gentle, almost as if he were comforting her, and she looked down at their clasped hands as the illuminations changed colour again, their stark white light almost hauntingly beautiful as the images chased each other.

There it was again—that jolt of awareness. And now she knew there was little point denying it to herself. There was definitely something going on.

It was as if her whole body was focused on their clasped hands and she was willing him to pull her closer, whilst conversely fighting the urge to take that step herself. Right now it wasn't only about curiosity, although that was a strand in the whirling, swirling urge that was willing her forward. There was also a need to give comfort, offer warmth, to chase the sadness from his eyes.

Surely, she could do that? Years ago she would have hugged him without thought, offered the comfort of friendship. Before that fateful kiss. After that, by tacit consent, they hadn't so much as brushed hands.

But that was then. Now she was a woman, a successful lawyer known for her bite, intellect and professionalism. Yet here she was, unable to give this man, a friend in need of comfort, a hug.

Not right.

She would give a Zayne a hug.

Not allowing herself to think, she stepped forward and put her arms around him. She heard his involuntary catch of breath and knew in that instant this was a mistake. Because now he was too close. *They* were too close. She could feel the lithe, lean hardness of his body through the layers of his clothes, could smell the expensive tang of bergamot.

She looked up at him and saw the unmistakable flash of desire in his brown eyes. A desire she reciprocated. She wanted him, had a reckless need to know what it would feel like to taste him, to loop her arms round his neck, to tangle her fingers in his thick black hair.

She stood on tiptoe and brushed his lips with her own. The sensation was so searing, so breathtaking that it took her by surprise, and she gave a small gasp of sheer pleasure—before the panic set in.

Panic engendered by the intensity of the desire that gripped her…the depth of pleasure from that brief simple contact.

Panic made worse by the fear that she had made a complete fool of herself.

This was Zayne. Her old friend Zayne, but also pres-ent-day Zayne: millionaire, yacht-owning, party-loving Zayne, who had dated women so beautiful, so dazzling, so successful...

So not Thea.

'I...' She forced herself to meet his gaze and felt a sense of relief touch her, because she saw a mirror of her surprise, shock and desire in his eyes. 'I don't know what to say.'

'Me neither,' he said shakily. 'So maybe for now we shouldn't say anything at all.'

'Agreed.'

Or maybe they shouldn't say anything ever.

So they focused on another swathe of illuminations as they lit up the temple, and the crowd gave a collec-tive sigh of appreciation.

Then he glanced at his watch. 'We should probably head to the restaurant now.'

She nodded, even as she put her fingers to her lips and realised they were still tingling.

CHAPTER SIX

ZAYNE DIDN'T EVEN try to come up with any small-talk as they walked to the restaurant. Right now all he could focus on was whatever the hell had happened back there, against the illuminated backdrop of the temple. He wasn't even sure it counted as a kiss, but it had provoked in him a reaction, a response, that had blown his mind.

So what now?

For once he didn't know—had no idea. The Zayne Wood playbook was coming up a blank.

Twenty minutes later they entered the restaurant. Its décor was basic and unfussy, and it was filled with people all seated on *tatami* mats on the floor at traditional low tables.

'Is this OK?' Zayne asked. 'They do have a section with Western-style tables if you prefer.'

'This is fine. It's called a *zashiki*, isn't it? I've actually got used to it.'

She sank to the floor in a graceful movement and smiled at the waiter, waiting for him to leave before turning to Zayne.

'Could we forget what happened back there? I don't want it to change anything.'

'Like last time?' he asked.

'Exactly. Let's eat and catch up and not complicate anything.'

'Works for me.'

After all, maybe he and Thea could rekindle their old friendship, be part of each other's lives again. As friends. In which case they needed to forget what had happened, pass it off as an inexplicable aberration.

'So, what would you like to eat? The *ramen* here is the best.'

'Then the only question is which one. Do I go vegetarian? Or shall I…?'

She frowned as she studied the menu and he grinned.

'What?' Thea looked up.

'You're so serious. It's like you're figuring all the angles on your menu choice.'

'Of course I am. Menu choices are really important. I may never have the chance to have *ramen* here again.'

'Then I have a solution. We'll order all six choices and share. Then we'll take anything we don't eat home with us.'

'That is a brilliant idea.'

'That's because I am handsome, charismatic *and* brilliant.'

She smiled, a genuine smile that flecked her eyes with amusement. 'Ha-ha!'

The waiter approached and Zayne ordered, trying out a few words of the Japanese he'd picked up.

'Impressive,' Thea commented, then raised her hand. 'OK… OK. We'll add linguist to your ever-growing list of accomplishments.'

'Feel free to keep going all evening.'

'If I don't, I'm sure you will. But I have to admit this is an excellent choice. It looks and smells amazing, and it's full of locals—which is always a good sign. How did you find it?'

'It was recommended by the guy who runs the café we went to this morning.'

Even as he said the last two words he questioned their veracity. Was it really only hours ago that he'd bumped into Thea? Somehow that didn't seem possible.

It felt so easy to be with her in so many ways. And in so many other ways it didn't. The simmer of attraction added an edge, an awareness, a whole new facet that enhanced the familiar. Because this Thea wasn't the Thea he'd known years ago. This Thea was sharper, more driven, and there were shadows in her eyes that hadn't been there before. He wanted to know why. All she'd told him about the past twelve years so far was to do with work. He wanted to know more.

'So, tell me more about what you've been doing? How are your family? How is Eliza?'

The memory of the time Eliza had been seriously ill was still vivid in his mind. The shock, the change to the happy, laughing Kendall household. The fear and anger that the eleven-year-old Thea had felt, the way she'd clenched her fists and vowed that nothing would happen to her little sister, the tears she'd cried just that once on his shoulder.

But now Thea's face lit up. 'Eliza is good. Better than good. She got the all-clear—no more hospital visits necessary.'

'That is fabulous news. You must all be over the

moon.' He sat back as bowls of steaming *ramen* arrived at the table. 'I am so glad, Thea. I know we were worried before I left for MIT; she was so tired all the time.'

'She did have a relapse soon after you left. Your parents decided not to tell you. They were concerned it would distract you.'

'That's ridiculous.'

Thea shrugged. 'They didn't think so. They thought you might want to come back to support me. I told them that you wouldn't do that, but they were adamant, and in the end I agreed not to tell you either.'

He studied her face, saw the wariness in her eyes, the slight tension in her jawline, and despite her direct gaze he sensed she was hiding something…some emotion she didn't want him to hone in on.

'You should have told me,' he said.

'There was nothing you could have done. Eliza was in hospital, with the best doctors and treatment.'

Her voice was stiff, as if she'd rehearsed the words in her head. Maybe she had.

'I'm sorry. I saw how hard it was the first time around. I'm guessing this was even more scary.'

'It was,' she said simply, and he could see remembered pain cross her face. She shook her head. 'But that's over now and we can all finally relax. It's five years since Eliza got the all-clear, and that is a pretty significant marker.'

'Then that is the most important thing. But I still think you should have told me, or my parents should have. Although they were right.' He helped himself to a second ladleful of the fragrant *ramen*. 'I would have come back. But it wouldn't have impacted my studies. I would have caught up.'

She froze, chopsticks halfway to her mouth. 'You'd have come back?'

'Yes, I would,' he said, his voice steady. 'Exactly like you would have come to my dad's funeral. I grew up with your family. I saw what it was like when Eliza was sick the first time. I would have wanted to support you.' He frowned as he saw a shadow cross her face. 'Thea? What's wrong?'

'Nothing is wrong.' She took a deep breath. 'But it shows your parents were right and it's good that you didn't come back. What if the world had been deprived of your brilliant ideas because you didn't graduate from MIT?'

What if he *had* come back? What would have happened then? With Thea?

'I'd have found another way,' he said. 'Anyway, that's a bit dramatic. I wouldn't have dropped out of MIT.'

'Well, what's done is done.'

There was a finality to her voice that he didn't understand, but for whatever reason it was clearly time for a subject-change.

'How is Sienna?'

'She's OK. She and her husband split up recently. I know, and so does she, that he wasn't the right man for her, but she's still hurting.' Thea's eyes narrowed and she stabbed at a piece of *tempura* with unnecessary force. 'That's why I sincerely hope she is sitting in the sunshine right now, a cocktail in her hand, watching the waves. And if there happens to be a gorgeous surfer around all the better.'

Zayne smiled at the protective note in her voice. He'd always admired and perhaps envied how close the Kendall sisters were.

'So Sienna's on vacation as well?'

'Yes.'

Thea didn't seem about to elaborate, and now Zayne's curiosity was aroused. He made a guess.

'And Eliza?'

'Yes.'

'So all of you are on holiday at the same time, separately, in the run-up to Christmas. That's a bit of a coincidence.'

Thea sighed. 'It's not a coincidence. It's a pact. A Christmas pact.'

'Tell me more.'

'Mum and Dad have gone on a cruise this year, to celebrate their fortieth wedding anniversary, so the usual family Christmas isn't happening.'

'Are you telling me that the Kendall family Christmas traditions have continued until now?'

'What's wrong with that?' she asked, her face creasing into a scowl at the surprise in his voice.

He'd forgotten how fierce and yet how cute her scowl was. The scrunch of those amber eyes and the pressing together of those lips...lips his gaze snagged on. Again.

'You know how important Christmas is to us,' she said.

'There's nothing wrong with it. I love the idea.' He truly did. 'Do you still watch Christmas movies in your pyjamas?'

'Absolutely we do. I'm in charge of the pyjamas, in

fact. I even made sure I packed some in Sienna and Eliza's suitcases.'

'So how does this pact work?'

'Eliza and I chose where to send Sienna, Sienna and I chose where to send Eliza, and they chose to send me here, to Japan. We all packed each other's suitcases and only found out where we were going the day we left. So Sienna is in Bora Bora right now, and Eliza is in Costa Rica. A client of mine, Matt, owns and runs a portfolio of eco hotels there, and he has promised to look out for Eliza. Sienna and I think she'll love it. There's plenty of adventurous things to do—she can really spread her wings and be independent.'

'Though I bet your client is under strict instructions to keep her safe.'

'Well, he promised his PA would, but Eliza messaged me. It turns out Matt has stepped up.'

'Does Eliza mind that you've detailed her a minder?'

'Nope. I think she's so used to us being protective she takes it in her stride. I just hope Matt is coping with her.' A small frown creased her forehead. 'I hope I'm right about Eliza and she doesn't mind. Maybe it was a bit over the top...'

Zayne could have kicked himself. He'd already overstepped earlier, over Thea's work ethic—now he was questioning her knowledge of her own sister.

'Of course it wasn't. Hell, what do I know? I'm an only child. I have no idea how having a sibling works. Eliza has been wrapped in cotton wool all her life, through no fault of her own, and it will be strange for her being out there on her own. I reckon she'll be glad of some back-up.'

Thea flashed a relieved smile at him, 'Thank you, Zayne. That was the absolute right thing to say.'

She reached out and covered his hand with her own. And, *wham*, sparks flew. He'd swear he could see them...could hear a little zing and a whoosh as awareness reignited in an instant and he was back outside the temple, her hands in his, her lips brushing his in exquisite sensation.

Say something...anything.

'And you've sent Sienna to Bora Bora? That's French Polynesian, isn't it?'

Yup, Zayne, show off your geographical knowledge, why don't you?

'We figured Sienna deserves to go on holiday somewhere *she* wants to go. Somewhere warm and sunny, where she can surf...or rather kite surf. That's what's she's opted for, and she'll love it. I just hope...'

'Hope what?'

'I packed her a brand-new designer bikini along with her usual trusty black one-piece. It's bronze and she will look stunning in it. I only hope she'll wear it.'

For a minute he couldn't help wishing they'd ended up on a sunny beach and it was Thea in the bikini.

Blinking the image away, he said easily, 'I'm sure she will. Because she'll feel bad if she doesn't, seeing as you sent it.' That was how the Kendall sisters worked. 'And your sisters sent you to Japan? What do you reckon their motivation was?'

'I think they wanted me to be far, far away from work and in a different time zone, so I couldn't sneak back to the office.'

Zayne raised his eyebrows. 'Yet you told me you're on a working holiday.'

'That's because I am. I can't take a two-week break. Simple as that. I only agreed to the pact because I could see how much it meant to Eliza. And I know it made my parents feel better too. Plus, Sienna needs this break. Obviously I haven't told my sisters how much I'm working. Though I will thank them at some point. Because it means I am on the spot for this client meeting. Which is a massive opportunity.'

'Plus, you got to meet me.'

'I still can't really believe that. I mean, what are the chances of it, really, after all these years?'

'The chances are pretty slim.'

'Almost unbelievable.' Her eyes narrowed suddenly. 'Unless…'

'Unless what?'

'Is it common knowledge that you're here?'

The question was laser-like, and he wondered where she was going with this.

'I didn't take a billboard out and announce it, no, and I wasn't expecting to stay so long. But there have been some pictures taken, and there may have been some coverage on social media. Why?'

'I was wondering if my sisters knew you were in the area. I mean, now I come to think about it, why Japan?'

Her face scrunched again, and this time the scowl was way more formidable.

'They didn't contact you, did they? This isn't some sort of elaborate plot to make sure I actually have a holiday?' She leant forward. 'Is it?'

Zayne looked at her, saw she was being serious, and understood why. The Kendall sisters were very close—it was something he could picture Sienna and Eliza doing. He thought he could even understand why they might have.

Thea's life seemed to focus utterly upon work, it was as though she was unwilling or unable to relax. He got that, and her drive and ambition were to be admired. But, as he'd been trying to point out to her, everyone needed to wind down. And the Kendall sisters would do anything for each other.

However, in this case...

'Not guilty.' He lifted his hands. 'Word of honour.'

He held out both pinkie fingers, as they'd used to do as children. It had been their own code to prove they were telling the truth. Their very own private system. He could recall sitting on the swing chair in the Kendalls' garden and eyeing her, ascertaining the truth or making a solemn promise.

'I mean it. They didn't contact me.' He pushed his hands further forward. 'I promise, and here's the proof.'

He needed Thea to believe him, to know she could trust him, and whilst part of him knew inviting further contact was foolhardy, right now that didn't matter.

For a second she hesitated, and then she lifted her own hands. They linked little fingers and Zayne felt a sudden breathlessness hit him, an intensity of feeling as their fingers entwined. The jolt and volt of sensation increased as they pulled away slightly, before pressing the palms of their hands together and withdrawing.

There was no denying it as they stared at each other.

The jolts and volts were continuing, even after the contact was broken, and something was fizzing through his veins.

All he wanted to do was lean forward and kiss her. The desire was so strong it tightened his chest and twisted his gut. And it wasn't just him. Thea was affected too. He could see it in the flush on her cheeks, in the way she looked down at her hands, the way her lips had parted slightly.

They were leaning ever so slightly towards each other. This time he knew for sure he wasn't imagining it.

Now what? Usually Zayne Wood would know exactly what to do, he had a series of moves in his playbook. But usually this situation came up on a bona fide date, with the rules known to both parties in advance, and usually there were two playbooks in play, with a recognised manoeuvre expected.

But this was not a date. This was Thea. No rules, no playbook, and Zayne had no answers.

He had nothing except common sense to fall back on. Common sense and data analysis—coding the numbers and looking at the possibilities.

Maybe the fact that he hadn't dated for nearly a year was having some sort of odd effect on his libido. So one look at an attractive woman and *kaboom*.

Only he knew it wasn't that. This was about Thea. This attraction was specific, and complete in its intensity. He knew it…she knew it. He could see that knowledge in her amber eyes, along with shock, wariness and panic.

This had to stop. There were way too many emotions

going on. There was a reason for rules and a playbook. It meant no shock, no panic, no unwanted rollercoaster of emotions.

It was time to take control of the situation and the conversation. Find some context. Zayne was in Japan trying to figure out where he wanted his life to go next. He was not getting involved with Thea in any complicated capacity. If they could be friends again, all well and good. And if that was a possibility they mustn't muddy the waters with attraction.

'Truly,' he said. 'Your sisters did not get in touch with me and ask me to fake an accidental meeting. And if they had—which they didn't—I wouldn't have faked a collision on the slopes. Too risky and too complicated. I'd have had to know when you were going on the slopes, which slope, and then I would have had to loiter, recognised you in a mask and goggles, and—'

'Fair enough. I overreacted.'

It was hard to know if she meant with the allegations or her reaction to his touch.

'It's just they've already messaged me multiple times, checking that I am having a holiday. And I wouldn't put it past them. But I accept the collision was a genuine accident and meeting you was a genuine coincidence.'

'I mean, there may be some factors at play...' He frowned, relieved to have something to focus on apart from the flutters of desire that were still rippling through him. 'Maybe Eliza and Sienna saw something that mentioned I was in Japan skiing, and it registered somewhere in their consciousness when they chose your destination. Or maybe it's fate.'

'Fate?' Her voice held surprise. 'Can this be Zayne Wood speaking? King of statistics, probabilities, numbers and codes?'

He'd regretted using the word as soon as he'd uttered it. 'I know... I know. But you have to admit that sometimes the inexplicable happens. You could argue that all those random things combining together to get us to collide on that mountain is what fate is. Me deciding to explore a new slope, you skipping breakfast, you trying out an intermediate slope today, me waking up at the time I did, you waking up at the time you did, those kids' parents booking this holiday... All those tiny decisions and happenings and chances combined in order for our collision to happen. Fate.'

She looked directly at him. 'I'm not buying it. I mean, why would fate bother? Fate surely has bigger things to worry about than getting us together for dinner and a catch-up.'

'Maybe fate got tired of waiting. I mean, we've had plenty of years to try and catch up.' He looked at her. 'Why didn't you ever contact me?'

She thought for a minute. 'To begin with we were so caught up with Eliza. And then...you hit the big time. You felt a bit unreal, not like my Zayne—' She broke off. 'Not that you were ever mine. I mean I couldn't really relate to the celebrity version of you. A Zayne who partied on yachts, a multi-millionaire Zayne. I couldn't contact you then.'

'Why not?'

'Because it would have looked pretty bad. As though I were a groupie. It would have felt fake. *Hi, Zayne, we lost touch, but now you're rich and successful and all over the news I thought I'd get in contact.'*

He stared at her. 'But I'd never have thought that of you, that you were after my fame and fortune.'

How could he have? This was Thea.

'You'd never want anything you hadn't earnt yourself. I know that.'

'It's how it felt to me. Plus, I figured if you wanted to contact me you knew where I was. And if you didn't, it was because you'd moved on into your new, glamorous life.'

'Now I get why fate took a hand in it all,' he said. 'It was the only solution.'

'Nope. Not buying it.' She shook her head and her auburn hair caught the light. 'We've survived and thrived for over a decade without each other. There was no need for fate to intervene.'

'How about we find out? Maybe there is a reason.'

'Such as?'

Scepticism creased her brow, but he saw curiosity in her eyes as well, as if she was wondering where he was going with this. In truth, he was wondering the same. Even as an idea began to take shape in his head...

He hesitated, glanced at their empty plates. 'How about I get our leftovers packaged up and we go somewhere for dessert and I'll tell you?'

That would give him time to work out if this idea was a dud or a doozy.

CHAPTER SEVEN

As they walked along the stretch of shops, most of them closed now, the bright pictures on the closed shutters formed a moving stream as they passed.

Thea wondered what on earth Zayne had in mind. She was aware of a hum of anticipation that somehow made the illuminations sparkle brighter, and as she looked up at the indigo blue of the sky the scent of snow seemed fresher, colder, sharper than before. The whole evening felt alight with possibility, even though she wasn't sure what those possibilities were.

She glanced up at him, saw the intent look on his face, and knew he was figuring out the idea that had come to him, assessing it. Out here, so many miles from home, walking next to him, the idea of fate somehow didn't seem so daft, and it sent a funny little shiver down her spine.

One she dismissed as they entered a small café and saw that the proprietor was about to close.

Zayne stepped forward, and after a quick conversation Thea saw the woman nod and smile.

'It's fine. She says we can stay.'

Thea smiled at the woman, hoping she'd sense her

appreciation of the kindness, and then followed Zayne to one of the small square black tables before looking at the menu. She saw that all the desserts were hand-made on the premises. Glancing round, she saw the packaged puddings, in small, simply decorated jars lined up on a shelf.

'I think I'll try the matcha one,' she said. 'It says it's "bittersweet and elegant", which sounds interesting. And I'll get the other four to take back.'

'Good choice. I'm going to give the sesame seed one a try.'

Once they had sampled their puddings, Thea said, 'Right. You've had long enough to mull your idea over. So spill—tell me what you're thinking. Why do you think fate has thrown us together like this?'

'To help each other.'

Thea raised her eyebrows. 'OK… You have my interest.'

'You're trying to juggle work with doing enough holiday stuff to keep your sisters happy, right?'

'Right.'

She knew her sisters would have put as much thought into her adventure as she had into theirs. Would be hoping that distance from the office would be enticing her to embrace the holiday experience.

'So that's where I come in. I can plan and organise fun things for us to do. That will give you more time to work and yet it will also maximise the holiday experience for you.'

She stared at him, and despite herself anticipation shot through her. 'Us?' she asked.

'Yup. I'm part of the deal. I bet Eliza and Sienna will be thrilled you have company. Especially mine.'

'And what about my thrills?' she asked.

Even as she said it she regretted it, as he smiled a sudden slow smile.

'They can be negotiated.'

Her insides seemed to go all gooey as she looked into his eyes, which had taken on a sudden dark intensity. She had to get a grip before she made a complete idiot of herself. Zayne was flirting because this was what Zayne Wood did. He had the smile and the lines and she would not fall for it.

'I am perfectly capable of organising my own fun.'

'Sure you are. But be honest. Hasn't today been fun? Haven't you done things you wouldn't have done otherwise? *And* got some work done?'

Honesty compelled her to nod.

'So what do you think?'

Her eyes narrowed. 'You said we could help each other. What's in it for you?'

'The pleasure of your company.'

She rolled her eyes. 'Is that a line out of the Zayne Wood playbook?'

'No—' He broke off and gave a sudden rueful smile. 'Maybe,' he modified. 'But in this case I really mean it. I would like your company, and more than that I'd like your insight, your opinion.'

'About what? I mean, what on earth could you want my opinion on? If you mean legally, I'm sure you have a swathe of corporate lawyers at your fingertips.'

'Nope. It's not legal advice I'm after.' He looked

almost embarrassed. 'I need a friend's advice.' He paused, scooped up a spoonful of pudding. 'It's a bit difficult to explain, but right now I feel like I'm at a crossroads. Maybe it's a cliché thing. I've turned thirty and I have decided to reassess.'

Thea shook her head, resisted the urge to roll her eyes. Talk about shades of the past… That was exactly what Ian had said. He'd been approaching thirty and he had 'reassessed'.

Only he hadn't asked Thea's opinion, or her advice, despite the fact they'd been together for five years and living together for three. Instead he'd reassessed for both of them. Changed the rules, changed the goal-posts, changed full-stop. She no longer blamed him, accepted that people changed, that he hadn't meant to lead her up the garden path. But she would never ever let a man do that to her again.

Zayne looked at her. 'What's wrong with that?'

'Nothing, but I don't get it. It's just a number. It doesn't need to change anything.'

'Then maybe that isn't the reason. Maybe I've done what I set out to do. I've achieved wealth and security. I took my idea and it worked. I built up a business and I took it global. I sold it for an obscene amount. So what next? I don't know.'

'And you think I can help. How?'

'You can be a sounding board. You know me, you know where I came from, how I grew up. You were part of my formative years. You are also trained to analyse information. Maybe you can help me weigh up my options?' He grimaced. 'I've been thinking about it by myself for weeks and I've got nowhere. So a second opinion could be the answer. From someone I can trust not to post our discussions on social media or give an interview.'

'An interview that could literally crash the price of the shares in any company you're involved in?'

'Yup.'

'And you trust *me*?' The idea warmed her.

'Yes. You always had my back, and you always kept my secrets.'

'I was a child then,' she pointed out. 'Things change.'

'Are you saying I can't trust you?'

'Of course not. You can. But I wouldn't advise you to randomly trust anyone just because they've been important in your life.'

'There hasn't really been anyone important in my life,' he said simply. 'Since you.'

The words seemed to take on a sonorous sense of meaning, and as if he sensed it he gave a light laugh.

'I mean not in this sense. Of course I have friends, business colleagues…people who are important in my life one way or the other. But I am talking here about implicit trust. How many people like that do you have in your life?'

'I have my sisters.'

'I mean outside of family.'

Thea thought, and realised anew how lucky she was to have Sienna and Eliza.

'I have maybe one close friend I'd maybe trust.'

But she could hear the doubt in her voice, and knew in reality that if push came to shove, if it was a really important secret, she wouldn't trust her friend Claire not to tell her husband, or have a glass or two too many and tell someone else. She realised, too, that in the past two years she'd seen Claire less…seen all her friends less.

'"Maybe" doesn't cut it,' he said.

'No, it doesn't. But the point is you can trust me.'

'I know. That's why I'm suggesting this deal. We spend some time together over the next few days. You fulfil your allocation of fun, get some good evidence to send your sisters. I get a sounding board. What do you think?'

Thea looked at him, and wished it was easier to actually think around him. 'I think it could work. But I need to make this clear: my priority is work. Especially my upcoming meeting.'

Even as she said the words misgivings hit her. She hadn't given that meeting a thought all evening, had been too caught up in Zayne.

'That takes precedence over any deal.'

Disquiet of another sort struck. How could it be right to put work above friendship? But that was how it was. She couldn't pass this opportunity up. For anyone.

'Got it. You fix the timetable. Tell me how many hours are available in your day for fun and discussion. We can always multi-task, maybe chat through my options over meals. I'll work around you.'

'You're OK with that?' She'd expected him to make more of a push to be in charge.

'Absolutely. So, is there anything you particularly want to do?'

'You mean for my fun tasks?' she asked.

Zayne sighed—an exaggerated noise that was half a groan.

'What?'

'Fun is not a *task*. Fun is meant to be... Well, fun. Not just something on your to-do list. Sometimes it is even possible to have spontaneous fun, not planned fun.'

He drew each word out in an exaggerated drawl.

'As I remember it, you're the one trying to figure out his life plan. How about you do that spontaneously?'

Zayne grinned. 'Fair point. But if you do have any ideas for fun let me know.'

'There is one thing... I'd like to go to an art gallery. The client I'm meeting is a fan of art. I haven't managed to find out much more than that, but I thought it would be a good thing to discuss.'

'Do you like Japanese art?'

'I don't really know. But it would be interesting to find out.'

He frowned now, and she looked at him questioningly. 'What's wrong? You did ask what I wanted to do.'

'Exactly. I asked what *you* wanted to do. Not what you should do for a client. What do *you*, Thea Kendall, want to do? Really want to do? Right here and now?'

With his words the atmosphere changed. She looked at him, saw the serious look in his brown eyes, and for a mad moment all she wanted to do was lean over and kiss him.

Giving her head a small shake to dislodge the

thought, she sighed and considered his question. 'I don't know.'

'Close your eyes and think about it.'

She closed her eyes. 'I'd like to read a book. A fictional book. Sitting in an outdoor *onsen* like the one you were talking about.' She opened her eyes, felt suddenly silly. 'That's a bit daft, isn't it? When I could be doing so many more exciting things.'

'It's not daft at all,' he said softly. 'I'll try and incorporate it into our fun timetable.'

'Thank you. And I haven't forgotten about you. How about we meet for breakfast tomorrow at my hotel and we can have a talk?'

'Works for me. So we have a deal?'

'We have a deal.'

He held out his hand and she looked at it. Suddenly the world seemed to shift slightly and all she could focus on was his hand. The size of it, the strength, the shape of his wrist, the tapering of each finger… Her mind streamed with images of that hand on her, on her body, and the thought of placing her hand in his sent a shiver of desire through her.

Before she could think further, she held out her own hand and braced herself as he enclosed it. The feel of it…the feel of him…intensified the desire and she couldn't help it. She tugged her hand free. They'd made a deal based on friendship, a friendship she didn't want to jeopardise.

'Deal,' she repeated.

'Good. Then let's head back now and I'll see you in the morning.'

* * *

By the following morning Thea had herself under control, and by the time she walked down to the lobby to meet Zayne she was sure she was restored to her usual professional self. This breakfast was more of a business meeting than anything else.

That comfortable conviction lasted for exactly as long as it took her to walk across the lobby. Both comfort and conviction were eroded the closer she got to him.

Dammit, the man had no right to look this good. His hair was slightly damp from the snowfall outside, and the chunky fisherman's jumper seemed to mould to the breadth of his shoulders. Hell and damnation. She could feel her poise starting to crumble.

'Good morning,' she said.

'Hey. Good morning. Sleep well?'

His voice was a low, deep rumble.

'Fine, thank you. Breakfast is this way. It'll be served in my room. I hope that's OK? I thought it would be more private.'

Did that sound suggestive?

'That way no one can overhear us,' she added hurriedly. 'Talking,' she concluded desperately.

'What else would we be doing?'

His tone sounded genuinely confused. She halted as he opened his eyes wide in what she now realised was mock innocence and then grinned at her. And she couldn't help it. She chuckled, and he laughed, and suddenly it was as if the years had vanished and they were two giggling teenagers.

Eventually they stopped and he followed her to her room, where breakfast was already laid out.

'This is definitely one of my favourite parts of the day,' she said and exhaled a small happy sigh as they surveyed the food spread out on the low table in the middle of the floor. Like Thea, Zayne had removed his shoes, and he sat down cross-legged on the floor. She surveyed the bowls of sticky white rice and the sheets of *nori*—the seaweed that she'd learnt to roll the rice into with the tofu and pickles. Then there was *miso* soup, and Japanese omelette.

'The omelette is my favourite, even if I'm not sure I am pronouncing it right. It's called *tamagoyaki*. Is that right?'

'Yup. I tried to make it and it's not that easy. Mine certainly didn't look so perfectly rolled.'

'How *do* you make it?'

She sat down opposite him and waited for him to help himself, knowing she couldn't risk even an accidental touch. Not when she felt as though the conversation and her hormones were under control at last.

'You have to roll together layers of beaten fried egg. So you cook a bit of the egg, but you can't let it set on top, and you push it to the side of the pan. Then you repeat, and kind of roll the first bit onto the second bit, and you keep doing that until in theory you achieve this.' He waved his chopstick at the *tamagoyaki*. 'Mine was less successful.'

'So where are you staying?'

Presumably not a hotel if he was cooking for himself.

'I've found a cabin. It's pretty secluded, right in the

middle of the woods. It belongs to a friend of one of the café's owners. He doesn't usually rent it out, but he has made an exception. It's quite basic, but it's got everything I need. I thought that isolation might help me think, and it has, but I still have no answers.'

'Then let's see if I can help.'

CHAPTER EIGHT

ZAYNE STUDIED THEA'S FACE, wondering suddenly if this was such a good idea as it had sounded the day before. But it was too late for regret. They'd made a deal, and Thea looked like a woman with a plan.

'Right, so how do we do this?'

Thea tipped her head to one side. 'First, I guess I need to ask the obvious question. What's wrong with the lifestyle you have? You've enjoyed it for the past twelve years. What's changed?'

'I'm not sure,' he said honestly. 'I think it started when I sold ZW, a couple of years ago.'

That was the company he'd built up from scratch.

'Why did you sell it?'

'For me, the joy was in creating my idea.' He grimaced. 'I know cyber security software isn't everyone's cup of tea, but my model, my program, was a game-changer and I knew it. I loved the buzz of selling the idea, getting the backing, setting up a company and growing it. But once the company got to a certain point I felt…restless. I'd done what I set out to do and it was time to move on. My whole heart wasn't in it any more and I knew it was time to go. So I sold it.'

'And since then?'

'Since then I've been dabbling. Investing in various new tech companies, making more money. I like new ideas, new companies, but it's not what I want to do for ever.'

'So do you have any idea at all what you want to do?'

'Nope. Not a clue.'

He'd been so driven to succeed, to achieve his dad's dream for him, that once he'd got there he'd had no idea what to do next.

'I have enough money that I don't need to work ever again. But I'm not ready to retire.'

'OK. I'm going to try something. I'm going to name some different options and you have to say yes or no. No thinking. Just gut instinct.'

'Got it.' He took a sip of green tea and nodded. 'Ready.'

She sat back. 'Doctor.'

'No.'

'Nurse.'

'No.'

'Firefighter.'

'No.'

'Magician.'

'No.'

'Trouble-shooter.'

'Maybe.'

'Mountaineer.'

'No.'

'Lecturer.'

'No.'

'Charity worker.'

'Maybe.'

'Parent.'

'Yes.'

Huh?

'I mean, no. I mean, maybe.' He raised his hand. 'OK. Stop. That was a trick. Parenting is not a profession.'

'I think you'll find there are a lot of stay-at-home parents who would disagree.'

'You know what I mean.' He was aware of a sudden urge to stand up and pace. 'That was not a relevant option.'

Thea raised her eyebrows. 'I disagree. Whether or not you want a family is utterly relevant to what you want to do with the rest of your life. You must have thought about it.'

'Not really.'

Her eyebrows rose higher. 'What does that mean?'

'It means I don't think that is something I can plan at this stage in my life. I am single, and I have never been in a long-term relationship, so it's not something I've ever needed to consider.'

'But clearly you want to be a parent.'

'You can't know that based on that one answer. A gimmick.'

'It's not a gimmick,' Thea said. 'Come on. Every other answer you made, even the maybes you came out with, were instinctive, and I bet they were all valid.'

'Well, yes,' he conceded. 'But parenthood is different. It's not that simple to decide to be a parent.'

'No, but it's simple enough for most people to admit it's what they want.'

'I don't *know* what I want.'

'I think you do.'

Zayne sighed, knowing that on some level Thea was right.

'It's not that easy,' he said. 'For a start it takes two.'

'Not necessarily. You could adopt or look at surrogacy.'

'There is nothing wrong with either of those options. But neither sits right with me. It's not as though I have a large family, so it doesn't seem right for me to become a single parent. If anything happened to me that child would be left on its own, and that doesn't seem fair. Plus, I think I like the idea of being a family. I want to give my children what I had…what you had—a happy family home.'

'I get that.' She smiled. 'We did both have that, didn't we? Your house was full of laughter. I remember that. I remember Bollywood movies playing and your parents dancing along and collapsing with laughter.' She nodded. 'I understand that you want to give your child the same. And I am sure it won't be hard for you find someone who would be happy to have a baby with you.'

'How?'

Thea frowned. 'What do you mean, how?'

'Well, first I have to meet someone I like enough and who likes me enough to even want to have a relationship. I've hardly managed that so far.'

She looked at him. 'But you haven't really tried, have

you? I mean, you've never stayed with anyone longer than a few weeks.'

'That's because it's what we've always agreed up-front.'

Thea stared at him. 'I don't understand.'

Zayne had an urge to cross his arms in what he realised was a classic defensive move, and reminded himself he had nothing to be defensive about. 'I make sure that the rules are understood before I start on a relationship.'

'Rules?' Thea echoed. 'You have rules? You agree when you're going to break up before you even start dating?'

'No. Or at least not exactly.'

'So how does it work, exactly?'

'I make sure that neither of us have any unrealistic expectations. That she knows I'm not interested in the long term. Because until now I haven't been.'

'Then I don't see the problem. Next time you date someone don't put those rules in place. Don't have any rules. Hell, Zayne, maybe don't date a beautiful celebrity just because you want to add another notch to your bedpost.'

'What the hell is that supposed to mean?'

'Exactly what I said. All these years you have been deliberately chasing short-term affairs with trophy girl-friends. Not that they're ever even girlfriends. I mean, what would you call them?'

Anger flared inside him. 'I would call them beauti-ful, successful women whom I liked and who liked me. Who wanted the same things I wanted and were honest enough to admit it upfront. Do not judge them or me. I've hurt no one. In fact I'm still in touch with some of them. They weren't trophies to me. Yes, they were all celebrities, but that made sense. There was parity. We were both rich and famous, both knew there was no ulterior motive to our relationship. Also, I won't date business colleagues or employees, so I tend to date women I meet in my social life. I won't apologise for any of that. I have liking, affection and respect for every single woman I've shared time with, and I'd like to think they would say the same about me.'

There was a silence, and then she nodded. 'I'm sorry, Zayne. You're right. I had no right to judge you or them.'

He saw genuine apology in her eyes.

She held out a hand. 'Friends again?'

'Of course. And I do know how it must look, but I promise I have never cheated on a woman, and I have never just moved on from one to another.'

She gave a sudden small smile. 'Let me guess... You have a rule—only two girlfriends a year?'

'Something like that, yes.'

'OK. Well, I can see now why you haven't ever had a long-term relationship—you've never let yourself. I mean, how can you if you've only looked for women who want short term.'

'I know. But in all these years I haven't wanted to change the rules. To begin with it was because I was so caught up with work that I didn't have the time. Hell, I also couldn't quite believe that I, Zayne Wood, a lad from Chiswick, was dating Hollywood stars. And I wanted to make sure all my ducks were in a row, that it was real. The security, the money, the wealth... I wanted to believe they weren't going to vanish.'

'And now you believe that. So maybe now you're ready for a long-term relationship. You need to change your criteria.'

'How am I supposed to do that? I can't tell a woman on a first date that I want to marry her. I'm not even sure I want to marry anyone. I don't want to raise expectations or lead anyone on. Our parents didn't do this. They met, fell in love and—*kaboom*—they were happy.'

'They were lucky,' Thea said. 'Maybe they were lucky because they happened to want the same things in life and so it all worked out. But love isn't enough.'

He heard the bitterness in her voice.

'There is way more than love to a successful relationship,' she said. 'You have to want the same things. That's why all your short-term relationships have worked. They were without drama and anger. It's even more important if you're looking for a woman to marry, a woman who will be the mother of your children. So, with the next women you date, don't tell them upfront that you aren't open to a long-term relationship. Tell them you are.'

'You don't think that will scare them off?'

'If it does, that's good. There's no point investing in something that won't work.'

'But what if *I'm* not cut out for a long-term relationship?'

'The only way to find out is to try. So we need to figure out what is important to you.'

'I'm not sure this is what I had in mind when we decided to brainstorm,' Zayne said.

Thea waved the objection aside. 'This is what we've come up with, so let's see it through. You need a woman who wants a family…'

Zayne frowned. He thought he'd heard the slightest of cracks in the steady tone of her voice.

'What else is important to you?'

He thought for a moment, looked out of the window at the flurry of snow, and wondered how the conversation had got to this.

For an instant an image played in his mind. Himself in front of a roaring fire, with a Christmas tree in the corner, two children with brown hair, a boy and a girl, looking up and laughing. A woman stood on a ladder, reaching up to put a star atop the tree as he threw another log on the fire. The woman was turned away from him, a cascade of glossy brown hair down her back. She turned her head to look down and he could see who it was. Thea.

He blinked. Hard. Twice. Told himself that that was ridiculous.

A little voice asked him why. Why was that ridiculous?

'Zayne?' Thea snapped her fingers and tipped her head to one side. 'I'm guessing you're conjuring up thoughts of your perfect woman. So tell me what's important to you.'

He pulled himself together, wondering what she'd say if he shared what he had actually conjured up. He knew he wouldn't. This was all about Thea helping him as a friend.

'I don't know. I suppose I should say love.' Only he wasn't sure. After all, love was a wonderful thing, but if you lost it, it caused pain and heartbreak.

'Not necessarily,' said Thea. 'I think shared values, beliefs, wanting the same things from life—they are more important. I mean, a lot of arranged marriages actually last, and a lot of love matches end in divorce. And there are different types of love. You said it yourself; you had liking, respect, even affection for the women you dated. Maybe you can build on that.'

'Maybe…'

Zayne blinked again, all too aware of that image that still hovered in the forefront of his brain.

'Attraction,' he said. 'That's important. In fact that is vital.'

And without him even meaning to do it his voice went suddenly deeper, as if the word itself had pulled up a reminder of the attraction that he knew still simmered under the surface right here and now.

'But attraction can be completely ephemeral, a temporary madness,' she said. 'Think of all the women you've been attracted to, slept with…that attraction didn't last.'

'That doesn't mean attraction isn't important in a lasting relationship. I believe in fidelity, and how can anyone be faithful to someone they aren't attracted to? However good a parent someone might be, there's not much point if they've got no interest in the act of making that baby.'

'But how can you know attraction is going to last?'

'You can't. But if it's strong enough and mutual I think you can make it last.'

'So, you need a woman you're attracted to, who wants a family, someone you like and get on with...'

'And someone who makes me laugh and gets my jokes.'

'For real?' She sighed.

'For real. You know how important laughter is in family life.'

He knew she did. He remembered her dissolving with laughter together with Sienna and Eliza over the silliest things. Recalled, too, the way Thea had made him laugh with her funny voices and her funny faces.

'You're right. I'll add it to the list.'

'I appreciate this, Thea. It's definitely given me something to think about.'

'Make sure you do think about it before you jump into a relationship,' she said. 'Because if you tell a woman that this is what you're looking for, you'd better mean it.'

He studied her face and saw sadness, anger, even bitterness there.

'Did someone tell you something and not mean it?' he asked gently.

'It doesn't matter.'

'It matters to me. Tell me, Thea. Tell me so I can understand, and tell me because I'm your friend. If you want to, that is.'

He paused as a knock on the door heralded the arrival of a staff member come to remove the remains of their breakfast. He waited, watching Thea's thoughtful face.

* * *

Did she want to tell Zayne?

Thea smiled at the member of staff automatically as she mulled over the question.

She'd never talked about her break-up with Ian to anyone. Not even her sisters.

Sienna's marriage had been in trouble so she definitely hadn't wanted to burden her big sister with her own problems. But it had been more than that. She hadn't known if Sienna would get it. Hadn't been sure that her sister wouldn't secretly side with Ian, even if she'd never admit it.

Sometimes Thea herself wondered if she had been the one at fault.

But Zayne? Maybe she could tell him. Should tell him. Because it would be a reminder to herself that she was far from the kind of woman he was looking for.

Because something strange had happened whilst they'd been talking. She'd found herself feeling a tinge of envy, a green strand of jealousy, towards this as yet unknown woman who would share Zayne's life. Which was ridiculous. It must be some side effect of their equally ridiculous attraction. Well, perhaps once he knew the truth about her it would kill any attraction stone-cold dead. Most significantly, it would reinforce to him how important it was to be upfront and honest.

So she nodded. 'I'll tell you. I met Ian when I was twenty-three and he was twenty-five. We met at a Law Society event. He was...well, *is* a fellow lawyer, and we hit it off straight away. We were both ambitious, driven, and we wanted the same in life. Things moved quickly. Neither of us saw any reason to wait. Pretty soon we were an item, and a couple of years after that we moved in together.'

Zayne nodded, but said nothing, and she knew he didn't want to interrupt the flow of her words. She remembered now what a good listener he was. Could see an echo of the young boy he'd once been, listening while she explained some petty school feud, or her disappointment at losing the netball finals, how as captain she felt she'd let the team down.

'We did talk about the future, but it was always around work, how we both wanted promotions, partnerships. Ironically, things started to go a little bit wrong when I got a promotion before he did. He minded. He pretended he didn't, but with hindsight something shifted.'

She should have seen the signs then, in the small put-downs, the sudden criticisms, the change in his expectations.

'He started getting annoyed that we got so many takeaways and said he wanted me to cook more. There'd be little put-downs in front of our friends, little gibes.'

She really should have seen it—she had been quick enough to spot the flaws in Sienna's marriage...the way Callum had treated Sienna.

'I made excuses, tried to understand the fragility of the male ego. Then he got a promotion too, and things were better for a while. Until I got more successful. A pattern emerged. Ian started to undermine my work plans, subtly trying to sabotage things so we'd have a late night before an important meeting, or he'd ask for my help when he didn't really need it but he knew I needed to prep for a case. Then, right before his thirtieth birthday, he dropped a bombshell on me. He'd been offered a transfer to Australia. He wanted me to go with him and he thought it was time we started thinking about having a family.'

Thea shook her head, reliving the whole sorry mess of that conversation. Remembering her shock on so many levels.

'I didn't even know a move to Australia was in the offing. There had been no discussion, no nothing. As for starting a family... I'd always been clear I didn't want children. Ian knew that; had always said he was fine with that.'

She heard Zayne exhale a breath and met his gaze, saw something cross the brown depths she wasn't sure she could identify. Surprise? Disappointment? But then it was gone, leaving his brown eyes clear and judgement-free.

'You must have been reeling,' he said.

'I was. I asked him to explain. He told me he'd changed, said that he wanted a family and was happy to be the provider. That we could start a new life together and it would be exciting and wonderful. He thought it was a great surprise, that I'd be happy. And when I wasn't he... Well, it all kind of went downhill.'

'What do you mean?'

'He said he'd changed and evolved and I hadn't. Said that he'd thought I'd change my mind about children, asked me what "real woman" wouldn't want a family. He told me that I was cold and ambitious and that any man would want more than that. He said he was happy to be a provider, he wanted kids, and he was going to find a warm, loving woman who would appreciate him.'

She could remember his words now.

'What is your problem, Thea? Why can't you take a step back? For a family? What's so bad about me wanting that? I thought you would want that—look at your family, how happy they are. Don't you want that? Instead of this obsession with a career?'

Ever since she'd wondered if there was something wrong with her. Told herself time and again that there wasn't. That she was right not to want kids, that the decision was a good one, a valid one. And if she did feel a pang when she passed by a park with a couple pushing their baby on a swing, if she sometimes tried to duck out of an invitation to a colleague's baby shower, that meant nothing.

Maybe her decision did cause her some pain, but it didn't make it invalid and surely it didn't make her cold. Or unnatural. She just wouldn't be a parent if she couldn't do it right.

'Anyway, Ian went to Australia and he's there now, happily married with a baby, I'm not sure, but I think he'd already met Lucy, his wife, whilst he was still with me. So it's all worked out for the best. My point is, if you're serious about wanting a family then you need to tell whoever you're in a relationship with and you need to be sure she is on board. Don't bank on people changing. Don't waste time like Ian and I did.'

'But it wasn't a waste of time.'

'What do you mean?'

'You and Ian—you had some happy times, didn't you? That's worth something. You experienced love and happiness.'

'And that led to unnecessary, avoidable pain. I believed Ian. I believed him when he said he'd support my career and agreed that it was OK not to have a family. I understand now that people change, and that's why I won't take a risk again.'

'Yes, people *do* change.' He paused. 'You may change your mind about children.'

'Not happening.' She removed her hand from his. 'That is not a possibility.' She wasn't maternal. She knew that. 'I'll settle for being the best aunt in the world.'

Because she hoped with all her heart that Sienna and Eliza would meet someone wonderful, who deserved her wonderful sisters, and then they could have a whole brood of children.

She looked at her watch. 'But now…'

'Now we'd better get a move on,' Zayne said, clearly getting it that the conversation was over. 'We're going to get a train to an art gallery.'

CHAPTER NINE

ZAYNE GLANCED ACROSS at Thea as the train made its way forward. Her head was bent over the work file she'd brought with her and there was a small frown of concentration on her face, her focus intense and absolute.

In that moment Zayne understood why her sisters had wanted her to take a break. He himself had to almost sit on his hands to fight the temptation to tug the papers out of her hands, to exhort her to look outside, see the landscape meandering by, experience the scenery of a different place and culture.

But he had no right to do that—not even as a friend. And he sensed that any attempt to question her priorities and her choices would be met by an angry defensiveness that he now understood. He knew that Ian's words would have hurt her.

He wondered why Thea didn't want children. He completely understood and accepted that not all women had a desire for a family. Hell, until today he hadn't been sure he wanted to be a dad. But he would have thought Thea was so family-oriented she'd want a family.

Which made him perhaps no better than Ian.

And yet he wished he knew why she was so sure. Why did it matter to him? Was it because of that strange vision he'd had? Had he been considering 'interviewing' Thea for the role of wife and mother?

Of course not. He wanted Thea back in his life as a friend.

The train slowed and he looked out of the window.

'Thea? We're the next stop.'

She looked up and his breath caught—she really was so beautiful. It was nothing to do with each individual feature, it was just *her*, Thea—the way her eyes sparkled, the gloss of her hair, the straight line of her nose and the curve of her lips…lips that called out to him. The attraction was as present, as real, as it had been before.

'Perfect.' She made a notation on the papers she was reading and then put the file into the backpack she had brought. 'Let's go.'

As they left the station, she looked round.

'So, where are we?'

'Obuse. It's one of the prettiest villages in the prefecture. It's famous for its chestnuts, and it also houses a museum dedicated to one of Japan's most famous painters from the Edo era.'

Thea looked up at him suspiciously. 'Chestnuts?'

'Yup. Apparently in 1367 a wealthy man planted the first saplings and it turned out the soil here was perfect. The area started to gain fame for the quality of its chestnuts. So much so that an offering was made to the *shogun* every year.'

'That's incredible. To think all those years ago someone did that, and now, hundreds of years later, people come here because of the chestnuts.'

'How about we take a picture outside this confectioner's of us eating a chestnut dessert? You can send it to Sienna and Eliza. Obuse is famous for its chestnut-related food.'

'Good idea.'

He could hear a soupçon of doubt in her voice. But how hard could it be for two friends to take a selfie holding a wonderful, decadent cake?

Once he came back out of the shop he nodded at her. 'Ready?'

'Maybe we could just send a picture of the cake,' Thea suggested. 'They'll enjoy seeing that. I've never seen a cake like it.'

They both regarded the beautifully constructed cake, encased in what looked like noodles.

'Those are actually made of chestnuts,' Zayne explained, 'and underneath there's a sponge cake and chestnut paste and cream. I think there may be ice cream involved as well.'

'Then let's send a picture of that.'

'Nope. They'll want solid photographic evidence that you are actually in Obuse, having fun.'

But as they stood there, and he angled his phone to take the snap, he was horribly aware of the tension in his body, of the way his whole being was in conflict, desperately trying not to get too close whilst simultaneously desperately craving her proximity.

Both of them practically sprang apart when he was done.

'Any good?' Thea asked.

He handed her the phone and she looked at the photo, then back at him. 'That's…'

'Pants,' he replied. 'We look...'

'Awkward and uncomfortable. And we definitely aren't smiling.'

'It's more of a grimace,' he agreed.

'A rictus and it looks completely fake. If I send this to Sienna and Eliza they'll think—' She broke off. 'I don't know what they'll think, but I do know what they won't think. That I'm having fun.'

'No,' he agreed. 'So we need to solve this.'

'How?'

'Let's go into the café, eat the cake and whilst we do that maybe we need to actually talk about what's going on here.'

'Do we?' Thea made a face. 'I mean, that's going to be awkward and not fun at all.' She gave a sigh and then, 'But it's probably necessary, or the next couple of days will be awkward and not fun too.'

He nodded, and they entered the café. They sat down at a small table and Thea took a bite of the cake, closed her eyes and sighed again.

'OK. This bit will be fun. This is delicious.' She took one more bite and then, 'So who goes first? I vote you, because you brought it up.' She closed her eyes. 'Oh, man... Anything I say sounds like a double entendre.'

It took him a second, and then he groaned. 'I wouldn't even have noticed.'

'I know. Neither would I. Normally. Anyway... Go ahead.'

'I want to try and resolve the issue. We need to be able to take good photos for your sisters, but we can't because we're terrified to so much as brush hands.

Maybe the issue is we're so busy trying to pretend the attraction isn't there, we're actually making it worse. So I suggest we face it.'

'How?'

'We admit it. I'll go first. Thea, I admit it. I am attracted to you.'

She took a deep breath. 'I feel ridiculous.'

'Exactly. Maybe we can make this into something ridiculous. Let's try.'

She took a deep breath. 'I admit it too. I, Thea Kendall, am attracted to you, Zayne Wood.'

The words took on a life of their own, reverberating around the small wooden table, bouncing off the surfaces and creating a shimmering, sparkling bubble around them.

Instead of ridicule they had conjured up a magical, glorious reality. Her eyes sparked now with dark amber flecks of desire, and his pulse rate ratcheted up.

'That didn't work.' He hardly recognised the hoarseness of his own voice.

'No. So maybe we need to remind ourselves why this attraction is a bad idea.'

'Sure.'

There was a beat of silence as they both ate more cake, until eventually he put his fork down and sighed.

'So why is it a bad idea?' he asked. 'Because right now all I want to do is kiss you. Properly. And it seems like a very good idea to me.'

'Well, it isn't.' She bit her lip and then gave a rueful smile. 'Though at the moment I can't think of any reasons why. However, I may not be able to think of them, but I do know they exist. Give me a second...'

She closed her eyes, then opened them and looked away from him, down at her plate, as if grounding herself.

'Right, it's a bad idea because surely we're rebuilding a friendship here. How can we do that if we let attraction get in the way? An attraction that can't go anywhere. I am not your type and you aren't mine.'

'Now, that *is* ridiculous. You are one hundred percent my type—that's why I am sitting here exerting every iota of control so I don't do something about this attraction.'

'The only box we tick is attraction. I don't want a family. You do. Ergo, you are not my type.'

'So what *is* your type?' he asked.

'What does that matter?'

'I want to know. Hopefully, the more I can tell myself I'm not your type, the easier it will make it to not kiss you.'

There was a pause as her gaze lingered on his lips, as if she was wondering what it would be like if she let him do exactly that.

'OK. Um... I don't really know. Since Ian I've steered clear of any type. I've preferred being single and answerable only to myself.'

There was defiance in her voice, and Zayne sensed it was deeper than that. Ian had hurt her more than she was willing to let on.

'But you can't let him influence the rest of your life. You must want a relationship at some point.'

Thea seemed to give this some thought, her nose slightly crinkled. 'I don't want a serious relationship, I want a convenient one. One where I live in my place and he lives in his. I want someone happy to let me focus on my career and fit around that. If that is selfish, I don't care.'

'It's not selfish—but...'

But it was a far cry from the Kendalls' happy family existence.

Thea had moved on from that. She was a single woman with her own life that she clearly loved. Yet something felt off.

'But are you sure that would be enough?' he asked.

'Of course. That way there would be no expectations. Perhaps this ideal man would already have kids of his own, and I wouldn't interfere with that at all. He'd be someone fun, but he wouldn't need me and I wouldn't need him. No expectations except for a good time. A kind of long-term casual lover.'

Not a role he could apply for. Nor would he even want to, because he knew it wouldn't be enough for him.

'So you see?' she said. 'You aren't my type and I'm not yours. If we want to reinstate our friendship we have to kill this attraction off.'

'We also have to work out how to take a convincing selfie. Which means we have to practise getting used to each other. Instead of flinching away from each other, let's try to be natural. If there are a few sparks along the way that's fine, because we've acknowledged the attraction and decided not to act on it. We'll just have to accept it and let the sparks fly as they will.'

He rose to his feet and held out his hand.

'Like this. Put your hand in mine. Let's see how it feels on our way to the museum.'

Thea eyed his hand as though it were dangerous, then hauled in a breath and put her hand in his. And there it was—the jolt and the warmth as he pulled her to her feet.

'Let's just go with it,' he said.

Thea glanced down at their clasped hands as they walked along the pavement, cleared of the snow that was still layered the roofs and roadsides. And as they walked it dawned on her that this wasn't the world's best idea.

Because although, yes, the sparking voltage of desire had simmered down, the result was an aching awareness and a sense of…connection…a warmth. She was trying to tell herself it was the warmth of friendship. That this desire could be reshaped, moulded into friendship.

'Nearly there,' Zayne said, and it was only then that it hit her.

She hadn't given the museum a thought, the museum that she was here to study, to research, to gain information for her meeting. This was work related, and she was wandering around in a haze of desire, thinking of Zayne.

Another reason to knock this on the head as they approached the curved walkway that led to the low-roofed modern building.

They entered the museum and Thea looked around

in awe at the sheer amount of work on display, its breadth and scope incredible.

'This is only some of Hokusai's work. The museum has to rotate it because there's so much. He was a true master of his art.'

Thea could hear the awe in Zayne's voice.

'I thought it might be useful for you to have some extra information about him,' he went on. 'So I did some research.'

The idea warmed her. 'It's incredible to think he created all this so many hundreds of years ago, in a different time and era. Tell me more about him.'

'OK, but stop me if I go into too much detail. I don't want to bore you.'

'You won't.'

He couldn't. She liked the sound of his voice, its deep baritone, and the way he occasionally moved his hands around to emphasise a point.

'OK. So, Katsushika Hokusai was born in 1760, and he started painting at the age of six. At fourteen he became an artist's apprentice, and worked on woodblocks creating prints of people—courtesans and actors.'

'So, like a celebrity photographer?'

'Yes, exactly and in some ways that is what makes him so interesting. Because from his twenties onwards he moved away from that. He started painting real life—people and landscapes. Which was groundbreaking, for him and for the whole genre. He changed the way art was seen. It's called *ukiyo-e*, a type of painting that shows life. It literally means "this world", and it's meant to demonstrate normal everyday stuff that people see and experience.'

Thea considered this. 'So he made people see that they mattered even if they weren't famous.'

'Yup and that's important, isn't it? From there he went from strength to strength as an artist. Then when he was fifty, Hokusai was struck by lightning. Oddly enough, it was after that he began to produce his most ambitious work and became phenomenally successful. He was in his eighties when he came to Obuse, and even then he was changing, improving. He never rested on his laurels. Whilst he was here in Obuse he painted some of the stuff you'll see here.'

They started to move around the exhibits and Thea studied them, took in the detail, the care that had gone into them, the differing styles over time.

'Look at these,' she said. 'They're festival floats. I didn't even know they existed back then.'

They studied the dragon and the phoenix, one on a scarlet background, one on a dark one.

'Apparently they represent yin and yang,' said Zayne. 'Opposing forces that create harmony. Two things that complement each other. If one person pulls, the other pushes. If one person presses, the other retreats, whilst still holding the other.'

Thea looked at the colours, at the visceral beauty and force of the images, and felt their power.

'But you need to balance those forces to achieve it,' he went on. 'If you don't then you create chaos.'

Thea blinked. For some reason his words felt important, meaningful, and the idea that an artist from so long ago could influence the way she felt about Zayne seemed profound. Too profound.

'Before we get too philosophical, I need to make some notes,' she said. 'Things to say to my client once I find out what she thinks about Hokusai.'

'Why does that matter? Will you agree with her opinion, whatever it is.'

'Yes.'

'Why?'

'Because I want to win her business.'

'Surely it doesn't work like that. It's more important to be honest. If I'm hiring a lawyer I want to know that he or she will tell me the truth. I don't want yes-people who will agree with me regardless, because I know sometimes I might be wrong.'

'I get that. And if it's a legal thing I would obviously tell it as it is.'

'Sure. But… Sometimes I may not want legal fact. I may want legal opinion, or a general opinion. Some of the best professional relationships I have are based on trust. I need to know that those people will disagree with me if necessary and tell me what they really think, not what I want to hear.'

Thea blinked at him and knew that he was right; the best way to create a lasting, professional, real relationship with a client *was* to be honest. Not rude, but honest.

'You're right. I know you're right. And that is how I operate.'

Or at least it was how she'd used to. When had she stopped? she wondered.

'Good. Because if you come across as trying too hard, wanting her business too much, it might have the opposite effect to what you want. Make you look needy. Keep perspective, and remember you're the best. She'll respect the fact that you've visited the museum, and she'll probably appreciate a genuine discussion more than a fake one.'

Thea nodded, aware that she wanted, *needed* to change the subject. 'Got it,' she said. 'Now, is it OK if we go to the nearby temple and see Hokusai's last work? It sounds incredible.'

Apparently it was a phoenix, painted so that wherever you stood in the room the mythical bird seemed to be looking down at you from the ceiling of the temple.

'That sounds like a plan.'

CHAPTER TEN

As THEY WALKED or rather strode to the temple, with Thea setting the pace, Zayne told himself he needed to let it go. He was meant to be helping her to have fun. Instead, judging by her rate of acceleration, he seemed to be stressing her out.

They were approaching the temple now, and he vowed to simply allow Thea to enjoy the experience. If she wanted to take notes, he wouldn't say a word.

But she didn't. Instead they both simply stood and gazed at the painting. Its sheer size made the intricacy of it even more inspiring, the colour, the impressions. Then, in tacit agreement, they moved around the room, their eyes still focused on the magnificent creation.

'Yup. It's true,' he said. 'The phoenix is one hundred percent looking at us wherever we go.'

'And Hokusai was eighty-nine when he did this? That is phenomenal. He truly was a man who dedicated his life to his work.'

There was a hint of challenge in her voice, but he had no intention of denying that or accepting the challenge.

'He was,' he agreed. 'And a man who left an amazing legacy behind him. On his deathbed he apparently said that he wished for five more years so he could become a real painter. Yet he changed a genre and has brought pleasure to people over the centuries. A man with a true vocation.'

Zayne wondered what it would feel like to have that.'

Thea glanced at him. 'What about his personal life?' Her voice was a touch over-casual.

'He was a real character. At one point he signed his work with *Painted by the madman of painting, Hokusai*. And he hated cleaning so much so that he kept moving—apparently about ninety-three times. He was superstitious. I read somewhere that he drew a Chinese dragon every morning and chucked it out of the window, because that was supposed to bring good luck.'

'You could argue that it worked! What about a family? Did he marry? Have children?'

'He had two wives, who both died, and five children, I think. One of his daughters was also an artist, who ended up living with Hokusai after she left her husband. His grandson was a gambler who lost all their money, and the family had to move into a temple for a while. So he made a difference to his family as well.'

Thea glanced upwards again. 'I wish I could travel back in time and meet him.'

'Me too.' He smiled at her. 'I'm glad you've enjoyed it.'

'I have. I've really enjoyed today.'

She took a deep breath and he nodded, because he knew what she was about to say and decided to pre-empt it.

'You're worried because your meeting is the day

after tomorrow and you want to prep for that, as well as do the other work that needs doing before Christmas.'

'Exactly—but I do want to keep my side of the deal and help you.'

'Well, how does this sound?' he said. 'We'll head back now. You can work on the train, and for the rest of today and all day tomorrow. Then in the evening why don't I cook you dinner and help you prep for the meeting?'

'You'd do that?'

'Of course. I understand how important this meeting is. I want to help.'

She hesitated and he raised a hand. 'Think about it. Figure out the angles. Take your time whilst we head back to the station.'

But in the end it was only a few minutes before she spoke. 'I would like to come to dinner. And if I need to prep with you I will. But primarily I'd like to try and help you…keep my side of the bargain. Plus, I'd like to sample your cooking. After all, I'll be the first person you practise your new-found culinary skills on.'

The fact seemed oddly significant, though he wasn't sure why.

'I guess you will,' he said. 'I like the idea.'

'So do I,' she said softly, and the words took on a sudden wealth of meaning.

It would be the first time they would be properly alone together. At breakfast hotel staff had popped in and out, at the temple and in the café, in the museum and now in the temple, there had been other people. But tomorrow night there would be no one—just Zayne and Thea.

The idea was full of promise, and a vortex of possibilities, each one spiced with anticipation.

'I'll look forward to it,' he said. 'Now, let's get back.'

Thea gritted her teeth, and realised she was daydreaming. Again. Picturing dinner with Zayne. *Zayne.* A shiver goose-bumped her skin. Again. Just as it had all day. Whenever she'd thought of him.

Ridiculous.

Yet now there was a goofy smile on her face.

Double ridiculous.

Zayne was cooking her dinner. No big deal. She'd tell him about the ideas she'd come up with about his future. Ideas to add to what she'd already helped him with—her advice to find a woman he loved, who would be a mother to his children.

Now the goofy grin fell from her face, and the words on her computer screen seemed to blur into an image.

Zayne, with a goofy grin on *his* face, looking down at the tiny baby cradled in his arms. Next to him was a toddler, a little boy with Zayne's dark hair, and there in a corner was the shadowy image of a woman, a mystery woman. And as Thea squinted her eyes, she'd swear that the woman looked like…

Thea blinked hard. *Whoa.* That woman could not be her and she wouldn't be foolish enough to think it ever could be.

That was not part of her life plan. She couldn't let it be…couldn't and wouldn't do that. Not to Zayne and not to those two beautiful babies. Babies who deserved a better mum than she could ever be, just as Zayne deserved a woman who could be part of the family he wanted.

She couldn't. But maybe, if their friendship flourished, she could be godmother. Only... That wasn't possible either, was it? Not whilst this attraction simmered and shimmered and invaded her very being.

So maybe she needed to see tonight as a finale. Because tomorrow was Christmas Eve, and she assumed that Zayne must be returning home. There was no way he'd leave his mum alone over Christmas.

In which case, tonight was it, the last time she'd see Zayne, perhaps for another twelve years, perhaps for ever. So the least she could do was get him a gift, a Christmas present. A thank-you for the past two days.

The last time... The words took on a bleakness, but they also gave Thea an urge to seize the moment. Whatever that meant.

She glanced at her watch, then outside, where snowflakes were fluttering down in a white kaleidoscope of flakes. Surely she could take a small break—a quick trip to the shops?

Zayne regarded his culinary efforts with a mix of satisfaction and worry. He wanted this to be perfect. For Thea. He knew that she'd have packed a phenomenal amount of work into the past twenty-four hours, since they'd returned from Obuse. She deserved a break before her all-important meeting. But it was more than that; he wanted her to truly relax, let her hair down. He wanted to look after her, pamper her, cook for her...

Do all the things her waste of space ex hadn't done.

And he wanted to show her too, that he did admire her drive and ambition,

Right. He took another look at the food. All he could do now was hope for the best, that it would taste the way he hoped it would.

He walked to the window and manoeuvred the Japanese curtain, the *noren*, so he could see outside. A glance at the sky outside showed a flurry of snow falling from the dusky grey sky and he frowned, wishing Thea had let him pick her up. But she'd insisted on getting a rental car, told him firmly that she was more than capable of a bit of off-road driving.

Nothing would be more calculated to annoy Thea than him pacing anxiously or staring out of the window. So in a swift movement he allowed the curtains to close again and did one final check of the room as he heard the sound of an approaching car.

A minute later he opened the door and his greeting died on his lips.

She looked almost unnaturally beautiful…like a conjured up illusion. Her hair was slightly damp from the falling snow, her bright red coat a splash of colour in the swirl of snowflakes against the looming trees in the shadowed background.

Blinking, he stepped backwards to let her in and she turned to close the door against the cold. On automatic, he stepped forward to take her coat, and then she turned round. He froze, coat in hand, as he took in her beauty close up.

'Too much?' she asked.

He shook his head, searched for words. She looked

stunning. The simple off-the-shoulder silver dress, accentuated at the waist with a flower motif to one side, shimmered down to just above the knee, showcasing the length of her legs. Her chestnut hair cascaded in waves past her shoulders, and a subtle layer of make-up emphasised the amber of her eyes and the curve of her lips.

'No. Not too much. At all.' His voice was a rasp. 'I could happily just look at you all night. So...um... come in.'

She entered and looked around, and now he saw the room through her eyes. The flickering fire, the sheepskin rug he'd bought in front of it, the candles on the table, the lilting melody of jazz in the background.

'Too much?' he asked, and she smiled.

'No. Not too much at all. I could happily stay all night.' She bit her lip. 'I mean—' She broke off. 'Sorry. I'm nervous.'

'Me too.'

He was so far out of his comfort zone that comfort was somewhere over the horizon. This wasn't something he'd done before. It was nothing like entering a high-end restaurant with a celebrity on his arm and a smile on his face for the cameras. This was warm, and cosy, and full of so many possibilities. He had no idea how the evening would pan out. No idea how even the next few minutes would.

'Which is absurd,' she said.

'Maybe. But right now my heart is pounding and my pulse-rate has ratcheted up. You can feel, if you like.'

Even as he said the words he realised exactly what they sounded like. A cringey chat-up line.

He groaned, even as she laughed—a genuine, spontaneous peal of laughter.

'If that's the line you use on all those celebrities I have no idea how you ever persuade them into any sort of relationship with you.'

'I promise I've never said those words before. Because they've never been true before. I'm not kidding. I feel…'

'Fluttery? Edgy? Unsettled?'

'All of those things. I can't tell what this is. It should be a friendly dinner, but it feels like a whole lot more than that.'

'Also absurd,' she said. 'We need to do what we did yesterday. Power through. Because we've made our decision. We will not act on this attraction.'

'Right. Power through. In that case, come in, sit down. I got champagne. I thought we should celebrate coming together after all these years.'

'That's always worth celebrating,' she deadpanned, and then gave a little gasp and raised a hand to her mouth. 'Sorry… I'm sorry. I didn't mean to say that.'

But now he laughed, and so did she, in genuine acknowledgement of the absurdity of the situation. When they stopped it did seem as though the laughter had cleared the air, and she entered, went and sat in one of the chairs by the fire, accepted the champagne he poured for her.

'Just half a glass. I'll need my wits about me to drive back. It was snowing the whole way here.' She sipped appreciatively and then raised her glass. 'Thank you. And now I'd like to talk about *you*,' she declared. 'I've done some thinking. Well, in fact I did some research. I thought maybe if I read some of your interviews and articles about you it might help give me some ideas.'

'And?'

'I came up with a big fat zero. You give nothing away. I mean nothing. I tried to read between the lines, but there was nothing to read. Just lines.'

'I don't understand.'

She tucked her legs underneath her. 'Your answers all sound really honest and open, like you've really listened to the question, but they don't say anything about you. About what makes you tick. For example, you say that your heritage is important to you, but you never say how.'

'I do. I say that I appreciate that my parents brought me up to be aware of my roots, but also embrace the country I was born in and the country I moved to.'

'That's what I mean. That sounds lovely, but it doesn't say what that awareness entailed. I know your dad took you to temple, and I know you celebrated Diwali *and* Christmas. I know your mum cooked the best Indian food in town, and shopped in Indian supermarkets *and* British ones.'

'Where are you going with this?'

'I don't understand what Zayne Wood cares about. I mean, not even hobbies. In your interviews you mention that you like cycling. But *where* do you like cycling? Off-road? By the beach?'

'There are some great biking trails where I live. That's where I go.'

'OK. And where *do* you live? I mean, I understand

you don't want to broadcast your actual address, but is it a flat? A mansion? A two-up, two-down?'

'I live in the first apartment I bought. It's not massive, but I love it. I could move, but to me the apartment represents something. When I bought it, it symbolised to me that I'd made it. I owned bricks and mortar. I'd arrived. I owned a place.'

It was his private sanctuary…a place he'd never taken a date to. It was his. And yet sitting here now he had a vivid image of opening the door and letting Thea in. Which was daft.

'I don't think you'd like it,' he said.

'Why not?'

'Because it's a bit cluttered. There are bikes in the front room, and I haven't ever replaced the furniture. I've accumulated things over the years, so it's a mishmash, really. Whereas I bet your home is minimalist, with a proper theme or design.'

'I… Actually, no, it isn't.' She looked almost puzzled as she thought about it. 'It isn't really anything,' she said in the end. 'It's a place. A place where I feel at home, in that I love that it's mine. But I haven't really ever got round to doing anything to it.'

She sounded almost wistful. Words hovered on the tip of his tongue—an offer to meet up the next time he was in London, to wander round the markets together. But he swallowed them down, unsure of how she would respond, unsure of what was happening right here and now. After all, he was supposed to be looking for a woman to marry, to have a family with. It was perhaps naïve to think he could do that *and* cultivate his friendship with Thea, a woman he wanted with an intensity he'd never experienced before.

As he watched her looking into the flames, the fire-light highlighting the glossy waves of her hair, he had to force himself to remain seated, not to move over and kiss her.

Instead he stood up. 'You stay there. I'll go and start dinner. We're having *pakoras* to start with.'

Her reaction was everything he'd hoped for.

'*Pakoras?* Really?'

'Yup. I got the recipe from Mum. Along with her recipe for vegetable *biriani*.'

'Seriously? Where did you get the ingredients?'

'Tokyo.'

'But that's a four-hour round trip.'

'I know.' He shrugged. 'I wanted to make these dishes. I know how much you used to love Mum's food. I had the time, and I needed to pick some other stuff up as well.'

'Thank you. And thank your mum as well. I can't believe you'd do this for me.'

Now she rose to her feet. Came over to him and placed a hand on his arm. She looked up at him, her lips slightly parted, and now the urge to kiss her was nigh on overwhelming.

As if she felt it too she moved her hand, stepped away, her eyes wide, the amber flecked with green. 'Is there anything I can do to help?' she asked.

'Keep your fingers firmly crossed whilst I fry up the *pakoras*.'

CHAPTER ELEVEN

THEA LET OUT a sigh of happy appreciation. 'Those *pakoras* were incredible. And the *biriani* was wonderful. Fragrant, spicy, but not overpoweringly hot. Exactly the right texture and consistency. So, either crossing my fingers really does make a difference or you have inherited your mum's culinary skills.' She gestured to the empty plates. 'That was a truly amazing dinner.'

And it had been—but it was about more than just the food. It was about the thought Zayne had put into the meal, the menu choice, the drive to Tokyo, the candles, the music and the ambience.

By tacit consent they'd talked about books and films and food, told jokes, laughed, and the whole hour or so had been relaxed and wonderful.

'But now we've finished eating, we need to return to the topic of you,' she told him. She really wanted to help Zayne, or to at least come up with an idea that would help him work out what to do next.

'OK. Shall we move in front of the fire?'

'Good idea.'

Once they were seated before the comforting warmth of the flames, she began.

'I have a question, well several questions.'

'Go ahead.'

'What do you care about? What makes you angry? What fires you up? What charities do you support?'

'My company made donations to several different causes—'

'Many of which were decided by employee vote,' she finished for him. 'I read the article. But I mean *you*, personally. Is there a charity you support?'

'Yes. I support a children's charity, one that helps children who are in care.'

'OK. Why?'

'Because it's a cause I believe in.'

Thea sighed. 'Which sounds like another anodyne answer for a magazine interviewer. This is *me* you're talking to.' She thought for a moment. 'I'm not prying out of curiosity; genuinely have a reason for all these questions. But I get that this is hard for you.'

'What do you mean?'

Thea thought about her words carefully. 'I get the feeling you protect your privacy pretty fiercely, so however outgoing you appear to be, you actually resemble an oyster.'

The more she thought about it, the more she knew she was right. Zayne had relationships that barely scratched the surface of emotional intimacy, he didn't have siblings to confide in, and she suspected his relationship with his mother had become one where he looked after her.

'To a degree that makes sense,' she went on. 'You're in the limelight, and the last thing you want is anything personal splashed across the papers.'

But she sensed it was more than that, Zayne didn't want to share anything personal. Full stop.

'Problem is, that isn't going to work here. If you want me to help then you have to open up a little bit. You have to trust me and you have to let me in.'

There was a silence. Thea knew he was considering her words and it gave her a moment to consider him. To study the planes and angles of his face, etched and shadowed by the firelight. The clean strength of his jawline, which made her fingers crave to trace it. The firm line of his mouth. The lips that suddenly seemed so accessible, so tantalisingly close. All she would have to do was shift her chair a bit closer to the fire, turn and...

'Thea?'

She blinked, refocused. 'Yes?'

Amusement lit his eyes, as though he knew where her thoughts had taken her. 'Sorry to interrupt your reverie.'

'No problem. Go ahead.'

Now his face was serious again. 'You're right. I've asked you to help and you need information in order to do that. So I'll try to be more forthcoming. Fire away.'

'OK... So, is there a more specific reason that you support that particular charity?'

'Yes. In fact you probably remember this. My parents fostered children. Just for a couple of years, when we were teenagers.'

'I do remember. They loved it, didn't they? Especially your dad. I went to the park with him and one of the foster children once. A little boy...about six or so.'

'Rahul,' Zayne said, and she nodded, the memory clear in her head.

It had been just after that infamous kiss and she and Zayne had been in full avoidance mode. She'd bumped into Arjun on his way to the park with a solemn little boy. He'd asked Thea to go with them.

'We played in the sandpit. Rahul was so serious about it, and your dad was so patient. We spent ages building a castle and a road and a moat.'

Zayne nodded. 'Dad was good with all of the kids, but Rahul especially. Rahul is why I support the charity.'

'Tell me.'

'When Mum and Dad started fostering, I didn't actually pay a lot of attention. It was mostly babies or toddlers, so I'd make the odd funny face, or play peekaboo, but I wasn't involved. I was busy with my teenage life and concerns. Then they took Rahul in. It was an emergency situation and it was meant to only be short term. But he stayed longer, and that did impact me more.' He shrugged. 'It was not my finest hour.'

'Tell me,' she said again, her voice gentle. 'I won't judge.'

'Rahul got into my room when I wasn't there. He must have been fascinated by the computer. I'd stupidly left a can of energy drink by the side. He knocked over the drink. It fried the keyboard, the monitor—everything. I came in and I lost it. I yelled at him and, moved forward fast, to try to save the computer. And Rahul panicked. Big-time. He was yelling that he was sorry. Then he whimpered and cowered away, curled up on the floor. I had no idea what to do. I froze, and then my dad came running in.'

Thea was almost there with him—could picture the young Zayne, standing stock still, the little boy on the floor, his hands over his head, his cries reverberating off the walls. She moved closer to Zayne, so she could reach out, cover his hand with hers.

'What happened?' she asked.

'Dad knew what to do. He went straight to Rahul. But before he did I saw him look at me, and for the first time ever I saw disappointment on his face. In me. He crouched down on the floor next to Rahul and he was amazing. He didn't try to pick him up or touch him. He sat next to him and he talked to him really gently, said that it was OK, no one was going to be hurt, not in his house. After a while he told me to go and sit on my bed, and then he asked Rahul if he wanted to get up. Told him that it was safe. He promised. After what seemed like ages Rahul did get up. But he wouldn't look at me, just edged closer to my dad.' Zayne shook his head. 'I felt like such a heel, Thea. I watched Dad take Rahul out and I didn't know what to do.'

'You couldn't have known how Rahul would react,' she said gently.

'That's what my dad said. He came back to my room and we talked. Really talked. It was as if I was seeing a new side to my dad. Really seeing him as a person. He told me about Rahul's background, the truly heartrending level of abuse he'd suffered. Said he hadn't told me before because he hadn't wanted me to be upset. But now he'd decided I should be told. I was old enough to know that the world wasn't always a good place. I'd never heard my dad so angry or so sad. He cared so much. Not just about Rahul, but about all the kids out there who through no fault of their own had been hurt, abandoned, betrayed by the people who should love them most.'

'He was a good man,' Thea said quietly.

'He was, and he wanted to make a difference. He'd planned to retrain as a social worker—the plight of these kids mattered to him.'

'And it matters to you too?' she asked.

'Yes. My parents wanted to keep Rahul, to adopt him but Social Services said Rahul needed to go to a family who would focus only on him. I wanted them to try and fight against that, but they decided not to.'

Thea sensed a slight withdrawal in his voice, saw the shadows that crossed the brown eyes as he looked back into the past.

'Hey. That's not on you. That was their decision. You were a teenager—a decision like that was way above your pay grade.'

'I get that. But I think they were wrong. I wanted them to keep fostering. I wanted to get involved, be part of it. I even thought about doing a social work degree, but both my parents went nuts at the idea. They had their hearts set on MIT.'

Thea glanced at him. She'd always believed MIT was what *Zayne* had had his heart set on. 'I thought that was your dream?'

'It was,' he said quickly, too quickly, almost. 'Of course it was. My parents worked so hard for me to get there, and it set me on course to the life I have now.'

He sighed. 'But I've always wondered what happened to Rahul. I just hope he found a good family.'

'So do I.'

She wrapped her fingers more firmly around his, sensing he didn't want to talk about Rahul any more. Sensing too that, for whatever reason, Zayne felt a responsibility towards Rahul.

'Hey,' she said. 'I got us dessert.'

'You did?'

'I got something called *onsen manju*. They're small buns with red bean paste inside them and they are apparently delicious. I thought of your dad, buying me *gulab jamun* when I bought them so maybe now is a good time to eat them.'

She rose and went over to her rucksack and took out the box of pastries.

'Thank you.' They both bit into the pastries. 'Dad would have loved these.'

As they ate Thea considered their conversation, her mind racing. 'Have you ever thought of fostering yourself?' she asked.

'Yes, I have, but it wouldn't work. It wouldn't be fair. How could I offer a child a lifestyle like mine? Even temporarily? How could I make them feel my lifestyle is in any way normal? Plus, what can I offer a child in need? I have no experience with children.'

It was a fair point, and Thea took another bite, staring into the fire as Zayne replenished the logs. She listened to the crack and sizzle as an idea sparked in her head. An idea that instantly filled her with excitement.

'Do you remember the other day, when I asked you

all those yes or no questions and you had two maybes? Charity worker and trouble-shooter.'

'Yes.'

'Well, maybe we could take charity worker idea a step further. I was thinking about you volunteering somewhere before, but now I'm thinking why not think bigger? Why not set up a foundation—run it like a business, a non-profit organisation? A foundation that helps kids in care. You could trouble-shoot as well. I bet there are loads of care homes and organisations that could do with an overhaul so they can do better. That could be part of what your foundation does.'

She watched his face, could almost hear the pop and whir of his brain processing the idea, and then he was on his feet, pacing over the sheepskin rug to the window and back again.

'I love it. I mean, I'll need to do a ton of research, but this could be amazing. I could make a real difference to so many kids. Outreach programmes, fundraisers, organised trips, community hubs, counselling... It'll mean a whole new start for me.'

She nodded. 'And you could help in so many different ways. You could help families adopt children, you could fight court cases, you could provide teenagers who have got into trouble with rehabilitation. There's so much you could do to help.'

'The good thing is I have the money and the influence to make a difference.'

'And the charisma and the passion,' she said. 'I can hear it in your voice already. You can make a difference and leave a real legacy behind you.'

For a fleeting moment it occurred to Thea that she wouldn't. This, what Zayne was talking about, was something real and inspired and, yes, worthwhile. Something she wanted to be part of.

She pushed the idea aside. This was Zayne's life choice. Zayne was at a crossroads, not Thea. And there wasn't room for Thea in his life. The person who would stand by his side and help him would be the woman he found to love and build a life and a family with.

But right now Thea was here, and for these few hours she could be excited, could brainstorm with him.

'I'd want to get involved with the kids on a personal basis,' Zayne continued. 'I mean, I know I'll need training, but I can do that.'

He grinned at her and, reaching out, pulled her to her feet. In a sudden deft movement he lifted her up and twirled her round. His happiness palpable, a sense that he'd found something positive and good and new. It made her dizzy and she laughed out loud, looking up at him when he put her down.

'Thank you, Thea. Truly. I mean that, hand on my heart. Thank you for listening and not judging and for coming up with such an amazing idea. I love it. It feels like a vocation.'

'I'm glad. Truly glad. It feels right.'

And it did.

'I know something else that feels right. If you'll agree?'

'What?'

'Will you spend Christmas with me? Here in the cabin? I know it's not the same as a Kendall Christmas, but…'

'I'd love to.'

The answer was utterly spontaneous, and it was only when she'd spoken that she realised the implication.

'But what about your mum? Surely you're flying back home tomorrow?'

She knew Zayne would never leave his mum to spend Christmas alone.

He shook his head. 'I'm not due to fly back until the thirtieth.'

'But your mum…?'

'Actually… Mum remarried. Just over a year ago.' His voice was over-casual. 'Didn't I mention it?'

He reached out for another pastry, his eyes on the small round buns.

'No, you didn't and you know damn well that you didn't.' Though he'd had plenty of opportunity to. 'But it's great news.'

'Of course it is,' he said quickly. Too quickly. 'Great news…great news. And she and Don, her new husband, are having Christmas together, with his two grown-up kids and their families. And, yes, I was invited. But Mum was fine with me not being there.'

'But you're not fine. I can see that; I can hear it in your voice. And that's OK. You can be happy for your mum whilst also having some less noble feelings and emotions.'

He shook his head. 'No, it's not OK to have negative thoughts. It's as though I'm begrudging her her happiness. Don is a good guy, and he adores her, worships the ground she walks on.'

'And your mum? How does she feel about him?'

'She's happy.' He paused. 'She loves him.'

Each word was clearly hard for him to say, and Thea's heart twisted.

'That's the hard bit, isn't it?' she said.

'Yes, but it shouldn't be. I don't even get why I'm so…conflicted. I am happy for her, truly I am.'

'I know you are. You love your mum. You would never begrudge her her happiness. And I know you've done all the right things.' She eyed him for a moment. 'Let me guess… You've done lots of kind things for them, like booked them a honeymoon, helped arrange the wedding…gave a wonderful speech.'

'Yes.' He looked at her, half smiling, half suspicious. 'How do you know all that?'

'Because I know you. You're a good person. And you love your mum.' She looked at him, wanting to help him. 'I think this is about your dad.' She hesitated. 'When he died, did you have any counselling? See anyone?'

Zayne shook his head. 'I didn't need to. My dad and I had a great relationship. I loved him and he loved me. I didn't think I needed to see anyone. I knew what I was going to do…what he would have wanted me to do. Look after Mum and achieve everything he wanted me to achieve. Everything he sacrificed so much for.'

'So you set about doing exactly that. And that turned you into the Zayne Wood you are now. A charismatic, successful, strong person. With a ready smile, and an aura of success and happiness. A man who could take on anything. But what did you do with all that grief?'

'I channelled it into making everything good, like he would have wanted.'

'And that's great. But whilst you used it to fuel you, you weren't dealing with how it made you feel, and all the other emotions surrounding loss. Maybe your mum remarrying triggered some of those feelings? Feelings of unfairness. It's not fair that your dad died so young.'

He looked at her and she could see the surprise on his face—surprise and acknowledgement.

'That's it exactly. It doesn't seem fair that Don is getting the life with my mum that my dad should have had. My dad died before he could benefit from my success, before I could give him the life of ease he deserved. I wanted to give *him* a wonderful holiday, I wanted to buy *him* a house, I wanted my parents to reaffirm their vows and I would have made *them* a speech.' His voice broke. 'I want him to still be alive...with my mum. To have had the chance to train as a social worker, or be here now to help me set up a foundation.'

'I wish he could be, too, Zayne.'

'And maybe he would be if he'd lived differently, if he hadn't worked so damned hard for me, all those extra hours, all that stress. All for me. If he hadn't done all of that, then maybe right now he'd be alive.'

The words were so full of pain, so poignant, that Thea sat in shocked silence, her heart twisting at the realisation that Zayne had borne this intolerable burden of guilt all these years.

Then in an instant she was next to him, her arm around him, holding him close.

She waited a while before she spoke. Then, 'I'm sorry that you've carried this for so long.' Eating away inside him. 'But I need you to listen to me now. What your dad did for you he did out of choice and love. You couldn't have stopped him. There is also a good chance that nothing could have prevented that heart attack. It could have been caused by genetic factors outside his or your or anyone's control.'

She took a deep breath.

'And genetics do count. My nana—the one who lives in Cornwall—has always said her genes are going to keep her going for ever, because her own parents died in their nineties and she's still going strong at eighty-seven. Your dad's heart attack, his death, they're not on you, Zayne. They're not. Yet since he died it's as if you've been try-ing to make up for it. You've done everything he wanted you to do. I believe, and I hope, that somewhere, some-how, he knows what you've done and he's proud of you.'

Zayne shook his head. 'But what was it all for, Thea? All that self-sacrifice so he could collapse and die be-fore his time? Just so Zayne Wood could make it big, make a few million, date some beautiful woman and live it up on a yacht.'

'No! It's not like that. You worked incredibly hard to build up your company. You used your talents to develop software that means something, that has done good. You employed hundreds of people. You *cre-ated* something. As for those beautiful women… I bet you've been spreading happiness with them for years.'

That did pull a smile from him.

'But your dad's life was about more than you. He had a life before you, and he had other people and other things in his life. His relationship with and his love for your mum. And after they had you he loved your family life, the love and the laughter and the happiness. It wasn't all sacrifice, not by a long shot. And, Zayne, you've done so much in his memory. You've striven and worked to fulfil the dream he wanted for you. That's something to be proud of.'

She took his face in her hands.

'He'd be proud of you. And now you're moving on to do something else. Something you want to do.' As she recalled his excitement about the foundation, she smiled. 'That's something he didn't expect you to do, but it's still something he influenced you to do. And that is part of his legacy. He taught you to want to make a difference. And I know you're going to. But promise me you'll at least try to let go of this burden of guilt. Don't let it eat you up inside or hold you back. Your dad wouldn't have wanted that.'

She stared into his eyes, willed the sadness to clear, and then he smiled—a true smile that crinkled his eyes and lit up his face.

'Thank you, Thea. Again. For listening and for helping me see the past differently.'

And now it was he who cupped *her* face in *his* hands and looked down at her. And all the emotions of the past hour, all the confidences, the pain, the happiness seemed to coalesce and trigger something else: a shimmering, hazy miasma of desire.

All she could think of, all she was aware of was the feel of his hands, the tilt of her head, the look in his brown eyes as their gazes meshed. And in that moment all the possibilities of this evening crystallised.

'Thea...?' His voice was so soft, so sensual. 'Can I

kiss you?' He gave a small half-laugh. 'If you want, we can sit down and discuss the pros and cons.'

'This time I don't care about the pros and cons,' she said. 'Right now I can't think of any reason not to kiss you.'

A small voice at the back of her head screamed caution, but then she looked at Zayne, saw the smile that tipped up his lips, saw the desire and warmth in his brown eyes, and she knew no matter what that this was all that mattered now and she could have no regrets.

Then his lips touched hers, and there was an inevitability in the glorious, wonderful sensations. No need to question or talk or discuss. There was only an overwhelming need to taste, to touch, to feel his touch.

Her fingers and lips were as greedy as his own. And then a kiss wasn't enough, and they tugged off their clothing, the layers ending up in a muddled heap, until finally they were gloriously naked, lying on the sheepskin rug in front of the fire, with the light from the flames flickering over the contours and the clean, muscular lines of Zayne's body.

And now her desire turned molten, twisting inside her with a need so great nothing could stop her. It was a need she saw mirrored in his eyes, in his urgent touch. In the heat and want of each caress. Each touch was a promise of further escalation, until she was lost in a crescendo of sensation, need and joy.

CHAPTER TWELVE

THEA OPENED HER EYES, aware of a hazy, wonderful sense of wellbeing, her body sated, her mind a dreamy fog of memory and happiness.

Somehow, somewhere in the night, they had moved across to the bedroom. She recalled now that she'd woken to the dying embers of the fire, safe and warm, cocooned in Zayne's arms. He'd opened his eyes, and she'd watched as he'd woken up, and smiled at her with a whispered, 'Hey, beautiful…'

She'd blinked, taken in the smooth, bronzed shape of his shoulders, contoured by the dying light of the fire, then reached out and run her hand over his bare skin, revelled in the fact that she could, that it was allowed…welcomed.

'Hey.'

He'd glanced at his watch. 'Do you want to stay?'

For a fogged moment she'd considered the prospect of getting up and leaving, but then her hand had continued, moving over his body, and she'd seen his eyes darken. Her own body—the body she'd believed to be sated—had come back to life, demanding, craving more pleasure, the pleasure she now knew was beyond her wildest imaginings.

'Yes.'

The syllable had been said with an urgent need that had made him give a low, rumbling laugh. He'd risen to his feet and in one lithe movement had scooped her up into his arms and carried her to the bedroom.

She exhaled on a happy sigh of contentment and remembered that today was Christmas Eve, December the twenty-fourth.

Thea blinked as full consciousness returned with a thud.

It was the day of her meeting.

She forced herself to remain still, glanced quickly at her watch, and took a deep breath of relief. It was later than she'd normally wake up, but there was plenty of time.

Something was nagging at the outer edges of her brain, trying to tell her something. Yes, it was odd that she'd slept so late, but… Well, last night had been busy.

She frowned as she worked out what was niggling her. Everything was incredibly quiet. But that was because they were in the middle of a forest. That was all.

Now she needed to get up and go. Back to the *ryokan* to prepare. Shower, change, read through her notes.

Careful not to disturb Zayne, she got up, realised her dress was still in the lounge, then left the bedroom and quickly pulled it on, giving a little shiver of cold. It was only now she realised how much heat the fire had generated.

She headed to the window, and divided the *noren*, looked outside and shock held her completely still.

All she could see as far as the horizon was a stretch

of white, a mountain of snow. The only colour was the glimpse of brown bark on the trees that peeped through the heavy white blanket. And the snow was still falling, in a dense swirl of white flakes that continued to pour inexorably from the sky. A curtain of beauty and a force of nature.

'What the…?'

Where were the cars? It took her a while to realise they were buried. Was that even possible? The answer was obvious. A better question would be how had she let this happen? How had she been so distracted as to make such a bad decision? She'd known she must focus single-mindedly on work, not let anything else get in the way.

She took a deep breath in and turned as Zayne entered the room, his dark hair sleep-tousled, clad only in jeans.

Zayne saw Thea, and relief, warmth and happiness cascaded over him, all engendered by her sheer presence. Memories of the evening, night and early morning streamed in his mind, along with the image of her smile, the sound of her laughter, the taste of her, the glorious sensation of her skin beneath his hands, her body against his, the magic and the wonder…

It would be impossible for him to regret any of that, but when he'd woken and realised she wasn't next to him panic had touched him. Because perhaps Thea regretted it, perhaps she'd flitted away, leaving nothing behind except the lingering scent of jasmine and a stray chestnut hair curled on the pillow.

But she was still here. And even if she hadn't been she was coming for Christmas, so his disquiet had been unnecessary.

'Good morning...' he began, and then saw that his smile wasn't mirrored on her face.

Her lips were pressed together and her amber eyes were stormy. Now he strode over to the window, pushed the *noren* apart and looked out. He saw the driving flurries of snow and whiteness everywhere, as far as his eye could see.

He cursed and pulled his phone from his pocket as his mind raced to assess the situation.

'We're stuck, aren't we?' she said, her voice low.

'Yes. There's no way we're going to be able to drive in this, even if we could get the cars out.' The dirt track was obliterated under a solid wall of snow. 'On the plus side, I think we'll be OK here. We've got plenty of wood. And I've got provisions for exactly this type of emergency.'

'Can't we call for help?' she asked. 'Get people out with snow ploughs or—?' She broke off. 'Sorry. That's selfish of me.' Her face creased in concern. 'There'll be people without fuel and provisions who need to be prioritised.'

He nodded. 'There may be people in danger,' he said. 'Trapped skiers... It depends. This storm wasn't predicted, so it's going to have caught people by surprise.' He thought for a moment. 'Go and call your client, although I'm not sure how long we'll be stuck for. I'll make some calls and see what I can find out.' He moved over to the light switch and pressed it down, glanced up at the light. 'Looks like the power is out. There's a generator I should be able to get going.' He nodded towards the bedroom. 'Help yourself to some of my clothes. We need to stay warm. I've got thick sweatpants and jumpers in there.'

'Sure. Thank you.'

Her response was mechanical and he knew how gutted she would be about her meeting.

'Thea. Your client will have to cancel anyway. I doubt she'll be able to get here.'

'Maybe,' Thea said, even as she shook her head. 'It's not important, Zayne. Not compared to what may be happening out there. On the slopes. I'll call her and then I'll come back and we'll figure out a plan.'

Zayne nodded, wondering what was going through Thea's head. The radiant, joyous woman of the previous night, of earlier this morning, had vanished. Now he couldn't read her at all. He sensed, though, that a wealth of emotions were roiling within her, but he knew she would prioritise the safety of others before her own needs.

He dialled the number of the man who owned the cabin.

Twenty minutes later he dropped the phone on the table, and looked up as Thea came in, clad now in a rolled-up pair of his sweatpants and a jumper with the sleeves pushed up.

'Did you reschedule?'

'She can't. She actually came to Nagano a day early and got into the village yesterday. I missed her email.'

And he knew why. She'd missed it because they had

been engrossed in each other, neither of them even looking at their phones. Because last night they'd shut the world out, been in their own bubble, whilst outside the snow had whirled down.

'She says she's pretty much snowed in at the *ryokan*, but they're clearing the roads.'

He nodded. 'There are some skiers missing, apparently, but one of them managed to send a text saying that they've found shelter and are OK, thank goodness. They're all together, and two of them are experienced skiers, so they should be all right. But the priority is still to get to them first. We can easily last for a few days.'

Thea nodded. 'I'm so glad they're OK.'

She looked around the cabin and he could almost see the previous night replaying in her head. They both looked at the candles, burnt down now, at his clothes still strewn on the floor by the sheepskin rug. Her gaze lingered on the rug and then she looked away with a jerky movement.

'Tell me what we need to do,' she said.

'Wood,' he said. 'We need to chop some wood. I can get the generator going, and then we can assess the food situation—prioritise what to use up first. I've checked our provisions and we have plenty of food. I stocked up when I got here, just in case. I bought a load of dried foods and things we can heat up, even if we end up warming them over the fire.'

'Sure. Great. Good thinking.'

Each word was a bite, a snap.

'Let's go and chop wood.'

They walked outside, through the snow, to the small shed at the back of the cabin. Thea picked up an axe and set to work, each chop a forceful blow, her anger palpable. He said nothing until she finally stopped, handed the axe to him.

'Want to tell me what's going on?' he asked.

'I'm angry,' she said.

'With me?'

'Yes. With you.'

She said it as though it should be obvious.

'If you knew there was a chance we'd be snowed in, why the hell didn't you tell me?'

'Because I didn't know. This wasn't forecast. It's a freak storm.'

'Then why are you stocked up? You said yourself that you bought provisions for exactly this type of emergency.'

'Yes, I did. When I first moved in here. Weeks ago. Before I met you.' He could feel his own anger rising up. 'What exactly are you accusing me of, Thea?'

'You should have told me the risks. When you asked me to dinner. Last night. And you didn't.'

'Are you saying I lured you here to sabotage your meeting?'

He could hear the ice-cold edge of anger in his voice, as sharp as the axe blade he held in his hands.

But she was as angry as he was, and she didn't back down.

'Not deliberately, no. I excuse you from that.'

'I'm flattered.' The syllables dripped sarcasm. 'So you think I subconsciously sabotaged your meeting?'

'Yes. These past days you have kept on telling me that I'm too ambitious, I should slow down, I've lost perspective.'

'No, I didn't say that. I admire your ambition and your drive. All I want is for you to have balance in your life, not to burn out. I would never sabotage your meeting, consciously or not. The reason I have provisions is because it makes sense for a worst-case scenario. I work the odds, just like you work the angles. It was an unlikely scenario, but I wanted to be prepared. Last night...yesterday...the weather didn't occur to me. I could only think of you. That's the truth.'

He held out his hands, pinkie fingers outstretched.

There was a silence, and then she shrugged and turned away. 'Let's get this wood inside.'

They worked in silence. Zayne chopped more wood and Thea carried the logs inside until they were all brought in.

Zayne entered a few minutes later, his face set. And she couldn't blame him, not really.

She waited until he'd lit the fire and then walked over to him.

'I apologise,' she said. 'I know this isn't your fault.' Now she held out her pinkie fingers. 'And I believe what you said.'

He studied her expression before linking his fingers with hers. That simple touch triggered a response, a memory of the night before, and desire rippled over her.

What was the matter with her? She still wanted him with a visceral intensity. Even when she'd been furious she'd been so aware of him. Out there, chopping wood, at the height of her anger, she'd still wanted him. Had been painfully aware of his every move, of the muscular shoulders, the lithe, easy swing of the axe, the glint of perspiration on his brow.

And now, as they stood still linked, the connection shimmered and grew. Unable to resist, she stepped forward just as he did, and then he was kissing her with a need and an urgency that matched her own.

'Come to bed.'

His voice was a rasp, and so full of the promise she knew he would fulfil. And how she wanted to…with all her heart and all her might.

'I can't,' she said, and used every iota of her willpower to step away from him, her breathing ragged.

'Why not?'

'Because… Because I can't. I can't let you—this—distract me from what's really important.'

God, she was making a mess of this. She saw a flash of hurt cross his face and who could blame him?

'I've screwed up. That's why I'm so angry. Not with you. With myself. For staying last night. For not going back when I knew I had an incredibly important meeting today.'

'Why did you stay?'

'Because I wanted to.'

Wanted to explore the insidious desire that had pervaded her since she'd bumped into him on the ski slope just a few days ago. Days that had tilted the world on its head, spun it and her out of control.

She shook her head. 'I wanted to stay.'

And it hadn't only been lust.

'I wanted to stay here with you. Sleep in the bed next to you, wake up in your arms.'

'I still say that decision was a valid one. You couldn't have predicted the storm. No one could.'

'Doesn't matter. I shouldn't have taken any risk at all. I should have left. But I didn't. I let myself believe something that I know isn't true. That I could have it all.'

'It's only because of a freak snowstorm that you couldn't leave.' She could hear the frustration in Zayne's voice. 'Plus, you may still meet with your client and win her business.'

'Possibly. But it's less likely now. She's due to fly out on the twenty-sixth.'

'Then if the snow clears, arrange to meet her at the airport. Or travel to Tokyo. Do whatever it takes. I know you can do that.'

Thea nodded. 'Sure. I will do all that.'

She would. Even though right now the prospect didn't excite her, but made her feel listless, dull, tired.

'But I shouldn't have to. If I'd gone back last night I could have met her. If I hadn't got involved with you at all I'd have been there.' She bit her lip. 'My boss will be livid.'

'I don't think your boss can blame you for a snowstorm.'

'No. But he can blame me missing that email. For not making sure I was back. And what am I supposed to say? *Sorry, I was in bed with an old friend and accidentally got snowed in.*' She shook her head. 'I messed up. Even if somehow I wing this, win the client, I'll know I haven't given it my best shot. I can't afford to take my focus off what I want. I can't be distracted.'

'So that's all I am to you? A distraction? Like an annoying buzzing fly?'

'No! It's not like that at all.' She wished it was that easy, but it wasn't. 'You're…important, but I don't have room in my life, even if—'

She broke off, horrified by the words that had nearly tumbled out.

Even if I'm falling in love with you.

No, that couldn't be happening.

'Even if…?'

Thea thought desperately, her brain scrambling to figure out the bombshell that had exploded within it. Love Zayne? No. Surely she could not have been so foolish.

'Even if you are important, you are still a distraction. And the same goes the other way. I mean what am I to you?'

CHAPTER THIRTEEN

ZAYNE LOOKED AT HER. 'It's a good question.' What *was* Thea to him? 'I mean, we didn't really clarify last night. We didn't set any rules...we didn't say what we were expecting or wanting.'

For the first time ever he'd not thought—he'd simply acted, without rules or boundaries. He'd acted out of instinct, and out of something else he wasn't sure he wanted to examine.

'So for once I don't know,' he continued. 'I haven't labelled you.'

'I'm a one-off, a super-temporary relationship, a one-night stand, a...' Her voice was slightly breathless.

He shook his head. 'You, *we* can be whatever we want to be.' He took a step forward and stopped, saw wariness and panic in her amber-green eyes. 'Maybe we don't need to decide that now, maybe we can see where it takes us.'

'No!' The word exploded from her. 'Didn't you listen to anything I said? There is no point in that. There is no future for us.'

'Why not?'

'What do you mean?' The question faltered out.

'Why can't there be a future for us?'

'Because you want a family. Remember the ideal woman we discussed?'

'That woman is a myth…a figment of the imagination. You're real.'

'I am not your ideal woman. I don't want a family. You do.'

'My answer was "yes, no, maybe". That's hardly definitive.'

'It doesn't matter. If there is any chance you want a family, then I am not the woman for you.'

Her voice broke slightly and she turned and looked at the cold fireplace.

'There is nothing else to say. So don't say anything foolish, anything we'll both regret. I am not the woman for you. I want you to move forward, set up your foundation, have children, fall in love and be happy. I won't make you happy.'

She took a deep breath.

'And you won't make me happy. I am not interested in a committed, meaningful relationship. I told you that. I want a casual lover and that's what last night was about.'

The words hit him, individual bullets of pain, and he was relieved that she had the grace to keep her head turned.

'What if I told you I would rather have you and no family? That I want to give us a chance?'

There was a silence and then she faced him, her hands clenched by her side. 'I'd tell you again not to be foolish. I can't and won't invest in something that has every chance of going wrong. I won't have you watching me, hoping I'll change my mind, looking at other people's children. I don't want to know you're wishing for one of your own and I'm the one stopping you. I won't let whatever we build erode and crumble.'

'I am not Ian.'

'I know you aren't. I know you'd support me, and I know you think you mean what you're saying now. But I won't take your dream away from you. You deserve the opportunity to be a dad, a good dad, like your dad was. You deserve to pass on that legacy, and your mum deserves grandchildren. I won't be the spanner in the works. You and I can't work. We knew that twelve years ago and we know it now.'

Zayne knew he had to hold it together, knew that this pain would pass. He tried to believe that Thea was right. He could see with certainty that she'd made her mind up.

'OK. I get it. But could you explain why? You said yourself that Ian had the right to change his mind— how do you know with such certainty that you don't want a family? That you won't change your mind?'

'Because I can't let myself do that.'

The words were taut with pain and Zayne frowned at the implication.

'I'm too selfish to be a parent,' she said. 'But I'm not selfish enough to have children when I know I can't give them what they need.'

Zayne stared at her. 'You are not selfish.'

'Yes, I am.'

'Give me one example of your selfishness.'

A shadow crossed her face, and then she nodded.

'OK. That's easy. Do you remember how happy we both were when we were accepted? You at MIT and me at Cambridge? How proud we were to have made it?'

'Yes, of course I do.'

'Well, it was very soon after that that Eliza relapsed, had her second bout of leukaemia. We couldn't believe it, or we didn't want to. But after the first shock faded all I could think was *What about me? What about Cambridge?* I knew what I should do. I should have given the place up, or at least deferred it. Stayed home and supported my mum. My mum who'd already sacrificed so much, her own career ambitions in the dust.'

Zayne frowned. He'd vaguely known that Lila Kendall had given up work when Eliza was ill, but he'd never really thought about it—mostly because Lila had gone into supply teaching, and if she'd mentioned her job it had always been in a positive way. Stories about kids she'd helped, or the way a child had written a brilliant essay.

But this wasn't about Lila.

He shook his head. 'Thea... You wanted that place so much. You had put your heart, body and soul into your studies, into interview prep, into everything. You were ready. It was what you always wanted. Your mum would have known that.' He'd known that.

'She did. She told me I had to go, that there was no point me staying, that Eliza would be in the hospital, in isolation, getting the best possible care. She said that there was nothing I could do even if I did stay. That she had Dad to support her.'

Zayne moved a step closer to her. 'And that all made sense…surely it validated your decision to go?'

'They were just words,' Thea stated. 'She was being selfless. I *know* she wanted me to stay. Even if she didn't, I should have. To support her. Because she was terrified she was going to lose Eliza. I knew how exhausted she was going to be. Juggling work and the emotional strain. I should have been there for her. Just once. Someone should have been there for her.'

'She had your father,' Zayne said gently, and now he put an arm round her, moved her towards the fire, hoping its warmth and his own would help her. 'They were a unit…there for each other.'

'I know, but Dad was scared too, and his job meant he had to travel. I know you're trying to make me feel better, but in the end the bottom line is I didn't stay. Knowing that she needed me, I went anyway. I left her, and I left Eliza. I left my dad, my whole family, and I went off and did my own thing.'

He heard the self-recrimination, the guilt, in her voice, and all he wanted to do was figure out how to show her the Thea he could see.

'But I'll bet you went home every weekend and that you were on the phone every day. I bet you sent gifts, sacrificed social events and all the things new students do so that you could go home. And I'm equally sure Sienna was there as much as she could be too.'

'Doesn't matter. Mitigating factors don't make a selfish decision OK.'

'I don't believe it was selfish. And I'm sure your family don't either. You're such a closeknit unit. Even now you've agreed to this Christmas pact because you knew it would make your parents feel better about going on a cruise, because you thought it would be good for your sisters.'

'Yes. But that doesn't compensate for everything my mother gave up…all the years Eliza lost to illness. Nothing can. At the time I had a chance to do something, I didn't. So there you go, that's what you asked for, an example of my selfishness.'

'I don't believe it qualifies. You aren't selfish. You care deeply about your family. Even now, in three different time zones, you and Eliza and Sienna are still checking in. You and Sienna are still protecting Eliza, but you've also let her go, let her spread her wings. You're a good sister and a good daughter.' He shifted and took her hands in his. 'Don't not have a family because you believe you should have stayed at home all those years ago.'

'It's not just that. What if I had a child who became ill, like Eliza? I wouldn't be able to do what my mum did. Abandon my career…give up everything I'd worked for. I couldn't do it. And if I can't do that then I'm not parent material.'

'Whoa!' He raised a hand. 'That's a massive leap. You don't know what you would or could do in that situation. Have you ever talked to your mum about this? Asked her how she dealt with it? How she felt?'

'No. I don't need to. My mum is an amazing, incredible person. I'm not like her. I'm just not. And I won't do that to a child, won't burden him or her with a parent who can't put them first. I know you can't have it all, and I've chosen a career.'

This time the break in her voice was clear, and he could see tears glisten in her green eyes.

'So there is no future for us. No point in seeing where we can go because I know the answer.'

Zayne heard the finality in her tone and knew that there was nothing he could say to change her mind. Knew he had to respect Thea's choices. However much that hurt.

'Then there is nothing more to say.' He managed a smile of sorts. 'Hopefully the storm will break soon and you can sort out your client meeting. I truly wish you well, and I hope that you get the partnership and all your other dreams come true.'

'I hope that all your dreams come true as well.'

Her voice soft, and he could see a pain in her eyes that mirrored his own.

Thea opened her eyes and blinked, her dream dissipating in the unfamiliar surroundings.

The image of a massive Christmas tree faded along with, the scent of pine, a pile of presents under the tree and the excited shouts of two small dark-haired children, a girl and a boy. To one side there had been a small empty glass and a plate with the remains of a carrot and a small pile of crumbs, just as she, Sienna and Eliza had seen every year—the remnants of what they'd left for Father Christmas and his reindeer.

Reality seeped in and tears threated anew. She was in Zayne's cabin. Snowed in with the man she loved.

But she could never tell him of that love. Because if he worked it out he'd try to persuade her to give their relationship a go, and Thea was terrified that she'd crack and agree.

That way lay misery, not only for her, but for Zayne as well. So somehow she would have to stay strong, continue to let him believe he meant no more to her than any casual encounter.

Closing her eyes, she wondered if she could summon more sleep. It was the first Christmas Day she had ever wished to stay in bed and sleep away Christmas.

For a moment she wondered what her family was doing, and then remembered the varying time zones they were all in. It probably wasn't even Christmas for her sisters. But that didn't mean they wouldn't know it was Christmas here.

Grabbing her phone, she quickly sent a message to their group chat, and dropped the phone back to the bedside table.

Scrunching her eyes closed, she tried to think about her client meeting, about getting back to work. Tried to think about what she would say to Riikka Itawa. But the images wouldn't come—worse, she didn't even care.

A quick look up at the ceiling and she tried again, tried to imagine her return to London, the frenetic work-day. But it was no use. Instead all she could see was the dream she'd woken up to, that daft, impossible illusion of herself and Zayne and a family. A Christmas of love and laughter.

His words echoed in her head. *'I hope that all your*

dreams come true.' Tears threatened again and she blinked them away, forced herself to push the covers back and get up.

After all, maybe the snow would have melted and she could leave. Worst-case scenario, she would have to be civil and wish Zayne a happy Christmas. After all, he was meant to believe that he had been a casual lover.

Memories of their night together, the intensity, the joy, the passion and the laughter, streamed through her mind with irony.

Once up, Thea faced the next dilemma—what was she supposed to wear? Her dress? The one that she had worn to dinner, the one he had removed from her body and tossed to one side, both of them stoked by that desperate, dizzying need for each other. Or Zayne's clothes, clothes that had touched his body.

In the end she opted for the latter, and left the bedroom. She entered the lounge and came to a halt.

Whatever she'd expected it hadn't been this.

She looked around the room as Zayne entered from outside, a basket of logs in his hand.

'Good morning and Merry Christmas,' he said.

'I…' Her vocal cords seemed to have gone on strike. 'I… How…? When…? Why…?'

'I'll get you a coffee,' he said.

'No. Wait. First explain.'

She swept an arm around the room, all too aware that tears were threatening again. Because she had no idea of the how, why or when, but somehow Zayne had transformed the room.

Fairy lights twinkled from the eaves and strings

of paper decorations festooned the ceiling. The table held a beautiful centrepiece—a tree-shaped crystal ornament, with three tapered layers. Each layer held a beautifully crafted miniature village, snow-covered cottages, pine trees, a tiny train running along a track.

'This is beautiful,' she said softly. 'But I still don't understand.'

'Let me get the fire going properly and we can talk.'

'I'll make the coffee.'

Ten minutes later the fire was roaring and they were sat at the table.

'OK. Talk,' she said.

He took a deep breath. 'When I went to Tokyo I'd already decided to ask if you'd spend Christmas with me. In the hope you'd say yes, I bought some decorations.'

'That explains why you have them. But why have you put them up? After yesterday…'

'Just because you don't want to take our relationship further, it doesn't mean Christmas has to be a complete wash-out. We are adults, we can either avoid each other all day or we can try and have a good Christmas. I know how important Christmas is to you, and how much you must be missing your family. I'm sorry if I've made it harder for you.' He smiled at her. 'So what do you say. Shall we try to make it a good Christmas?'

Thea looked at him and warmth rushed over her, warmth and love. She realised that Zayne was wrong. Right now, however bad it sounded, and however unbelievable it was, she didn't miss her family. She wouldn't swap this snowbound Christmas Day with Zayne for anything. Not even a Kendall Christmas.

'I'd like that,' she said. Perhaps it was foolish but she wanted to store every precious memory, wanted to remember she had spent one Christmas with the man she loved.

'Perfect,' he said. 'I've managed to figure out a Christmas breakfast. How about pancakes with sweet chestnut paste?'

'That sounds delicious.'

'And after that I have a Christmas tree.' He gave a rueful smile. 'It's not up to Kendall standards, and it's artificial, but it's a tree and I bought decorations. So if you like we can decorate it. Or I can box it up and—'

'No! Don't box it up. Of course I want to decorate it. Bring it in here and I'll put it up while you make the pancakes, and after we eat we will make it the best tree ever.' Realisation struck. 'I even have some presents for you. I was going to give them to you after dinner yesterday, but...'

'Events took over,' he said, and gave her the most gorgeous, wickedest smile imaginable. 'Well, I have gifts for you too, so let's get cracking. We'll have to cobble a Christmas dinner together, as I thought I'd have time to shop for that on Christmas Eve. But I do have crackers. We'll manage.'

'Of course we will,' she said, as excitement bubbled up inside her.

She wouldn't think about the next day, or the future. She'd focus on now. And as she put the tree together and surveyed the boxes of beautiful baubles and ornaments Zayne had bought, some with intricate Japanese paintings on them, others plain red and gold, as they ate the delicious pancakes he'd made, a bittersweet happiness threaded through her.

Just as they finished the last mouthful Zayne's phone rang.

Thea watched as he answered, saw the smile drop from his face even as he nodded.

'Thank you. That's great news. We'll get shovelling.'

He dropped the phone into his pocket and smiled again, but she could see that it was forced.

'Right. The roads are cleared. The storm has stopped. All the lost people have been safely located, none the worse for the wear.' He looked at his watch. 'So, if we get shovelling, there's even a possibility you could catch your client before she heads off.'

Thea looked down at her empty plate, waited for the buzz of excitement at the prospect of meeting Riika. But there was nothing. Just a sense of bleakness. Even the fairy lights seemed to have lost their sparkle.

'I…'

He looked at her questioningly.

'I don't want to go. I want to stay.'

She knew she couldn't have it all, knew there was no future with Zayne, but surely she could have this day, this snowbound Christmas with Zayne? Looking towards the window, she almost willed the snow to start again, just here, in this bit of the forest.

'Is that what you want?' she asked.

After all, why would he want to stay if he didn't have to?

But his answer was instant and unequivocal, even

though his face retained its seriousness, his eyes dark and intense.

'Yes. That is what I want. But what about your client?'

'I'll contact her. See if we can meet tomorrow. It's Christmas Day. She'll understand.'

'And if she doesn't?'

Thea thought for a long moment. 'Then so be it.' A sense of almost recklessness possessed her as she continued, 'There will be other clients.'

'You could go and meet her and then come back,' he said softly. 'You don't have to choose between me and a business opportunity.' He took a deep breath. 'Go and call her. Then I think we should talk.'

Thea's heart seemed to pound in her chest. What did he want to talk about? Why did he look so serious?

In that moment she knew she was staying there, staying put, that her meeting with Riika Itawa was not as important as whatever Zayne had to say.

Zayne waited for Thea to return, paced the room in an attempt to steady his nerves. He wondered if he had made the right decision—knew he had. Knew he had to talk to Thea.

Finally the door to the bedroom opened and Thea came back in. His heart gave a funny little hop, skip and a jump. 'How did it go?'

'I've arranged to meet her on the twenty-seventh. In Tokyo.'

'Could you have seen her today?'

'Yes. But I chose not to. My choice.'

Her voice was almost dismissive, her amber eyes wide, the green flecks showing so many swirling emotions.

'So, what do you want to talk about.'

Zayne opened his mouth. Closed it again. Every bit of charisma and charm had deserted him. 'Us,' he finally managed. 'I want to talk about us.'

'We've already done that.'

'No. Or at least I didn't say everything I wanted to say. Especially the most important thing.'

'What's that?' Her voice a whisper.

'I love you.'

Three such simple words, and he could only hope she heard the sincerity behind them. He wasn't even sure when he'd realised it himself, but when he had, it had seemed so obvious, so real, so right.

'I wanted to tell you before, but I didn't want to make things even more difficult for you when you were stuck here with me. Now if you feel awkward you are free to leave. But I wanted you to know. I love you. Exactly as you are.'

He wanted to try to make her believe that they did have a future.

'That is more important to me than having a family, and that is my decision to make, not yours. If I have children I want it to be with you. Or I would prefer not to have them at all. I am not going to go and find the perfect woman, because I already have. I'm not Ian. I don't resent your success. I don't need to be the provider. You are a real, gorgeous, wonderful, beautiful woman. Full-stop. Exactly as you are. So if you don't love me—if you don't think you and I have a future, just you and me together—and if you can't trust me to stand by you and our love, then fine. Walk out of the door. But if you feel anything for me then please give us a chance.'

He saw tears balanced on the end of her eyelashes, saw hope and doubt war in her eyes.

'But what if our love erodes? What if—?'

'Whoa! Hang on. *Our* love?' Happiness and disbelief suffused him. 'You mean…?'

She gave a shaky laugh. 'Yes. I mean that I love you. I love you with all my heart, Zayne. I don't know how it happened, when I was trying so hard not to let it happen, but it did. I fell in love with you. Hook, line and sinker.'

'Then yesterday, why did you say we have no future?'

'*Because* I love you. I couldn't bear to be the one who makes you unhappy if we don't have a family.'

He registered the word 'if', but that wasn't important now. 'Your love could never make me unhappy. You are my world. You light up my life…you light up any space you are in. You make me laugh…you make me happy. You're thoughtful and you're clever and you're kind. You know what you want and you go for it. I love your drive and your ambition. I love the way your forehead creases when you're thinking and your whole face scrunches when you scowl. I love every single millimetre of your gorgeous body. I love the way you laugh. I love *you*.'

'But what about children? A family?'

'I want *you*. There is no point in me having a family unless you are part of it.'

'But…'

'There aren't any buts, Thea. You. I want you. As for a family, there are so many things I could say to you. For a start, I don't think anyone can predict how having a child might change you, or how you might feel once you're holding your baby in your arms. Also, if the only reason you don't want children is because you think you're too selfish to be a mum, then I will do everything I can to show you that you are wrong.'

He tried to pull his thoughts together, to understand her deep-seated fear that she would be a bad mum.

'Because you aren't selfish,' he said. 'The very fact you are willing to not have children for their sake, not your own, shows that.'

An arrested look crossed her face. 'That's what my mum said.'

Zayne raised his eyebrows. 'She did? When?'

'Just now.' Thea smiled. 'I called her after I called my client.'

'Why?'

'Because I took your advice. I decided to ask her how she did it, how she sacrificed her career so selflessly.' Thea hesitated.

'What did she say?'

'She said having kids turns all your preconceived ideas on their heads, that you truly cannot predict anything. She said she'd always believed nothing could be more important to her than becoming a head teacher. But when Eliza fell ill it stopped mattering. Just like that. Turns out my dad felt the same. They both wanted to give up work. In the end she felt bad for my father. He was the one who kept climbing the career ladder, because in the end they decided that was the better option for the family as a whole. She told me that sometimes life changes but it works out for the best. She actually loved being a supply teacher—she got to meet a variety of children, she didn't have all the pressure and the bureaucracy of being a head teacher, and she was able to be truly happy in her family and in her career. She said that sometimes you have to go with the flow and how you feel about people. And that the most important thing is to realise life isn't set in stone.'

'Your mum is a very wise woman.'

'I know. And I know she's right. Because loving you has made my whole perspective on the world change. Just like that. Becoming a partner... It's still something I want, but it's no longer the be all and end all. And it's you loving me back that's making my head spin with happiness.'

She moved towards him, looked directly into his eyes.

'But I still can't guarantee that I'll want children. I just don't know.'

'And that's OK. We can find out together. And if you truly don't want children that's OK too. I love you, and you are enough for me, Thea. Just you. That won't change. My love for you is an absolute, a foundation, a bedrock. You have to decide if you can believe in that. But please don't walk away from our love because you think it's the right thing to do. I will not go and find another woman, nor will I marry someone just to have children. The only person I will marry is you.'

'Is that a proposal?' she asked, her voice shaky.

'Nope. Let's call it a statement of intent. When I propose to you I plan for it to be a lot more romantic than this.'

'This feels pretty romantic to me,' Thea said, and she gave him a beaming smile. 'You can propose to me wherever and whenever you want, Zayne, and the answer will be the same. A great big yes. That's *my* statement of intent.'

'For real?'

'For real. I love you and I trust you. With all my heart. I do believe in our love, and I believe in our future. And I know one of the things it holds is heaps and heaps of happiness. I love you, Zayne Wood. I love how special you make me feel, I love your kindness, your sense of humour…'

'Don't forget my devilish good looks and charisma,' he put in.

'I was getting to that.' She smiled at him. 'Though obviously I'm marrying you for your other skills.'

He wiggled his eyebrows. 'I like the sound of that.'

'In the kitchen,' she said.

'I like the sound of that too. Dining table or worktop?'

It took her a second, and then she giggled. Suddenly they were laughing, and then he picked her up and twirled her round, and knew he had never been so happy.

Once he'd put her down, she smiled up at him. 'I am literally dizzy with happiness.'

'Me too. Now, let's decorate the tree.'

So they did, managing to fit every single bauble on before Thea placed the star on the top. Then came the presents.

'Here you go,' Zayne said, and watched, breath held, as she opened the package and pulled out matching his-and-hers Christmas pyjamas, liberally printed with Christmas trees on a red background.

'I can't believe you remembered,' she said. 'They're perfect. Now open yours.'

He opened the slim, rectangular package, and it was his turn to smile as he looked at the DVD of a Bollywood film.

'Thank you. There's even a DVD player here.'

'So we can watch a movie in our Christmas pyjamas?' Thea said.

'Yup. And I got you this as well.' He handed her a second gift, watched as she opened it to reveal a book, a recent bestseller. 'It's for you to read when I take you to an outdoor *onsen*.'

'Because that's the thing I said I wanted to do.' She snuggled in closer to him. 'Thank you.'

She reached for the last gift. 'And this is for you.'

He opened up a print of one of Hokusai's paintings, and felt warmth touch him at her thoughtfulness.

'It's a souvenir of our time in Obuse,' she said.

'I love it.' He grinned at her. 'It can hang in our bedroom. Wherever we end up living.'

'We can choose all the furniture together—it will be so much fun. And for your information I don't mind if it's all higgledy-piggledy. As long as we choose it together.'

She turned to face him.

'I feel so lucky, Zayne.'

'So do I.' He got up. 'Wait here…'

He returned a few minutes later with two glasses of champagne and handed one to Thea. Then he raised his own.

'To fate,' he said.

'To fate,' she echoed.

And as Zayne saw her face light up with her beautiful smile, saw the love in her eyes, he knew he would spend the rest of his life being thankful that fate had brought them back together again. For this perfect Christmas, that he knew would be the first of many.

EPILOGUE

December 31st

THEA GLANCED LEFT and then right, first at Sienna, then at Eliza, both sitting next to her on the swing seat in the Kendalls' back garden in Chiswick.

She and Zayne had arrived back that morning. Eliza and Matt had arrived the previous day.

Eliza and Matt—she really hadn't seen that coming when she'd asked Matt to look out for her sister. But the smile that lit her baby sister's face when she looked at Matt and the answering love in his were clear to see.

And then there was Sienna… She had a radiant glow about her, brought about by Kai Hunter and his little daughter Kinny, the most adorable toddler Thea had ever seen. Already she could see the bond between Sienna and Kinny; as for Kai, he looked at Sienna as if she was his world.

'Wow!' Thea said. 'My head's whirling with everything that's gone on.'

The sisters had exchanged messages, trying to keep each other in the loop, but Thea had wanted, *needed*, to see her sisters' happiness with her own eyes. Now she had, and the three of them had sneaked out to their much-loved favourite talking place.

'Mine too,' Sienna agreed. 'But I think I'm dizzy with happiness as well.'

'Do you think they're all OK in there?' Thea asked.

The sisters had left their parents, newly back from their cruise, inside with Zayne, Matt, Kai and Kinny.

'Mum and Dad will be fine,' Eliza said.

'I'm not worried about Mum and Dad,' Thea quipped.

'Matt will be fine,' Eliza said, a dreamy look on her face.

'I'm sure he will,' Thea said.

Sienna grinned. 'If he survived a fortnight in the jungle with you, meeting Mum and Dad will be a walk in the park. Plus, they'll be so happy you're home in one piece they'll be awarding him gold stars.'

'Matt was more worried about what Thea would do to him,' Eliza said. 'I'm pretty sure that at one point I heard him muttering about how you'd skewer him on a stick if he didn't look after me.'

'That was probably after the zipwire. So I would have done. But seriously...' She looked at Eliza. 'You're happy?'

'I am more happy than I can put into words. I feel like we're meant to be. It's that simple. And I know you'll all love him, and so will Mum and Dad.'

'As for Kai,' Sienna said. 'He won't have to say a word. Kinny will win Mum and Dad over in a heartbeat.'

'No arguments there. She is beyond cute.'

'She is. And she's... I can't really come up with the words,' Sienna said. 'I love her, I really do. I know it sounds mad, but it felt like an instant bond, as though I'm meant to be in her life and she in mine.'

'And Kai?' Eliza asked.

'Kai is everything I've ever dreamed of. I mean, when I first saw him I thought...' Sienna went a little bit pink and both her sisters laughed.

'We get it. No words needed,' Eliza said. 'And now...?'

'Now I love him. He sees who I really am and he values it.'

'And he loves you,' Thea said with satisfaction 'He's also got great taste,' she added. 'Your ring is stunning.'

Sienna held her hand up and the gorgeous emerald surrounded by diamonds sparkled in the winter sunlight.

'Thank you. Now, enough about us. What about you and Zayne?' Sienna gave a slightly smug older sister smile. 'I always knew you were meant to be.'

'I think maybe we were. We just didn't realise it until fate threw us together,' Thea said with a laugh. 'Literally. He's changed me, you know? And he says I've changed him. Now I feel like the world is a place full of choices. We have so many plans, and I can't wait to see what the future brings. As long as he is in it.'

Eliza grinned. 'So we can definitely say that the Christmas pact was a success?'

'I think we can.' Sienna rose to her feet. 'Now, we'd better go back in. Kinny needs some lunch.'

The three sisters re-entered the house, and Thea smiled at the tableau that greeted them.

Kinny was sitting with Zayne, who was playing

peekaboo with her, and she could hear the little girl's giggles as Zayne made a funny face. Kai was nearby, one eye on his daughter, whilst he engaged in conversation with her mum. Thea heard the words 'education', 'importance of play' and 'milestones', and knew her mum was in her element. A little further away Matt was deep in discussion with her dad, both men clearly interested.

She watched as her sisters headed in. She saw Kai's arm automatically stretch out to pull Sienna close, and Sienna's quick glance to make sure Kinny was OK. Saw Matt turn his head and smile at Eliza as she approached, a smile that signalled love and welcome and a sense of togetherness.

Then she headed towards Zayne, and happiness tugged at her heartstrings as he glanced up, his brown eyes so full of love that she could almost cry. She kissed the top of his head, felt warmth filling her as he put a hand up to clasp hers.

She smiled down at Kinny and covered her face with her hands to join in their game. 'Boo!' she said, and her heart warmed at Kinny's smile.

Before repeating the game Thea took another look round the room. She wasn't sure what next Christmas would bring, but she did know that wherever they all were the day would be filled with new traditions. And the most important ingredient would be there too. There would be love.

* * * * *

MY UNEXPECTED CHRISTMAS WEDDING

RACHAEL STEWART

MILLS & BOON

To all the Christmas lovers.

This one is for you. xx

CHAPTER ONE

Elena

'YOU WANT TO tell me what's going on, Adie?'

The man in question rakes an unsteady hand through his dark blond hair, the carefully groomed locks returning to their swept-back state as his tormented gaze flits to me. He smiles, but it's small and out of step with the sadness still lurking in his vibrant green eyes. A sadness that's swept through me too.

Why is it that I feel everything this man does? It's a connection that runs far deeper than anything else I've ever known, and we've had it all our lives. Best friends since birth, thanks to the friendship our mothers formed on the maternity ward.

And now he's here, like this.

Aiden Monroe. Infamous billionaire and infallible too. Head of Monroe Wealth Management, with a face as instantly recognisable as my own but in very different circles.

I'm an opera singer, renowned in my field. I don't have his wealth, but I have his media appeal, and that makes our meeting potential fodder for the press. Something I'm not prepared to deal with right now.

We've fended it off in the past, the gossip, the rumours, but coming off the back of a recent break-up, messy in the eyes of the press, I'm in no mood for it. Only... Aiden isn't infallible right now, and that far outweighs my concern for the rumour mill.

His eyes are bloodshot and shadowed. The grooves either side of his lips cut deep beneath the fashionably short beard. I haven't seen him in a year—a *year*—and to see him like this…

My hands itch to reach for him but I keep my distance. Even in our discreet corner of the hotel bar, I don't dare move closer. For many, many reasons. My heart being one, our notoriety being another.

This is Milan, and this hotel is as exclusive as they come, but it doesn't mean a hungry reporter won't have found a way in, or a bystander won't take the opportunity to snap a surreptitious pic on their phone.

'You're the only one to ever call me that.'

'What?' I say, losing track of the conversation.

'Adie…or any other pet name, for that matter.'

The minor fact shouldn't elate me, but my heart revels in it regardless. 'Is it a problem?'

'No.'

He laughs into his glass, takes a swig of the dark and amber liquid. Whisky, at a guess. No ice. Another thing out of Aiden step.

'Not at all.'

'Good.'

I feel relieved. I don't know why. It's not like it matters. We've been friends for thirty-five years and will continue to be friends for evermore. But there's an edge to him tonight… an edge that I can't get my head around.

And I normally know this man—better than I know myself at times.

He falls quiet again, no explanation forthcoming, and I sip at the gin and tonic he ordered before I got here. Give him the time he needs even though I'm driving myself half-mad trying to second-guess what's going on.

'I hope I chose right?' He gestures to the drink in my hand. 'I wasn't sure, but it's a single, not a double. I knew that much.'

His voice trails off, and his uncertainty is as worrying as

the rest of him. I take in his state of dress—shirt unbuttoned at the collar, tie slackened as though he was part-way to stripping it off entirely and forgot. Aiden's never undone, never unsure.

'It's fine, thank you.' I bite my lip, then, 'You're not, though...'

He holds my gaze for a breath-stealing second, a moment when I wonder if he will say anything at all, before, finally...

'What gave me away?'

'What didn't?'

He gives a soft huff. 'How long's it been, Elena?'

Not the response I wanted, not the one that gets me any closer to the bottom of this, but...

'Since we last saw one another?'

A year, one month, two weeks and three days, but who's counting?

Our longest time apart. I've been on tour and he's... Well, he's been Aiden. A billionaire workaholic with a sister and a mother to worry over and a global enterprise to lead, making money for others while investing in medical research that can never bring his father back but may save many more.

Is there anything this man does that doesn't make my heart soft, my knees weak...?

I adjust my skirt, smooth it down even though the fabric is smooth enough already. I'm fidgeting, and if I'm not careful he'll pick up on that too, and know he has me on edge. And I don't want to be. We're best friends. He shouldn't put me on edge... It's my own feelings that are doing that. Feelings that I can't control or suppress, and not through a lack of trying.

'About a year.'

He nods slowly, swirls the drink in his hand as he eyes the mini whirlpool he creates. 'Your mum's birthday party.'

I give a small smile. He remembers.

He's stressed, not losing his memory, Elena!

'Her sixtieth,' I say, ignoring the inner scorn. 'Though she still thinks she's twenty-one...'

'Don't they all?' He throws back more of his drink, gives a wince and gestures to the bartender for another.

I frown. I don't like this one bit. I rarely drink much, if at all. In my line of work vocal cords are sacred and alcohol is the devil. But Aiden rarely hits it hard either—not like this.

'Come on, Adie, what's going on?'

He drags his gaze back to me, takes an unsteady breath. 'It's Mum.'

My heart sinks. 'Margot...?'

'She's sick.'

A chill spreads through my limbs...my gut rolls. 'How sick?'

Though I know the answer well enough...

'Very.' He takes another breath that shudders through his broad frame, the hand around his empty glass trembling as he sets it down. 'Cancer. Stage Four.' He shakes his head. 'And you know what makes all of this so much worse...?'

It's rhetorical. He doesn't need my answer and I wouldn't be able to give one. My throat is too choked up with his pain, his news.

'I've spent millions over the years investing in hospitals, research centres, doing the only thing in my power to try to save others, but my own mother... I feel so damn helpless. I can't...'

He fists his hand and strikes it side-down against the polished wood, swiftly, repeatedly, silently fighting the force of emotion within, and I forget my need for self-preservation as I reach out.

'Oh, Adie.' I cover his hand with mine. 'I'm so sorry.'

His anguished gaze flits to me, his throat bobs. 'She underwent experimental treatment over the summer, but...'

'The summer?' I lean closer. 'But that was *months* ago. Why didn't you ring me? Why didn't you—?'

'You were touring. I didn't want to interrupt.'

'But this is your mother—this is *Margot*!' A second mum to me. And the idea that she is suffering, that she might not have long… I swallow the lump in my throat. 'Does my mum know?'

'No. No one does. Save for me, the doctors, and now Avery.'

'*Now* Avery?'

'We didn't tell her at first.'

'At first—? How could you not? She's your sister…'

His eyes collide with mine and he retracts his hand, breaking the physical connection as he leans back in his seat. 'How'd you think?'

'But something like this…you can't…'

'It was losing Dad that sent her off the rails in the first place.'

'But she was a child, a teenager. She's a grown adult now. You can't protect her from everything, and something as important as this…'

'Now you sound like Gabe.'

'So Gabe knows? You missed him off your need-to-know list…'

I throw back more of my drink, try to suppress the sting of it, the sting of his retraction too… And for Gabe to know and not me…

'I needed his help over the summer.'

'What kind of help?'

'To give Avery a job—keep her away while Mum underwent surgery.'

'And he was okay with that? All the secrecy, I mean?'

'No.'

There's more he's not telling me and he turns away, his eyes distant, his head elsewhere…

'They're together.'

It takes me a second to register that he's spoken, another to say, 'Who? Who's together?'

Because he can't mean—

'Avery and Gabriel.'

I choke on my drink. 'Are you—? No way.'

'It's true.' The hint of a smile—a genuine smile—touches his lips now. 'You should see them together, Laney. It's quite nauseating, really.'

My laugh is as stunned as I feel. The shift in topic as jarring as the news itself.

'I'm not sure what surprises me more. Your laidback reaction or that Gabe is in a real relationship—at least, I'm assuming it's real, because you wouldn't be this okay if Avery was just another one of his fleeting fancies.'

'I didn't say I was okay with it…not entirely…but he knows the score.'

'What? Break her heart and you're done?'

'Break her heart and we'll be more than done,' he fires back at me.

'Hey, easy tiger.'

Though seeing him come alive is a relief. *This* Aiden I can deal with. The broken man of before…that's something else.

'I'm sure Gabe wouldn't have let anything happen if it wasn't the real deal.'

'I know. They're in love. Or so they say. And I've no reason to believe it won't last.'

'Save for Gabe's reputation with the ladies and Avery's penchant for failing to stick at anything long enough to make it matter.'

'She's changed.' The small smile makes a return, reaches his eyes too. 'Turns out I never gave her the chance to be who she wanted to be. Now she's doing that, free of my involvement, she's as committed as they come.'

'Interference, you mean?'

'Involvement, interference, protection… However you want to look at it…'

He plays the big brother card so well and my heart swoons. It's sexy and endearing and I'm powerless to protect myself in the face of it. Powerless to protect myself from the pain that remains too.

Poor Margot. Poor Aiden. Avery…

I force my focus back on the conversation. 'She's still studying jewellery design, then?'

'She is. And she's impressive, Elena. Wait until you see her work. Mum's bowled over by it too. You should see them together, poring over her designs…'

His voice thickens with his words, its gruff edge tugging at my fraying heartstrings.

'And Gabe?' I say, pressing on. 'Has he changed?'

'Put it this way, I've never seen him like this over a woman before.'

I smile softly. 'There's a first time for everything, I suppose.'

'Indeed.'

His eyes lift to mine and something in their depths has the smile fading from my own, beads of sweat breaking out across my nape. He isn't done.

I lift my long black hair away, press a cool hand to the heated flesh. I should have worn cotton rather than wool. The fit of the fabric is flattering, and perfect for casual drinks with an old friend, but right now it's far too hot.

He's making me far too hot.

I look away and sip at my drink, roll a small piece of ice around my mouth, let it melt and cool before I meet his gaze once more.

'You should have called me, Aiden. I would always make time for you. You and your mother. You're family in all the ways that count.'

'I know—which is why I left it until now.'

'So I wouldn't break my commitments?'

'Guilty as charged.'

I shake my head. Always the thoughtful one. Always putting others first. Can he ever put a foot wrong in my eyes?

He does where women are concerned…

I ignore the unhelpful remark while also acknowledging

that it's not fair either. He's always very clear that he has no interest in forming a real relationship outside of the bedroom, and I probably understand his reasonings better than he does. Fear of loss, fear of not being enough, fear of—heaven forbid—having someone else depend on him...

This is the last thing I should be thinking of—Aiden and the bedroom and his closed-off feelings—but then I've been celibate since my break-up with Enrique two months ago.

Oh, who am I kidding? We hadn't slept together for months before that. Our relationship rocky long before it came to an end. He blamed my intense work schedule, while I blamed this. My feelings for Aiden that just won't quit.

Maintaining our friendship while also moving on has proved impossible. Hence the avoidance, the year apart...a year where it seems I have failed him completely.

Not being there when he needed me the most.

'I truly am sorry, Adie.' I nip my lip. Wish I could change it. The past, my feelings...my failings. 'I'm grateful you came all this way to tell me in person, but never keep something as important as this from me again. Please.'

He barely blinks as he absorbs my plea—is he even hearing me?

'It's not the only reason I've come in person, Laney.'

The tiny beads of moisture return. Why is he looking at me like that?

I swallow, but there's nothing to take down. 'No?'

'No.' He leans forward in his seat, brings himself that bit closer. 'I have something to ask of you.'

I force myself to hold his gaze, wishing my heart wouldn't pulse every time he looks at me. After thirty-five years I should be used to it. Or maybe that's the problem. It's been thirty-five years in the making. Feeling this way. And never has it been more concentrated than in the last few—ever since I was forced to accept my love for a man who refuses to ever be touched by the emotion.

'Anything,' I murmur. 'You know that.'

His mouth quirks to one side, stretching out its fullness, enhancing the dimple to one cheek that peeks through the stubble.

'You say that now…'

My heart races that bit faster. 'To use the age-old adage… if you don't ask, you don't get.'

'Perfectly put…'

And still he asks nothing.

'Adie, unless you plan on finding me a replacement for tomorrow night's performance, I suggest you—'

'Marry me, Elena?'

Aiden

I've done it. I've said it. I've asked her.

Now to explain. Only I can't seem to find the words. Probably because this is a crazy idea. I know it is, and yet it makes sense.

In black and white, it's the perfect solution to my current problem, and she's the only one I trust with it. The only one who will understand what I'm offering and what I'm most definitely not—a real relationship, a real marriage, romantic love.

She blinks across the table at me. Her rich brown eyes wide and confused. 'What did you just say?'

I interlock my fingers on the table. 'Just hear me out…'

'I swear you just asked me to…'

'Marry me, yes.'

She shakes her head, wrestling with her thoughts as the bartender appears with my drink. He sets it down and she waves an unsteady finger at it.

'What on earth is in that drink? Because I really don't think you need another.'

'Thank you,' I say to the bartender who nods and takes the empty glass away. I barely give a second's thought to what he makes of her remark, grateful that he wasn't within listening distance when I reaffirmed my hash of a proposal.

What had I been thinking? To blurt it out like that? I'd intended to lead up to it, deliver a gentle opening…

'I know how it sounds, but—'

'Do you? Because you've just told me Avery and Gabe are together, which is crazy enough. Now you want me to marry *you*. Just what are you playing at, Aiden?'

'I know what you're thinking.'

'I doubt that very much.'

I lean back, drag a hand down my face and take a breath. Maybe this wasn't such a great idea after all. But then I think of Mum. Think of the worry on her face. And resolve runs through me, solidifying my stature, adding strength to my voice.

'This has nothing to do with Gabe and my sister. I'm not trying to outdo them, or any such nonsense.'

'The thought hadn't occurred to me, but now you mention it…'

'Love isn't catching. I can promise you that.'

Her lashes flicker, the solitary lit candle between us playing in her eyes, turning their brown depths molten with gold and hypnotic with it…

God, I've missed her eyes, her smile, her laugh…it's been too long.

And the realisation stirs something deep within me. Something I don't want to examine.

'So, what is this about?' she asks.

I clear my throat, shake off the confusing haze with it.

'It's about Mum.' I say it like it's all the explanation she needs.

'What's Margot got to do with…?' Her voice trails away as her brows lift, her eyes lightening with realisation. They really are quite captivating.

And you really are losing the plot.

'I don't believe this. She wants you married, and you want to give her that in case—in case she… Aiden, come on. You can't be serious.'

'Deadly.'

'Not the—'

'Wisest choice of words? No. But the truth. It's been on her mind for a long time and she's made sure everyone knows it. Even the household staff are aware of her desire to see me married off, settled… You should see the looks I'm getting. Every unattached female now fancies themselves a candidate, thanks to her oversharing.'

'A candidate?'

'Perfect wife material.'

She laughs, her chuckle soft and disbelieving as she shakes her head and lifts her drink to her lips, takes a sip. And another. She opens her mouth but it's more choked laughter that she gives.

'It really isn't funny.'

But my voice is distant, distracted, my eyes inexplicably drawn to the trace of pink gloss she leaves against the glass edge. The shape of her mouth, feminine and soft and full of appeal.

Is this what happens when I don't see her in too long? The lines of friendship blur, and my awareness of her as a woman gets dialled up by a thousand…?

I've always thought her attractive, her beauty is impossible to ignore. But she's still Laney. My best friend Laney. And the way I'm reacting is so far from okay… Hell, she's practically *family.*

'Aiden?'

'Yes.' I snap to attention, blame my crazy proposal for my even crazier reaction.

'Where did you go?'

'I'm right here.'

'Physically, yes. But your head was long gone.'

'It was?' *It really was.* 'What did I miss?'

'All this talk of candidates and wife material…it sounds like it's not just your mother who's been thinking about this for a while.'

'How can I not? Especially now she's so ill. Before, it was simply a case of her passing comment on my lack of passion for anything but work. Then she got her diagnosis, and when she should have been focusing on her health, and getting better, she became obsessed with the idea of leaving me behind with, to use her words, "no one to lean on".'

'You have Avery.'

'I know that. She knows that. But it's not the same and she's made sure I know that too.'

'So she's badgering you into getting married?'

'Badgering, dropping not-so-subtle hints, deploying emotional blackmail—they're all one and the same, right?'

She shakes her head, looks at me like I've lost mine—not that I can blame her.

'Since when do you do something because someone else expects it of you…? Actually, don't answer that.'

Because we both know the answer. It happened the day my dad died and left me in charge. My whole life became about the expectations and demands of others.

'But this is marriage, Aiden. You can't marry a random woman just to make your mother happy.'

'I'm not talking about marrying someone random, I'm talking about marrying *you*. Think about it, Elena. When we were growing up our mothers joked about it, but at the heart of that joke was a real hope that one day it would happen. And my mother isn't stupid. If I came home with just anyone, she'd know it was a ruse, a fake engagement to keep her happy. But if I come home with you… Well, then it's her dream come true and she won't question it. She'll take our word as gospel.'

'Our word?' she repeats quietly. 'And what word is that?'

'That we're in love.'

The ice clinks inside her glass and she sets it down. The tremor in her hand too obvious to miss as I push on, desperate to convince her, desperate to ignore the weird sense of chaos within too.

'That we've been in love for a long time but we didn't want to tell anyone until we knew it was a dead cert.'

She shudders. 'Will you quit it with the dead word?'

'You know what I mean.'

'I do, but I still don't understand why you would do this.'

'Because I can't bear it, Laney. Dad died, and a part of her died with him. She's never been the same. And now she's sick, and I don't know how long she has left, but I'd like to know that I did what I could to bring her some joy once more. Joy and peace and everything in between.'

'Isn't it enough to see her daughter settled?'

The inner chaos morphs into an ache, resonating deep within my chest. 'You'd think so. After everything Avery went through…after everything we went through with her. But no. It's not enough.'

She frowns, her eyes raking over my face as she seeks out something in mine.

'She's scared that without a woman you'll work yourself into an early grave…'

I flinch. Her supposition is so on target. And she knows it too—thinks the same, even. The way she states it as fact rather than a question.

'And you think the same?'

Her silence is answer enough.

'My mother saw the inherent workaholic in my father and spent their life together trying to ensure he found balance. Trying and failing. So I can understand why she would think it of me. But you?'

'Come on, Adie, ever since your dad passed away work has become your life—you know that. Everyone knows that.'

'Because I care what happens to the company.'

'Of course you do. It's your father's legacy.'

'And I won't fail him.' It erupts in a rush, my hand balling into a fist.

'You could never fail him.'

I scoff. 'Were you not there when I was a kid? An adult, even? You saw the pressure…the need to excel. It wasn't enough to pass, to just be good enough. I had to do better, be the best.'

'And you did. Look at you, Adie. Look at Monroe Wealth Management. You're at the top of your game.'

'And I'll make sure I stay that way.'

'But to what detriment?'

I force my hand to relax. 'You don't understand.'

'Of course I understand. I was there. I understood the pressure. I also understood that you were loved. And your father wouldn't want you to sacrifice your life for his work.'

'It's my work too.'

'Because it was forced upon you. You forget I remember those days when you used to dream of doing something else—*anything* else, almost. Are you saying you don't have those thoughts any more? That Monroe Wealth makes you feel happy and fulfilled?'

'It's not a question of happiness. It's a question of looking after my father's legacy—my family's too. It's about keeping the future secure for the hundreds and thousands of employees who work for me.'

'You have people you can trust to continue that work and free you to pursue other interests. Take Gabe's new business. You could step in there…do something with your best friend. Or those charities you support—just think what they could achieve with you dedicating your time and expertise to a cause that you truly care about.'

Her words tease at the fringes of my mind, at age-old dreams long ago forgotten as the necessities of life took over. As grief for my father became an overwhelming need to do right by him. To prove my worth and ensure he didn't die in vain. To never fail him.

'Monroe Wealth is my responsibility.'

'But it doesn't need all of you, Adie. It will always be a part of you, but you can choose to have more in life. You just need to open your mind to it…and your heart.'

I stare back at her, ignore the flicker of light that comes alive inside me as I try to find the words to deny it, to deny her.

'Look what happened with your father,' she says. 'He was far too young to—'

'He had an undiagnosed heart condition,' I cut in, aggressive, defensive.

'Exacerbated by his lifestyle. His work.'

'There's nothing to say the same will happen to me.'

'You can't know that.'

'I've had a thorough work-up. Believe me, if there was a risk I'd know about it.'

'You're missing the point.'

'I'm not missing the point. I'm addressing it head-on.'

'Is this really how you want to spend the rest of your life, Adie?' She looks sad, sad and concerned, and it skitters over my skin. 'Working all hours to—'

'I'm not working all hours—not now Mum is sick. I've been home more. I've had to be.'

'But when she's gone? Who will give your life balance then? Avery has Gabe. Who will you have?'

The conversation has come full circle. 'You think her concern is valid?'

'I think her concern is valid, yes, but I don't think you getting married is the answer.'

'How so?'

'I'm sorry, Adie, but I don't think there's a woman out there capable of making you change. That has to come from you.'

'At least on that we agree.'

'No one could change your father…not your mother and not you.'

She says it softly, so full of meaning, and I know it's because she sees it. My own guilt. My own failing.

'It wasn't your fault your father wouldn't stop. You tried…'

I shrug, but it's awkward, stilted. I did try. On all those father-and-son trips when he was supposed to be getting some R&R—Mum's orders. And yet he'd still have his phone to his ear, his laptop within reach. All those weekends where he'd skirt around the edge of the pitch, one eye on my game and the other firmly on his phone. I performed for him, eager to distract him, rarely succeeding. He was proud of me, and he loved me, and my sister, my mum…just not enough to give work a rest, take the rest his body needed.

'It doesn't matter now, anyway. I can't change the past.'

'No, but you can change the future. *Your* future.'

'This my life, Laney. Whether I like it or not, I choose to live it this way.'

Her gaze is intense, her rich brown depths questioning and assessing, filled with doubt and disappointment too. Not that I'll react to it.

'So why do this, then?' she says. 'If this is really how you want to live, why are you bending your life rules with this crazy proposition?'

'Because my mother doesn't agree. She sees marriage as the answer and that's all that matters.'

'Is it?'

She wets her lips, crosses her legs. Her knee brushes against mine beneath the table and I have the strangest urge to maintain the contact. I cover the echo of her touch with my hand, dismiss the thought as quickly as it occurs.

'Yes. I'm not seriously contemplating marriage because I think she's right. I don't need another person to feel responsible for, to depend on me.' I wince. 'No offence, Laney.'

'None taken.'

Because she gets it. She gets me. And that's why it has to be her.

'I'm proposing a front—a pretend relationship to quit her worrying over me so she can focus on what she should—getting better. And if she doesn't…if I'm to lose her…then at least she'll leave this world thinking I'm okay.'

Elena stares back at me and I take up my drink, give her time to mull it over.

'You really want me to be your fake wife?'

'No, a fake fiancée will suffice.'

'Suffice?' she chokes out. 'Have you heard yourself?'

I grimace. 'Sadly, yes. And I know how it sounds—I do.'

'And what if she survives, Aiden? Have you thought about how we manage that?'

I swallow, feel the blood inch from my face. 'The chances are slim…'

She touches a hand to her mouth as the tears make a return.

'Life is so unfair…' She waves a hand at me as I try to apologise, hating that I've put her in this position, but hating the situation that led us here more. 'Not you. I don't mean you and this. I mean your mum. I mean her illness. To have gone through all she has and now this.'

'It's why I want your help, Laney. To make the best of an awful situation. You know I wouldn't ask if there was any other way. And you're the only person I can ask…the only person I can imagine by my side.'

'I…'

My heart flutters up inside my chest, my head lifts…

'I don't know.'

The slump is real—the disappointment, the desperation. 'Think about it, Laney. It's not like it doesn't help you too. After what happened with Enrique—'

She reacts as though I've slapped her, and I bite my cheek, curse the low blow I've delivered. Does the man still have the power to hurt her so much?

'I'm sorry. I didn't want to mention him.'

'But you did anyway?'

'You know it makes sense. It'll get the press off your back, stop them pitying you and speculating over your feelings now that he's with—'

'I couldn't care less what they say, and I'm happy that he's happy.'

'Are you?' I don't believe her—not for a second. 'Because you don't look it, and I'm sure your mother worries over every printed word.'

'Is that going to be your constant defence when it comes to this crazy idea? Our mothers?'

'It really isn't so crazy—not when you give it proper thought.'

'We'd be lying to the world, Aiden.'

'But not to each other.'

'And you think that makes it okay?'

'You're one of the few people in this world I care about, Elena. Lying to you is an impossibility.'

'But lying to our mothers, your sister, Gabe?'

'The latter are too loved up to care and the former will be too ecstatic.'

'And when we expose it for what it is?'

'We won't. We'll simply part amicably. Like any normal couple.'

'And what about the press? You say this will help me now, but don't you think the press will have a field-day over our eventual break up? Especially as they've been dying for this story for far too long.'

'We'll control the narrative together, and our PR teams can take care of the rest.'

'You make it sound so simple.'

'Because it is.'

'Can you really be so cold and matter-of-fact about it?'

'I'm being anything but cold, Elena. I'm doing this for my

mother and hoping it will help you too. Aren't you sick of the press speculation? Aren't you sick of the weekly, if not daily, phone calls from your mother, checking in? Worrying?'

'How do you know about those?'

'Because I know you and I know your mother.'

She chews the corner of her mouth and I force my eyes up, hold her gaze.

'It really does make a lot of sense.'

'In an Aiden world, where everything is black and white.'

'What's that supposed to mean?'

'What about the shades of grey?'

'I wasn't talking about us getting into bed together, Laney.'

Her cheeks flame, and I know I shouldn't have said it. It was too close to the knuckle, too much of a tease when this is a serious conversation. But…

'Neither was I, Monroe,' she quips back, my best friend through and through. 'I meant, what about when things get complicated, messy…?'

'How so?'

'I don't know. But if we're to convince people we're in love, they will expect us to…you know…'

'So you *are* talking about the bedroom?' I hold my hand up when her eyes flare. 'Sorry, not the bedroom. But you are referring to physical shows of affection?'

'Yes!'

I can't resist the slow smile I give. 'Does the idea of kissing me turn your stomach that much?'

CHAPTER TWO

Elena

'DOES THE IDEA of kissing me turn your stomach that much?'

I almost miss my cue as I recall his question from the night before and I race to correct my mistake, praying the world doesn't notice. I say world, but it's an audience of two thousand—an audience that will spread the word faster than I can quit the theatre if I don't get back in time and stay there.

'You're only ever as good as your last performance,' my mentor, the late, great Valentina, whispers in my ear, and I roll back my shoulders, breathe and sing. Sing my heart out like I'd wanted to last night.

Kissing Aiden.

The number of times I've imagined it, dreamed of it...

I push him out, but he returns just as quickly, defeating the lights that shine down on me, the music that beats through my veins. If I hadn't known he was here in the theatre, my body would have told me so.

I sing to the audience, but I sing for him.

To the world, he's just another billionaire. To me, he's my best friend, and the man who took my heart before I even knew what love was. And now he wants to marry me. Marry me for appearances' sake.

And I left him hanging. A hurried 'Let me think about it' all I'd been able to give.

I understand why he's asked me. Why he's chosen me. Because I get it—I get him. I get what this is and what it isn't. I only wish my heart would get the message, because then maybe I'd be able to move on from this hopeless, unrequited love and find Mr Right. A man who can love me in return.

Enrique had come so close. I'd almost thought he was the one. And then Aiden had appeared at my mother's birthday party, effortlessly sexy, effortlessly distracting to my heart, which was all too keen to remind me of all the ways in which Enrique wasn't him.

Cue several months down the line, with a disgruntled Enrique bemoaning my heavy work schedule and the arguments that had then ensued.

I was hiding myself in my work, hiding from the truth, and I couldn't blame Enrique—not for a second. That was all on me. And if Aiden knew the true reason I'd been so horrified at the mention of Enrique he'd have been as pale as me.

I know I can't carry on like this. I won't. I need to find a way to move on. And if that means saying yes to Aiden's proposal, guarding my heart while opening his to another way of living and loving, then I will. If I'm not the woman for him, he cannot be the man for me.

Absence didn't hammer the message home; I can only hope proximity will.

Foolish, perhaps. But I can't say no.

Not when he needs me.

I've failed him these past few months. I won't fail him again.

I close my eyes, let the music consume me, let his presence fuel my performance, feel my skin come alive under his watchful eye.

This is the last night of my world tour and the opulence of my surroundings, the history, speaks to my very soul. The Teatro alla Scala, all red and gold, with the glamour of yesteryear and the spirit of every performer who has come before me feeding the ancient rafters. It's magical. Monumental. A highlight of my career...

It should be everything to me.

Only *he* is…

The cadenza is my time to shine, and though I can't see him, my head tilts to where I imagine him to be. I give him my all and forget the nerves that accompanied his note to my dressing room before I came on stage…his note and a bouquet of glorious red roses.

Forgive me, Elena.
I am here to see you sing, no more.
Your friend always,
Aiden x

In all the years I have performed, I can count the number of occasions he has watched me on one hand. The number of times he has sent flowers even less.

Guilt is his driving force. But I don't need his guilt. And the sooner this performance is over, the sooner I can tell him my decision and put his mind at rest.

I think ahead to the festive break I had planned, only it's going to be a very different Christmas from the one I envisaged. So very different from anything I've ever imagined…

Or not, if I was to think of my unattainable dream.

To win the impossible.

Aiden Monroe's heart.

Aiden

I don't move. I'm not even sure I've breathed since she came on stage—not fully. Not until the end, when the applause sounds up around me, urging me into giving the same. And even then goosebumps still prickle across my skin, my ears still ring with the beauty and the power of her voice.

Elena Martinez.

She's not my best friend—not now. On that stage, she's a

superstar. And glorious with it. If only my mother had been well enough to come…

My mother…the woman who has driven me here. When the woman who should've lured me here on her own merit is the one upon the stage.

I curse the way I treated her the night before. Curse the way I came right out with it. Asking something so huge of her and crossing a line I had no right to.

To expect her to agree, to come with me and give up this life for however long…

I knew her schedule before I asked. I knew she intended to take a break. A prolonged spell away from the stage, resting her body and her voice. I knew the press had been hounding her, and her break-up with Enrique was still front-page news on certain gossip sites.

But none of that can excuse what I did.

Rising with the audience, her standing ovation hard-won, I zero in on the blush touching her cheeks, the way her eyes sparkle and her whole face shines with joy. Regret slices through me. Regret that I stole some of that from her last night.

I never should have come.

No. That's not right.

I should have come. I should have come to watch her perform years ago, like the good friend I claim to be. What I should never have done is put her on the spot. Our first reunion in a year and I did that to her.

She told me she'd think about it as she raced away, unwilling or unable to refuse me—both just as bad. *Selfish*. I'd been *so* damn selfish. Manipulative too.

My fingers curl into my palms and I turn away, leave her to her fans and her glory, regretting every step I've made since arriving in Milan. I leave the privacy of my box and debate heading backstage, before realising I'll only intrude more.

I'm going around in circles mentally, and the journey to my car is taking far longer than it should as I'm plagued with uncertainty.

I'm never uncertain. I choose a path and I stick to it. Only deviating when it works for me.

Before my ridiculous proposition, I would have gone straight to her dressing room, congratulated her on a performance well done, taken her for after-show drinks before heading back to the States.

Maybe it's that realisation which has me pausing under the theatre's grand stone portico. Or maybe it's the chill of the outdoors, the wind whipping up, that wakes me up to myself and the situation we're now in.

I can't leave Milan without knowing we're okay. And the only way to do that is to look her in the eye and have her tell me we are.

'Aiden?'

I spin on the spot. The soft hesitation in her voice, so far removed from the powerhouse of a voice that not an hour ago filled the rafters of the great theatre behind her, makes my heart ache. The way her heavily made-up eyes blink across at me, hesitant and unsure, intensifying the sensation.

She must have raced to get here, throwing a fur-trimmed shawl around her shoulders to protect her from the bracing cold as the delicate satin of her stage dress leaves too much of her exposed. I have the overriding urge to step forward and protect her, and if not for the presence of one too many bystanders already eyeing us with open curiosity, I would.

'You're leaving…?' she whispers.

'Yes. No. I mean…' I clear my throat. 'I wasn't sure you'd want to see me.'

'Yet you came to see me perform?'

I step forward, rake a hesitant hand through my hair. 'I couldn't leave without seeing you perform, Laney. I should have come sooner.'

I touch a hand to her elbow as I lean in and kiss her cheek. A platonic kiss in greeting, wholly acceptable, but for some inexplicable reason it feels like more. She smells of happiness and roses, and I'm breathing her in before I realise I'm making it into more, letting it feel like more. What is *wrong* with me?

'You were incredible tonight.'

I mask my inner ramble with a smile as I step back.

'But you were going to leave without saying goodbye?'

I can hear the wound I've unintentionally created in every soft-spoken word.

'Not quite.' My smile twists to one side. 'I was coming back.'

'You were?'

She doesn't believe me. I know that look of old. The folded arms, the cocked brow… It's the one she'd throw my way when I promised to be on best behaviour around her friends when we were in our teens, or promised not to sneak the last piece of apple pie when she wasn't looking.

'I really was,' I insist. 'I wondered if I could take you for a drink…a proper goodbye before I fly. That's if they can spare you…?'

I gesture towards the theatre, where I'm sure her absence will already have been noted.

'I'd like that…' She eyes the onlookers, adding quietly, 'We can talk about your proposal.'

I raise a hand to cut her off. 'Forget I even asked. Please.'

Her brows pinch together. 'You've changed your mind?'

'I never should have put that on you.'

I remember the way she fled, all flustered and uncertain, claiming she needed her rest before tonight's performance. Not a total lie—she's an elite athlete, to all intents and purposes, careful with what she eats, what she drinks, what she does and how much she sleeps, especially when on tour. But she would've stayed longer had I not done what I did.

'Can you give me time to change?' she says, her sudden smile so warm and reassuring it coaxes one out of me in return.

'Of course. Let me know when you're done and I'll have my car ready.'

'I won't be long.'

And in a billow of red satin and black fur she disappears inside.

I nod to a gawping woman whose husband is trying to get her attention, smooth out my tux and stride for my waiting car. I'll do a circuit and come back for her. Hopefully the on-lookers will be few and far between by then. They've never concerned me before—Laney and I have faced plenty of spec-ulation over the years—but they do now.

Whether it's the proposal hanging in the air between us or my feelings that aren't so clear-cut any more, I feel exposed, vulnerable to their keen gaze that's capable of seeing far too much.

And making sure the world knows it too.

Elena

Aiden's chauffeur-driven black Mercedes pulls up within min-utes of my text, and his driver's opening my door before I can get to it. I give him a smile as I climb in, and hold it steady as I meet Aiden's eye.

Shame I can't do the same with my breath. Aiden in a suit always gets to me, but Aiden in a dark tux does something else entirely. I feel my cheeks warm beneath my make-up and pray the light is so low he won't notice.

'You really were incredible tonight, Laney.'

The raw appreciation in his voice has my cheeks burning deeper, my lower belly too. I touch my fingers to my neck, to the skin that tingles just behind my ear.

'Thank you.'

'Are you being coy with me?'

I give a nervous laugh. 'Of course not.'

Because that would mean I care about his opinion more than I should. That it affects me more than it should.

His eyes remain on me, the question persisting even though I've brushed it off.

'What happened to us, Laney? We used to be so at ease, so comfortable around one another...'

I stiffen. 'What do you mean?'

'I'd blame my selfish proposal last night if it weren't for the fact things have felt a little off for a while now...these last few years I feel like something has changed.'

'We've both been busy, Aiden. Our careers are full-on, and time is a luxury we don't have a lot of.'

'And some have even less.'

I know he's talking about his mum and her diagnosis, and I curse my choice of words. 'I'm sorry.'

'I'm the one who's sorry. You always make time, Laney. You always check in with me, even if it's just a message, or an email. You're always there. I'm not sure you can say the same of me.'

If he truly thinks that, then why didn't he tell me about Margot? Why didn't he feel he could come to me? He explained it away last night, blaming my work schedule, but that only makes me feel worse.

'You've supported me plenty over the years.'

'From afar...'

'And what's wrong with that? I know you're there. I know I can call you if ever I need you. And, let's face it, the past decade you've been filling your father's shoes and I've been pursuing my dream to sing in places such as this. I'd say we've done well to achieve all that and still have what we have.'

'And what is that?'

I purse my lips as I eye him. 'Our friendship! Or are you being deliberately obtuse?'

'Never.' He gives a low chuckle that reverberates through me, the intimacy of the back seat and his proximity working together to elevate my pulse and sensitise my skin.

I clutch my hands in my lap, look away to the passing streets that I still find stunning, no matter how many times I visit, and cling to the scenery rather than the mood within.

'You know, I could stare at that building all night.' I gesture to the Duomo, all lit up, its gothic beauty resplendent.

'That's good, because we're getting out.'

'We *are*? Already?'

We've been in the car minutes at most. Is he suggesting we take to the streets for a *walk*? Even at this late hour the pavement is bustling. Does he really want to attract that kind of attention?

'I have a suite at the Galleria.'

He points to the nineteenth-century shopping arcade beside us—the same arcade we could have accessed directly from outside the theatre.

'You're joking?'

'Not in the slightest.'

'And we needed the car because…?'

'It makes a good decoy. No one would expect us to do a loop and get out across the way. Had I simply walked you over the road everyone would have seen and known what we were about.'

I smile. 'Sneaky.'

'Well-practised.'

'Still, I would have put you somewhere like the Hyatt or the Armani…'

'Would you, now? And what exactly are you trying to say about me?'

'That of all the places I expected you to stay in Milan, a shopping centre isn't one of them.'

He laughs. 'Not just any shopping centre. It's an iconic structure—and more art gallery than hotel.'

'Oh, I know that…and I appreciate the appeal.'

'I thought you would.'

I eye him. Did he book it because of me? He couldn't have… wouldn't have…but… 'I'm surprised it tickles your fancy, though.'

'Most things don't, but there's something quite unique about the Galleria Vittorio Emanuele II.'

'You mean besides its once-coveted seven-star status?'

'There is that. But, no, it's the history, the architecture, the people-watching… Being able to exist in the centre of it all without being spotted and instantly outed. You'll see what I mean—and you'll love the view from the master bedroom, too.'

'Is that so?'

And why is he mentioning the master bedroom…the master bedroom I don't intend to see. Why does he say it so easily too? Without any hint of suggestion?

Because you're friends. Just. Friends.

'It has the perfect vantage point to take in the front of La Scala.'

'Are you spying on me, Adie?'

He grins as the car comes to a gentle stop, my breath with it.

'Now you mention it, it is a bit stalkerish.'

He's teasing—of course he is. But the idea that he would book it to be close to me…

The driver opens my door and I don't have time to think on it any longer as we move at pace, the hood of my cloak pulled up and my head down to avoid catching anyone's eye.

He leads me through a narrow entrance that I'd never have noticed, and a laugh escapes, all silly and girly. But he makes me feel young and giddy, as though we're on some little adventure only the two of us are privy to. Like when we were kids and he'd come up with a fantastical story as we rampaged through the grounds of his vast family estate in the Canadian Rockies. I loved it there…just as much as I love being on stage now.

We enter a rectangular lobby and I halt in my tracks. A bronze sculpture takes centre stage—Auguste Rodin's *The Thinker*. And all around us, floor to ceiling, is a black and white fresco of entwined bodies, moody and dramatic and seriously intense.

'Okay, I take it back,' I say, lowering my hood and turning on the spot. 'This place is perfect for you.'

'I daren't ask why.'

Though he knows, I'm sure. The playful spark in his green

eyes telling me he's on the same wavelength as he guides me through the contactless entry and we walk through halls immersed in art, ever-changing. Bold murals, striking sculptures, the colours vibrant and in some cases clashing.

There can be no denying it has a certain appeal, tapping into the artistic heart of Milan, its history and its culture. Every wall a canvas. Every corridor an exhibition.

And his suite is no exception.

'The presidential suite?' I say as he pushes open the door and gestures for me to go ahead.

'Only the best.' He steps in behind me, tosses the keys onto a twisted metal console table as he shrugs out of his jacket. 'You hungry?'

'Not particularly.' I slip the cloak from my shoulders and drape it over a nearby chair—part sculpture, part cushion—and step deeper into the space, taking in the wild canvases on the walls, the eclectic style. 'I try not to eat after eight.'

'Ah, yes, I remember. Champagne, then? A celebration of sorts?'

'A celebration? And just what are we celebrating?'

'The end of your tour, for one thing? Our reunion for another?'

'It has been a while…'

'And I'm sorry for that.'

'Can we lay off the guilt? We're both to blame.'

My unavoidable feelings for him are right up there with our busy careers, our busy lives…not that I can tell him that.

'No guilt. No blame. So…champagne?'

I laugh, the sound lighter than I feel. 'Sounds poetic and perfect.'

I walk into the living area and take a moment to appreciate the suite's glorious position. Perched in the rafters of the Galleria, the floor-to-ceiling arched window takes centre stage on one wall, and looks out over the intersecting walkways of the famed four-storey shopping mall and the few wanderers still out at this late hour.

Subtly lit in a golden hue, the glass-vaulted arcade with its mosaic floor, its murals in the rafters and gold stone carvings in the walls, is a piece of art itself. And this high up no one would even notice us, let alone care.

It's a vantage point many a celebrity would treasure, and I'm no different.

'You're right about this place. Privacy amongst the masses is kind of special.'

'I'm glad you like it.'

He pops the cork on a bottle that seems to have appeared from nowhere, and I fall back into a giant fur bucket seat that is so un-Aiden it has me laughing again.

'This decor, though...' I pluck at the super-soft white fur.

'I don't know...it could work. Especially at the lodge.'

'At your lodge in the Rockies, yes... But here?' I cock a brow as he hands me a glass.

'It'll work when the place is adorned for Christmas, I'm sure.'

I look back to the view and imagine it.

'You're right. With the giant Christmas tree in the heart of the arcade, it'll make the perfect backdrop.'

'I'm surprised it isn't already up. Most places I've visited recently are already in full festive swing, despite it being mid-November.'

'They wait for the feast of Sant'Ambrogio, patron saint of Milan, on the seventh of December, to officially start their Christmas celebrations. Then they go all in. The tree outside the Duomo is particularly stunning. Have you ever seen it?'

'Can't say I have.' He lowers himself to the seat beside me. 'Will you still be here for that?'

I swallow the bubble of nerves that rises up as he inadvertently brings the conversation to its all-important pinnacle. 'Well, that depends on you.'

'How so?'

'Your proposal...'

He raises his hand to wave it away. 'Please, say no more, Laney. I never should have asked.'

'Are you saying you regret it?'

'I'm saying I regret putting that on you, yes.'

'But you don't regret the idea itself?'

I study him intently now, needing to know his answer before I give him mine.

'No, Laney.' His eyes are as serious as his tone and my heart shivers. 'I can't imagine having any other woman by my side to present as my wife-to-be.'

Another tight swallow. 'Good.'

One dark brow lifts. 'Good...?'

I nod and force myself to reach across, take his hand in mine, knowing the sparks will fly but needing that contact, as a way of grounding myself in the present and my decision.

'I'm in.'

His fingers pulse around mine, his eyes narrow. 'You're...*in*?'

'I'll be your wife—your fiancée. I'll help take care of Margot too. Whatever you need.'

His lips part ever so slightly, but he says nothing, his eyes hesitating over my face.

'Say something, Adie. Anything will do?'

I pull back and he tightens his grip around my hand to stop me.

'Are you serious?'

'I think I was the one asking you that last night...'

'I mean it, Laney...'

The intensity of his green eyes, the way he runs his teeth over his bottom lip, has me struggling to breathe past the heat that fractures right through me.

'Are you sure? Because you don't have to do this. You're my oldest friend—you will *always* be my friend. You don't owe me this. You don't owe me anything.'

Am I sure? No. But do I want to do it...? With every fibre of my being.

Time away hasn't eased my love for him...perhaps time together will. Perhaps it'll give me a real insight into what life is like living with him and his untouchable, work-focused heart, and mine will get a wake-up call. Open itself up to finding someone else. Someone who can love me in return. Someone who isn't him.

And I'm not naïve, or stupid. I know the risk. I know this could see me falling deeper and my heart torn in two. But it's a risk I have to take. Because he needs me, and I need to find another way of moving on.

'I want to, Adie. I want to do it for you, for Margot. And you're right—it will be good for me too. Some happy press after a spell of despair.'

'*Are* you despairing, Laney? Truly? Because the idea that you would be broken over him is…'

I shake my head, squeeze his fingers. 'No. Enrique is in the past. You're my future…as far as the world is concerned.'

And I'm never going to admit that Enrique and I were doomed from the start, because my heart already belonged to Aiden.

Aiden

This is what I wanted. What my mother wants for me.

So why the thrumming sensation in my gut, the unease…?

I hold her gaze, read the sincerity, the compassion, the love there.

'We're really doing this?'

'We really are.'

I smile, purposefully ignoring the weird churning within. 'In that case, a toast.' I lift the glass in my hand and focus on the end game. *Why* we're doing this. 'To happy mothers and happy lives.'

'I'm sure the phrase is happy wife, happy life.'

My smile widens at her jest, and the sparkle in her eyes is as golden as the champagne bubbles in her glass.

'That too. Thank you, Laney, from the bottom of my heart. Thank you.'

CHAPTER THREE

Elena

I TWIRL A strand of hair around my finger, eye the approaching runway with trepidation.

Not over the flying. The Monroe private jet is comfort at its finest. Plush leather, soft creams and warm wood. Nothing is too much for the stewards on board.

No, what has me fidgeting is what will greet us on the ground. We're almost two hours out from his winter home in Banff. Two hours out from his mother and showtime.

I need to give the performance of a lifetime off the stage and I'm not ready for it.

'Nervous?'

I lift my gaze to the snow-capped mountains, their beauty accentuated by the glow from the setting sun, and manage a small smile before I turn to him.

'A little.'

He nods. 'You always did that with your hair when you were nervous.' He gestures to my finger, currently covered from base to tip in glossy black. 'I didn't know my mother scared you so much.'

I give an unsteady laugh. 'Your mother doesn't. But *this*... the pretence...does.'

He eases my hand free of my hair, the contact working its magic and warming me through.

'It's not too late to change your mind.'

I shake my head. 'No. We're doing this. If I can perform in front of thousands, I can perform in front of a select few.'

'But it's different. I know that, Laney.'

His green eyes are dizzying with understanding, spellbinding with their compassion. This is what's so hard with Aiden. He cares. Deeply. About his mother, his sister, Gabe, me. It's hard to believe he refuses to love when he's capable of this. Hard to remind myself, too, that the look in his eye means nothing more than the love of a lifetime friend.

'I want to do this, Adie. I promise.'

He studies me a moment more.

'You'll be needing this, then...'

He reaches inside his jacket and pulls out a small velvet box. My eyes widen, my breath catches. It doesn't matter that I know this isn't real, my heart is all over it.

'I hadn't— I didn't—'

'What? You didn't think I'd buy you a ring?'

'I—I guess I hadn't thought about it.'

Every word is a struggle to get out and my heart is strumming too fast, too loud. I'm convinced he can hear it.

'It is customary, you know.' He gives me that charming, endearing smile that makes me weak at the knees.

Fall out of love with him?

My heart would be laughing if it wasn't toeing such a dangerous line.

'And my mother would have my head if I proposed without one.'

He starts to open it and I place a hand over his to stop him. 'I can't take it.'

'But you can't walk in without one, Laney. And asking you in front of them is an added pressure neither of us needs to endure.'

'You make it sound like torture.'

I'm not upset. I'm not. He's right. To do the whole proposal with an audience—no, thank you. But... I blink at him, my brain racing for a good enough reason not to take it.

'If you're worried you won't like it, we can change it.'

'No, it's not…'

'Worried you'll like it too much and won't want to give it back?'

He's teasing, but he's so close to the truth—not for the reason he thinks…for the reason I cannot give.

Get a grip and take the ring, Elena! Before you give your heart away!

I wet my lips. 'No. I'm just… I'm being silly.' I lift my hand away, rub at where the contact still echoes through my skin and smile wide. 'Ask away…'

'Laney…'

His expression shifts, his eyes raking over my face. Something's changed, and I don't know whether it's all in my head, whether I caused it with my response, or if it's all in him, but there's an intensity about him now. An intensity I fail to gauge.

'I am indebted to you. Please take this ring as a symbol of my unwavering affection and gratitude.'

'Wow…' I say, breathless with it all. 'You really know how to make a non-proposal into something very real.'

'You told me to ask.'

'I know, but…'

Words fail me. What am I trying to say? What am I trying to do other than not freak out entirely? I nod, the move rapid and uncomfortable, and I feel dizzy. So very faint and close to tears.

Take a breath.

And so I do. Breathe and remind myself why we're doing this—for his mum. And what he's offering me is his truth and a beautiful ring…perfectly acceptable.

He opens the box and I look down.

'Adie, no—I can't!' It blurts out of me, my eyes wide as they instantly mist over and launch back to his. 'It's too much!'

'It's a ruby, Laney. You didn't think I'd forget, did you?'

'But, Adie—!'

'You always said it had to be a ruby. When we were kids you said—'

'We were *kids*, Adie. That was *years* ago.'

'Changed your mind in the interim?'

'No, but this isn't for real…'

'Don't you like it?'

'Like it…?'

I shake my head, gaze down at it in wonder. A cushion-cut ruby flanked by leaf-shaped diamonds sparkles back at me. It's perfect—more perfect than I ever could have imagined—and he bought it. For me. *Especially* for me.

Not your typical diamond solitaire or anything close.

I press a hand to my throat, release my trapped breath with my words. 'I love it.'

'I'm glad. And it's yours to keep.'

My lashes flutter up and my eyes lock with his. 'Keep?'

'I mean it.'

He slips the ring from its bed of velvet and takes my hand in his. My head continues to revolve as if I'm on the waltzer, and I tell myself it's through lack of oxygen, though I know it's more than that. His touch is soft, yet firm, as he smooths the ring over my finger. An exact fit. As if it's meant to be…

'I really can't keep it, Adie.' I lift my hand, tilt the ring so it catches the light. 'It's too beautiful, too precious, too *expensive*.'

'You can and you will. It's made for you.'

I dare to meet his eyes again and the look is back—that strange dark intensity that I really can't read and have never witnessed in him before. Maybe it's the grief, the worry over his mother, the guilt over the lie we're about to tell…?

'Are you—?'

'Mr Monroe, sir?'

A steward enters the cabin and I press my lips together on the question I want to ask, on my desire to check that he's okay too. Her smile is bright and polite. She seems oblivious to our little exchange and the mood hanging in the air.

'Prepare for landing.'

He clears his throat. Nods. 'Thank you.' And the look is gone before he comes back to me. 'Let's get this show on the road, shall we?'

I smile and ignore the wriggle of doubt playing havoc in my stomach. 'It'll be just like all those times we played house as children.'

He chuckles. 'Trust me when I say that ring isn't edible, though.'

I waggle my fingers. 'More's the pity.'

And just like that we're friends of old again, with more memories than I can count and a future that blurs. A mishmash of fantasy and reality.

Never have I needed to keep my wits about me more if I am to help him and help myself while I'm at it.

I flex my fist, eye the ring, and my wary heart hardens.

You've got this.

Aiden

The ring is perfect.

Just as I knew it would be.

Yet it had taken me the entire flight, ten hours and counting, to present her with it.

And still I can't calm the nervous buzz in my veins. We're almost at our destination. The lodge where I've spent every Christmas for as long as I can remember. My mother and sister both await us there, neither have a clue of the news we're bringing, and I'm struggling to release the hold around my chest.

My fierce grip around the steering wheel, nothing to do with the snowy terrain I'm now navigating and everything to do with her...us...*this*...

If it was a genuine proposal, I'd understand.

But it isn't, and she'd already agreed *before* I presented her with the ring. So why the nerves? Why that inexplicable moment just before I opened the box…and after too…when things had changed? Things had felt…different?

The mood, the way she looked, how I saw her… She wasn't just Laney, my friend of old, staring back at me. She was a woman with trust and love in her eyes, and my body responded of its own volition and in kind. Disturbing the status quo.

I run a finger through the collar of my shirt, roll my shoulders back.

'Now who's nervous?' she asks.

'Not at all.'

'You can't lie to me. You know that, right?'

I meet her gaze and realise the truth of it. 'Look at that. Perfect marriage material.'

She gives a high-pitched laugh. 'I don't know… I don't think I fancy a husband who looks like he's been caught with his hand in the cookie jar.'

I choke on a laugh of my own. 'Is that a euphemism for something?'

'No!' She shoves my arm, her cheeks flaming as she snatches her hand back. 'It's an accurate depiction of how you look, and if you want to convince your mother that this is real—even more so your sister—you need to lose the nerves.'

She's right. Any sign that this isn't the real deal and my sister will be on it quicker than we can even announce it.

'Point taken.'

But knowing it and acting on it are very different things… especially when my gut is entertaining an all-out rave.

'I'd forgotten just how beautiful it is here,' she murmurs, her soft observation a welcome distraction as I take in the view with her.

The craggy mountains with their snowy peaks. The jutting forests of pine, larch and fir. The turquoise blue waters that change with the season.

It is indeed beautiful. Beautiful and familiar, soothing and stunning, and everything in between.

'It's been a while.'

'It's been too long,' she says, seemingly on autopilot, and then she turns to look at me, mitigates her remark with a smile. 'It's good to be back.'

I return her semi-smile just as the road opens up and the Monroe lodge comes into view. Rising high at the water's edge, its sympathetic design—warm wood, pitched roofs and vast, stretches of glass—manages to blend while taking advantage of the view.

'I'm glad to have you here.'

And I am. Beneath the nerves, her presence is as reassuring and soothing as the familiar grounds we're in. Giving me the courage I need as I bring the car to a gravel-crunching stop outside the lodge.

'You ready?' I say, turning to face her.

'As I'll ever be.'

But her smile falters.

I reach across to touch her thigh, feel the contact zip through my fingers, overly aware of her warmth beneath the denim.

'I won't make you go through with this,' I say, focusing on what she needs to hear rather than how I feel, how she's unintentionally making me feel. 'Not if you're unsure.'

She wets her lips. 'I want to do this, Adie. I promise.'

I hesitate, search her gaze a second more, and nod. 'Okay. Let's go.'

I swing the door open and step out, suck in the frigid air twice over as I wait for her to join me. The cold shouldn't surprise me, but after the heat of the car and her proximity it does.

I rub my hands together as I eye the freshly cleared and gritted path to the lodge. I wonder whether Avery did it or if they called in extra help. We've never had staff here. It was always part of the tradition for it to be just us. Just family. Even after Dad…

'You okay?'

I focus through the painful avalanche of memories threatening to descend, and see Laney looking up at me, steam lifting from her parted lips, her big brown eyes soft with concern.

I don't answer but I do take her hand, absorb her warmth as I lead us up the broad wooden steps and dig around in my pocket for the key.

'Aiden!'

Avery bursts out of the door, sending it swinging on its hinges as she yanks me into the tightest hug.

'And Elena! I had no idea you were coming too!' She thrusts me away to pounce on her. 'What a wonderful surprise!'

'It's lovely to see you, too!' Elena chokes out.

'Squeeze her any tighter and she'll expire on the spot, Avery,' I tease but my smile is unsteady in the face of their good cheer. A moment. I just need a moment. 'I'll get the bags.'

I turn back. I'm not sure why, but the sense of being suffocated from within is taking over and I'm not ready to head inside. Seeing Avery, being here, knowing Mum is waiting…

'Oh, no, you don't. Mum's desperate to see you!' Avery tugs me back towards the house, Elena too. 'We can fetch them later.'

I swallow down my refusal, knowing it's selfish and unfair. 'How is she?'

'She's good. Tired, but good.' I see the sadness lurking in my sister's gaze and beat back my own. 'She's reading by the fire. If you want to go on through, I'll get the kettle on. It really is so lovely to see you again, Elena. It's been a long time.'

'You too.' Elena smiles. 'I'm also very happy to hear the news of you and Gabe.'

My sister touches a hand to her auburn hair and blushes. 'Your reaction certainly beats my brother's.'

'Ah, but he's had the good sense to come around,' Elena says, flicking me an amused look.

'Eventually!' my sister drawls.

'Speaking of Gabe…' I'm already switching focus and wondering just how long we have before we face the ultimate test—convincing my best friend that I'm in love. 'Is he due to arrive soon?'

'He had some business to take care of, but he should be back in the next few days.'

'Great.'

So we have some time at least...though my relief is short lived as we enter the entrance hall and I halt in my tracks. There are boxes *everywhere*.

'What's going on here?'

My sister scans the very same mess, her hands twisting together.

'Avery...?' There's an undercurrent to my voice, a warning...

'It's the Christmas decs.'

'Why?'

'Why, what?'

'Why are they here, Avery?'

I'm stating the obvious as I stare at the dust-covered mountain as if I can will it to miraculously combust.

'Because it's the first of December tomorrow and I thought it might be nice... You know, to decorate like we used to.'

'We haven't decorated in years.'

I'm no more specific. I don't say, *Since Dad died*. The words a destructive trigger for my sister. And though she's so much better now, it's a force of habit. A protective tic.

'Does Mum know?'

'Kind of...'

'Avery...'

'What, Aiden? Dad's been gone for almost a decade. Don't you think it's time we enjoy the season again?'

The fact she can say the words without flinching speaks volumes, so why on earth am I the one freaking out?

And *enjoy* the season? Did she seriously say *enjoy* it?

The very idea is an impossibility. I see a lit Christmas tree and I see the light leave Dad's eyes. I see my mother hunched over in grief. I see her wasting away, locking us out. I see teenage Avery, lost and devastated in the corner, drunk and disorderly, not knowing what to do, where to run… And I see me, not sure who to help, how to help, what to fix first, all the while being surrounded by the 'joy' of the season.

I feel a hand slip inside mine and my instinct is to flinch away. I almost do. But then the fingers take hold, firm and re-assuring. I focus on the present to see Elena, her sympathetic gaze and smile urging me to let it go. The pain, the panic, the unease…

I swallow the tightness in my chest, look back to Avery as I release Elena's hand. 'We'll talk about it later.'

'There's nothing to talk about, Aiden. It's happening.' And with that she turns on her heel and strides off towards the kitchen. 'Now, go and see Mum before she wonders what's taking you so long.'

I watch her go, shake my head. 'You'd think she would be easier to manage now she's on the straight and narrow.'

'Your mistake is thinking you can manage anyone out of your employ, Aiden. Which is wrong on so many levels, but now isn't the time to argue it out.'

'Is that so?'

She nods. 'It absolutely is so. And, for the record, to my mind your sister knows exactly what she's about and you'd do well to listen to her.'

I choke on a laugh.

'You can laugh all you like, so long as you listen and take note. You used to love Christmas—you all did. And if I'm spending mine here, we're decorating. Now, if you don't mind, I'd like to see Margot.'

'Why? So all three of you can gang up on me?'

She doesn't answer, only smiles, the sparkle in her eyes doing all the talking for her.

'Roll on Gabe's return,' I murmur.

'Ha! Something tells me he'll be far too smitten to take anyone's side but Avery's.'

Is she right? Probably. But…

'There is a code between brothers, you know.'

She laughs. 'You going to get all street on me, Aiden?'

'Bro code is a thing—no matter what side of the tracks you're from!'

'I know, but if you think he'll take your side over Avery's, you're delusional.'

'You haven't even seen them together.'

'You've told me enough… I think you used the term *nauseating*?'

I did. And they are. And she's right.

Gabe isn't going to take my side…not for a second.

With one last look at the boxes I haven't seen in almost a decade, I let her drag me into the living room. Mum's favourite place in the lodge…once Dad's favourite too.

The floor-to-ceiling glass is a picture window to the lake and snow-capped mountains outdoors, while inside the fire crackling in the open grate warms the entire room. Including Mum, who is positioned before it, her head in a book, her grey-streaked auburn hair covered with a russet headscarf, spectacles on her nose, a flush of welcome colour in her thinning cheeks.

She's aged more in the last six months than she has in years. The headscarf has become a constant accessory, hiding the way the treatment has ravaged her hair—not that she's ashamed of it, more that she's aware of how others feel seeing it. A constant reminder of something she doesn't want to be constantly reminded of. And she always opts for colour—something bright and cheerful. Just like those glasses, with their brightly coloured rims—another recent necessity, now her eyes are tiring far too quickly, but something she uses to express the personality that's still in there. Fighting strong.

'Hey, Mum.'

'Aiden!' Her head snaps up and that's when I realise she was likely dozing. 'Darling!'

She slaps the book closed and starts to rise.

'Stay there, Mum.' I'm upon her in a second, but she's already on her feet.

'Don't be silly, darling! I may be old, but I'm not incapable!'

She hugs me as I kiss her cheek, but no sooner have I done so than she's reaching around me to take in Elena.

'Now, *this* is a surprise!'

'Hi, Margot.'

I step away, give the women space to greet one another, and get a grip on the fear that's risen within me. Fear that the clock is ticking far too fast and I'm not ready. Nowhere near.

They wrap one another up in a hug that goes on and on.

'It's so good to see you again, Elena. How long has it been? Much too long, I'd wager!'

'Definitely. You must forgive me.'

'All those fans of yours, keeping you busy?' my mother teases, her green eyes alive with obvious joy as she presses Elena away to meet her gaze.

'Something like that.'

She cups her cheeks. 'I don't blame them at all. It's been years since I've seen you perform. You remember your mother and I came to London, the Royal Opera House? It must be five years ago now.'

'I remember—how could I not…?'

Elena smiles, but I can see the concern in her eyes. She hasn't seen Mum since her own mother's party. The decline is obvious enough to me, and I've lived through it with her, but for Elena… I should've warned her.

'Oh, it really is lovely to see you…' My mother's voice quivers, and her fingers are trembling as she releases Elena to touch them to the corners of her eyes.

'Oh, don't cry, Margot. I'll wish I hadn't come.'

'I'm just being silly…ignore me.'

She waves away the tears, the concern, as she gingerly sits back down. Takes a breath that sees her visibly straightening and lifting her chin, composed and elegant through and through.

The old Margot Monroe is back. The one who hosted so many amazing functions by her husband's side when he was alive, and the one who bravely put on a front for the outside world when he passed. Not so much the mother who crumbled behind closed doors. The broken woman I remember as clear as day and live in fear of emulating.

'So!' She pats her knees. 'To what do I owe this unexpected pleasure? Is your mother coming too? I'd love to see her.'

'I'm sure she'd love to see you…'

Elena looks to me and there's a question there—*Are we going to tell her? Is this a good time? The right time?*

And my mother isn't blind. She'll see the ring soon enough, and ask her own questions.

'We have something to tell you, Mum.'

'You do?' Her eyes narrow as she grips the arms of the ancient wingback chair that was once my father's favourite. 'This sounds ominous…'

She looks genuinely worried, and I can't blame her—not with the way life has been of late.

'Not at all,' I rush out. 'It's good news, I assure you.'

I reach for Elena, wrap my arm around her waist and pull her close, feel her warmth and feed off her strength as we face Mum together.

'It's *very* good news, Margot,' Elena says emphatically, and I smile at her before looking back at Mum.

'We're getting married.'

The book she'd placed on the side table hits the deck as she thrusts off her glasses and shoves them away, her eyes darting between us.

'Did you just say…? No… Aiden? Elena? Are you—?' She shakes her head, her disbelief obvious. 'Okay, I'm clearly delusional, because I swear you just said you're getting married.'

'We are.'

'But *w-why*?'

I chuckle, low and tight. 'Why does anyone get married?'

She looks to Elena. 'Are you *serious*?'

'Yes.' Elena crouches down beside her, rests her hand on my mother's knee as she looks up into her eyes. 'Very much so.'

'Sorry, I'm just—' Mum looks at me as Elena does the same. 'I didn't even realise you were together.'

I should be saying something—anything. But faced with my mother and the doubt in her eyes—the concern, even—I know I should have anticipated it, planned for it, had the words to convince her at the ready.

Elena bites her lip, turns back to my mother. 'It's been something of a whirlwind,' she says, her voice strong and admirable and everything I need in that moment as she gains my mother's focus so I can breathe.

'A whirlwind?' My mother gives a choked laugh. 'My dear, it can hardly be a whirlwind when you've known each other for ever. What's changed?'

Elena gives a smile that snags at the breath I'm trying to take. 'Everything.'

'Are you saying you're in love?' Hope comes alive in her wise green eyes and Elena nods.

'I'm saying I love Aiden very much.'

My heart twists inside my chest...pulls a manoeuvre I don't understand.

I try to clear my throat. Like a fish caught on a hook, I'm reeled into the sentiment, the mood Elena has created. And seeing my mother's eyes well up anew, seeing the joy there, I fear I'm about to choke.

That's when my mother spies the ruby.

'And this is your engagement ring?' She takes hold of Elena's hand. 'Did Aiden choose this for you?'

'Yes.'

Elena meets my gaze, her brown eyes shining with so much emotion that I can't tear my own away.

'Adie always knew it had to be a ruby.'

'The moment I saw it,' I say, 'I knew it was the one.'

It's the truth. And it seems the truth is all I'm capable of giving in the face of our lie.

'I can't believe this is happening!' Mum reaches for my hand, takes Elena's in her other. 'Your mother and I…oh, how we joked about it. Teased you both mercilessly when you were younger. But now, after all this time, to hear you say those words, to have you realise just how perfect you are for one another…'

A solitary tear trickles down her cheek. Her breath rattles through her as she shakes her head.

'Does your mother know?' she asks Elena.

'Not yet.'

'But she must!' Mum launches to her feet once more. 'She must come—and we must celebrate!'

'Celebrate what?'

Avery appears with a tray of biscuits and tea, her green eyes, so like mine and Mum's, narrowed and instantly suspicious.

'Never mind tea, darling!' Mum clasps her hands together, presses them into her chest. 'We need champagne—and lots of it!'

'We need—? *Why?*'

My sister sets the tray down and I'm grateful, because I don't fancy it going the same way as Mum's forgotten book.

'I know it's great that Aiden's home, and has brought Elena too, but your treatment…'

'They're getting married!'

Avery chokes on thin air, her laughter as deranged as I'm starting to feel. 'This is a joke, right?'

'No. No joke.' I find my voice, look down at Elena, who meets my gaze in return. 'We're engaged.'

Avery steps forward, stops, cocks her head. 'Is this because Gabe and I are together and you need to get in there first, big brother? Is this some weird sibling rivalry thing?'

I tear my gaze from the steadying effect of Elena's and stare my sister down. 'How old do you think I am, Avery?'

She folds her arms, her lips pursed, her eyes dancing. 'I

really can't believe this. My brother is giving up his bachelor ways and tying the knot.'

'Believe it.'

'Will wonders never cease?' She laughs wholeheartedly this time, her grin lifting her entire demeanour. 'I'd given up all hope that you two would see sense and realise how made for each other you are.'

Her words are so like Mum's they steal my voice, my sanity. Where is this whole 'made for each other' thing coming from? I get that our mothers used to rib us about it. But I figured that was them being all sentimental about their own friendship, and how perfect it would be if their kids were to marry and make us one family. But my *sister*?

'Well, as they say, better late than never.'

And then she's running at us, scooping up Elena and pulling me in, embracing us both.

'Congratulations!'

'I'll get the champagne!' Mum starts to move, but Avery's already breaking away and racing ahead.

'No, you won't. You stay right there. I'll be back.'

I watch my sister go, feel Elena take an unsteady breath beside me.

'Do you think we should call my mother?' she asks.

'Let's video call!' my mother pipes up. 'I'll get the laptop.'

You okay? I mouth as Mum sets about finding a device.

Elena nods.

Sure?

She presses her palm to my chest and nods, and her small smile is everything I need to calm my pulse, which hasn't evened out since we set foot in the lodge.

One hurdle overcome—two if you count convincing Avery.

It's a good start.

Positive.

Easy.

Perhaps a little *too* easy…

CHAPTER FOUR

Elena

'WHEN I ENVISAGED the challenges ahead for us,' I say, staring at the bed as if it might suddenly come alive and walk off by itself. 'I hadn't anticipated this one.'

Aiden takes a ragged breath, blows it out slowly. 'You and me both.'

We're standing on the threshold of the bedroom—*our* bedroom—both trying to work out how to make this okay. And in my head all I can hear is my mother's excited squeal over the video connection. All I can see are my parents' happy faces on the small computer screen as they congratulate us over and over. And I try to quash the guilt but it's no use. It's still there. The squeal, the happy faces, all the guilt.

'I swear the bed has shrunk in the time I've been gone,' he murmurs, scratching the back of his head as I shake mine, shaking off the immobilising anxiety with it.

I stride in. One of us needs to get a grip before his sister or his mother or—worse—the pair of them find us on the threshold, looking suspect.

'Don't worry, I'll take the couch.'

I'm already raiding the room, looking for a blanket that I can throw over it. There's a tartan fleece I can take from the bed…

'No, you won't.'

He swings the door closed, rakes a hand through his hair

that's steadily gone more awry throughout the day and I try not to stare. There's a part of me that likes him like this, slightly unkempt, more rugged, sexy...

'I will!' I blurt out, the force courtesy of my wayward thoughts as I tug a matching throw from the chest at the end of the bed. 'I'll be fine.'

'If anyone's taking the couch it's me.'

'You think all six foot three of you is going to fit on that?' I point at the threadbare antique couch that is more chaise-longue than plush sofa and has certainly seen better days.

'I've endured worse.'

I pop a fist on one hip. 'I don't believe you.'

'Okay, so I haven't. But that's not to say I won't survive it.'

'You won't be able to walk, come morning, and I don't want your sister—or your mother, for that matter—questioning what we were up to all night to cause it.'

He chuckles, and I'm delighted to see a touch of colour in his cheeks.

'Considering we're still in that loved-up phase, I think a broken look will aid our cause, don't you?'

And now it's my cheeks that are burning as my head races with far too many explicit images to count. None of which are helping our cause. I push them out and murmur a swift, 'If you insist.'

'I do.'

So why are neither of us moving? Instead, we're facing one another off, both looking rather flushed, and my head is dipping back into its forbidden X-rated territory.

And hell, it's ever so trope-tastic!

To be here now. With him. And only one bed.

One bed, people!

The thought makes me giggle—or maybe it's the nerves. Either way, I collapse back on the aged sofa and let it all out. By the time I sober up he's staring at me, his dark brows drawn together, his midnight-blue sweater making his green eyes pop.

'What's so funny?'

I throw my hands out. 'This!'

'Which bit about this?'

I shake my head. 'Never mind. You wouldn't understand.'

'Try me.'

I look around the room. At the writer's desk with photos of him and his family when he was younger. The skiing trophies among the books on the bookcase. The paintings of the Rockies in various seasons on the wall. The tartan throws and matching cushions on the old sleigh bed. They're all things I recognise and feel comfortable in the presence of... Save for him, for us, and this new dynamic we've thrust upon ourselves.

'We either laugh or we cry, right?'

He drops to the bed, grips its edge as his head falls forward. 'I refuse to be beaten, but I'm not sure I see the funny side.'

'You're sitting on it.'

His head flicks up. 'The bed?'

I stand and close the distance between us, sit down beside him and ignore the way his nearness makes me feel. This moment is about him and making this okay. Making the man I've always known to be stoic and strong okay.

I saw the way he blanched in the face of all the boxes, the impending return of Christmas and the painful reminder of all he's lost. I witnessed him wrestling with the lie, struggling to get it out when faced with his mother's obvious fragility and rapidly declining health. I saw the concern he had for me in it too. And I want more than ever to make this Christmas special. For him, for his mum, for them all.

'Only one bed...' I cock a brow. 'It's a classic romance trope.'

'Are you likening this scenario to one of those books you like to read?'

'For my amusement, yes.' I grin. 'You've got to admit it is kind of funny.'

He gives a laugh of disbelief. 'I'm glad you think so.'

'You don't?'

'Hell, no.'

I try to keep my smile light, try to keep the tension out of my limbs…

'I never considered the sleeping arrangements…not once,' he says.

'Well, we can hardly feign a traditional stance now. Not when we've moved ourselves in.'

'I guess I was hoping Mum might insist…'

'Like she has with Gabe and Avery?'

'Fair point.'

'Or your previous girlfriends?' I hate to say it…to acknowledge it, even…but it's the truth.

Another unhinged laugh. 'There haven't exactly been many of those of late.'

'Lothario taking a holiday? I'd never have believed it.'

His mouth quirks to one side. 'No time…nor the inclination.'

The slight pleasure I take in his singledom is promptly forgotten as he sags forward, elbows on his knees, head in his hands, and he rubs at his face, exhaustion etched in every crease.

'Which makes me doubly safe in this huge bed,' I say, back to lightening the mood. 'And besides, it was fine when we were younger…'

'It was fine when we were just friends.'

'And we still are, right? We can do this. We can even build a wall, if it will make you feel better.'

Now he gives a real laugh. 'A wall?'

'A pillow wall. It's a classic defence move.'

'Are we talking about your books again?'

'Yup. A couple ought to do it, and no one will be any the wiser.'

I will be, though… And I'll be lucky to get any sleep with him lying alongside me. But I'll do it if it means we both avoid the couch and any risk of our duplicity getting out. Because seeing Margot for myself, seeing how her sickness has eaten away at her physically, seeing how our news gave her such a glorious boost...

'Besides, I could sleep for a week after months on tour and dealing with all the press nonsense over Enrique, when I wanted to be front-page news for my voice.'

'*Was* it all nonsense?'

'Huh?'

'Did he break your heart?'

His eyes rake over my face, concern bright in the tired green depths.

'Were you in love with him?'

My heart chokes up my throat, chokes off the lie I'm unable give.

He curses under his breath. 'I'm so sorry, Laney. I should have contacted you. I should have been there for you.'

I shake my head, look away before he sees the prick of tears that come from nowhere.

'The man was an idiot,' he says. 'To have you and play away like that...so publicly too.'

'It wasn't his fault. I was rarely around...always too busy with work...and he felt like he was in constant competition with it. It wasn't healthy for anyone.'

'That sounds like a familiar complaint.'

I give him a teasing smile. 'Another thing that makes us so perfect for one another.'

'Now you sound like my sister and our mothers. I swear I've heard that phrase a hundred times over today.'

'Best not question it when it works so well in our favour.'

'Indeed. But are you really going to sit there and make excuses for the way he treated you?'

The vehemence in his tone surprises me. Why does he care so much?

Because you're his best friend. He's going to care—just as you would care about him being treated in such a way. It doesn't mean he's jealous. It doesn't mean more.

'Laney?'

'I'm not saying it's right, what he did,' I hedge, coming to my senses. 'But he's a man who doesn't like to be alone—or single, for that matter. So I get why he did it.'

He shakes his head, gives a scoff. 'Lining up women to take your place before he moved on...'

'Before I *made* him move on, yes.' The strength returns to my voice, the memory of kicking Enrique out of my apartment in London fuelling my words. 'And I am *not* broken over him, Adie. I can promise you that.'

'Good.'

And he means it, the weight behind that simple word making me smile.

'Anyway, as I was saying, after the pressures of the last year I could sleep for a week. And if I snore, don't hold it against me.'

He chuckles, his tight expression finally easing. 'Still a snorer, hey?'

'You were the snorer, not me.'

'Now, that's a lie if ever I heard one.'

'We'll see...'

He gives me a lopsided grin, his eyes warm as they lock with mine. 'You're one of a kind, Laney.'

I struggle to swallow, to speak. There's too much going on behind his eyes. Too much care, too much passion. 'How so?'

'For doing this...for being there for me, for us.'

'I'll always be there for you, Adie. Always.'

I know it. My heart knows it. It doesn't matter that I know the risk I run by being here.

He lifts a hand to my hair, strokes a strand behind my ear, and for one breath-stealing second I think he's about to kiss me. I'm *sure* he's about to kiss me. The lines of our friendship blur, my lips part, my body leans that bit closer...

'Why don't you take the bathroom first?' He's on his feet

quicker than I can blink, striding away. 'I have a few calls I need to make.'

It takes me a second to recover, another to release the breath I've held.

I check my watch. Calls? 'But it's so late.'

'Money doesn't sleep, Laney.'

'You need to, though.'

He shrugs. 'When your company is global, you get used to functioning twenty-four-seven.'

'And when you run said company, don't you think you should trust that you have the right people in place to ensure you're not?'

I press my lips together. It's similar to what I said to him in Milan, only now it feels like I'm crossing a line. Doing exactly what his mother wants and trying to curb his workaholic nature. Doing exactly what I want too. To make him see his life differently, even if it does mean I'm playing my role far too well.

The nagging, interfering wife-to-be.

But he doesn't have to like what I say. It's not as if I'm trying get him to fall in love with me… I'm just opening his eyes to the fact that he could make room in his life for love. Even if that love isn't for me.

He shoots me a look that I can't read and I'm not sure I want to.

'It won't take long.'

Aiden

I wake with a start, the rap on my bedroom door coinciding with the hinges creaking open and a loud, 'Wakey-wakey! Rise and shine!'

'Mum!' I shoot up in bed with a curse, toss the soft wall of cushions aside and almost toss Elena out with them.

'Sorry, darling, I was struggling to knock and carry.'

'You shouldn't be carrying anything at all, Mum!' I say,

spying the heavily laden tray and flipping the quilt back as I meet her two steps in, take the tray of food from her hands.

'*Margot?*'

Elena slips her eye mask up, her voice and eyes groggy, her long dark hair a wild halo about her head. The sight does something to me...something I'm unwilling to acknowledge as my mother smacks my arm.

'I'm capable enough, thank you very much.'

'Seriously, Mum!' I scowl down at her. 'We're not children. We can fetch our own breakfast.'

'I know.' She beams. 'But since I want to send you on an early errand, I thought a wake-up call might be nice.'

'What kind of an early errand?'

If I didn't already have goosebumps over my bare back, I would now. There's something about the way she says it that tells me I won't like it. Not one bit.

'I want you to take the truck over to Old Jimmy's and fetch us a tree.'

'A—a tree?'

'The biggest and fullest you can find. Elena's parents will be here in a week, and I want the lodge to look as festive as we can make it. Starting with a tree.'

'Right.' I swallow, my eyes flitting to Elena. 'A tree.'

'Sounds wonderful to me.' She smiles, her warmth taking the edge off my sudden chill.

'So you'll go, darling?'

I nod. Only this time Dad won't be with me. It was our tradition—every year from when I was a very young boy. Mum would stay at home and bake. Dad and I would fetch the tree. Then Avery came along—something of a surprise, being over ten years my junior—and it would be Mum and Avery baking, Dad and I tree-fetching, and then we'd all come together and decorate it.

'Soon?' my mother presses, all hopeful.

'It's the crack of dawn, Mum.' My voice is hoarse, and I pray they'll both attribute it to sleep.

'The best trees don't hang about. Every Tom, Dick and Harry will be there for the best pickings.'

'I can always chop one down myself—we have plenty.'

'And how long has it been since you wielded an axe?'

About as long as it's been since my last visit to Old Jimmy's farm. Before Dad died but I'm not about to say as much.

'One from Jimmy will be just fine. Besides, the last time your father tried to chop down one of our trees he ended up taking out the truck.'

The memory is so vivid, so real—as is my sudden laughter. Surprising in its force and its presence, pushing out the sadness completely.

'Now, that *was* funny.'

'For you kids maybe…' She shakes her head, a subtle hint of tears in her eyes, but her smile is true and wide. 'Now, I'll leave you two lovebirds to your breakfast. Let me know when you set off.'

She turns and I watch her go, happy to have shared a memory with her and not to have felt the pain, the grief of losing him. I can't remember the last time she spoke of him with such lightness. The tears were there, but there was also joy in the memory, as bittersweet as it must have been…

'Aiden?'

'Elena.' I turn and smile, ready for a reset. 'Good morning.'

Her eyes rake over me, her cheeks flush deeper, and I'm suddenly acutely aware of how naked I am. Every millimetre of exposed skin prickles awake. Maybe I should have worn more than boxers to bed.

I hurry to the bed, slide the tray between us. 'Sorry about the wake-up call.'

'It's sweet.' She presses herself up as I get back under the quilt.

'That's one word for it… Coffee?'

'Please.'

She tugs off her eye mask and smooths out her hair as I pour her a mug with a splash of milk, no sugar.

'Just how I like it.'

'I know.'

I send her a smile which she returns, her eyes lighting up and drawing me in. She looks kind of cute in the morning, her face all warm and puffy, her lips too… Cute and fresh and…

And what am I even doing, debating how she looks?

I tug my gaze away, pound the pillows behind my back under the pretence of getting comfy, and take up a piece of toast.

'So…' she murmurs, lifting a piece for herself and settling back too. 'Tree-shopping?'

'Tree-shopping.' I sense her grin before I even turn. 'You're enjoying this, aren't you.'

'Aiden, I haven't settled in any place long enough, let alone big enough, to house a family-sized tree in too many years to count. I'm in my element.'

I wish I could say the same, but seeing her brown eyes sparkle back at me, and with the memory of my mother's grin too, I can't deny that there's a part of me that takes pleasure in theirs. And to feel that thrill over Christmas again…even if it is just a subtle flurry, deep in my gut… It beats the chill of the last decade by far.

'Besides you owe me—so indulge me.'

My mouth twitches. 'There's nothing I can say to that, is there?'

'Nope. You might even enjoy it.'

'I wouldn't go that far.'

'We'll see…'

Elena

Two hours later, I'm tugging on my woolly beanie and gloves, ready to step out of the truck, when Aiden turns to me and says, 'Leave the negotiating to me, okay?'

'Negotiating? We're buying a Christmas tree, not undertaking the deal of the century.'

'If I remember Old Jimmy right, he'll see us coming and wallop on an extra zero or two.'

I laugh. 'Quit being such a Scrooge. It's not like you can't afford it.'

'That's what he'll say.'

I just laugh harder, stepping out of the truck without paying attention to the ground, and suddenly I'm slipping, the door swinging out as my legs go under—*'Woah!'*

Two strong hands reach me before I hit the deck, gripping me beneath my arms as they set me back on my feet.

'Oh, my goodness!'

Hand to chest, I turn to thank my saviour and find myself eyes to a chiselled jawline, a full mouth stretched into a dizzyingly bright white grin, a straight nose and piercingly blue eyes.

'Thank you!'

'You're welcome.' The deep voice matches the big strong frame. 'Names Brett.'

'It's nice to meet you, Brett. I'm Elena.'

'A pretty name for a pretty lady.' He adjusts his beanie over his shoulder-length blond hair and my cheeks burn, my giggle ridiculous.

'Who happens to be my fiancée.'

Aiden comes up behind us, the possessive edge to his voice unmistakeable, as is the palm to my back. What on earth...? I turn to look at him, but he's far too busy staring Brett down.

'I wasn't expecting to see you here, Brett. Is your dad about?'

'Aiden.' Brett gives him a restrained nod. 'I've been chipping in here for a few years now, since we expanded with the year-round garden store. I've not seen you in a long time, though. Back for Christmas?'

'Something like that.'

I almost roll my eyes. Could he be any more enigmatic?

'So, what can we do you for?'

'We're looking for a tree.'

'How big are you thinking?'

'Big!' I pipe up, my obvious excitement earning a scowl from Aiden and a return of Brett's supremely friendly grin.

'It's for the living room back at the lodge,' Aiden explains, far less exuberantly.

'Ah, that's a cracking space. I remember when your parents used to host the annual Christmas party. It wasn't Christmas until that bash kicked off the season...it's been a while, though.' He frowns, scratches his forehead beneath his hat. 'Though I guess it's hard...without your dad an' all.'

I give a minute shake of my head, glance at Aiden, who manages a grunt in response.

'Right you are, then,' Brett blurts, pocketing his hands as he rocks on his feet. 'You want to follow me?'

Aiden doesn't move. 'Is your dad not about?'

'Not today. He's semi-retired now. Comes in occasionally, but mainly to get out of Mum's hair. You know how it is.'

I grit my teeth. For all Brett is good looking, he certainly lacks in the emotional intelligence department, and I find myself slipping my gloved hand into Aiden's, cosying up to him as we trudge through the gravel that's been neatly cleared of snow.

Like something out of a Hallmark Christmas movie, this place is a holiday lovers delight. With its snowbanks and thick woodland, a hut that looks like it came from Lapland, with signs for Santa and his elves on the door, and a pop-up Christmas store too. Kids running between the buildings, whooping with excitement as parents chase close behind.

I drink it all in as Brett leads us past the garden centre and takes us into a huge warehouse filled with trees. The scent of pine and festive magic carries on the air and my grin reaches ever wider.

'If there isn't one here you like, I'm sure we can cut you a fresh one.'

'One of these will be fine.'

Aiden's answer is almost a grumble. Does he fear the flexing of Brett's muscles in my company...the prowess he was forbidden from demonstrating by his mother?

Is he really, truly, jealous?

The idea has me stifling a giggle and he sends me a sharp frown.

'You're right,' I hurry to say. 'I'm sure one of these will be perfect.'

I practically skip towards the back of the building, taking him with me as I seek out the biggest, most impressive... Every shape and shade of needle is on display but it doesn't take me long to find the one. A perfect triangle, all bushy and tall.

I halt, causing one attached Aiden to jerk to a stop too. 'This is it!'

Brett grins. 'Good choice.'

'Let me guess,' Aiden says wryly. 'The most expensive?'

'Isn't your fiancée worth it?' Brett challenges him, and I purse my lips on another giggle.

The tension coming off Aiden is palpable, but it has nothing to do with his father and his sadness now...this is about me—*us*.

'Of course.'

Brett whistles to a hovering member of staff and gestures for him to wrap it up. 'It'll be ready shortly. Meanwhile, if you'd like to check out the pop-up store...?'

'Not particularly.'

'That would be wonderful, thank you!' I say, talking over Aiden, my full-wattage smile enough to make up for his scowl. 'Come now, darling. I'm sure your mother would love some new decorations to put out this year.'

New memories too—happier ones to replace the last decade of nothing.

I'm already tugging him away, and I swear I hear Brett chuckle.

Please don't hear him...please don't hear him.

But one peek up at Aiden's deepening scowl and I know he has.

It should dampen my mood—instead I'm elated. Whether Aiden recognises it or not, he was staking his claim, he *was* jealous, and my long-smitten heart is far too ecstatic. Even if it doesn't mean more, it does mean *something.*

Besides, I'm on a mission to help his family have the perfect Christmas, and that means getting Aiden into the spirit of the season too. No matter how impossible that might seem.

In fact, I'm not sure what's more of a challenge—convincing everyone we're in love, or convincing Aiden that Christmas is worth loving again.

But I'm all over both.

Aiden

What is wrong with me?

You're jealous!

I am.

I'm jealous of Brett over Elena.

And what kind of madness is that?

She flits between the tables and shelves within the pop-up store, her delighted gaze taking in every item. She's a flurry of colour—bright red woollen coat, cute cream scarf and beanie, dark hair flowing out beneath, rich brown eyes sparkling, cheeks flushed pink with excitement.

I can't blame Brett for taking a liking to her. Any red-blooded male would. She's beautiful.

And she's not mine.

Not truly.

So why the possessive spark? The heat that I couldn't quash in the face of Brett's obvious attraction...?

'I just *love* this place!'

I grunt my response, thankful that Elena's festive cheer is enough to offset my lack of it. She's as dialled up as the cheesy Christmas hits playing over the static-filled speaker system. They really need to fix that...

I'm about to say as much when she thrusts some knitted fluffy thing in my face.

'Look, Adie! How adorable is this? We have to get it. Everyone needs a gonk these days.'

'A *what*?'

She turns it in her hand, plays with what I now realise is a beard with a round pink nose sticking out. 'A gonk.'

'Looks like a gnome to me.'

'They're kind of a mix between a gnome and a hobgoblin.'

'Is that so?' My smile threatens to make an appearance.

'They're a Nordic thing. They bring good luck and fortune and protect the home...but only if you're nice enough.'

Why does that sound like a playful threat...?

'What happens if you're not nice?'

Her eyes spark up at me. 'If you're not nice you'll soon know about it. They cause all manner of mischief.'

'Something tells me I'm in for that, regardless.'

She blinks, wide eyed and innocent. 'Are you saying I'm bringing mischief your way?'

'I'm saying that right now, with no Gabe and three women under my roof, I'm facing all the mischief a man can manage.'

She laughs—and damn if I don't laugh too, far too entertained by her and the story she's relaying.

'But this one will look perfect by the fire, don't you think?'

I don't think, just nod, as she tugs at its cone-shaped hat which is four times as big as its body and bright red—her colour.

'I think we should get one for each bedroom,' she says.

'Really?'

'Really. Blue for you—still your favourite, right?'

I huff. She's right. Of course she is. 'I'm saying nothing…'

'Can you grab us a basket or two?'

There's no arguing with her when she's like this. Far better to just do it.

When I return, a basket on each arm, she's singing away to the music, her exquisite voice a vast improvement over the sound coming through the speakers, and I hang back and just listen. Listen and watch and feel how lucky I am to have her.

Especially when my plan is working. And all because of her.

Mum is happier and livelier than she's been in months.

I'm happier, which is an unexpected bonus.

And it's all thanks to her. Elena.

She turns to me and smiles, nips her lip. I don't know what that look's about, but I feel it teasing at a part of me I don't understand. The same part that came alive this morning when she was all mussed-up from sleep and in my bed.

It warms my soul, makes me smile from within.

'You have my permission to go wild.'

She grins. 'You know I was going to anyway, right?'

I chuckle, low and slow. 'I had a fair idea.'

And then she launches herself up to plant a kiss on my cheek and the contact whips through me, hot and fleeting.

'Far more fun to have you on board, though…'

She skips off and I'm rooted to the spot. Immobilised by her easy affection, drunk on her pleasure, and shaken by the desire to pull her back in for more…

I shake my head, smother a curse.

She's Laney. Your best friend Laney.

Not your partner. Not your fiancée.

Not yours to be jealous, possessive, or any other such crazy notion over!

I stride after her, paste on a smile and play the dutiful fiancé, carrying whatever her heart desires.

Play being the operative word.

CHAPTER FIVE

Elena

I BUSTLE INTO the hallway, my arms laden with bags, and sense Aiden freeze behind me. My happy smile freezes with it.

'What's wrong?'

'That smell…'

I breathe in the warm air of the lodge—woodsmoke and Christmas and… I sigh.

'Mulled wine?'

'No, it's—'

'Fabulous timing!' Margot appears, wearing an apron that would do Mother Christmas proud and with a tray of steaming baked goods outstretched before her. 'I've made your favourite, Aiden.'

'Butter tarts?'

His voice is small, quiet, and she smiles, her cheeks all flushed, wisps of auburn hair peeking out beneath her red headscarf. She looks bashful, suddenly uncertain.

'I figured I'd best get a practice batch in before our guests arrive.'

'But—but you haven't made those in years.'

He sets his overflowing bags down—with escaping strands of berries, decorative branches of evergreen, tufts of gonk beard—and frowns at the tray.

'Hence the need for a practice run. They should keep us

going while we decorate the place, don't you think?' He doesn't respond and she follows his gaze, taking in the glossy-topped pastries with a frown of her own. 'I only hope they're as good as they used to be.'

'I'm sure they'll be delicious, Margot.' I rush forward to get a closer look, stepping in for Aiden. 'They certainly smell like it!'

I know it's the scent that's getting to him. The scent and the memories it's evoked.

'May I?'

'Of course, dear. Careful, though, they're hot.'

Gingerly, I take one up, nibble its edge as Aiden slowly regains some of the colour he's lost. Sweet baked pastry and syrupy butter—a culinary delight for my neglected tastebuds that get denied far too often.

'Wow, these are good.' I cover my mouth as I say it, look back to his mother, who's now beaming with pride and relief.

'I'm so glad.'

'Gee, you two took your time.' Avery wanders in with a box of decorations and slows to a halt when she spies the bags. 'What's all this?'

I give a sheepish smile. 'I think I may have got carried away.'

'And Aiden let you?'

We're all looking at him now, and he comes alive, tugging his woollen beanie from his head and raking a hand through his hair, although his eyes avoid us.

'There was no stopping her.'

Avery and his mother laugh.

'Good woman,' his mother says.

'Shall we take it all through to the lounge and go grab the tree?' I say.

'Give it two mins and Terry will be over to help,' she replies.

'You called in the neighbours?'

Again, Aiden is surprised, and again, his mother simply smiles.

'Terry offered. Plus, he's doing the outside lights for us. We'll have that roofline twinkling come nightfall.'

Aiden shakes his head. 'In that case, I'll leave you to it and catch up on some work.'

'Oh, no, you won't—it's Sunday,' I say, hooking my arm through his and holding him back. 'A day of rest.'

'You call *this* rest?'

'Of a sort…' I paste on my most persuasive smile.

'And there's no way poor Terry can lug that tree in on his own—you did get a huge one, right?'

Avery is looking at me rather than her brother.

'Sure did.'

'Fabulous!'

Avery heads into the living room while I take another bite of the butter tart and moan with delight.

The sound earns me a peculiar look from Aiden. 'What?' I say, defensively. 'They're really good.'

He steps out of my hold, eyes the tray hesitantly before taking one. 'Is there mulled wine too?' he asks.

'You know me so well, darling. I'll just set these down and go fetch it.'

'No need, Margot. You go on in and we'll get it. Won't we, Aiden?'

Not that I'm giving him a choice as I take him with me, following the scent of festive spice to the kitchen, where a pan is gently heating on the stove.

'She must have been at it the entire time we've been gone.'

He looks both concerned and surprised as he places his untouched tart beside the mountain of ingredients on the flour-covered work surface.

'She seems okay, though. I'm sure Avery would have stepped in if she was worried about her overdoing it.'

His hand is back in his hair, the grooves either side of his mouth deepening.

'You can't expect her to just sit around, Adie,' I say softly.

'It's what she has been doing…'

'Well, maybe she's feeling a little better. You said her last treatment was a couple of weeks ago? Maybe the symptoms are easing.'

'Until the next lot.'

I step up to him, rest my hand on his heart. 'Hey, come on. This is what you wanted. To bring her some joy…a new purpose, even.'

'I didn't expect her to bring Christmas back in all its glory.'

I frown up into his haunted green eyes. 'Is that really such a bad thing?'

'No. Yes. Hell, I don't know.' He grips the back of his neck with both hands. 'But walking through that door…that scent… They were dad's favourite too, you know? Not just mine.'

'And she hasn't made them since he passed?'

He shakes his head.

'And it's made you remember. Just like everything Christmas-related makes you remember?'

His throat bobs, his eyes fall to my lips, and his 'yes' is a husky acceptance of his grief.

He curses, thrusts himself away. 'What is wrong with me?'

'Nothing's wrong with you, Adie. Christmas is hard for families, regardless of when they lose their loved ones, but you lost your dad at Christmas. The anniversary of his death is wrapped up in a time that was once full of love and joy…a time that was important to him. And it should be important to you still.'

'But look at me, Laney! I mean, *look* at me! Thirty-five years of age, successful, revered—feared in some circles, even. Yet stick a butter tart under my nose and I'm reduced to this!'

He's shaking, his words husky with confusion, desperation,

and I close the distance he's created between us, reach up to cup his face and hold him steady.

'You loved your father and you lost him, and you didn't get to grieve. You had to pick up all the pieces. You had to take care of your family. You had to run the company. Fill his shoes in every way. And now your mother is sick, and there's nothing you can do about it but try to bring her some happiness. Ease her discomfort. You're allowed to break, Aiden.'

He tries to shake his head, but I won't let him. 'You. Are. And you're allowed to enjoy Christmas again.'

'It doesn't feel right.'

'Why? Because you feel like you're moving on? Like you're somehow belittling the anniversary of his death by letting yourself enjoy the season again?'

He doesn't answer but I know I'm right.

'It doesn't need to be the same. In fact, I guarantee it won't be. But we can make new memories, new traditions, mix it up. But don't block those memories of happier times. Of family time, with your father front and centre. He loved Christmas—you all did. You owe it to his memory to find a way to enjoy it again. Just as he would want you to.'

I sweep his fringe out of his face, search his gaze as I plead with him to listen to what I'm saying. And then something in the air seems to shift…catches at my breath. We're close, *too* close like this, and I feel hot. Our outdoor layers and the heat of the kitchen, working with the heat building deep beneath my skin. It coils its way through my limbs, my abdomen, as he takes my wrists in his hands.

I think he's going to move me away, but he doesn't.

He holds on to me like an anchor. His lashes lower and his gaze rests on my mouth—dark, dizzyingly intense. I should say something, anything to break the moment, but I can't find my voice. I wet my lips, desperate to do something…anything. If he was anyone else…if *we* were anyone else…

'Laney…'

'Come on, you two!'

Avery comes stomping in and Aiden jolts away.

'Terry's going to be here any minute, and Mum's bemoaning the lack of beverage.'

My cheeks burn deeper and I clench my fists against the heat still penetrating my palms. Not that I have any reason to be embarrassed in front of his sister. We're supposed be intimate. Supposed to be in love.

But that's just it.

Supposed to be. Not *actually*.

And, as much as I hoped this time with Aiden would encourage me to distance my heart, every second in his company is doing the complete opposite.

How am I supposed to move on if my heart won't listen to my head?

And can I blame it, after the way he behaved at Jimmy's? That possessive streak, the jealousy? I told myself it didn't mean anything. But what if it does? What if there's a chance? Living with Adie, doing these family-orientated things with him, helping him move on from the past... What if it does bring us closer? What if it does open his heart up to the possibility of love?

Not with anyone, but with *me*?

Aiden

'You coming?' my sister asks, when I make no attempt to move.

She has the tray all ready. Five glasses of steaming mulled wine on board. One for the arriving Terry. All garnished with fresh orange slices, star anise and cinnamon sticks.

'I'll be right out,' I say, and Elena looks at me. 'You go. I won't be long.'

She hesitates and I force a smile, trying to reassure her that I'm fine.

Or at least I soon will be.

I wait for both women to leave and collapse back against the counter. I take a steadying breath, and another, my eyes on the ground. My head...my head is spinning.

I don't recognise who I am right now.

Unsure. Unsettled.

And disturbingly, yet undeniably, attracted to my best friend.

It's wrong. It's messed up. But it's true.

And if it hadn't been for my sister's timely interruption I would have kissed her!

I think back over the years, from our friendship when we were kids to what it is now... Granted, we haven't spent as much time around one another as adults. We went to separate universities, and then her career took off and Dad passed away—after which everything became about work and my responsibility as the man of the family. Avery's breakdown. Mum's...

Have I been so lost in all of that, that I've failed to see the woman she's become? I always knew she was special. Caring. Intelligent. Talented. Beautiful. But this attraction runs far deeper than that. Far deeper than anything I've felt before.

And it's inching out of my control.

I thrust a hand through my hair, grip the back of my head. Christmas...the anniversary of my father's death...my mother's illness...our play-acting... They're all working to mess with my head, my heart, and I need to get a grip on it all.

Before I do something really stupid.

It's one thing to have Elena agree to this. Another entirely if I abuse that friendship, that trust, that loyalty, by taking advantage. By succumbing to this, whatever 'this' is.

Because then where would we be?

I can't lose Elena too.

The very idea rattles through me with my breath. No, I need to get a spine, get my strength back, and act more like myself.

In control. Unemotional. Big brother and dependable son. Elena's best friend and the man of the Monroe family. I don't have time for anything else—any*one* else. Not at the level someone like Laney would demand—no, *deserve*.

My father proved you couldn't be everything to everyone and survive. I'm not fool enough to think I'm any different.

I will, however, put on a festive front and make this Christmas one to remember. Not just for my family, but Elena too—the one woman who truly understands me, better than I understand myself at times.

Common sense tells me that she's right. That celebrating Christmas again doesn't diminish my father's memory, lessen the sense of loss, betray him. But I can't help the way I feel.

It's impulsive and difficult to shift. Emotional conditioning. A learned reaction to something that long ago became associated with so much pain. I know what it is, and why I feel like I do, but that doesn't mean I can change it.

I can, however, take a leaf out of Happy Loved-up Laney's book and at least pretend…

As for the way I'm starting to feel around her, I'll find a way to manage it. I have to.

For our friendship's sake.

Elena

'Elena… Elena!'

Avery waves a hand in front of my face and I almost drop the glass bauble I was unwrapping when Aiden walked past the window, lugging a set of ladders.

'Sorry, did I miss something?'

Her auburn hair flounces about her shoulders as she shakes her head, her grin wide. 'Only the last five minutes… He'll be back in soon, you know.'

'You think it's safe? Climbing those ladders in this weather?'

'We're not due another flurry of snow until this evening.

He'll be fine. Besides, Terry is an old hand at this. He'll look after him.'

'But maybe I should—'

'Maybe you should help me get this tree finished, else we'll still be doing it when Gabe arrives. And frankly—' she sneaks a peek at her mother, who's now dozing before the fire, her book forgotten in her lap '—there are other things I'd rather be doing then.'

She gives a wink that tells me exactly what she means, and the assumption that I'll understand—empathise, even— is clear.

'I thought he was away for a few days?'

'He was…' she bends down to search the box for another ornament '…but when I told him your news—it's okay that I told him, right?'

'Of course,' I say, forcing a smile as she looks up at me.

'Cool.' She goes back to the box, picking out what she wants. 'So, yeah… When I told him he decided to cut his trip short.'

'Why?'

She straightens, eyeing the tree for the perfect spot. 'Beats me. Maybe he just wants in on the champagne.' She laughs. 'Or maybe the news has made him miss me all the more and he can't bear the separation any longer.'

I laugh with her, though I know there's more to it than that. He's coming to see it for himself—me and Aiden—but why the urgency? It's not like we're going anywhere…

'So when is he arriving?' I ask casually, hanging my own decoration on the tree.

'He should be here for dinner this evening.'

'So soon?'

'Yup. And I can't wait.'

'No…' I crouch over the box, focus on rummaging through it in the hope that she won't notice the worry on my face. 'I bet you can't.'

I can, though. Because one thing is for sure.

Gabe won't be as easily fooled.

Not for a second.

Aiden

Several hours later, I can no longer feel my fingers or my toes, but the women in my life are content. At last.

'It's perfect,' my mother sighs.

'It really is,' says Avery, one hand pressed to her chest, her head resting on Mum's shoulder.

'It really, really is,' says Elena, snuggling into me, her performance as my loved-up counterpart spot-on.

Terry and I share a satisfied smile.

Even I have to admit the lodge looks pretty special, with nature's snow all around and the sun dipping behind the mountains, allowing the Christmas lights to come into their own.

White lights chase across the roofline and sparkle in the bauble-adorned tree on the front lawn, where a family of illuminated reindeer graze at its base. A trail of candy canes light up the pathway to the lodge, and the swing at the far end of the porch is wrapped in a holly and berry garland with its own twinkling fairy lights.

The latter something that Avery and Elena whipped up together, the two thick as thieves and looking like elves themselves, with their bobble hats on and cheeks all aglow.

Mum dusted off her craft skills too, making a festive wreath. The circle of spruce, cones, cinnamon and berries, with its velvet red bow, takes pride of place on the front door, where Elena's new additions—two long-legged gonks nicknamed Little and Large—stand guard.

'Admit it—you love it!'

Elena nudges my chest with her head, her perfume rising with the chilling breeze, and I smile over the weird dance it sets off within my chest.

'*Love*'s a bit of a stretch.'

'Ha! I knew it,' Avery murmurs. 'Hard on the outside… mush on the inside.'

'You talking about me?' I say. 'Or the lodge?'

'I thought she was talking about me,' Terry jokes, his blue eyes twinkling and crinkling at the corners, his grey beard lifting with his grin.

'Oh, you as well, Terry,' Mum says, giving him an affectionate pat on the chest. 'You know, I think we've all earned another glass of mulled wine.'

'I'd love to, but I should be getting back.' He adjusts his hat and knocks the snow off his boots. 'Isla promised she'd call by with the kids this evening.'

'Oh, how lovely! I can't wait until my pair treat me to some grandchildren.' Mum hunches her shoulders, and her smile at us is as much playful as it is serious. 'I'm just saying…'

My jaw pulses, my smile frozen to my cheeks. 'Off you go, Avery,' I say.

'I'm not the one engaged to be married.'

'She has a point, darling.'

My smile is tight, and tighter still as I acknowledge the odds are stacked against Mum ever seeing grandchildren of any kind.

'Jostling for position, hey?' Terry's chuckle is a grateful distraction. 'I will admit they're exhausting, but so much fun. And it's always good to know you can hand them back.'

Terry and my mother laugh, but I fail to see anything funny in the matter. Especially as Elena has gone unusually quiet, her eyes distant. Is she worrying about Gabe's imminent arrival or is it the talk of children? Maybe her head has travelled down the same depressing road as mine.

'Laney and I will get the mulled wine on,' I say, keen to get some breathing space, 'if you want to see Terry off, Mum. Thanks for all your help, Terry. Not sure I could have done it without you.'

'Any time, son. It's great to see the lodge all lit up again.'

My smile falters. I don't think it's a dig, but it feels like one. Or maybe that's my own guilt working its way to the surface for not having done it sooner. For Mum's sake as much as for the rest of us.

'It *is* good to see it like this,' I admit. And better late than never...before it truly is too late.

I glance my mother's way, but she's busy walking Terry down the path.

'Lovely to see you, Terry!' Elena calls after them, smiling once more. 'I hope we see you again soon.'

'I'm sure you will. And if I could trouble you for an autograph while you're here, my daughter would be ever so grateful.'

'Of course.' Laney beams back at him, graceful as any star, but down-to-earth with it.

We head inside and I shake off my coat, hang it with my hat on the stand beside the door as Laney does the same.

'Do you ever get sick of being asked?'

'For an autograph?' She frowns at me. 'Not at all. It's an honour. I get tired of the press, and their intrusion, but in general the public are sweet and kind. It's not like I'm a pop sensation shrouded in gossip... Enrique was an exception,' she hurries to add. 'I couldn't have coped with what your sister had to go through.'

I huff. 'I don't think she did cope. Not really. And all that attention came from the people she chose to hang around with, rather than her place within our family.'

'Still, it can't have been easy... But she got through it and look at her now. You'd never know what she's been through.'

'She's come a long way.' My smile lifts to one side. 'And now she has Gabe...'

The faint sound of an engine has me looking out the window to where the lights of an approaching car weave along the drive.

'Speak of the devil…'

She follows my gaze, her brows drawing together as she worries at the corner of her mouth.

'What's wrong?' I ask.

Her eyes flit to mine.

'Elena…?'

'Don't you think it odd that he's brought his trip to an end early?'

I frown. 'You think it's because of us?'

'Don't you?'

'I'm sure he's just wrapped things up quicker than he anticipated.'

'You don't think it's because he wants to talk some sense into you? Into us? Or, worse, because he thinks this is all an act?'

'No. And even if he did, what could he hope to achieve by coming early?'

'I don't know, but…'

The car pulls to a stop outside and Avery's excited squeal reaches us through the door.

'I think you're worrying about nothing. Just listen to them. It's likely he's missed Avery more than he anticipated, that's all. The pair have been inseparable since the summer, and unbearable with it.'

'Perhaps…'

'No "perhaps" about it. Now, come on, there's a mulled wine with your name on.'

'I hope you're right,' she says, following me.

'I'm always right.'

'Ha—you wish!'

She digs me in the ribs, and instead of feeling the friendly poke, I'm struck by two things—one, that she's right. Gabe is never going to believe this is the real thing. And two, that actions speak louder than words.

I halt, causing her to stumble. 'Follow my lead, okay?'

I can hear footsteps approaching on the porch, sense their hands on the door…

'Follow your…?'

She frowns up at me, and before I can question my next move I step her back against the wall and claim her startled gasp with my kiss.

A kiss that isn't what I anticipate at all.

Her body softens against me, her lips too. Pliable, yielding, succumbing to my pressure.

What began as a sudden move, a quick demonstration of our togetherness, becomes a moment of exploration. I'm kissing her not because I want to prove something, but because I can't seem to stop. Something animalistic has taken over, a driving force I can't contain, and as her hands move to my hair my fingers fork through hers. It's silky, luxurious…just like the rest of her. She tastes sweet and forbidden and unlike anything I've ever known.

And now I'm not just kissing Elena.

I'm *kissing* Elena.

Deeply. Passionately. And with my all.

CHAPTER SIX

Elena

OH, DEAR LORD, this isn't happening...

Only it is, and I'm a hot mess. My knees have turned to jelly and my entire body is moulded to his, making the most of every glorious, hard millimetre pressed against me.

Save for his lips. His lips are soft and coaxing, and he tastes of the sweet pastries we've been consuming. He smells of the cold outdoors and fresh pine, and the feel of his stubble beneath my palms as I comb my fingers into his hair is as tantalising as I always imagined.

And he doesn't stop.

He delves deeper, his tongue teasing inside, a tender sweep, and I instinctively reach for more. My whimper is as desperate as I feel and I swear he groans in response.

It's a blur...an electrifying, dizzying blur. His hands turn rough and eager as they travel down my sides, his thumbs hooking into the belt loops of my jeans as he tugs me closer.

I don't care that this isn't real, that I'm following his lead in a performance of his choosing. I'm all over it...under it. I'm hot under my clothing, fizzing all over with it...

'Seriously, you can't get the staff these days!'

A frigid blast of air sweeps down the hallway along with Avery's mock outrage.

'They're supposed to be fetching the mulled wine!'

I break away, find sanity where there was none, press the back of my hand to my thrumming lips and give a hiccupped, 'Oops...'

'I'm sorry,' Aiden whispers down at me, green eyes ablaze.

Did I put that look there? Was he as lost in it as me? Less act. More intense, mutual desire.

I give the smallest shake of my head, indiscernible to prying eyes but enough to reassure him.

I know why he's done it. I do. And it's fine. Honestly.

Even if it has shaken me to my very core.

'It's all good,' I say—only my heart is racing, my body burns. I want him. With every fibre of my being, I want him.

He stares down into my eyes for a second longer and I wonder what he's thinking. I wonder if his pulse is as off the charts as mine, despite his innocent intentions. Surely something this potent can't exist in me alone?

'Gabe...'

He turns away, calm and collected, his grin so very easy, and I have my answer.

'It's good to see you.'

I ignore the way my heart sinks, the way my body wants to slide down the wall, and straighten my spine, smooth out my voice.

'It's been a long time, Gabe.'

The man himself smiles, but his eyes are as sharp as ever. 'You haven't aged a day, Elena.'

Aiden slips his arm around my waist, the move seemingly so natural and electrifying despite my sunken heart. 'What can I say?' I manage to smile. 'It's all in the genes.'

We close the distance between us and I give him a peck to the cheek.

'This news has been quite the surprise,' he says to me before turning to Aiden and the pair give each other a manly back-pounding. 'Of the good kind, of course.'

'You know how it is when love catches up with you.'

Aiden sends me a doting look that I can't bear to connect with, his words taking the remaining wind out of my sails.

'That I do.'

Gabe tucks Avery back into his side, kisses her hair, and she beams up at him. The intensity of the connection between them is thrumming through the air around us.

'Shall we go and get your bags unpacked?' she murmurs, that spark fully alight in her green eyes. 'We'll come and join you for wine shortly.'

She doesn't look at us as she says it, and Gabe's choice is made for him as she starts dragging him off towards the stairs.

'But you haven't got any bags…' Aiden waves at their empty hands.

'It's code, darling. Leave them be.' Playing my part to perfection, I tug him towards the kitchen and the wine we're supposed to be tending to. 'We have mulled wine to heat.'

'Shouldn't I at least help by bringing the AWOL baggage in?'

I laugh—or at least I try to. 'I don't think Gabe is going to miss it just yet, do you?'

He gives a tight chuckle. 'I guess not.'

The smack of envy is sudden and unexpected. I don't want to be envious of what Gabe has found in Avery. And I say it that way around because he's our age…he's spent as many years as us alone.

I don't want to be envious. But I am.

And maybe it's because the man I want is right next to me. The man I want has just kissed me into oblivion and has no idea of the effect it's had.

I release him as promptly as he slammed me against that wall, his urgent desire a pretence that felt far too real, and head into the kitchen, set about pouring the prepared wine into the pan that's waiting on the stove.

'I like how you're so at home here,' he says, resting against the counter and leaving me to it.

'I am at home. You know how often we were here as kids, right? I learnt to ski here, remember.'

I learnt to ski with him by my side, egging me on or teasing me to distraction, and I loved every second.

'Aye, those were the days. Life was so much simpler then.'

He'd had his father, for a start…and no responsibilities other than making him proud.

'We were children. It was as it should be.'

He gives a silent nod. Contemplative.

Then, 'It's nice.'

'What is?'

'Having you here…having you so at home here.'

I stir the pan more vigorously than it needs.

'It *is*,' he insists. For my benefit or his? I'm not sure. 'I don't have to worry about you…whether you're okay, whether you're enjoying yourself, whether you have enough company, enough stuff to do.'

I laugh, my body warming with his words. Is he trying to make me feel special…?

'I think we've known each other long enough to just *be*, Aiden.'

'To just be… I like that.'

I continue to stir the pan as the steam starts to lift, and he comes up behind me, breathes in the scent of it.

'It's been a long time since I could smell that spice and not feel an overwhelming sense of sadness.'

'I know.'

Not that I know what it's like to feel the kind of pain he does. I still have my parents. As deeply in love and as doting as ever. And a part of me feels guilty that he has suffered so much loss when I haven't.

'It's thanks to you, though, Laney. You and Avery.'

'I haven't done anything.'

He touches a hand to my hip, and the contact is so unexpected that I jump.

'Sorry, I didn't mean to startle you.'

'No, it's fine. I…'

I just ignite every time you touch me. I shouldn't, but I do…

'It's fine.'

I turn to him and my heart flutters over his proximity, the look in his eye.

'I'm sorry I kissed you like I did,' he says.

I shake my head, sweep my hair out of my face—anything to keep busy. 'You just wanted Gabe to witness how close we are.'

'I did.'

'But it's going to take more than a kiss to convince him… Your mother and sister are blinded by what they want to see. Gabe's spectacles aren't so rose-tinted.'

'No, I know. But thank you.'

'For what?'

He wets his lips and I don't want to notice… I don't want to feel…

'For going along with it—the kiss, the relationship…all of it.'

'You're my best friend. If you can't do these things for your soul mate, who can you do them for?'

He frowns and I curse my choice of words.

'Your soul mate?'

Stand by it, Elena. For goodness' sake.

'Yes.'

'I've never heard that phrase used in a platonic sense before.'

'Google it!'

He laughs, low and slow. 'I will.'

'And anyway, there'll come a day when I'll call it in.'

He cocks one sexy brow. 'Call it in?'

'The favour, Adie.'

'And I'll do it—whatever it is,' he says, his eyes as earnest as his voice. 'I'll do it.'

My breath catches and my heart begs me to tell him the truth. To ask him for the one thing I know he cannot give.

To make this real.

'I think it's ready…'

'Huh?'

He nods over my shoulder to the wine and I nearly knock the pan off the hob in my eagerness to turn away.

'Well spotted. You want to fetch the glasses?'

I get myself back under control… I press my lips together and count to three, grateful that he doesn't seem to notice. Not the rising colour in my cheeks, nor the confession I swear is blazing in my gaze.

Aiden

I take the wine into the living room, grateful for a job to distract me from everyone else.

From Mum, who still hasn't made it back inside after seeing Terry off, though I know she's okay as she's messaged to tell me so. Apparently they're just catching up…after already being in one another's company for several hours today. I don't dare ask.

From my sister and Gabe, who have yet to make it back downstairs. Again, I don't dare ask.

And from Elena, who has excused herself to go to the bathroom, when I believe there are numerous reasons she doesn't want to be around me right now, my invasive kiss being right up there as number one. And yet again, I don't dare ask.

What had I been thinking?

You weren't thinking, and that's the problem.

No, my brain had exited the second my lips had touched hers, a primal instinct taking over that I was powerless to stop. I wasn't kissing her to convince my best friend we're together. I was kissing her because I wanted her. And that whimper that she gave—*man!* It pulses through me even now. Making me want, making me crave…convincing me that she wanted it too.

And she can't possibly.

You don't go from a lifelong friendship to this.

It's just some kind of madness.

Utter madness, and the verdict revolves around my brain, failing to land.

Because it didn't *feel* like madness. It felt all too real, and normal, and sane, and right. The passion, the love…

But it can't be.

I must be more unhinged than I thought. More desperate to see Mum okay. More eager to ensure the bubble of our home life is as perfect as it can be.

Because I can't love Laney. Not in that way. And even if I *was* falling for her I'm not the right man for her. She deserves so much more than I could ever give. Than I could ever *want* to give. Because that kind of love…when you lose it, it breaks you. You end up like my mother. Curled in a corner, sobbing away your heart, your life, broken for ever…

And I can't go there.

I have responsibilities—people to take care of, a company to lead. I have to function. I have to perform…keep a clear head, stay in control.

'What's wrong?'

I turn so sharply my head spins. Elena's in the doorway, her narrowed gaze on my hand, which is gripped around a glass, my knuckles flashing white.

I force a smile. 'Nothing.'

She walks in slowly, tentatively. Her fluffy hair courtesy of her recently stripped off bobble hat, or my hands—I'm not sure which. Her cosy sweater and jeans are suddenly as sexy as the skimpiest of outfits, and I swallow, try to wrestle with this newfound awareness as she steps ever closer.

'You could have fooled me.'

I lower my gaze to the glass, ease my grip. 'You know Mum's still out?'

'I guessed she might be. Her and Terry get on well.'

Her words jar me a little. It's not like I don't already suspect the potential for something to happen there…but for Laney to think it too?

'He's a good guy,' I say simply.

'I gather he lost his wife a few years back?'

She pours herself a glass of wine as she asks, her focus on the action rather than me, and I wonder if it's her way of giving me space. Typical Laney, forever the empath.

'Yeah.' I clear my throat, stare out at the frozen lake. 'A car accident. Far too much pain in so small a neighbourhood.'

'But something they can understand in one another?'

'I guess…' I shake my head as I think about where she's heading with this, where my thoughts have been heading, too. 'Though with her illness, Laney, it's just… I don't know.'

'You can't expect her to put her life on hold completely.'

I choke on a laugh. 'I think a new relationship should be the last thing on her mind.'

She nods, but says nothing, and for that I'm grateful. I can barely get a handle on my feelings for her, let alone on the thought of my mother starting a new relationship when her own life hangs so tentatively in the balance.

'Okay, so where's this mulled wine your sister is raving about?'

Our gazes snap to the doorway, to a smug-looking Gabe. In jeans and a sweater he looks far more relaxed, and that works for me.

'Ave's on her way—she's just popped out to check on your mother.'

'Great.'

I'm glad one of us is capable of doing so. I pour him a glass as he joins us.

'Congratulations on your tour, Elena,' he says. 'The reviews are exceptional, as always.'

'Thank you.'

I hand him his glass and lift my own. 'Here's to a successful tour and to a Christmas all together. I assume you're staying, Gabe?'

'If I'm welcome?'

'You really need to ask?'

'I don't know… I wasn't expecting you and your wife-to-be and all of this…' He gestures around us at the decorations. 'Have to admit, though, it makes a nice change to see you Monroes back in the Christmas spirit.'

Elena doesn't take her eyes off me. Is she wondering if I'm okay? I don't want her worrying about me—not when she's done so much for me, for *us*, already.

'I will admit it's a nice surprise for me too.'

Gabe grins. 'In that case—to nice surprises.'

We raise our glasses, clink them together and take a sip.

'Now, that *is* good.'

'Mum's recipe. I'm sure Avery will share if you ask her for it.'

'I will.'

And then he's back to studying us intently. So many questions blazing in his blue eyes. Is he hoping we'll just come out with it if he stays quiet long enough?

'I'm surprised you haven't any events to perform at between now and Christmas, Elena,' he says eventually, breaking the loaded silence. 'Your schedule seems to have been quite full-on this past year?'

I read between the lines.

Too full-on for you two to have spent any real time together.

'I've had a break in my schedule planned for a while now,' she says smoothly.

'Since your recent break-up with that musician…what was his name?'

'Enrique,' I supply, and want to cringe at the tightness in my voice. No time in the schedule, a break-up that's two months fresh…

'That's the one. Enrique.'

'No. My break was on the cards long before we split.'

The message from Elena is clear. No man runs or ruins her schedule. Not for a moment. And I'm so grateful that she has control of this, because I don't.

'It's been a tiring few years, and I'm overdue an extended holiday.'

'Well, I can't blame you for spending it here. It's the perfect place for Christmas.'

'As perfect as the man I choose to spend it with.'

She hooks her arm in mine, smiles at me adoringly, and I feel my own lips curve of their own volition.

'What can I say?' I murmur. 'The timing's perfect all round.'

'Perfectly convenient.'

Gabe sips at his wine, his other hand buried in the pocket of his jeans and my fraying nerves reach breaking point.

We can't carry on like this. I need to have it out with him, but now isn't the time. Not in front of Elena, and not when my hackles are already up, my feelings for her so deeply confused.

'Tell you what—why don't I give Avery a hand while you men catch up, man to man?' says Elena.

'Hang on, Laney.' I step forward, but she's already placing her drink down.

'It's fine.' She walks off, waving a hand. 'You guys have much to discuss.'

'She's not wrong,' Gabe says into his glass.

'As annoying as it is for me to admit it, in my experience women rarely are.'

He chuckles. 'Now, that's a point we can debate until the cows come home.'

'I'm up for that…' I turn to face him. 'If it'll save me from the conversation you have brewing.'

'No such joy, my friend. No such joy.'

I knock back my wine and almost choke on a stray clove. 'I didn't think so.'

Elena

I gulp down the cold air, wishing it could chill the heat inside me.

Did I call it right? Leaving them to address the elephant in the room?

I don't know. But I couldn't stay there any longer.

Gabe knows. I'm sure of it. Which means he also knows that kiss was all an act. On Aiden's part, at least. But mine? Does he know how I feel? Is he in there right now, telling Aiden my deepest, darkest secret?

God, no. I hope not. Just because he's finally in touch with his own emotions, owning his love for Avery, it doesn't mean he's capable of seeing the same in me. Does it?

I blame a drunken conversation we had many years ago. One that I'd hoped he would've forgotten in the haze of the night. I'd been young, foolish, my hope to be a world-renowned opera singer still a pipe dream, and I'd been drowning my sorrows after my latest stage rejection in cheap cider and karaoke. My unrequited love for Aiden had spilled from my lips as steady and strained as the lyrics to 'All by Myself' and this feels just as humiliating.

At least back then it could be dismissed as a foolish crush. But now...?

What am I doing?

Why am I opening myself up to potential heartache and pain?

I tug my beanie further down my head, bury myself deeper into my coat, wishing I could hide my shame just as easily. I look this way and that, seeking out Avery and Margot in the snow. It really is dark, even with the Christmas lights all aglow, and they seem to hinder rather than help as I look for their shapes in the distant darkness.

And that's when I see them. Or their silhouette. One leaning into the other, their breath lifting like plumes of smoke into the dark sky above.

I hurry forward. 'Avery, Margot…are you okay?'

'We're fine, darling.'

'Can you give us a hand, Elena?' Avery says over her mother's flustered response, her own voice soft with worry.

'Of course.'

I wrap my arm around Margot's slight waist from the other side and together we walk.

'I told you that you were overdoing it,' Avery murmurs.

'And I told you I was fine—because I was. It just came on all of a sudden.'

I look at Avery's face over her mother's head, see the concern in her eyes beneath the rim of her bobble hat.

'The doctor said you needed to take it easy.'

'He also said I should do whatever I feel up to.'

'Within reason, Mum.'

'Look, darling, I may not have all that long left in this world, and I plan on making the most of it while I still can.'

She gasps on the last word and we all stop, give her a moment to recover as Avery takes an unsteady breath herself.

'I wish you wouldn't say that.'

Margot touches a hand to her daughter's. 'It's the truth, darling. Not saying it doesn't make it go away.'

'I know, but…'

Margot pats her hand. 'I know, love. I know. But…' She smiles wide, her eyes glistening in the moonlight. 'Just look at us now. If you'd asked me a year ago if I thought I'd ever see the day that both my children would be settled and happy… Seems miracles do happen—and I could be yet another one of those.'

Avery nods, her eyes still damp.

'Now, come on,' Margot says with a sudden burst of gusto. 'Let's get inside before the men send out a search party.'

And so we do. We move in step together, and I realise that this family needs me more than ever. That I can't back out. I can't take this away from them. It's a moment in my life, but it's everything to Margot, and not even Gabe's presence can take that away.

I won't let it.

Aiden

'I don't know why you can't just accept it, Gabe.'

Accept it and stop digging, so we can all move forward with Operation Keep Mum Happy for as long as necessary.

Maybe I should just be straight with him. Explain the whys and wherefores and be done with it.

I'm not sure why I don't. I just know I'm not ready to shatter the illusion.

Mum and Avery are readily treating us as a couple, and the ease with which we've slid into that role…

Having Gabe in the know would ruin that.

'If you were anyone else, I would,' he says.

'What's that supposed to mean?'

'You've never expressed any interest in settling down and getting married before. Hell, you've never even had a relationship that lasted long enough to warrant a ring.'

My brows lift. 'And coming from anyone else maybe I could stomach that observation, but from you…'

He raises a hand. 'Yeah, yeah… I know. But I'm not the one proposing marriage.'

'Yet.'

He nods, his smile small. 'Yet.'

'Something tells me you will be…'

'And you'll be the first to know. But right now we're talking about you, not me.'

'And when the roles were reversed, and you told me about your love for my sister, I believed you. So can't you credit me with the same?'

'Two things, Aiden.' He turns away from the window to

face me head-on. 'One, I told you I loved her. You've said no such thing about Elena. And two, I had a whole summer with Ave to come to my senses and realise that I was in love with her. You've had—what? All of five minutes.'

'I've known Laney all my life.'

'That's just it! Where was this proposal when you actually spent time together? You haven't seen her in months...a year, even. And now you're getting married?'

'I met up with her in Milan.'

'So I hear. And what happened? Did you have an overnight epiphany? Because we all know she's been on tour, travelling the world for months, and you've been nowhere in sight. I know we've lived through a pandemic, and video calls are all the rage, but seriously, Aiden. Are you telling me that's what did it for you and Elena? A long-distance relationship over the internet? Because I don't believe you. Not for a second.'

'Why not?' I bite back. 'She's a great woman, Gabe. Talented. Kind. Loving... Sexy as hell.'

It's the truth, and I'm not holding back as I deliver it. Even if the words brand me at the same time, heartfelt and burrowing that bit deeper.

He gives a soft huff. 'You'll hear no argument from me.'

I give him a sharp look.

'Save for the sexy remark, of course, I only have eyes for your sister.'

'I don't think I need to hear either remark.'

I scratch the back of my neck, which feels weirdly sensitive at the unexpected turn our conversation has taken. And it has nothing to do with my sister and his feelings for her and everything to do with the way I feel about Elena.

'But you get my point. It's not that I don't think she's good for you, or that you don't make a great couple. It's that I don't believe this sudden turnaround. I wish I could, but...'

'Can't you just go with it?' I resort to pleading with him now.

'Give me a good reason.'

'There—*okay*?'

I gesture out of the window to where Elena and Avery are returning with Mum and fight the urge to join them. I know Mum won't appreciate the extra fuss, but I can see the effort the walk is costing her.

'We're doing this for Mum—satisfied?'

His brow furrows in confusion. 'I get that she wants her children to be happy—any decent parent would. But marriage?'

I know he adds the word 'decent' because his own father couldn't care less, and there's a small part of me that feels guilt over resenting my mother's overzealous interfering when it stems from her love for us. When others, like Gabe, are far less fortunate.

'Happiness and love are one and the same for her. And she's been a different woman since we gave her the news. All of this, Gabe—the mulled wine, the baking, the Christmas decorations everywhere… Mum's driving all this. Her and Avery. Do you know how long it's been since we've been able to do this and actually enjoy it?'

'So is that what this is? Some weird, twisted "last Christmas" hurrah?'

I wince, give up on the drink I was about to swig as my gut rolls.

'I'm sorry, mate. I don't want to be blunt, but I'm worried you're doing this for all the wrong reasons.'

'They seem pretty sound to me.'

'But—'

'Gabe!' I interject, swallowing down the fear as I think about the latest report from Mum's oncologist. 'Please. We don't know how long she has left. Not even the specialists know. This treatment is too new, too unknown.'

'But she's in the best hands—thanks to you.'

I nod quietly.

'And your proposal to Elena…?'

'What about it?' I don't snap. I just sound weary now.

'Three months ago you took some convincing that Ave and I were in love. Actually, let me rephrase that, you took some convincing that *I* was in love. Coming from you, I could understand it. We've never set out to find love, marriage, a family of our own. I've known Avery all my life, but it took a summer with her to realise I was wrong about a lot of things. Love being one.'

'I know you love her. We don't have to go over that again.'

'I'm not finished.'

I raise my glass to him in apology. 'Talk away.'

'I'm serious, Aiden. Ave made me realise I've been living a half-life without her in it. I want to believe it's the same for you. That somehow Elena has opened your eyes to it. But…'

He scans my face, shakes his head, his disappointment ripe and my spine stiffens, my grip around the glass with it.

'I don't need your judgement, Curran.'

'You need something—and I don't think a fake wife is the answer.'

'Fiancée.'

'Fiancée…wife.' He shrugs, takes a sip of his wine. 'Same difference.'

'They're very different things.'

'Legally, yes. But as far as your feelings are concerned—'

'There are no feelings,' I blurt.

His brows inch up. 'You sure about that?'

'I know how I feel.'

Liar.

'And what about Elena? Are you sure you know how she feels?'

'Of course I do. She's doing this for Mum.'

'She's doing it for you.'

'She's doing it for both of us. And in a few months—a year…whatever—we will go back to being just friends.' I'm tired with the façade now, tired of arguing it out even as I admit it all. 'No divorce needed. Just an amicable breaking off of the engagement, with no one any the wiser.'

He nods, his mouth twitching at the corners. Is he *amused*?

'Right.'

'Why are you saying it like that?'

'If you can't see what's right under your nose, there's no point in me spelling it out.'

'What's that supposed to mean?'

'Nothing, Aiden.' But even his eyes are dancing now. 'Nothing at all.'

Oh, hell...

'You won't say anything to Avery, will you?'

'Ave and I don't have secrets.'

'You did before.'

'That was before. And I didn't like it then. I like it even less now.'

'You don't have to like it. You just have to keep quiet.'

'No can do, Monroe. When you decide to share your life with another—I mean, *genuinely* share it—you'll understand why you can't ask that of me.'

I curse. 'What happened to good old-fashioned loyalty?'

'You're my best friend, my brother in all the ways that matter, and you have my loyalty. But so does she. She's my partner and the love of my life, Aiden, and there's nothing I'll keep from her. Nothing at all.'

'Then why hasn't she got a ring on her finger?'

'There are many reasons. For starters, you're the man of the Monroe family, and you haven't been around to ask.'

I choke on a laugh. 'Like you need my permission.'

'Be that as it may, it feels right to ask you first.'

'My sister wouldn't agree.'

'I think she would appreciate the sentiment and the tradition.'

'And what if I said no?'

'Well, then I'd marry her anyway.'

Now we both laugh.

'At least you're honest about it. And the other reasons?'

'She's got a lot on her plate. Finishing her course in London while still being there for your mum. And, let's be frank, I'm no jewellery aficionado. Buying the right engagement ring for a jewellery designer is a pressure like none other.'

'She'll love anything you buy her because you chose it.'

'Perhaps. But what it really comes down to is time.'

'The one thing we don't have…'

'And the one thing I think you're banking on.'

'What's that supposed to mean?'

'You think this engagement is okay because your mum won't be here to see the relationship fall apart.'

I ignore the way his words prick at the very heart of me. 'I told you—there will be no falling apart. We'll just go back to how things were.'

'Are you sure about that?'

'Of course I'm sure.'

'And what about the press? Have you thought about—?'

The front door opens and we both turn.

'Aiden… Gabe?' my sister calls out. 'Will one of you fetch Mum's blanket from upstairs?'

'I can get my own blanket,' the woman herself insists, though her voice is worryingly weak.

'Mum, will you just let us look after you, please?' Avery mutters, guiding her to the chair by the fire.

Elena looks to me. Hesitant. Concerned. About my mother? About my conversion with Gabe? Both?

'I'll go,' I say, needing a moment to myself.

We've covered the press angle, haven't we? We're going to manage it. Elena isn't naïve—she knows the risks. We both do. And seeing Mum like this, weak but still fighting, only emphasises *why* we're doing this.

I can only hope it persuades Gabe, too.

CHAPTER SEVEN

Elena

'YOU LADIES HAVING FUN?'

Aiden comes up behind me in the kitchen, his hands gentle on my hips.

You'd think after a week of living as husband and wife-to-be I'd be used to his touch by now. Immune to it, even.

I'm not.

The slightest sweep of his fingers, the merest glance in my direction and my pulse races, my heart warms and I give myself away. I'm sure I do. Which is fine. Because to his family we're in love. And to him and Gabe I am simply performing.

Performing all too well.

My body instinctively leans into him at every opportunity, turning a single touch into a prolonged connection of outward affection, and I lose myself in every devoted look he sends my way.

It doesn't matter that it isn't real…it's all too comfortable, too easy.

Because it's not an act. Not for you.

'Always,' I say, looking up into his eyes, returning the devotion with every fibre of my being. 'Your mum is an excellent teacher.'

'Elena is an excellent pupil,' Margot says, smiling at us as I lean back into him.

'You can tell that to her parents, who are just pulling up.'

My stomach turns over. 'They're here? *Already?*' I turn so quickly he stumbles back. 'Sorry, I… But they're never early. My mother's never early for anything.'

I wipe my flour-covered hands on my apron, my panicked gaze on the clock.

Margot laughs. 'Some things in life are worth being early for, and your daughter's engagement is most certainly one.' She pulls her apron off, smoothing her festive headscarf back into position. 'Come on, let's go and greet them. This batch can wait.'

'And this batch is ready, right?' Aiden reaches for a steaming butter tart off the cooling rack.

'Oh, no you don't!' His mum smacks his hand away. 'You'll spoil your dinner.'

'That's not what you said the other day.'

'Today is different. Today your lovely fiancée has cooked, and you need to save yourself.'

'When you put it like that,' I say, shoving the rack closer, nerves rife in my belly, 'you should definitely fill up on as many tarts as you like.'

He gives me a look of mock horror. 'Are you saying you might poison us?'

'Poison you? No. But I don't think you'll be going back for seconds.'

I don't feel like I'll be going in for firsts either. What if my parents see us in the flesh and work it all out? Worse, what if they see my feelings for what they are and Aiden's lack thereof…?

'Nonsense, darling,' his mother says. 'The casserole smells delicious.'

'It's my father's favourite,' I say, distracted.

'Are you trying to get him on side?' Now Aiden looks worried. 'I thought he was merry enough when we told them the news. Did I miss something?'

'You don't know my father... Actually, scratch that. You do.'

'And she is his only daughter—only child, even,' Margot reminds him, successfully stripping the last of the colour from his cheeks.

'Thanks, Mum.' He pops the tart he's successfully swiped back on the rack. 'I think I've lost my appetite.'

Margot laughs and shoos us out of the kitchen. 'When they see what I see you'll have nothing to worry about...nothing at all.'

Aiden and I share a look and he takes my hand, gives it a squeeze as he leads me into the hallway, where Avery and Gabe are coming down the stairs.

'I thought I heard a car pull up,' his sister says.

'You did,' Aiden replies. 'Elena's parents are early.'

She grins. 'Bubbling over with excitement for the upcoming nuptials, I'm guessing.'

The way she says it makes it sound so very imminent, and my smile takes on a frozen edge as Aiden's palm pulses around mine.

'I can't wait to talk weddings with your mother, Elena,' Margot declares, excitement a fizzing aura all around her. 'We've long dreamed of this moment.'

'So you keep saying, Mum,' Aiden says under this breath. 'So you keep saying...'

'Tired of wedding talk already, big brother?' Avery teases, and he gives her a look which she promptly ignores, skipping ahead and tugging open the door. 'Aunt Angie! Uncle Peter!'

She disappears outside with a bemused Gabe and a grinning Margot close behind.

'Do you think she's doing it on purpose?' Aiden asks me.

'What? Your sister?'

'Yes.'

I laugh softly. 'You are her annoying big brother, after all. Winding you up is part of the deal.'

'For my sins.'

I shake my head. 'Come on—let's get this over with.'

I tug him forward, my smile firmly in place, and we step outside and are promptly engulfed in chaos. It's the only way to describe the greeting that is a frenzied blur of hugs and kisses, tears and squeals, handshakes and back-poundings, and what feels like a thousand congratulations.

There's, 'Oh, my goodness, is this really happening?'

With a bit of, 'Oh, I love the deer!' and 'Look at that tree!' mixed in.

And, 'Oh, the ring…it's exquisite, just exquisite!' being played on repeat.

There's so much cheer and excitement that I feel stupid for thinking they'd doubt us.

We enter the house in a flurry of activity. Bags are disposed of, drinks are poured—champagne all round—and we're finally settled in the living room.

Aiden and I stand beside the Christmas Tree, his arm locked around me. Dad is standing before the fire—warming his toes, he claimed, but I think it's more to distance himself from my mother's over-excited flapping. Avery and Gabe cosy up in the love seat by the window and both mums sit on the sofa, so close together it's as if they can't bear to have any air between them.

Their differences are more marked than ever. Mum with her big brown eyes, dark hair, smooth and glossy to her shoulders, plump cheeks and a tan from her recent travels. And Margot, green eyes bright but cheeks drawn, pale and frail.

Their eager glow and festive sweaters match though. And the look in their eyes is identical as they stare at us expectantly.

'So…' My mum grins, and I get the distinct impression Aiden wants to disappear into the tree. 'What have we missed? You haven't started planning without us, have you?'

'Planning?' he virtually squeaks out.

'The wedding planning!' she says, as if it's obvious.

'Yes, the wedding planning, dummy,' Avery says.

Her grin is worthy of the Cheshire Cat and it's making me wonder, not for the first time, just how much she knows. Has Gabe said something? Aiden suggested he might, but…

'Well, we…' Aiden's voice is unrecognisable, and he clears his throat, tries again. 'I mean, we only got engaged a couple of weeks ago. We haven't got into discussing the finer details.'

'I don't know why I'm surprised. It took you long enough to realise you were made for one another. If we leave it to you two we'll be lucky if we get a wedding at all.'

'Hey, go easy, love.' My dad comes to our rescue. 'They've only just got engaged. Give our daughter time to get used to the ring on her finger before you go sticking another on there.'

I swallow, wishing I hadn't taken a swig of champagne, because the bubbles alone feel too big to get past the wedge in my throat. Getting engaged is one thing, but planning the wedding…a wedding that's never going to happen…

'Do you at least have an idea of what you want?' my mother says, completely oblivious to any tension.

Aiden clears his throat again. Shrugs.

'Like Dad says…' My gaze drifts back to Mum. 'We're still enjoying the whole being engaged thing. I'm finally off tour, and it's nice to get some real downtime together.'

I don't mention that I think wedding planning is the last thing Margot needs with her health.

'Well, it's lucky you have us, then—isn't that right, Margot?'

Her voice softens as she looks at her friend and I see the love there, the concern too. I know seeing Margot like this will have shocked her and she's doing her best to keep it in.

'We're full of ideas, aren't we, honey?'

'You can say that again.' Margot's smile lights up her eyes as they clink champagne glasses. 'We'll have the wedding planned in no time, and all you two need do is say "I do". How does that sound?'

I feel the tension ripple through Aiden's arm. Did all the air just leave the room? Because I swear I can't breathe.

'Lucky us,' he says. 'Did you say you needed to check on the casserole, Laney?'

'Yes!'

'I'll give you a hand.'

And, like caged birds set free, we flee.

Aiden

I close the door and turn to face Elena, who is pacing up and down the kitchen, her elbow propped in one hand, a thumbnail caught in her teeth.

'It'll be okay, Laney.'

She shakes her head. 'What are we going to do, Adie? If they start putting money down on things…venues, caterers, cake bakers…'

'We won't let it get that far.'

'But how do we stop them?'

'We'll deflect…put it off…'

'What if we can't? You *saw* how excited they are. How excited your mother is.'

I rake a hand through my hair. I have no answer for her.

'We'll string them along, fail to make any decisions…'

'And you think that's fair?'

'Nothing about this situation is fair, Laney.'

It's harsh, cut from the chill of my reality, and she stalls mid-step.

'I've already lost my father, now my mother is dying, and there's nothing I can do about it. Nothing!'

Tears come from nowhere, choking up my chest, and frustration vibrates through me.

'All that money I've thrown at medical research over the years—and for what?'

She's across the room in a flash, her hands on mine, which are balled into fists and shaking.

'For all those lives you've saved.'

'But what about *hers*?' It's raw...broken.

'You're doing what you can, and the experts are doing what they can. You don't know what the future holds, Adie. No one does.'

I try to breathe in her words, her reassuring warmth.

'But you do know you've made her happy—that *this* has made her happy.' She takes a steadying breath of her own, gives a nod as though making her mind up on something. 'So we do this. We go along with it, string it out, whatever it takes.'

I swallow the boulder in my chest. 'I won't let your family spend a penny.'

She gives a small smile. 'I'll let you fight that out with my father.'

'I'm serious, Laney. You're already giving up so much for me.'

And I feel so guilty. She's too good, too special. She doesn't deserve this mess I've put her in.

'And right now there's nothing I want to do more. Nowhere else in this world I'd rather be than by your side, helping you through this.'

'I'm so lucky to have you.'

She smiles up into my eyes and I feel the world right itself beneath my feet.

'Always.'

Elena

We survive dinner with barely a mention of the wedding. I'm not sure whether it was our sharp exodus that led to our mothers reining it in, or if my father has had a word. But it's a pleasant meal, filled with chatter. Everyone is catching up on the last few years, and everyone is enjoying the food—thank heaven—and by the time we retire to the living room and the butter tarts make a return I'm feeling relatively relaxed.

'That was delicious, darling,' my father says. 'You did your mother's recipe proud.'

'That you did, love,' my mother says, giving my father's hand an affectionate squeeze. 'It's nice to know Aiden will be eating well when you're married.'

'Mum! Men do cook in this day and age.'

'You should tell your father that.' She sends the man in question a loving but pointed look, and he clears his throat.

'I'd prefer you to live, love.'

We all chuckle, and Aiden leans in to give me an unexpected peck on the cheek—either the perfect demonstration of a loving fiancé, or a discreet way of stealing the last butter tart, which he snatches up in the same sweeping move.

'On that note, Gabe and I will clear away the dishes.'

'I'll give you a hand, son.'

My father starts to rise, but Aiden waves him back.

'No need, you've had a long journey and should rest up. Gabe and I have this. Besides, we need one man in here to keep these women in check.'

'Hey!' I try to poke him and he artfully dodges me, snatching up my hand and kissing it instead.

'What?'

He eyes me innocently and I sense our mothers watching. They might as well have tiny little hearts floating around their heads.

'I'll get you later.'

'Is that a promise?'

Any answer is silenced by the heat unfurling within me, and I snatch up my water, try to douse it, as he and Gabe take off to the kitchen.

My mother gives a blissful sigh. 'It's so lovely to see you both like that at last.'

Here we go again...

'They do say the best things in life are worth waiting for,' Margot adds.

'And what about you and Gabe, Avery? Any sign of…?' My mum waggles her ring finger.

'Mum!'

'What, darling? I'm just asking.'

'I'm sorry, Avery, I think my engagement has gone to my mother's head.'

She laughs. 'It's fine. We've talked about it, yes. When the time is right, you know… Besides, we can't be stealing Aiden and Elena's thunder, can we?'

And just like that the focus is back on us.

'True,' my mother says. 'Though a double wedding…now, there's an idea.'

I choke on my drink and Avery splutters over hers.

'I need a ring first!'

'You're right. Best to get your brother married off first, and then it can be all about you. So, darling…' Mum looks back at me. 'You must have ideas. Big, small? Church, hotel? Traditional? Contemporary?'

Mum's excited chatter continues on and I think of Aiden in the kitchen and wonder if he's having an easier time of it than me…

Aiden

'What are you smiling about?'

Gabe is at the sink, washing the dishes that won't go in the dishwasher, and yet he looks as if he's doing something far more entertaining.

He shakes his head, his smile widening. 'I can't believe your mother was right.'

'About what?' I take the dish he hands me to dry.

'When you told me she was convinced a woman would bring you happiness, I was worried the medication had messed with her senses. You've never seemed the type to enjoy having one around on a permanent basis.'

'And you're saying I seem that type now?'

'I'm saying I've never seen you like this.'

'And what exactly does *"this"* mean?'

'In the time I've been here you've laughed more, worked less and—no word of a lie—appeared happier than you've been in a long time.'

I scoff as I slot the dish away and take up another. 'It's Christmas. The season of joy and laughter and all things merry.'

'But it's not been like that for you—for any of you—in a long time. I get that your mother has driven it, with her reignited vigour for the season, but you can't fake the way you've been this week. Not twenty-four-seven. And the difference isn't in your mother, and the way she's being, it's in you and it's because of her. Elena.'

I try to shrug it off. 'It's nice having her here. It's nice spending real time together.'

'Nice?' He stops scrubbing and looks at me head-on. 'You seriously don't think it means something more?'

'It means my mother is happy and not worrying about me. It means my sister is settled and with you. It means everything is just as it should be, and for the first time in almost ten years we're going to have a Christmas to enjoy and remember rather than forget.'

'And that's all it is?'

'What else?'

He shakes his head, goes back to washing up. 'If you can't see it for yourself, it's pointless me telling you.'

I give a choked laugh. 'That's the second time you've said something like that to me. You want to explain it this time?'

'Have you seriously never considered it?'

'Considered what?'

'You and Elena. For *real*?'

'Me and Elena? Come on, Gabe, she's my oldest friend—practically family. We're so close it would be…'

So why am I reliving that kiss right now? Why is my body on fire with it? With her? Why am I unable to quit thinking of her in ways that are anything but platonic?

'I could never give her what she deserves,' I admit. 'And I won't jeopardise our friendship by trying.'

'That's probably the most honest you've been since I got here.'

I shake my head. 'Whatever…'

'You're wrong, though.'

'I'm—'

The door swings open and Avery bustles in, cutting off my denial.

'What on earth is taking you two so long?'

'Why?' I blurt. 'You missing me?'

'No, dear brother, but I reckon Elena is.'

Something about the way she says it has the hairs on my neck standing to attention and I toss the tea towel down.

'Why? What's happened?'

'I may have deflected the attention off me and Gabe and put the focus back on you two and the W word.'

'The W…? Oh, for Pete's sake, Avery.'

'Don't look at me. It wasn't my fault. They were getting into double wedding territory, and I panicked.'

'And there was I, thinking you *wanted* to marry me,' Gabe teases.

'You know I do.' My sister wraps her arms around him. 'But that lot in there are talking dates, and every one of them is this side of Christmas.'

'They're *what*?'

She ignores my outburst and reaches for the tart I propped on the side earlier. 'Are you not eating that?'

I'm already walking out the door.

'We'd best go too,' she says, pulling Gabe with her. 'Moral support and all that.'

She's enjoying this—I know she is. Probably payback for all the years I spent 'controlling' her, to use her descriptor. I prefer to see it as looking out for her and wanting the best for her, but each to their own.

I enter the living room and find Laney's father has taken up a book and is sitting by the fire, minding his own business. While Elena, flanked by both mothers on the couch, is looking distinctly pale and out of sorts.

'Ah, Aiden, darling. Excellent timing,' my mother pipes up. 'We were just discussing dates.'

'So Avery tells me.'

I don't take my eyes off Elena. She has her bottom lip caught so tightly in her teeth I fear she's about to draw blood. I have to fight the urge to walk over and tug the poor flesh free.

I force a smile and think of the plan we hatched earlier—deflect, delay, don't make a decision.

'There's plenty of time for that. Let's get Christmas over with first, and then we can concentrate on wedding planning.'

'And where would be the joy in that?' My mother shares a conspiratorial look with Angie over Elena's head. 'Don't you think a festive wedding is just the most splendid idea ever? I hadn't considered it, but now Angie's mentioned it, it would be crazy not to. We need to make the most of the season. It will be beautiful, with the snow and the holly and the ivy.'

'You sound like you're about to break into song, Mum.' My words are light but my tone is anything but.

'I rather feel like it,' she says, pressing a hand to her chest, her eyes welling up.

'But Christmas is less than a fortnight away...'

'Ten sleeps,' Gabe supplies, earning a dig in the ribs from Avery and a very definite look that says, *Zip it!*

'All the more reason to get started with the preparations right away,' Angie says.

'Come on, ladies,' my sister intervenes, finally taking pity on us. 'They've only just got engaged. Let's not railroad them down the aisle just yet.'

'Exactly what I was saying,' Peter pipes up from behind his book.

'But I don't see the need to wait.' My mother looks at me then, sharp as an owl. 'If you're in love, and you know you want to get married, why wait?'

And then I see it. The pleading desperation in her gaze. Her illness—the ticking clock that no one can stop. How can we possibly insist we have all the time in the world to get married when time is the one thing my mother may not have...?

I'd hoped this would be enough—the ring, the engagement, an intention to settle down—but it's quite clear it's not.

'And we're not suggesting anything huge or fussy,' Angie says. 'Just a small affair. That way we can keep it something of a secret...out of the press's eye, so to speak. Unless you'd want the press involved? An official statement, perhaps?'

'God, no,' Elena hurries to say.

'We could even do it right here,' Angie adds. 'That way you wouldn't have to exhaust yourself with travel, Margot, and we can make all the arrangements from the comfort of this very sofa. It really is a magical location—just look at that view out there, and with that tree too. We could release a photo after the event, breaking the news—don't you think?'

'That would be nice.' Mum looks from Angie to me to Elena, and back to me, a frown forming between her brows. 'Of course if you need more time,' she says, quieter now, 'we could plan it for later. Maybe in the New Year. Though I have my next treatment scheduled for just after Boxing Day, and I... Well, I'm not sure...' She swallows, twisting her hands in her lap. 'Maybe you're right. It is rather a rush, and I wouldn't want you doing something you're not comfortable with. Not when it should be one of the happiest days of your lives.'

'And it will be the happiest of days, Margot, don't doubt it for a second.' Angie takes Elena's hand, gives it a squeeze. 'If it's the planning you're worried about, love, don't be. We will help with everything, and we have people we can call upon to create as small or as big a wedding as you'd like. It will be extra-special, I promise.'

'Special?' Elena nods numbly.

'I promise. We could even do it Christmas Eve!' Angie sits bolt upright, scans the room as if the idea has just come to her. 'How perfect would that be?'

All eyes look from me to Elena and back again…

'Christmas Eve?' I say.

'Christmas Eve?' Elena repeats.

'Is that a yes?' Her mother leans forward, as does mine.

Faking an engagement is one thing, but a *wedding*…?

CHAPTER EIGHT

Aiden

I CAN'T SLEEP, so I work. By the low light of the desk lamp I trawl through my barrage of emails and try to concentrate on something that isn't the train wreck of my life.

How could I let this happen?

I look over my shoulder, at Elena fast asleep, her features relaxed, her hair a dark cloud around her head. She truly is beautiful and kind and everything a man could ever want in a wife...

An ache kickstarts low in my gut.

Envy.

I envy those men who can love so freely. Give up a part of themselves to another and not live in fear of the day it gets ripped away. Like Gabe.

My mother's illness has only emphasised the fragility of life and the lack of control we have over it. All we can hope to do is protect ourselves.

But what if in protecting ourselves we end up hurting those we care for most?

Elena

I know he's working. I can hear the gentle tap of the keys, detect the lamplight through my closed lids.

Aside from him, the only noise is the gentle creak of the

house at night. I peer at the old clock on the bookcase, make out the time. Just past midnight. I hate that he works so late, but something tells me this has more to do with the day's affairs than it does with a necessity to get the job done.

By the time we'd come to bed I hadn't the energy to thrash it out with him—and what was there to thrash out, really? We were hemmed in by two mothers desperate to see us married, both keenly aware of time ticking away, and neither of us could come up with a reason not to be—other than the truth. That this was never meant to be the real deal.

Aiden and I…married. Husband and wife.

He blows out a breath that has his broad shoulders sagging. Naked from the waist up, he's hunched over his childhood desk, which is dwarfed by the man he has become. His hair is in disarray—a sign that he's thrust his hands through it one too many times. As if on cue, he does it now. Wherever his head has gone, it isn't a happy place.

'Adie?'

He spins in the chair, his eyes finding mine in the low light, their torment shining through.

'Laney! I'm sorry…did I wake you?'

'What's wrong?'

He stares back at me, the lines of worry etched so deep in his face.

'Adie?'

He lowers his gaze to the desk, closes the lid of his laptop. 'What's right?'

I press up onto my elbow and toss the pillow wall aside. 'Come here.'

I pat the bed beside me, but he doesn't move.

'I really don't bite.'

He gives a tight chuckle, my tease chipping away at the walls he's erected as he rises up and steals my breath in one.

Overwhelmed by his masculine beauty and the vulnerability that cuts right through it. His powerhouse of a physique barely concealed by his low-slung pants and eyes that tell a thousand tales, too many a burden. I feel his pain and my need for him combine…a twisted heat deep inside my chest.

He gets into bed beside me, leans back against the head-board, and I do the one thing I haven't done in so long. Since the one and only night I witnessed him cry over his father. I wrap my arms around him and rest his head against my chest. I hold him.

'It'll be okay,' I say.

He gives a soft huff. 'You didn't sign up for this.'

'We don't sign up for a lot of things in life, but we get through it. And, let's face it, a Christmas Eve wedding is fairly harmless in the grand scheme of things.'

'Not what I was expecting you to say…'

I shrug. 'We're not religious…we're not swearing an oath to God, only to each other, and the truth is we'll always have each other's backs, in sickness and in health. So is it really all that bad…? It's not even a lie when you look at it that way.'

'You've twisted that quite expertly.'

'I know.'

'But the news reports, the journalists… They'll have a field day over the eventual divorce. Controlling the narrative over a failed relationship is one thing, but a marriage?'

I ignore the way that word stings—*divorce*. 'We don't need to worry about that now.'

'I am worrying about it. They'll probably accuse you of being on the rebound and breaking my heart in the process.'

'Aw, will you be suitably heartbroken over me, Adie?' I try to tease.

'Don't joke, Laney. I'm serious.'

'And so am I. I can take care of myself.'

'But you shouldn't have to.'

If life was fair, I wouldn't have to. He'd love me as I do him and we'd live happily ever after. But that's on me, not him.

'And you know you'll come off worse,' he goes on. 'I'll do

everything I can to make clear it was amicable, mutual…turn myself into the villain of the piece if I have to. But they'll still paint it every which way they want, and make you suffer in the process.'

'I don't care.'

He looks up at me and I hold my ground, though the temptation to look away when he's this close is overpowering…to look away or do something worse, something foolish.

'How can you not care?'

I wonder how he can't see it. The love. Or maybe he does see it and chooses to be blind to it?

'Because I choose to care more about you than the opinion of the gossip-hungry press and the people they influence. So long as our family understand, that's all that matters.'

'And what if Mum makes it through this…?'

'Won't that be the most wonderful problem to have?'

I sense him smile as he leans back into me.

'Promise me something, though?' I say, my tone as sober as my thoughts.

'What?'

'You'll find some balance in your life, regardless. No more working twenty-four-seven.'

'Ah, the reason we are in this mess…'

'Your mother has a point.'

'I've hardly been working twenty-four-seven of late.'

'Because you've had me and your mother to lure you away. But when we part…?'

I hate to think of it, but at some point I have to come to terms with the fact that this will end and we will go back to how we were.

He shrugs. 'It's all I've known for so long. I'm not sure how else to live.'

'But you're not living, Adie, you're working. There's a difference.'

He yawns. 'And you're the expert?'

'When your work is your hobby it's a little different…'

'So tell me—what does an opera singer do when she wants to unwind if singing is her hobby?'

'I go rogue.'

He chuckles softly. 'How so?'

'I sing what I like, however I like, and act as though no one is listening.'

'Like the Christmas tunes?'

His voice is thick with sleep, his head heavy against my chest.

'You caught that?'

'Everyone caught that. When you sing, people can't help but listen. Here. At the shop… I think you dip into song more than you realise…'

I cringe. 'Sorry.'

'Don't be. I love it. It's you.'

My heart skips a beat. *Love. You.* Words said so close together, but not close enough.

'You won't be saying that once we're married.'

He gives a sleepy huff. 'And what do you do when you can't sleep?'

'I hum.'

'I should've guessed.'

And so I do. I hum until his breathing deepens, evens out. I hum until my own body relaxes into the sheets and I drift off to sleep with him. Our bodies as entwined as my heart already is with his.

And it feels right.

No act. No performance. Just us.

Aiden

I'm walking between row upon row of chairs filled with faceless people, all turned towards me—watching, waiting, pointing, laughing.

Why are they here? What's their problem?

My father is waiting for me. I know he shouldn't be here. He's long gone. But his smile is so familiar, so real. His dark hair lacks the streaks of grey...the lines in his face are softer. He's dressed for a wedding. Dark suit and tie, a red rose for a buttonhole...

I pat my chest, realise I have one too. I don't understand... I don't know why I'm here...

He reaches out, grips my hand and pulls me closer.

'I'm proud of you, son.'

His eyes sparkle.

'We couldn't have chosen better for you.'

I turn to see my mother behind me. Her cheeks are plump and glowing, her hair shining, eyes bright and happy.

'You may now kiss the bride,' comes a transcendental voice, and I spin on the spot.

It's Laney... She's wearing her dress from the stage in Milan, only it appears sheer, enhancing her curves. Her make-up emphasises her big brown eyes, the fullness to her lips. She hooks her hands around my neck and my body fires with the contact, stealing my breath...

'Adie...' she whispers, her mouth inching closer. 'I do.'

I wet my lips, groan in anticipation. This is what I've wanted for so long...wanted and wouldn't let myself have.

I lower my head, surrender to the desire pumping thick and fast through my veins...

And freeze—frown.

There's a weird tapping...a knocking...

My eyes flare open, two things hitting me at once—I'm pinned down by a sleeping Elena, and I have a blasted erection!

No, make that three things. The noise, the knocking, it's someone at the door.

I curse and tug the blanket over us just as the handle shifts and the door swings open.

'Wakey-wakey! Rise and shine!'

'Not again, Mum! Seriously!'

She chuckles. 'I've seen it all before, Aiden.'

Elena shifts beside me, slowly coming to. 'Margot...?'

'Morning, my dear, I have such great news! Your mother has arranged a morning appointment at the bridal boutique in town. They're opening early especially, to fit you in.'

'The b-bridal boutique?'

'Why, yes, dear. We can't have you getting married in rags, can we?'

'You shouldn't be fussing over us, Mum,' I say, taking the focus off the wedding talk and on to the tray that's loaded with food.

'I didn't cook it. Angie did. I'm just the waitress.' She slips the tray on to the bedside table. 'You'll be setting off in an hour—plenty of time for you to enjoy yourselves first.'

And with that bold statement, wink and all, she walks away, leaving a blushing Laney and an equally blushing me!

'I'm so sorry.' Elena presses herself up and off me.

'What for?' I ask. 'The drool or the—?'

She gives me a shove, her hand on my naked chest far more provocative than it should be, and I curse the lustful remnants of my dream. Though the way she snatches her hand back suggests she feels it too. And I don't have the mental capacity to process that right now—not when I'm still half naked, hard, and in bed with her.

'I don't drool.'

'My chest begs to differ.'

That's it—stick to the playful teasing, the kind a best friend would dish out in spades, because it's far safer than what I really want to do.

Thank heaven she's dressed. Though the white vest top with its thin fabric and delicate straps is hardly hiding much.

I snatch my gaze away, pick up the OJ. 'Want some?'

She stretches her arms above her head with a yawn, pulling my gaze back, and I swallow a curse.

'What was that?' Her arms flop back down as she frowns at me.

'Nothing.'

She eyes me, unconvinced.

'OJ?' I offer the glass, almost sloshing the thing at her.

'Just coffee for me, thanks. If I'm trying on dresses today the last thing I need is Mum's pancakes.'

'You look great—I mean, the pancakes look great!'

Idiot!

She gives me the side-eye.

'I mean you both look great…the pancakes and you…so you should definitely allow yourself to have some. Here.'

Oh, God, I sound like a fool, and she's laughing at me. I can see it in her eyes, in the way she purses her lips.

'Thank you… I think. But I only look like I do because I don't eat pancakes for breakfast.'

'That's sacrilege!'

She laughs.

'And you say I'm working more than living? If you're denying yourself these delights for breakfast, you're not living either.'

She runs her teeth over her bottom lip, eyes the plate that I'm still holding out.

'You know you want to.'

She shakes her head. 'A bite! Just one!'

I grin, pleased with my small win—even if it means I'm now forking up some pancake with lashings of maple syrup and feeding it to her. In bed. Just the two of us.

Not erotic in any way.

But by God, her unrestrained hum is…the way she closes her eyes, tilts her head back, scoops an escaped dribble of maple syrup from her chin and licks her finger clean.

'I'll be right back,' I say, throwing off the covers and fleeing to the bathroom before my body can give me away. 'Save me some pancakes!'

I close the door and lean against it, drag in a stifled breath, and plead with the heavens to give me strength.

Elena

I step out of the changing room, my head still very much in bed with Aiden, my body in the town's delightfully sweet bridal boutique. We've been plied with champagne since our arrival—it's never too early for bubbles, according to Mum—by the two equally sweet stylists, Gemma and Jemima.

They've oohed and ahhed on cue, and offered up so many dresses I've lost track of what I do and don't like.

And the truth is I don't care.

Or rather, I don't want to care.

'Oh, my goodness, darling! That is...' Mum dabs at her eyes with a tissue. 'That is stunning.'

'You said that about the last one—and the one before that.'

'But this one...'

I walk into the middle of the room that's designed to show-case your dream dress with its careful lighting, the arrange-ment of mirrors, the muted colours and plush seats. I do a twirl and take in my reflection.

Not too dramatic or flouncy. Quite pretty... The strapless ivory ballgown with its slim-fitting bodice and tulle skirt, skims my hips and drapes to the floor, with a sprinkling of pearls that look very much like the snow falling outside.

I turn this way and that, but can't seem to settle. Not on my feet, nor within. The crazy dance Aiden kickstarted in my gut that morning just won't quit. He's acting weird. It's the only way I can describe it. Racing to the bathroom like that, then returning and failing to make eye contact, even when I planted a kiss on his cheek to wish him farewell in front of his mother.

I'm surprised my mother didn't comment on it—not even when we were safely alone and en route to the boutique. Me be-hind the wheel of Aiden's truck, her my over-excited passenger.

Not that I would have known what to say.

Was it our conversation during the night? The idea of me wedding dress shopping today? Or our entwined bodies when we woke this morning…another reason that my pulse is so quick to race.

I don't know, but it's hanging over me and I can't shift the feeling that something's wrong.

'Honey?'

Mum's suddenly beside me, her hands soft on my shoulders, and that's when I realise they're bunched around my ears, and my hands are in fists at my sides.

'What is it?'

Her question cuts through all the pretence, teasing at the truth, and I'm helpless to stop the tears from forming.

'Oh, darling!' She turns to Gemma and Jemima. 'Could you please give us a moment, ladies?'

The two discreetly step out, and she offers me a fresh tissue while wiping at the tears herself.

'Tell me, darling.'

I shake my head, unable to meet her eye. It's not as if she can read the truth in me, but I'm scared I'll spill all anyway.

'I know it's a lot…getting married so quickly, making decisions…'

'It's not that.' I sniff, wondering why I denied it when it's probably my best defence. My *safest* defence.

'Is it Margot's illness?' My mother's voice thickens with her own sorrow, her own rising tears. 'Because seeing her for myself has really brought it home to me, too.'

'Oh, Mum, please. Don't you start.'

She gives me a watery smile. 'I'm sorry. I just can't imagine a world without her in it. We've been friends for so long…like sisters, really…' She takes a shuddery breath. 'Well, what will be, will be. But this—this wedding—it's the one saving grace.'

'Don't say that, Mum.'

'Why not? It's the truth. Having you both come to your

senses at last…it's a dream come true. And for Margot to be here to see it, too…'

I nod. 'I know. I know.'

And it makes me want to cry all the more. Because it's not just their dream, it's mine…my impossible dream…so close to becoming a reality, only not close enough.

'You really do look beautiful, darling.'

I take a shaky breath and flick out the skirt, focus on the dress. The practical, not the personal.

'It isn't me, though.'

'Then what is, honey? Because you only have to say the word and we'll do everything we can to find it for you.'

I peer back into the shop. There is something…a glimpse of fabric I caught earlier…

'Stay right there,' Mum says. 'I'm going to fetch the girls and you're going to start over, and this time, think about *your* dream dress, darling. Not mine or what you think people want to see, *yours*. Because you only get to do this once—in my book, at least—and you need to get it right.'

'Thanks, Mum,' I say, but it's tight with guilt, and my un-requited love for a man who is about to become my groom whether he wants to or not.

But maybe Mum's right. I do only get to do this once, with the man I have loved for more years than I can count, so I might as well get the details right…

Starting with the dress.

CHAPTER NINE

Aiden

THE HOUSE IS in chaos. Caterers, decorators, florists, delivery drivers—all dashing about. Christmas decorations have
now taken on a wedding twist and multiplied tenfold. Even
my morning coffee featured a glittery sprinkle of something
decidedly unpalatable.

And all for what?

A wedding that is as fake as I feel.

And I don't just feel fake—I feel ever more selfish, guilt
weighing heavy on my chest. Because I haven't been able to
look Elena in the eye since that day just over a week ago. All
because of that dream that had felt far too real.

And it wasn't just the sucker punch of desire—the kind that
you can sate between the sheets and then move on—but the
deeper, more emotional need to share my life with another.
To tie myself to her so completely.

It's everything I've fought against since my father died,
leaving me emotionally adrift, broken, lost. Leaving me responsible for so much. For my family and a company I didn't
even want but felt I had to take on.

And I don't want to depend on another. I don't want to need
another, yearn for another, cherish another. Love another. Not
like that.

But what if there is another way? What if Elena's right and

I can offload some of that responsibility, claw back time… time I could give to her, time to explore this?

And then what?

She might not feel the same. And if she does, the risk remains.

What happens if it all goes wrong?

Can I really risk losing the one woman who understands me so completely, who has been there since day one, quite literally? A woman whose friendship I *do* cherish and the only woman aside from my family that I have ever loved.

To risk hurting her, losing her… I just can't.

And so I've avoided it. I've avoided her.

I rise before her in the morning. I go to bed long after she's asleep. I use work or exercise to excuse me from the frenzied wedding planning and I hide behind the chaos. Keep my confused feelings buried beneath a front.

'Will you get your head out of that laptop and tell me which colour—navy or green?'

'Huh?' My mother is standing over me, a napkin hanging from each hand.

'Which one for the wedding breakfast?'

'I really don't mind, Mum.'

'Please can you have an opinion on *something*, Aiden? I'm beginning to think you don't care for this wedding at all.'

'You were the one who—'

No, don't go there, that isn't fair.

'Sorry, Mum.' I look at the napkins. 'Why not have red? We have a Christmas theme after all.'

'One can have a little too much red, don't you think?'

I raise my brows, unable to believe I'm even entertaining this mundane conversation when inside my head it's a mess and on the outside my life is no better.

'Green, then. The traditional colour of Father Christmas!'

She beams back at me. 'Great…' Then she pauses as she

eyes them anew. 'Though maybe the navy complements the silverware better...'

'Mother!'

'Chill out, darling!' She peers at my screen. 'What are you up to anyway? Not work, I hope.'

'No.' Because I'm not working. I *can't* work. My brain won't string a coherent thought together. It doesn't mean I wasn't trying, though. Trying and failing...

Much like you are when it comes to being a good friend to Elena right now.

'I'll just go and see if Gabe needs a hand shifting the furniture.'

'Great idea. Make sure he puts the officiant's table beside the tree, won't you? And can you drop a couple of things down to the cabin? There's a little something I'd like Elena to have. Tell her she doesn't need to wear them, but they may come in useful tomorrow.'

'Okay.'

I'm already heading for the door, running yet again.

'And there's a hamper with breakfast for her and her parents—though I can't imagine the girl will want to eat a thing. I've never seen a bride-to-be quite so jittery. I didn't think she was the type, but...'

Jittery?

Either her voice trails off or I'm no longer listening, because all I hear is her worrying depiction of Elena's current mental state.

Is she really that bad?

You'd know for yourself if you'd actually paid her some attention of late.

And that's probably *why* she's so bad.

So much for not hurting her...

I fist my hands until my nails bite into my palms.

'Don't hang about, mind!' My mother calls after me. 'It's bad luck for you to see the bride the night before the wedding.'

'I don't believe in any of that stuff,' I mumble.

'Humour me?'

This whole thing is about humouring you.

The words are there, selfish and silenced. Because they aren't fair either. This was my idea...my plan that's got wholly out of my control.

And what a joke that is?

I crave control. Control over my life. My emotions. Yet here I am, without it. With no one to blame but myself. And right now I owe the person at the centre of it all an apology.

'Always, Mum.' I do an about-turn and pull her to me, kiss the top of her head. 'I love you. Gotta run!'

She giggles, all relaxed and happy after my flourish of affection. 'Don't forget to take the things.'

'I won't.'

'And give her my love.'

'I will!'

Elena

'Elena, honey!'

Mum calls through the bedroom door, intruding on the dulcet tones of Frank Sinatra doing his rendition of 'White Christmas'—one of my favourites—and my supposed restful soak in the copper bathtub.

'I've brought you a mug of Dad's chocolate eggnog, to see off those last-minute nerves.'

'Or make me vomit them up,' I whisper to myself because how can I say that when it's the eve of my wedding...? The eve of Christmas Eve!

'Thanks, Mum,' I call out and she eases the door open as I sink beneath the bubbles.

I give her a smile above the foam that I fear doesn't quite reach my eyes.

'Oh, my, this place really is very beautiful.' Her eyes devour the master bedroom that's been carved out of the cosy cabin's loft space. Exposed beams, wooden floors and glass that takes up an entire wall, where a balcony acts as a private viewing point over the snowy woods beyond, with trees so tall they dwarf the cabin itself.

'What a romantic place to spend your wedding night,' she says, popping the mug on the varnished tree stump that acts as a table beside the bath.

I make what's supposed to be a murmur of agreement, but it sounds more like a squeak.

It is very romantic—in a rustic, snowy, secret hideaway kind of a way. Nestled in the woods that surround the Monroe lodge, the main dwelling is close enough to get to by foot, but far enough away to feel as if you're all alone in the world.

And then there's the bed—the huge, low-slung bed—with its soft brown furs and big plush pillows...pillows that will make an excellent wall tomorrow night.

But a pillow wall is no defence for my heart.

'I was concerned about your lack of honeymoon plans, but you know what, honey? This feels like the ideal place for you to spend your early days as husband and wife.'

She beams at me now, and I try to return it.

'Is the soak helping?' she asks.

'It was a great suggestion, thanks.'

But it's not helping. Nothing will help. My best friend is pretty much ignoring me, and tomorrow we'll be legally wed.

Nothing about this is okay.

'You just give me a shout if you need anything else.'

'I will. Thanks, Mum.'

With one last concerned smile she leaves, and I blow out a breath that sends soapsuds floating through the air.

I really should get out. My skin is prune-like and my head is in no better a state. Not even the cosy room and the open fire in the grate can warm the chill left by Aiden's sudden withdrawal.

And tomorrow he will be sharing this room with me.

Our first night as husband and wife.

Will he speak to me properly then? Look at me properly, even?

I take a breath and try to use the mulled spice from the scented candle to remind myself of the joy of Christmases past. Try to pretend that this is like any other.

A Christmas with a twist…

Sinatra has moved on to the very apt 'Have Yourself a Merry Little Christmas', and I wonder if he's right. Will next year be better? Will our troubles be miles away? Will Aiden be miles away, his mother gone? And our friendship—what will that look like?

Approaching tyres crunch through the snow outside and I turn to the window, not that I can see. Another delivery, perhaps? More wedding paraphernalia being ferried between the houses?

So much has gone into this day and I can't believe we've managed to pull it off in such a short space of time. I say 'we', but it's been our mothers. Happy to be together once more, planning their dream wedding and using it as a much-needed distraction from Margot's illness.

It's done what Aiden set out to do, and for that I can only be happy.

The front door opens downstairs and I can hear the soft murmur of my mother's voice, indistinct through the wooden floorboards.

'I just need to have a quick word.'

Aiden's voice permeates clear as day and I bolt upright, water sloshing out of the bath.

'I won't keep her long.'

He won't *keep* me…he wants to see me! Right *now*?!

'You best not,' my mother is saying as footsteps approach. 'It's unlucky for the groom to see the bride the night before the wedding.'

'So my mother says.'

He chuckles, the sound working its way through me as I scrabble for a towel.

'Don't worry, I'll be in and out. Scout's honour.'

Aiden

I take the stairs two at a time, my need to see Elena and fix things driving me on.

I thrust open the door, stride right in and—

'Elena!'

She grips the side of the bathtub—half in, half out, eyes wide, her mouth a gaping 'O'.

'Oh, heavens!' I turn and face the door that has closed with the momentum I generated on my over-excited entry. 'I'm sorry!'

A second's delay, then, 'Ever heard of knocking, Aiden.'

Water sloshes this way and that, and I visualise her moving…every naked inch. Some I've now seen, some my imagination is quick to fill in, and I mutter another curse, try to quit the visual and the crazy effect it's having below my waist.

'I wasn't expecting you to be naked.'

'I don't know of many people who take a bath clothed.'

'It's the afternoon.'

'People take baths at all times of the day, Aiden.'

I shake my head, find another defence. 'But your mother didn't say.'

'Why would she? She thinks you've seen it all before.'

And now I nearly have.

I press my head into my hand, as if it's somehow going to push the evocative picture out.

'I'm sorry,' I repeat dumbly.

'You can look now,' she says, her voice soft and uncertain and—I don't like it. She shouldn't be uncertain. Not with me. Not ever.

Slowly I turn, hold my breath as I take her in. Wrapped in a towel around her middle, her wet hair reaches all the way to her waist. Her eyes are big and round and over bright, her cheeks are flushed pink, while the rest of her glows gold in the firelight. Soapsuds weaving a downward path over her skin that I'm helplessly captivated by.

I force air into my lungs, force my eyes to meet hers in their wounded state.

'I'm sorry.'

It blurts out of me, my desire to see her stripped of that look overriding all else.

'So you've said.'

'No, not for the bath and the intrusion.' I step forward in my desperation. 'Which I'm sorry for too, of course. But I'm sorry for being an arse. A complete and utter arse.'

Her brows inch up. 'You are?'

'Yes!'

She looks as perplexed as my heart feels. 'Is this where you explain your weird behaviour this past week?'

I rake a hand through my hair. 'Yes. Or at least I'll try to explain, but it hardly makes sense to me either.'

She gives a small shudder and I grab one of the dressing gowns from the back of the door, wrap it around her and try not to lose myself in the way she looks.

Bashful and sweet. Her lashes look darker, thicker now they're wet, and as she looks up, I swear the room shifts.

The punch to my gut, my heart, so visceral I forget what I'm about.

'Adie?'

'Right, yeah…' I tug the robe together at the front and step back abruptly. Rake another hand through my hair.

'So, yeah… I'm sorry, Laney. I freaked out. I panicked. I feared where we were heading.'

I stride up to the fire, but I'm already too hot, and the bed is too near, and then there's the bath, and her, and she's still too naked, and... God, why can't I think straight?

I launch myself at the glass, stare at the cool white world beyond and plead with it to chill me.

'I thought I'd done something.'

'No—God no.' I spin to face her, needing her to see that I mean it. 'You've done everything you can to be there for us, and that's what makes my behaviour even more deplorable.' I rake both hands through my hair. 'I can't lose you, Laney. I can't lose our friendship. I just can't.'

She secures the robe around her properly as she steps towards me. 'You could never lose me, Adie.'

'But this whole situation... I thought it would be okay—not easy, but okay. We would act the part, and behind closed doors we would be us...friends, like always. But then we kissed. And I had this crazy dream. And...'

'You had a dream?' Her mouth twitches, her eyes sparkle.

'It wasn't that funny.'

'I can't comment if you don't tell me what it was about.'

I shake my head. 'You don't need to know.'

'You mean you'd rather I didn't know?'

'Yes.'

I hate the look that comes over her face and reach out to cup her arms before I can think better of it. Her body heat through the gown is like a torch to my skin, but to break the contact as swiftly as I made it would only hurt her further.

'It was just a messed-up dream and it freaked me out— made me question what I want from my life, what I'm doing with it. And now more than ever I need to be certain. I need to be in control and to do what's right. By you, by Mum, by the company...'

'I don't think questioning what you want from your life is bad thing. It's what I've been trying to get you to do, too.'

'I know.'

'But you're still not ready?'

'I hardly think now is the best time for me to re-evaluate anything.'

Because re-evaluating might make me want it all the more, and that scares me enough in itself. I need to focus on Mum, on her health, on getting her through this and then, failing that, picking up the pieces all over again, being there for Avery...

Elena gives me a sad smile. 'I worry that you'll always find a reason to avoid thinking about it.'

'That's not true.'

'Isn't it? I think you fear change, Adie. You fear the unknown. You've lived your life desperate to control everything for so long, to keep it stable for your family, your employees, for you. You've thrown money at your mother's illness, determined to get her the best care, to control an outcome that with the greatest will in the world you can't. And you did everything you could to control the life your sister—'

'I was trying help her, to keep her safe. Why does everyone see it as a bad thing?'

'Because you can't control everything, Adie! People make mistakes and they grow from them. By determining who Avery could and couldn't see, what she studied, where she lived...'

'It was to keep her safe.'

'You stifled her and made her rebel. You pushed her away when you wanted to bring her closer. But look what happened. She made mistakes and she grew from them...she's better for them, even.'

'I know.'

'Do you? Because if you truly know that then why aren't you doing the same? Why aren't you taking chances? Reaching out of your comfort zone and your carefully controlled life to see what else is out there for you?'

She's staring up at me, those big brown eyes penetrating my very soul, and my heart is screaming.

Tell her precisely why. Tell her the truth. Tell her that she's the one you want to take that chance on.

And run the risk of losing her completely? my head argues back. *Are you really that much of a fool? And you know full well she deserves more.*

Lifestyle change or no, you have no idea what you're capable of truly giving someone like her.

Do you really want to risk your friendship when you don't know for sure you can give her what she wants, what she deserves, make her happy?

What if she doesn't feel the same and you send her running for the hills?

Or, worse, what if this is just a blip, an emotional response to the current situation and you change your mind?

You've already hurt her enough.

'I don't know, Laney,' I say truthfully. 'I just know that the way I've treated you this past week is wrong, and I hope you can forgive me.'

Something inside me shrivels, but doesn't quite die, and I ignore it as I press, 'Can you? Forgive me, that is.'

My voice is hoarse, panic setting in when she doesn't answer straight away.

'Laney?'

'You hurt me, Adie.'

'I know. I know and I'm sorry. I'm sorry it took me so long to realise it too. I was selfish and confused and…'

I release her, but she pulls me back. 'You were an idiot,' she says, softening her words with a tentative smile, her eyes brimming with emotion. 'But I get it. You've faced a lot in your life, Adie, and if you'd come through all that without any scars you wouldn't be human. Of course I forgive you.'

I wet my lips, my chest tight. 'What did I do to deserve you?'

'You were you—which is a better man than I think you realise.'

I hold her gaze, search it, feel that shrivelled part of me start to beat, to warm. 'Laney, I—'

A rap on the door cuts me off. 'Right, you two.' Peter's voice penetrates the heavy wood. 'Time to say goodbye. The sun is setting and I won't be held responsible for your mother's actions if you stay in there a moment longer, son.'

Son. Even that word does something strange inside. Warms, but chills.

'Do you think she's about to come in here with a whip or something?' I ask, reaching for our old camaraderie, desperate for it.

She laughs, the sound so free and easy, the spark in her eyes a balm to a wound I'm not sure how to heal and likely never will.

'I wouldn't put it past her.'

I give a mock shudder that sees her laughing more. 'In that case I'd best be gone...'

Then I remember the velvet box in my pocket.

'Oh, I almost forgot. Mum asked me to give you this.'

I pull it out, noticing the gold initials embroidered into the top—my great-grandmother's initials.

'What is it?'

'No idea.' Though I have an inkling now as she takes it from me. 'She said you don't need to wear them, but they may come in useful tomorrow.'

She opens the box, a smile touching her lips. 'Something borrowed...'

'Something what?' I frown, lean over to see inside.

Nestled in black velvet is a diamond necklace and a tennis bracelet to match.

My mother's handwritten scrawl on a small ivory note rests in the lid.

Something borrowed x

'Old too,' I say, recalling the tradition. 'They were my great-grandmother's.'

She looks up at me. 'I can't take these.'

'It's only for a day, Laney,' I say. 'Not for ever.'

And why does that feel so depressing?

I shake off the sensation as her father raps on the door once more.

'Final warning!'

'I'd best go.' I pull her into my arms and hold her close. Breathe in her familiar scent, her warmth, her kindness, and my emotions rise up and spill over. 'Thank you for doing this, Laney. I love you so much.'

Oh, hell, where did *that* come from?

She freezes in my hold and I can't blame her.

Get out of there.

I lean back, force a smile. 'Soul mates, right?'

She nods, her lashes flickering, her eyes damp. 'Always.'

'See you tomorrow?'

It's phrased as a question, and her nod is silent, but definite. I hesitate a second more—I'm not sure why. To hear her voice again? To say something…?

And now you're just freaking her *out!*

'Sleep well, Laney.'

And then I leave, my heart never more confused but beating ever louder…

CHAPTER TEN

Elena

'You can stop now, Mum.'

She's been fussing and flapping since her alarm went off at six... In fact, I'm not even sure she slept. Which makes two of us.

'I know... I know. I just want it to be right for you, darling.'

'It is right. Everything is right.'

I'm getting good at this lying. My insides wince. I'm not proud of it. Just desperate.

I think back to Aiden's parting words the day before. His heartfelt *'I love you so much'* that felt like so much more than a platonic declaration. For the briefest second my heart had soared with hope, only to be shot down, obliterated by his strained smile and his hurried proclamation of *'soul mates'*— my words—hammering the message home.

'I really wish you'd invited at least one of your girlfriends to be here. I know it's last-minute, but...'

'I told you, Mum, they're all busy. It's Christmas Eve and everyone wants to be with their families.'

'But I'm sure Pippa would—'

I give her a look that sees off the rest of her negativity. And I'm not lying now—not entirely. Part of me doesn't want them here—not when most of them know how I feel. How I *really* feel. It's enough that I know, walking into this. I don't need their eyes and their judgement on me too.

'Oh, careful, honey. If you squeeze that bouquet any tighter you'll break the stems.'

I eye my vice-like grip around the festive arrangement of red roses, holly berries and pine, and force my fingers to relax.

'I was the same on my wedding morning…worrying about whether I'd get my words out straight…would your father jilt me at the altar…'

She laughs on the last, but I don't find it funny. Is there a chance Aiden won't show? That he'll realise this is a mistake and pull out. Would he do that to me?

Prior to a week ago I wouldn't have thought it for a second. But his behaviour recently…the way he avoided me…

I know he's explained and apologised. And I get it. I do. I didn't take it lying down though. I pushed back, eager to make him see how different his life could be.

Did I push too hard?

Hell, despite his *I love you*, could I have pushed him away altogether?

'Not that Aiden would do such a thing, of course,' my mother hurries to say as if she's read my mind, hands still fussing over my dress as a knock sounds on the door.

'Ah, that'll be your father now. You ready to let him in?'

I nod and feel my hair tickle the bare skin of my back. The carefully crafted waterfall braid creates a flowing effect down my exposed spine that the stylist deemed 'feminine and subtly sexy'.

I'm used to being made up for the stage, but I feel different, vulnerable.

I don't know whether Mum senses it, but she stops and tilts her head, tears pricking, her fingers fluttering before her lips.

'You look stunning, darling. The make-up, the hair, the dress… It's so perfectly you.'

I turn to the full-length mirror I've avoided until now and the world around me falls away. It's just me and my reflection and the magnitude of what I'm doing. I'm a bride.

My breath catches as I peer closer. The blush to my cheeks, the blood-red lips and the dramatic eye make-up all work in harmony with the striking colour of the fabric. The dress that I knew would be the one the second I caught a glimpse of it on the rack...

Everyone else had been far from sure. Until I'd put it on. And then the gasps that had dwarfed the previous oohs and ahhs had settled it.

My father strides in and stops just as quickly. 'Oh, my...'

I stiffen. 'What is it?'

He gives a small shake of his head, a strand of grey hair falling across his forehead which he quickly smooths away.

'Are you—are you *crying*?' I've never seen my Dad cry. In all my thirty-five years he's been loving and encouraging, never overly sentimental, but always there for me. And now... now he cries?

He clears his throat. 'No.'

Mum touches a hand to his chest. 'You always were a big softy...it's one of the reasons I fell in love with you.'

'You can't cry, Dad! You'll set me off.'

He chuckles, tugs at the lapels of his dark jacket and pats his pocket handkerchief. 'That's what this is for—it's not just for show.'

I smile. 'Ever the practical one.'

'Indeed. This, on the other hand...' He toys with the but-tonhole, a mini version of my festive bouquet, with its deep red rose, holly berries, spruce and a tiny fur cone 'Not prac-tical in the slightest.'

'But it looks the part, Peter,' my mother coos.

'And that's all that matters, so I'm told.' He looks back at me. 'Are you ready?'

I take a slow breath for courage. 'Ready as I'll ever be.'

I lift my skirt and step forward in a rustle of fabric. 'Oh, wait!' I spy the velvet box on the dressing table and hurry over to it. 'I almost forgot... Could you do the honours, Dad?'

I pass it to him and turn, scooping my hair up as he opens the box.

'This is quite special,' he murmurs.

'It's my something old and something borrowed, from Margot.'

'And the dress is something new,' Mum says, as Dad lifts the necklace over my head and fastens it in place. 'But what about the blue?'

'I have just the thing…' Dad tugs the deep blue handkerchief from his chest pocket and I wave it back.

'You can't give me that.'

He grins. 'I have another. Margot sent four on the off-chance.'

'Of course she did.'

'A second something borrowed doesn't outweigh the first, does it?' he asks.

'I'd say it's double the luck.' Mum takes out the bracelet and secures it around my wrist. 'Or triple!'

'But where am I supposed to keep it?' I say, turning the satin over in my hand.

'Your mother will show you. It's what she did on her wedding day, and I seem to remember it came in handy for her too.'

'You remember?' Mum says, genuine surprise and love soft in her voice.

'How could I forget?'

Dad turns away as Mum helps me slip it inside the front of my dress.

'Easy access…just in case.' She presses a light kiss to my cheek. 'Now, go get your man.'

Aiden

'It's not too late,' Gabe leans in to say.

'Are you kidding me?'

I look dead ahead, my smile firmly in place for the officiant and her colleague, although they're too busy taking in the snowy view beyond the glass, looking out for the arrival of the bride.

'You've loved every minute of this wedding prep and *now* you tell me I can run?'

'That was until…'

I turn my head, frown over the serious look in his eye. 'Until?'

'Until you both started walking around like you're on death row. Now I'm thinking you should release Elena from this madness and come up with some other plan to ensure your mother's happiness.'

I discreetly check behind me, make sure she hasn't over-heard, but she's still smiling, her hands folded in her lap. The green satin of her wraparound dress and matching headscarf enhance the colour of her eyes. Eyes that positively shine. No, she's happy, and I intend to keep it that way.

'That was before,' I say, sounding just like Gabe.

'Before…?'

'You want the quick version?'

'Not particularly…' his dark brows quirk up '…but, judging by the approaching officiant, you have seconds at most.'

My body tenses, all my senses attuned to Elena's imminent arrival as I fire back, 'I messed up. Acted like an idiot. Went to see her. Apologised. Explained. Fixed it. Okay? We're good.'

'You took the blame?' He grins as he settles back into position, hands clasped, shoulders back. 'Good on you.'

'You sure you don't want to rib me some more, there, mate?'

'Not at all. Sounds like you've paid your dues.'

I shake my head, give a tight chuckle.

Have I? Because I don't feel like it. I feel like there's a whole heap of unfinished business between us…business I have no place thinking about, let alone addressing.

'If we can all be upstanding for the bride…?'

The music being played by the string quartet changes and I take a breath that stutters as I recognise the song.

It's not…

It can't be.

But it is.

My smile grows as the memories hit me all at once. In every one of them she is there by my side. The TV is on, the tree is beside it, presents underneath, excitement is in the air. We're watching *Home Alone*, and everything feels bright and easy.

The joy of Christmases past warms my very soul, fuelled by the lyrics to 'Somewhere in My Memory', and I want to laugh, to cry, I want to tell her, *What a song!*

I turn just a little and her mother catches my eye, her teary smile wide. I try to return it, but I'm struggling to regain my breath. There's so much emotion swirling within my chest that there's no room for air.

Past and present combine.

Me and Laney.

What we've always had and what the future holds.

One is known, safe. The other…?

Tiny gasps sound from the rows of people, some sighs too, and I turn further, seeking out my…

Laney?

My jaw and my heart switch places, the former hitting the polished wood floor, the latter rising until I can do nothing but stare.

She's a vision. An absolute vision. And all dressed in red! In a ball gown fit for the vibrant star that she is. Slender straps fall into a heart-shaped bodice that enhances her curves and cinches her in at the waist. The dress flows to the floor in an abundance of colour. A festive delight!

I choke on a laugh that's half surprise, half desire, all pride. She's exquisite and all her. My Laney.

I face her fully and I don't care how I look—foolish, starstruck, lovestruck, even. Because in that moment she deserves it all. I don't blink until she's before me, her smile soft on her lips, her warm brown eyes sealed with mine.

'You take care of her, son,' her father murmurs, before turning to kiss her on the cheek. 'I love you, sweetheart.'

'You too, Dad,' she says, so softly I only just hear.

And then it's just us, at the head of the aisle, face to face. 'You look beautiful.'

'You approve?'

She sounds vulnerable...*looks* vulnerable.

'Not that you need me to, but *yes*. It's you and it's perfect.'

She blushes, and her mother rises up to touch a hand to her shoulder. 'I'll take your flowers, love.'

She twists to give Angie the bouquet, gifting me a glimpse of her back, of the way the fabric dips to the base of her spine, the way her hair trails over her rich olive skin and my mouth is dry. That dogged desire...so new and so impossible to suppress.

I tug my gaze away and mentally count to ten.

'Struggling there, bud?' Gabe murmurs, and I almost smack him one.

Dealing with my messed-up feelings for Elena with his teasing on top is too much.

'Are you ready?' the officiant whispers.

I give her a sharp nod, sense Elena do the same, because I cannot look. Not any more.

'Welcome, friends and family.' She smiles to the room, to us. 'We are gathered here today to witness the marriage of Elena and Aiden, to share in their happiness as they start the next chapter of their lives together...'

I feel as if my heart is trying to escape my chest. Sweat is breaking out from top to toe...cloying. I don't know whether it's the words, the heat of the room, or the heat of Elena herself...her presence, her proximity...just *her*.

'Today they express before you the love, respect and true friendship they share.'

I run a finger through the collar of my shirt, roll my shoulders back. The words are true. I feel them to my very bones, each and every one. Not a lie but an honest declaration of how I feel. So why do I feel suffocated? As if the room is closing in? As if I...?

Soft fingers brush the back of mine. Our hands are lightly touching. Did I move? Did she?

I turn just a little, take in her smile...hesitant, but present. Her eyes big and warm and open to me. To us.

'Together, they will be stronger, to face whatever the future holds.'

Oh, God, make that be so...

'Now for the vows. Please repeat after me...'

And so we do, we declare swiftly and smoothly that we know of no lawful impediment to our marriage.

Then, 'Do you, Aiden James Monroe, promise to give Elena Rosalie Martinez your honour, your devotion, and your love?'

I stare down into Elena's eyes, lose myself in their rich brown intensity as my body responds on cue. 'I do.'

Her lashes flutter, her blood-red lips part—to let in air or to release the tiniest of gasps? I'm not sure. Did my declaration cause it? Or the anticipation of her own?

'And do you, Elena Rosalie Martinez, promise to give Aiden James Monroe your honour, your devotion, and your love?'

She closes her mouth, the golden skin of her throat bobbing as she nods.

The officiant gives a soft laugh that's echoed by the people behind us. 'I'll need the words, Elena.'

'Sorry...' She bites her lip. 'I do.'

'Wonderful. Now for the rings...'

Gabe steps forward, palm outstretched with the two tiny circles of gold that carry so much weight.

'Aiden, if you'd like to...?'

I take up the smallest band, willing my fingers to steady. I never thought I'd see the day...

And you're not really seeing it now, either. This is an act, remember? The performance of your life.

And yet...

'A ring is an unbroken circle. It has no beginning and no end. It is a symbol of infinity and of your undying love for one another...'

Swallow. Breathe. This is all fine...not a lie. You will always love Laney. You will. She's your oldest friend.

As for the alien desire, the dream, the sudden need to wake up to those eyes each and every day... A blip? A momentary lapse of judgement that started the second I saw her in Milan and hasn't yet let up?

And maybe it never will. Now that my heart has made itself known, will it prove impossible to ignore?

'Each time you look at this ring, be reminded of this moment, of your commitment to one another and the love that you share. Aiden, place the ring on Elena's finger and repeat after me.'

I clear my throat, turn to her as she lifts her hand to mine. I smooth the ring onto her finger, savour the warmth and calming influence of her touch as I take the officiant's lead.

'Elena, I give you this ring as a symbol of our marriage...' I lift my gaze to hers, telling her with my all '...and as a token of my love and lasting friendship, always and for ever.'

'Wonderful. And now Elena...'

She takes the ring from Gabe's outstretched palm.

'Place the ring on Aiden's finger and repeat after me...'

I don't hear the officiant, only her, as she slips the ring onto my finger and softly declares, 'Aiden, I give you this ring as a symbol of our marriage and as a token of my love and lasting friendship...' She wets her lips, her voice thick with emotion but her hands around mine are steady and sure. 'Always and for ever.'

'Well done, both of you. Before these witnesses you have pledged to be joined in marriage and sealed that pledge with your wedding rings. Now, by the authority vested in me by the Province of Alberta, I pronounce you husband and wife. You may kiss the bride!'

She steps towards me and I reach for her. My dream comes back to me…reality takes over. I cup her face, feel her warmth beneath my palms, seek permission in her gaze to follow this through.

Instead of answering she presses her sweet mouth to mine.

A cheer goes up around us. A cheer that's driven away by the fierce pounding of my heart, the heat that encapsulates us. I feel like I'm drowning in a sea of sensation, of emotion. I don't know which way is up…where the ground is beneath my feet. I lose sight of where we are, what we're about—everything but the feel of her lips against mine and her hands in my hair…

It feels so right, so natural, and I want to lose myself in it completely.

Only I can't. I mustn't.

I pull back as we turn to face the room, hands clasped together, our stellar performance earning us smiles all round while inside I accept that, for me, it was no performance at all.

CHAPTER ELEVEN

Elena

WE'VE DONE IT.

Said our vows.

Sealed them with a kiss.

Dined and toasted with the room.

Gabe's roasted Aiden, and Dad's played the suitably gushing father of the bride.

And we've danced—danced until my feet hurt and it's still only eight in the evening, but I'm worried about Margot. I can see she's flagging.

Sitting at the edge of the makeshift dance floor, the soft-lit Christmas tree standing proud beside her, she's chatting with my mother, her posture steadily weakening.

'You okay?'

Aiden is sweeping me around to Justin Bieber's 'Mistletoe', his movements effortless, his ability to read my shifting mood all the more so.

'I'm fine...but I'm worried about your mother.'

He twirls me on the spot, follows my gaze. 'She does look tired.'

He eases us back together, leads us closer to her.

'You know she won't leave until we do,' I say.

'So, let's do it.'

'Do what?'

'Leave.'

'Like an over-eager, freshly married couple?'

'Why not? We wouldn't be the first newly married couple desperate to get some alone time.'

Alone time.

A thrilling shiver runs through my middle, as does trepidation. What happens when we're alone? Will I lose the doting, affectionate man I've been beside all day? The one who has lured me in along with our guests and left me wondering where the act ends and the truth begins?

Yesterday, he told me he loved me. Today, he pledged his love to me several times over in front of one and all. And I know he clarified his meaning the day before, but… I don't know. Something feels different. He seems different.

Have I just got too wrapped up in the excitement of the day? The abundance of love in the room? The glorious wedding and all the festive feels…

'You're glowing, Laney.'

'Am I?'

'Yes.'

He grins down at me and I realise he thinks I'm pondering our prospective alone time a little too intently. I elbow him in the ribs as we come to a stop in front of our mothers and he only grins more.

'All right, you two. Save those antics for later,' my mother teases.

'Mum!'

'What?' My father chooses that moment to sidle up. 'We were young and in love once too.'

I shake my head. 'Not what I want to think of right this second.'

'Wise, my dear,' Margot says, her accompanying chuckle tired, but happy. 'Very wise.'

'Has it been all you hoped it would be?' Mum asks.

'We should ask you both that,' Aiden says. 'You were the main orchestrators.'

They look at one another, their smiles easy and full of joy. 'It's been wonderful. But has it been the same for you?' Margot says. 'Because that's what matters most.'

'It's been great,' Aiden says, pulling me into his side with such ease that it feels natural, and normal, and so easy to believe we're a happily married couple about to embark on our next chapter together. 'And now we're going to call it a night on a high.'

'Already?' his mum says. 'I hope you're not worrying about—'

'Let them go, Margot.' My mother touches her hand, gives her a far too obvious wink which has Margot laughing once more.

'Right you are, then.'

'We'd say sleep well, but…'

'Mum!'

She waves down my repeated admonishment as she stands and pulls me into a tight hug. 'I love you, darling.' She releases me and tugs Aiden to her. 'I love you both.'

Dad is less gushy with his words, but no less emotional as he hugs us both too. 'Sleep well.'

'We've already covered that, Peter,' my mum teases.

'Night-night, Aiden, darling.' Margot stands and he bends to kiss her cheek.

'Night, Mum. Thank you for everything.'

'Any time, my love.'

They share a look that squeezes at my heart and brings tears to my eyes.

'Your father would be so proud.'

He gives a small smile. 'I know.'

'And you, Elena, sweetheart…you are everything we ever wanted in a daughter-in-law. I am so, so happy and proud. I love you.'

Oh, God. If I wasn't breaking down before, I am now. 'I love you too, Margot.'

'Shall we?' he says, forking his fingers through mine, his

eyes unreadable but blazing with something. Something strong and profound.

Was it the mention of his father, the affection of my parents, the love of his mother…or is he fiercely battling the lie?

'Your carriage awaits,' Margot says, tugging my attention back to her.

'Our carriage…?'

'You'll see,' she says.

Aiden says nothing as he leads me outside and I'm drawn up short, my gasp smothered by my palm. Waiting for us are two shire horses, a coachman, and a sleigh adorned with thick blankets and festive garlands.

The coachman hurries forward with a fur cloak that Aiden wraps around my shoulders and I laugh, steam rising from my lips.

'I can't believe this.'

'Believe it.' He adjusts the cloak around me. 'Are you going to be warm enough?'

'With you and this cloak I'll be deliciously toasty.'

Something flickers across his face…something I fail to read yet again and it's driving me crazy.

'This way, if you please…' the coachman says, gesturing towards the sleigh.

I shake my head as I walk in step with Aiden, struggling to keep a hold on reality. This is too surreal, too beautiful, too romantic. We climb aboard and Aiden pulls a blanket over our thighs as the coachman reaches for the bottle of champagne nestled in the front.

'I've got this,' Aiden says, and the coachman nods, returning to his box seat.

'I really shouldn't,' I say as he uncorks the bottle.

'Scared you've had too much already?'

'That's a given. You know I'm a lightweight.'

He grins as the cork pops free. 'You're safe with me, Laney.'

More's the pity.

It's only when his brows rise that I realise I've said it out loud and I curse, my cheeks flushing pink. 'That's not— I didn't—'

The sleigh lurches forward, breaking the awkward moment, and the coachman turns. 'Just some snow stuck under the wheels,' he tells us. 'It will be smoother now we're moving.'

I squeak some inaudible response. Smoother? How could it possibly be smoother when I'm already losing control of my tongue and we've not been married a day…?

Aiden silently offers me a glass, and I sink deeper into the gloriously soft cushions and pray he doesn't press.

And then I see the fairy lights in the trees that line the track connecting the main lodge to the small cabin and shoot back up.

'Adie!' I gasp out. 'When did they…? How did they…? Without us noticing, too!'

'This one is on me and Gabe,' he says, watching my reaction. 'I knew you'd love it.'

Just like he knew about the ruby...

'You always talked about a horse and carriage… I figured a sleigh was the next best thing. As for the lights…how could I not give you a winter wonderland to travel through when you've given me so much?'

'Adie!' Tears spike anew, my happiness overflowing as I wrap my arms around him, champagne flute and all, and kiss his cheek. 'It's magical!'

'And it's all for you, Laney.'

'Considering how much you hated doing the Christmas lights, to have done all this for me…'

His smile dazzles my racing heart and I have to look away before I say something stupid that I can't take back.

'It couldn't be more perfect,' I whisper, snuggling down into his side and cherishing it for what it is.

A gesture of friendship, of gratitude, just as the ring had been.

'No.' He presses a kiss to my hair. 'No, it couldn't.'

Aiden

I'm suffocating with it. Whatever it is. I couldn't even tell you.

All I know is that it's there, like a bursting weight trying to escape my chest, and no matter what I do it keeps on expanding.

As I help her down from the carriage, her face aglow, her eyes bright as they lift to mine, I can feel it rising up inside me, choking off my ability to breathe, making me dizzy.

'You okay?' she asks, taking her hand from mine and gripping the cloak together at the front.

I swear I was asking her that question not an hour ago, on the dance floor, when she was looking rather pale. Is that how I look now? Pale? Ill at ease? Ready to run?

'I will be when I get out of these clothes.'

She gives a small smile. 'You do look rather handsome, though.'

I thank the driver and he urges the horses on. The bells on the back of the sleigh jingle into the night, and the *JUST MARRIED* bunting draped across the back dances in the fairy lights, taunting me further.

'It's a little over the top, if you ask me,' I say.

And just what are you referring to? Your clothing or the whole day?

'If you think *you're* looking over the top, how do you see me?'

I let my gaze trail over her, as if I need a reminder of how attractive she looks, sinfully so in scarlet, and I swear I don't breathe.

She tilts her head to one side, her breath escaping her blood-red lips in a twisting cloud, her big brown eyes dark and pinning me in place. Her cheeks turn rosy—from the cold or the look in my eye, I'm not sure.

'There isn't a single word capable of summing up how amazing you look, Laney.'

She presses her lips together. 'Good answer.'

'I mean it.'

'I know.'

Does she know? Like, truly know?

Because if she does, surely she wouldn't be walking into this lodge with me alone.

Because I don't feel like her best friend right now.

I don't want to be her best friend right now.

I want to be so much more. I want to cross that line, and to hell with the consequences. Because I want her. More than I want my own soul.

'You fancy a nightcap?' I say tightly, knowing full well I don't need more to drink, but needing to say something to distract myself from the rising tension in the air.

Tension I've put there with my wayward thoughts.

Thoughts that don't belong where Laney is concerned.

'Sure, why not?'

We head inside the lodge and she heads to the stairs, stripping off her cloak and hooking it over the newel post.

'Bring me one up, won't you?' she turns to say, her lashes lowered, her mouth softly parted.

Is she...is she *flirting* with me?

I open my mouth to say yes, but nothing comes out. It's bone-dry at the sight of her. The dress dipping low at her back...her hair skimming the exposed skin that shimmers gold in the lamplight... I fist my hand against the itch to caress her just there.

'I will.'

It's barely audible as she disappears up, the train of her dress leaving a seductive red trail to follow.

You're losing it!

It's this blasted day. This blasted suit. Her exquisite dress. The string of congratulations and 'we knew you were made for each other' remarks playing havoc with my control.

I stride to the drinks cabinet and pour us both a bourbon,

knock mine back and refresh it just as quickly before heading up the stairs.

Kicking open the door, I head on in. 'These clothes have to go...'

'My sentiments exactly.'

She's standing before the mirror, eyeing me in open horror as she registers the words that came out of her mouth.

'That's not— That wasn't— I was just...'

'Are you lost for words, Laney?'

I try to laugh. I *want* to laugh. I want to pretend that the first thought that hit me wasn't to cross the room and free her of her own clothes.

'I meant I was trying to get out of this thing, but it isn't a one-person job.' The colour in her cheeks deepens. 'That sounded better in my head too.'

Okay, so we're on the same wavelength...

Though she's talking about necessity. You're talking about your libido.

Very different things.

'One second.'

I pop our glasses on the bedside table, try not to notice the rose petals sprinkled liberally over the furs and plush pillows.

'I think that might have been Avery's doing...' she says, spying my focus.

'Right...'

Cheers, sis.

'Very romantic.'

'You can't blame her—it's really quite sweet.'

I come up behind her, urge my pulse to steady, my fingers too, as I focus on the hidden fastening she's struggling to undo.

'What's wrong?' she says, sweeping her hair over one shoulder to grant me better access...a better view too. 'Adie?'

'Huh?' I force myself to meet her gaze in the mirror.

'You look like you're heading into battle.'

I give a tight chuckle. 'I don't know...' I eye the innocent task at hand, though it feels anything but. 'This looks fairly complicated.'

She laughs too, the sound rippling along her delicate spine, the warmth of her body teasing at my fingers.

'I'm sure you're quite capable...and let's face it: it's not the first time you've undressed a woman.'

'It's the first time I've undressed you...'

It comes out unthinkingly and now I am thinking of it. Thinking of it and so much more. And I'm done for. Damned.

'Not true—or have you forgotten that night in college?'

'Ah, Elena Martinez...drunk and disorderly. Those nights were few and far between.'

'And for that my hangovers are grateful.'

I take a breath, try to use her easy camaraderie to drag myself back from the brink. Instead I get a hit of her scent—sugar and spice and all things nice.

'So...?'

'So?' I repeat, strained, desperate.

'Are you going to...?'

Her brows lift, and her eyes are dark and sparkling with gold as she wriggles, her luscious rear brushing against my sensitised front. Electrifying. Tantalising. Distracting beyond measure.

It takes my all to force my body to follow instructions.

Unhook the dress.

Unzip the dress.

Don't catch her skin—her soft, warm, enticing skin...

I curl my fingers into my palms, press back every urge. 'Better?'

I step away quickly, avert my gaze from her and the mirror, knowing it'll be written in my face—the heat, the desire...

'Thank you.'

Her voice is low, hesitant, as she turns to face me, clutching the dress to her chest to keep it in place. And still I daren't look. Neither can I move further away. I feel as if I'm caught in a web…a web she's unintentionally spun.

'Aiden?'

I don't answer, and she takes a small step forward.

'Aiden?'

'Elena, I don't know what's going on,' I blurt, 'but I don't trust myself around you right now.'

It comes out in a rush, unplanned and too honest.

'Why?'

I can't answer her.

'Adie? Tell me.'

You have to give her something…

My gaze collides with hers and the truth spills from my lips. 'Because I want you.'

Not what you should be saying…

'And I know I shouldn't, and that this is messed up, and it makes me the worst kind of friend imaginable, but right now…with you…us…like this…' I wave a hand between us. 'I can't be here.'

I jerk away and she tugs me back, her dress hitting the deck in the same swift move. She's naked save for a strip of white lace low on her hips, white stockings up to her thighs. Her bare breasts are undulating with her shallow breaths, their tawny peaks upturned to me.

'Yes, you can.'

Desire whips through me, my brain rapidly piecing together her meaning and the look in her eye. 'What are you saying?'

'I'm saying…'

She takes another step, her gaze and her hand locked with mine, and I can read her answer before she says it, soft but sure.

'I want you too.'

An elated rush consumes me, forcing out a growl-cum-curse as I pull her to me in one sharp move. Our mouths collide in a mashing of lips and a clashing of teeth. It's wild and frenzied, and so far from skilled, but it is the sexiest damn kiss I've ever shared.

She shoves my jacket to the floor as I kiss her this way and that, changing angle, desperate for more, unable to get enough. *Never* enough.

She lifts her stocking-clad thigh to wrap her leg around me, pull me closer. Her breasts push up against my shirt, her nipples needling my clothed chest in an accidental tease that's as provocative as her eager mouth against mine.

'I can't believe how much I want you,' I rasp.

'I can.' Her eyes are hungry as they rake over my face. 'Because I feel it too.'

And then she's kissing me, pulling my tie free as I unbutton my shirt and flick it away, not once breaking the kiss that still isn't deep enough.

I fork my fingers through her hair, curse the pins that hold the braid in place. I want them gone. I want her hair flowing into my hands, its lustrous thickness spilling over her naked shoulders.

I want her above me, under me, every which way…

But this is Laney, comes that inner voice. *Laney!*

'Are you sure about his?' I say against her lips, the words rough, my mouth rougher still.

'Never surer.'

But what happens after?

She palms my groin, and the question disintegrates in a burst of heat.

If I'm going to hell, she's coming with me, and I can't think of anyone I'd want beside me more. Not in life, not in death, not ever.

I loop my belt free as she presses me back towards the bed, unzip my trousers, thrust one leg out, then the other. I drop back onto the mattress, strip off my socks, and then she's there above me. Knees planted either side of my hips, her sweet and perfect breasts at eye level.

My fingers tremble as I caress one, then the other, roll the hardened peaks with the pad of my thumb, cherish the way she arches back, her moan sinfully rich.

'You are exquisite, Elena. Impossibly so.'

She rocks over my hardness, her eyes all chocolate and fire. 'I want you, Adie.'

I flip her under me in one deft move, kiss her lips that have the power to make me feel so much. I trail my hand down her front, stroke away the rose petal that has made a home in her belly button, feel her skin prickle and her body writhe, urging me lower. I reach the lace band of her knickers and hold her gaze as I slip inside. She rocks back into the pillow, her lip caught in her teeth as her eyes glaze over. She's wet. So very wet for me.

Never more my Laney.

I roll over her beaded clitoris, treasure the way the colour in her cheeks deepens, the way she whimpers. One hand claws at the bedding, the other at my shoulder.

'You are beautiful, Laney.' I keep up the caress, driving her higher, my breath hitching with hers, my body tensing as she pulls taut. 'So beautiful...'

She shatters beneath me, her cry everything to my confused heart, which can't make sense of this connection. And right now it doesn't want to.

Elena

Everything about this moment is perfect.

The connection, his words, the orgasm that has rocked me to my very core.

But still I want more. I want him.

I press him back into the bed, kiss him slowly, savouring him, reacquainting myself with his mouth, his taste, his tongue.

Whether I'm on borrowed time or not, I treat him like I am.

I trail kisses down his chest, every ridge an avenue to be explored, teased, cherished. I reach the band of his briefs and ease them down. His groan is rough, like gravel, his need for me spurring on my hunger, my confidence, my love.

I tug the clothing aside and stroke my hands back up along his thighs, relish the way his muscles flex beneath my touch. His strength is a turn-on like none other. And then I take hold of his erection and he bucks up, his hand reaching into my hair.

'Careful, Laney.'

I smile up at him. 'I'm always careful…'

I kiss the tip and he shudders, gives a hiss between his teeth as he fists the sheets either side of him. His eyes burn into mine, follow my every move as I travel the length of him, kissing, tasting, taking him all. His breaths shorten, his body pulses…

'Laney?' he rasps out, his hand cupping my jaw, forcing me to pause.

I rise up, meet his eye. Though I'm not sure what he's asking, and I'm not sure he even knows.

'I'm on the pill,' I say, making a guess.

He runs his teeth over his bottom lip, his eyes grazing over my naked skin, his cheeks streaked with colour and so sexy with it.

'I want you.'

Happiness, pleasure, desire fizzes through my veins. The idea that he can't stop saying those three words is an intoxicating cocktail that I never want to be without.

'I want you too.'

I lower myself over him, eyes locked on his, devouring his every reaction as I devour him. The corded muscles in his neck, his grip on my thighs, the green eyes that blaze and burn, and the low groan that makes me feel empowered, owning my feelings for him just as I own the desire that we clearly share.

He fills me so completely, in every way imaginable, and as I move with him I feel it. All the love, all the desire, building within me. Such pleasure coils through my body as my heart beats wild and free, finally permitted to express how it feels in the most intimate of ways, with the one and only man I've ever loved and will always love.

'Oh, my God, Laney. I can't—I can't hold back.'

'I don't want you to hold back. I want you to let go. I want you to let go for me.'

And, crying out my name, he thrusts into me, his growl so fierce I swear it shakes the very rafters.

I find my release with his. My body pulsing as the words slip from my lips unbidden. 'I love you, Adie.'

I collapse forward, my body limp over his, and sense the moment my words hit home.

The moment the tension seeps back into his body.

The moment he realises that my 'I love you' is very different from his 'I love you' of the day before.

But it's okay. Surely, it's okay now. We've just *made love*!

'Adie?'

He says nothing and I press myself up on his chest, our bodies still entwined.

'What is it?'

He's staring at the ceiling as if he's keeping it in situ with his mind.

'Say something Adie...*please.*'

'What is there to say?'

'I don't know.' I feel a spark of anger. The sudden shift in him, dizzying and unsettling, and anger is far better than the hurt I don't want to let in. 'Something like, *What a perfect end to a perfect day.* That would suffice.'

'We had sex.'

'We had sex on our wedding day, yes.'

'Our wedding day that isn't real.'

I give a choked laugh, fear rising within me that I'm desperate to quash. Because he has to see it. Doesn't he? That this—us—works.

'The consummating of it certainly felt real. In fact I can still feel you right—'

He rolls from under me in a heartbeat. His feet hit the floor and the muscles of his back bunch together as he grips the edge of the bed.

I reach out, touch a hand to his shoulder. 'Adie…?'

He flinches away and it's like a chilled spear straight through my heart.

'That was a mistake.'

I force my mouth to close, swallow… I didn't hear him right. I couldn't have heard him right. I feel like I've been doused in ice, goosebumps spreading across my skin as I pull the sheet to my chest.

'It didn't feel like a mistake. Not to me.'

He shakes his head, chokes on a laugh that's filled with anguish. 'This whole thing is a mistake.'

'Thing?'

'Us! This act! It's gone to our heads. We've lost sight of who we are. What this is.'

'I hate to tell you, Adie, but I've always known what this is for me.' I lift my chin, force the truth out. Because I owe him this just as much as I owe it to myself. 'I've been aware of my love for you for a very long time.'

He twists his head, his sharp frown pinning me in place. 'What do you mean?'

Panic flutters up my throat. I don't recognise him like this. His face so contorted. The walls going up. The rejection too.

'What do you mean, Elena?'

Lie, for heaven's sake, lie.

I can't. I'm done with acting. I'm done with pretending this is something it's not.

'I'm in love with you, Adie. I've been in love with you for years.'

'You *love* me?'

I give a weak smile. 'It's not so different to what you said to me yesterday.'

He blinks, as though remembering. 'But that wasn't— I didn't mean… You know I didn't mean it in that way.'

'Do you see what we just shared as platonic, Adie? Seriously? Because if that's how you treat your female friends, I feel pretty disappointed to have missed out all these years.'

He shakes his head. 'This isn't funny, Laney.'

'No. It isn't. But it's the truth. You can run from it all you like, but I'm in love with you. And I think if you're honest with yourself, you'll realise that you're in love with me too.'

It's brave—arrogant, even. But today I witnessed it in him. I'm *sure* I did.

'You're crazy.'

He presses himself up off the bed, stalks to the window. The snow-dusted trees shimmer in the moonlight, the scene a dark contrast to his naked body, all golden in the lamplight.

'I'm no crazier than I was when I agreed to this marriage.'

'You *can't* love me,' he says to the glass, his voice hoarse.

I ease myself out of bed, tuck the sheet around me as I close the distance between us.

'That's where you're wrong,' I say, leaving a trail of fallen petals in my wake. 'I'm the one who's lived with this for as long as I have. I'm the one who's failed to have a decent relationship all these years because my heart was already yours.'

He shakes his head, chokes out, 'It's not possible.'

'Why?'

'Because you *know* me, Laney. You *know* I could never love you back—not in the way you would want, not in the way you would deserve.'

'I know your reasoning, Adie, and I know why you've shut love out. I know you say you don't want it, that you can't—'

'I don't just say it. I feel it.'

'I think you feel more than you care to admit.'

Again I offer a reassuring hand, and again he flinches away.

I swallow the bitter tang of rejection and try again, 'If you'd just—'

'Don't, Elena. Whatever you think you see in me, you're wrong! I won't do this. I won't risk what we have for something I can't give you.'

'Then why make love to me?'

His jaw pulses…the muscles in his back twitch. 'Because that's the kind of selfish bastard I am.'

If he'd struck me I couldn't be more winded. 'Don't say that.'

'Why not, Laney?' He spins to face me, his tormented green eyes piercing in their pain. 'Because you don't want to hear it? You don't want to accept the cold, hard truth?'

'You're no bastard. Selfish or otherwise.'

'And you're either a fool or a liar. Because this is the man I am. *This!*' He pounds his chest. 'Not the fantastical creature you have me painted as in your head, but the cold, manipulative bastard who never should have taken advantage of your good, kind heart and embroiled you in all of this!'

'Stop it, Adie.'

'Not until you see the truth! I will always put myself, my family and my company first.'

I lift my chin. 'You've never put yourself first, Aiden. Not in all the years I've known you.'

His laugh is harsh, grating my every nerve.

'I played on your good nature and abused our friendship. Asked you to give up your life for months, possibly more. To lie to those you love, to put your reputation at risk, the public's opinion of you, the press. All because I needed you to make my mother happy.'

'For your mother—not for you.'

'Tonight certainly wasn't about my mother. That was about me taking what I wanted for myself and to hell with the consequences. I knew the risks to you, to our friendship, and I did it anyway.'

'Have you forgotten that I wanted you too?'

'Because you thought there was something in me that doesn't exist!'

He has my heart in a vice-like grip, every word squeezing it tighter.

'You say that I can't tell you how you feel, Laney. Trust me when I tell you it works both ways. I can never be the man you need me to be, and it's better you see it now, rather than months down the line, when you've convinced yourself that this farce of a marriage can work. Unless…'

A shadow flickers across his face and the hairs on the back of my neck prickle.

'Is that—? Did you say yes in the hope you could *change* me?'

I open my mouth but nothing comes out. I refuse to lie to him, but the truth will only condemn me further.

'Is that what all this has been for you? Making out you were doing it for me, when really it was some twisted attempt at changing me, hoping that I'll—what?—see the light and *fall in love with you*?'

The scorn in his voice cripples me…his accuracy too. 'It wasn't like that.'

Only, it was…in part…

And what a fool I am.

'No?' He gives a disbelieving scoff as he rakes an unsteady hand through his hair, paces away. Curses. 'How could I have been so stupid? So blind to it too? All those conversations delving into my past, the future, trying to make me question…'

I fall forward a step, my knees threatening to buckle as I seek to make a connection—any connection that isn't this.

'I did that because I care. Because I wanted you to take a proper look at your life. I wanted to remind you of those dreams you once had…before your life got chosen for you.'

'And all the while you knew how you felt? All these years

you've been harbouring these—these feelings for me and never said a word?'

'Because you wouldn't have wanted to hear it.'

'And I don't want to hear it now!' he throws back at me.

I stare at him hard, fire warming my veins, my truth an antidote to his chilling rejection.

'Well, tough. Because I'm telling you. You want the truth? A reality check, even? I'll give you one.'

Because he has one thing right. I should have owned up to my feelings long ago. Owned up to them, dealt with them and moved on.

'All these years I kept it to myself because I was scared it would push you away. And you meant too much to me to take that risk. I decided that I'd rather have my best friend in my life than nothing at all. So I agreed to this marriage, knowing how I felt, knowing that it would bring me so much closer to my dream, and that walking away from it when the time was right would break me. I did it because I love you. I did it because helping you was more important than protecting myself. I did it because that's what love is, Adie. It's taking a risk on the unknown, putting someone else first and trusting your heart with them completely.'

His pallor deepens with every word, his eyes awash with thoughts I'm not privy to and likely don't want to be.

'Even when they don't deserve it, Laney?' he says quietly 'Even when months down the line you'll resent me for my work, the time I spend away…? Or, worse, you'll love me for it regardless, waiting in vain for the day I'll put you first and make you happy in return.'

'You're talking about your parents…'

'I'm talking about them and every relationship I've ever been foolish enough to form. I refuse to let that happen with you.'

'So you won't even try?'

'My father tried and it killed him.'

'No, your father was a workaholic, with an undiagnosed heart condition as you were quick to tell me. But he loved your mother…he loved you and Avery. He let love in and—'

'And failed to be enough.'

'Adie, you can't—'

'This wasn't what I wanted, Laney,' he insists, talking over me. 'None of this.' He sounds defeated, broken, but resolutely unchanged. 'It was meant to be safe, this whole arrangement. This marriage. Secured by our friendship. A known entity. No surprises. No one was supposed to get hurt.'

'That's life, Adie,' I say, frustration and pain giving me the strength I need. 'Full of surprises, horrid or otherwise. We don't always get what we want, and you know that better than most. But at least I'm finally brave enough to own up to my feelings and risk what comes next. Can you honestly say the same?'

He stares back at me, naked, ghost-like, and so very lost.

'I didn't think so.' I shake my head, look away. 'Just go, Adie. You've delivered your message, loud and clear. Consider me a fool no more.'

My voice cracks and he steps towards me, reaches out. 'Laney…'

'Don't!' I can't handle it. Not his pity. 'Just go, Aiden. Run like I know you want to.'

I hold my breath, grip the sheet to my chest so tight I know it will be bruised come morning. But it gives me something to focus on. Something that isn't his quietly exiting form and the aching void he leaves within me.

I brought this on myself. All these years I've spent secretly hoping, secretly dreaming, failing at relationships…

Well, no more.

It's time to move on—starting now.

CHAPTER TWELVE

Aiden

I SLEEP IN the spare room. Or rather, I spend the night there.

Snatches of sleep, induced by bourbon and terrorised by nightmares that have too much bearing on reality.

Reliving her words over and over. Haunted by the way she looked wrapped in that single sheet. Haunted all the more by the words I tossed her way, carelessly and callously.

She's never going to speak to me again.

I never wanted to lose Laney, and yet I've done exactly that. Pushed her away. Because she's right. I am scared. I'm freaking terrified.

'I'm in love with you, Adie. I've been in love with you for years.'

And I mocked her. Ripped her apart when she was at her most vulnerable. All because I couldn't face up to it. The truth. The real truth.

That I'm hopelessly in love with her too and fear she'll be my greatest ever failing.

Because to love Elena and not be enough—I couldn't bear it.

But to lose Elena so completely...

I shoot up in bed. Clench my head in my hands as if that can somehow do away with it all.

I need to go to her.

I need to explain myself better.

I need to make it right.

Above all, I need to win her back.

It's the one thing I cling to as I tug on the clothes from the day before and head to her room. *Our* room.

I knock gently. Unsure.

Knock again. More certain.

No answer.

She doesn't want to see you, comes the inner voice.

I push open the door as I defy it, stride in, 'Look, Laney, we can't—'

I freeze. She's gone. No trace of her in sight.

The bed is still crumpled from where we lay, darkened rose petals mixed up in the sheets. I see flashes of her naked above me, beneath me, standing in the pool of her dress...

It all feels surreal now, in the deserted room.

No toiletries, no clothing, no paraphernalia on the dressing table.

But it's her lack of presence I feel most. No warmth. No scent. No noise. Just...nothing.

And that's when I spy the glint of gold on the bedside table. Two rings, one resting at an angle on the other. The ruby engagement ring and her wedding band.

I grip the ring that still resides on my finger, squeeze it tight.

'Laney...' It croaks out of me. Hoarse with fresh pain. She can't have gone. She can't.

I turn away, stumble for the door, race down the stairs, call her name as I check every room even though I know she isn't here. I can feel it in the emptiness within.

I thrust the main door open and it bounces on its hinges. I cry out her name to the forest, barely aware of the chilling wind that assaults me.

I feel ravaged. Bereft.

But you brought this on yourself.

Rejected her love and my own in turn.

And I called *her* the fool, the liar...

You're the only lying fool here.

I trudge towards the lodge, the forest dark in the early dawn as my gaze darts this way and that, seeking any sign that she came this way.

But who am I kidding? She left long ago and fresh snow has fallen in between.

I reach the house, suck in a breath as I head inside and pray that she's here, that I can fix this. I don't care that I'll have questions to answer. I only care that she's here.

'Elena! Elena!'

I scour the hallway, the living room, the kitchen. I hit the stairs two at a time, catching my shirt-tail on the banister garland and ripping it free.

'Elena!'

My mother's door opens and she appears, pulling on a dressing gown, her hair all mussed up and exposed. The thinning layers obvious without her headscarf and my mounting despair robs me of my breath.

'Hush, love!' She hurries forward. 'Do you want to wake the whole house?'

She frowns as she takes in the state of me, ushers me back downstairs before Elena's parents can get wind.

'What's happened? Why are you still dressed in that and where's Elena?'

'I don't know.'

'What do you mean, you don't know?'

We head into the kitchen and I sink onto a stool, my head in my hands as my body shakes with the truth.

'She's gone…she's gone and I have no idea where.'

'What have you done?'

There was a time, a place when I would have replied on impulse 'why do you assume it's me?', instead I look up, meet her concerned gaze, and say, 'What *haven't* I done?'

'Oh, darling.' She pulls me to her chest, kisses my head as I shudder and shake. 'I'm going to make us some tea and you're going to tell me everything.'

'You don't need to hear this, Mum.'

'That's where you're wrong. And the longer you take to tell me, the worse my imagination will get.' She moves away and sets the kettle boiling, then turns to face me, arms folded. 'Tell me, Aiden, and don't spare a detail. Because it can't be any worse than what I'm currently thinking.'

I swallow. Can't it? Is she sure about that? Because I'm not.

'Aiden, please. I'm your mother. I love you and I love Elena and I want you both to be happy. That's all I care about. And whatever this is, I'm sure we can fix it.'

I wish I had her confidence.

And so I do. I tell her everything. From my fake proposal— oddly, she doesn't even flinch at that—to Elena's acceptance and our wish to keep up the act, to keep everyone happy, right up to last night's argument, and my fear that though I love her I can never be enough.

'Oh, my dear boy, you've always been clever—a complete over-achiever, working all hours to keep the plates spinning. Just like your father.' She gives a sad smile as she places two steaming mugs of tea before us. 'And he was a good man, Aiden, truly he was. When I lost him I was devastated, un- able to see a way of living my life and enjoying it again. And I know I made it so much harder for you.'

'You were heartbroken,' I say, struggling to see where this is going.

'But I should have been stronger. For you and for Avery. We should have been cherishing our memories of Christmases past, not avoiding making new ones. Your father gave me so much joy over the years, and I loved him with all my heart. I know we fought. I know I wanted him to work less, be with us more. But my biggest regret is the pressure we put on you. Making you feel like your life was mapped out for you. Your father was so blinded by the idea of his legacy being yours that I fear he lost sight of whether it made you happy.'

'It was *his* father's legacy before that…'

'And he knew no different. But he wouldn't want you putting your dreams on hold for his. And he certainly wouldn't want you passing up on a life with Elena because of the example he set. Just because your father couldn't let work go, it doesn't mean you have to be the same, darling. But then you know my thoughts well enough, since it drove you to this point…'

'It's not your fault, Mum. You didn't force me to put a ring on Laney's finger. I did that all by myself.'

'Regardless, I should have put a stop to it.'

'You couldn't have known.'

Her mouth purses and she looks off to the side as she sweeps a stray lock behind her ear and avoids my eye.

'Mum? You *didn't* know, did you?'

Her gaze inches back to me, her lips press together.

'Mum…'

'It's not how you think.' She starts clearing away the tea we haven't even drunk. Then she stops. Looks back at me. 'Actually. It is how you think. Angie and I suspected there was something going on. That you weren't telling us the whole truth and that it had more to do with me and my—my health, than it did your love for one another.'

'And you didn't say anything?'

'Because I hoped that given time, you'd see what we always saw…'

'That Laney and I were made for one another.' I repeat the phrase I've heard over and over and curse. 'I don't believe this.'

'I'm sorry, darling, it was wrong of me…of us. If I'd known it would end up like this, with the two of you so hurt…' She shakes her head. 'We never should have pushed you into marriage so quickly…we should have given you both more time. But I…' she swallows.

'Next you'll be telling me you faked your whole illness just to see me married off.'

It's a low blow, but I'm feeling sick to my stomach. I put

Elena through all this for nothing and now I've lost her. My best friend and the love of my life. My wife.

Mum gives a sad laugh, touches her hand to my arm where the cuff of my shirt hangs loose.

'No, darling. I think we both know that's very real.'

I see the sadness in her eyes, and I see something else too… something akin to hope.

'As real as your love for Elena.'

'And now I've lost her.'

'You haven't lost her.'

'But those things I said to her…they were real too. The hurt I inflicted…how can I take it back?'

'You can't. You face it head-on. You take accountability for your actions and you explain yourself. Elena knows you, love. She knows those words were born of panic. Tell her the truth. Tell her how you really feel and bring her back here. Where she truly belongs.'

'But I don't even know where she is.'

'I think I can help with that.'

Our heads snap to the open doorway, to where Elena's mum now stands, her face as pale as her nightgown.

'But you need to convince me of your intentions first.'

Elena

I peer out of my B&B room window and shudder. It's funny. In all the time I've been in Banff I've not felt the cold once. But now, without Aiden, I feel it. And not even my thick roll-neck sweater can keep out the chill.

I wrap my arms around my middle and step away from the window, screwing my face up. Okay, so maybe the snowy scene of the town outdoors is preferable to the view within. This dingy room above the Irish-themed pub was the best I could get with Christmas in full swing, but it beat waking up on Monroe land this Christmas morning.

I'll show my face there later and then I'll clear out. Somewhere hot and sunny and as far away from the memories of this past month with Aiden as I can get.

I head to the small desk, push aside the lamp that swings precariously on its base and pick at the breakfast I ordered. It looks the part. A full English and the perfect hangover cure. Only it's not an abundance of alcohol that's making me feel nauseous. It's love.

And there's nothing worse than the unrequited kind.

Especially when I can't bear the thought of losing him so entirely.

Maybe another year and we'll see fit to be on good terms again.

Good terms.

It sounds so cold and unfeeling, when not twenty-four hours ago we couldn't have been closer, our naked bodies irrefutably linked and love—or what I thought was love—spilling from our every pore.

But hindsight is a wonderful thing. I know the old romantic in me put that love there, and I'll never be so disillusioned again.

Aiden couldn't have been clearer about the way he felt. The way he *feels*.

It was me who forced love into the equation. It was me who moved the goalposts on him. Shifted the dynamic so completely.

It was me who ruined it by pushing him into acknowledging something that only existed for me.

But I'd been caught up in the moment. In the beauty of the day. My feelings overflowing, out of my control, and all because he wanted me.

I should have known better. I should have known that sex didn't mean more—not for Aiden. He swore off love long ago, but never sex. And I'd been just another notch.

My stomach rolls anew and I throw down my fork, head back to the window. Take in the walkers with their happy, festive faces, kids running around with shiny new toys, a couple who pause to kiss under the sprig of mistletoe hanging from a lamppost. Their loved-up gaze cutting through the very heart of me.

And then I see a man—a man who looks so much like Aiden I don't breathe for a spell. He scours the buildings, eyes peering out beneath a charcoal-grey beanie, cheeks flushed pink from the cold and the collar of his coat pulled high. Snow clings to his lashes as he pauses and blinks up at my window.

It is Aiden!

What is he—?

How is he—?

Why is he—?

I turn away from the window, then peer back, but he's gone. I hear the entry bell on the door downstairs, the murmur of voices through the floorboards and heavy boots on the stairs.

The thick Irish burr of the landlord's voice comes through my door, along with a sharp knock that has my body jumping and my heart kickstarting.

'Miss Martinez, you have a visitor. Says his name is Aiden Monroe.'

I take a shaky breath, run my suddenly sweaty palms down my jumper.

'Miss Martinez?'

'Coming!' I call back.

I pat at my hair, glance in the cracked mirror on the wall and wince. I look as bad as I feel. But what does it matter? He has little interest in how I look. Although the fact he's here must mean he still cares. Even if it's just a little.

I pull open the door before I can hesitate any more, and sure enough there he is. Standing over the landlord, his green eyes piercingly bright in the dark hallway.

'Thanks for showing him up,' I say, my gaze unable to leave Aiden's.

He mutters something about playing butler, and asks where do these posh folk get off as he walks away, but I'm too aware of Aiden…too aware of my heart trying to break free of my chest.

'Merry Christmas, Laney,' he says gruffly.

Merry Christmas?

Is he serious?

I shake my head, step back to let him in. 'How did you find me?'

It's not the most important question, but it's certainly the least contentious.

I close the door and stand before it, keeping my distance as he takes in the poky room with its single bed, the damp patch in the ceiling, the fridge that sounds like it might take flight and a sink that has seen better days.

'You're staying here?'

I cross my arms once more, fending off a very different kind of chill. 'There aren't a lot of vacancies at Christmas. Too many folk in town, visiting family.'

'Which is where you should be.'

I give a soft huff. 'I didn't feel welcome any more.'

'You'll always be welcome with the Monroes, Laney. Don't ever doubt that.'

I fight the uncontrollable warmth his words trigger—a warmth that only makes me want to cry more.

'Be that as it may… I needed space last night and I was lucky to find this place.'

'I wish you'd come to me first.'

'What? So, we could share a proper goodbye?' I laugh at the very idea of it. 'No, thanks. Like I told you, I got the message loud and clear. I thought you'd be relieved to see me and my foolish heart gone.'

He curses under his breath. 'Laney, please…that's the last thing I wanted.'

He sounds honest enough, and he looks remorseful enough. But neither matter. Not with his cutting rejection still so fresh within me.

'Why are you here, Aiden?'

He steps towards me and I back up.

'You can say it from there.'

He stops, hesitates, pulls the hat from his head and clutches it before him. 'I don't know where to start.'

My laugh is a scoff. 'You had plenty to say last night.'

He blanches, his throat bobbing. 'And it was all wrong.'

I frown. 'Which bit, exactly? Where you accused me of being crazy? A fool? A liar, even?'

He winces with every word. 'All of it. Laney, I can't even— I'm so sorry.'

I can feel my resolve weakening in the face of his contrition and I move before any more damage can be done, reaching to unlock the door.

'Apology accepted. Consider yourself forgiven. You can leave now—though I'd appreciate you making yourself scarce when I call by later to see—'

'I love you, Laney.'

It's so quiet, so soft, I'm not even sure I hear him right. I lift my gaze to his and feel his hand cover mine on the lock.

'What did you just say?'

Slowly, he peels my fingers away so that he can hold them. Takes my other hand in his as he steps closer.

'I'm in love with you, Laney. You were right about everything. I know I don't deserve you, but I can't stop myself from loving you and wanting you. And I'm selfish enough to come here now, knowing what I said last night, hoping you can forgive me, because I can't bear the thought of a life without you.'

I shake my head, not believing what I'm hearing, nor trusting the emotion blazing in his gaze. I believed in its existence once and look where I ended up—humiliated and rejected. I'm not ready to go there again. No matter what he says.

'Is this about your mother? Has she discovered the truth and you've come running to—?'

'No—God, no. Although she knows. She knows everything.'

'Everything?'

He nods.

'The marriage?'

'Yes. She already knew. They both did.'

'Both?'

'Your mother. My mother.'

'They knew all along?'

Another nod. 'It was your mother who tracked your phone to here—not that she would give me your location until she was convinced I was going to do the right thing.'

'Which is?'

'To make this fake arrangement real. To be brave enough to come here and tell you how I truly feel. Because you weren't the liar or the fool. I was, Laney. In rejecting your love, I was rejecting my own, breaking your heart even as I broke mine. I played the fool and I lied to you. But no more, Laney. I am head over heels in love with you and I need you to know that.'

'But I don't understand…what's changed?'

'Everything and nothing. When I woke up without you this morning my life fell apart. In twenty-four hours, I'd gone from being a man who had everything and didn't even know it, to a man who had lost it all because you weren't there to share it with.'

He cups my face in his palms, his intense green eyes urging me to see the truth.

'I don't want to wake another morning without you, Laney. I want to make changes—real changes. Starting with us…with you. I may not have had time in my life for a relationship before, but I sure as hell want to make that time now. I want to carve out a great big Elena-shaped hole and fill it with all the love I feel for you.'

I shake my head, feel the tears rolling down my cheeks. 'You're serious?'

'I've never been more serious about anything in my life.'

I give a choked laugh. 'I can't believe this is happening.'

'Please believe it. Do you need me to get that landlord back up here to witness my declaration? Because I'll do whatever it takes, Laney. Shout it from the peak of Mount Forbes, if I must. Make sure it's printed in every gossip magazine. Have it tattooed across my chest. Whatever it takes, I will do it.'

I'm laughing freely now, his desperation and crazy suggestions going to my head.

'Just kiss me.'

'Kiss you? Are you sure you don't want it tattooed? Because—'

I silence his words with my kiss, fill it with all the happiness and love I feel inside.

'That was far less painful than a tattoo,' he murmurs against my lips.

'Well, now you mention it, I always have had a secret love of ink…'

'You have?'

'No.' I hook my arms around his neck. 'But it was fun seeing your reaction.'

'You little minx.'

'You love me really…'

He sweeps his nose against mine. 'That I do.'

'And I love you. You may be a fool, but you're my fool, and I'll take that.'

His chuckle warms my very soul, and the kiss that follows sets it alight.

I wanted to make this Christmas perfect for the Monroes… Never did I anticipate it would be truly perfect for me too.

With my biggest wish coming true and our love, the greatest gift of all.

CHAPTER THIRTEEN

Aiden

'WILL YOU GUYS quit making up and get in here? We're waiting to do presents!'

I force myself to release Elena, though it's entirely against my will. Hers too, judging by the little grumble that she gives.

'Do you think Avery meant to say making *out*?'

I chuckle, bury my hands deeper into the rear pockets of her jeans, reluctant to move from our little alcove in the hall.

'I think she sees our inability to keep our hands off one another as an extended kiss and make up session.'

'Ah, in that case I like her thinking.'

She pops up on tiptoes, her mouth sweeping against mine, as my sister's bright red mop appears around the door.

'I'm serious! If you don't get back in here now, I'll start opening *your* presents.'

'I'm sure that's a crime,' I say, sweeping Elena into my side and ushering her forward. 'And just for being so impatient, I say we go first.'

'It's usually youngest first,' my mother pipes up from her chair by the fire. 'Or should that be guests first?' She looks to Elena's parents. 'It's been so long since we've had people here for Christmas I think I've quite forgotten.'

'Well, if it's okay with everyone,' I say, 'I'd like Elena to open the first gift.'

Avery grins. 'You'll hear no argument from me. She certainly deserves it for putting up with your antics.'

'Avery!'

'What, Mum? It's not like you're not all thinking it.'

'She's got a point,' adds Gabe.

'Cheers, bro!' I say, and they all laugh, taking great delight in my discomfort. 'It's not like you did so much better by my sister. If I remember rightly, you took some convincing too.'

'He's got a point...' Avery smirks, using her own man's words against him and following them with a peck to his cheek. 'The wait was worth it, though.'

I shake my head and stride up to the tree, mumbling, 'And on that delightful note...'

I ferret around at the base, find what I'm looking for and turn.

'Can you come here, Laney?'

She looks at everyone, eyes perplexed, her steps hesitant.

'I promise I won't bite.'

She laughs softly, her eyes lifting to mine and reliving a moment in this very house when she'd said a similar thing to me. Trying to reassure me that marriage was the right move.

Was it really only a week ago? It feels like so much has changed, and yet some things remain the same.

'My darling, Elena...'

I lower myself to one knee and raise the little box, open its lid. Inside, the ruby sparkles in the twinkling fairy lights, the wedding band too. All the women give a happy sigh, bar Elena, who looks as if she's forgotten how to breathe.

'Will you make this a Christmas to remember and take these rings as a symbol of our very real marriage and as a true token of my love and lasting friendship, always and for ever?'

She presses a hand to her throat, tears dancing in her eyes. 'As if you need to ask.'

'So, you will?'

It's gruff. I didn't realise until this moment just how much

I need to hear her say it. To know it's what she wants. No pretence. No end in sight.

'Yes, Adie!' She rushes forward and I leap up, squeeze her to me. 'Of course, yes! I love you so much!'

'I love you too.'

'Gee, bro… Giving her pre-used goods for Christmas?' Avery pipes up. 'Surely you could have gone one better than that.'

I break away long enough to send Avery a look, but she's already upon us, wrapping her arms around us.

'I'm so happy for you both!'

And then everyone is up, hugging us, kissing us, congratulating us. It's another five minutes before I have the chance to take Elena's hand and slip the rings back where they belong, where they've always belonged. On Elena.

My wife and my best friend.

Always and for ever.

My Laney.

My love.

EPILOGUE

Elena, four years later

'DO YOU THINK we should go and help them?' I ask.

Avery sips at her hot cocoa. 'And spoil our fun? Are you crazy? This is far too entertaining.'

'I never took you for the cruel type, Ave.'

'Cruel?' Avery laughs. 'It's just a bit of snow and tangled Christmas lights—they'll survive.'

'I give it twenty minutes before they call in the cavalry.'

'You mean Terry?' she asks.

'Yes! That's if they can tear him away from your mum. They've been inseparable since her remission.'

She beams. 'I know—ain't it cute? I think Mum didn't want things to progress until she felt more sure of things.'

'But Terry had other ideas anyway. When he started bringing dinner to her, it was only a matter of time before she caved and agreed that they were dating.'

'I know… It really is too cute. As for us helping with the decs—Gabe's already fussing enough. If I venture too far off this porch he'll have an absolute hissy fit.'

I smile as I take in the bump straining against the zipper of her bright red ski coat. 'A week overdue is no mean feat. How are you feeling?'

'Nervous. Excited. Terrified. All of the above. Maybe the little one knows and figures it's safer to stay inside.'

'Nonsense! You're going to make the perfect mother, Ave. Just as you've made the perfect aunt, twice over.'

A male expletive has us both biting our lips and looking back.

'Maybe your husband had a point after all,' I murmur. 'It looks like he's going to be sporting a sore bum, come morning.'

Gabe clambers back onto his feet, rights the illuminated deer he flattened in his fall, and brushes off his snow-covered behind—though I'm sure it's mainly his pride that is hurt.

'Next time our wives want extra lights put up,' he grumbles, 'we get them to untangle them first.'

'Sounds fair to me,' Aiden agrees, just as the front door bursts open behind us.

'Mummy! Daddy! Look what I made!'

Our eager three-year-old races out onto the porch, a small pastry delight in her outstretched podgy palm, her dark locks flying out behind her.

'Daddy's fav'rit!'

'Oh, wow, Rosie,' I say, dropping to my haunches to greet her. 'That looks delicious.'

'They taste quite perfect too,' says Terry, appearing in the doorway, the Rudolph's nose on his Christmas jumper flashing away.

'I figured there's no harm in passing down the legacy early,' Margot says, following close behind, her red apron covered in flour and my baby boy asleep in her arms. 'He was starting to stir, and I couldn't resist a quick cuddle before getting the dinner on.'

She gives me a sheepish smile that I laugh off. 'You never can resist a cuddle, Granny. Lucky for you, you'll have another tiny babe to enjoy soon.'

I take him from her and he immediately nuzzles in, looking for his food.

'Someone say dinner?' Gabe says, coming up behind us.

'Look, Daddy!'

Rosie trots up to Aiden and he lifts her into his arms, eyes the tart she thrusts under his nose.

'Is that for me?'

She nods proudly and he takes a hefty bite, chews it with relish. 'That's even better than Granny's.'

Rosie giggles. 'No one can make them as good as Granny.'

'Does this mean we're done with Christmas lights for today?' Gabe asks hopefully.

'Uncle Gabe,' I say, heading for the door, 'you know Rosie won't sleep properly until she's sure Father Christmas can see us all the way from the North Pole.'

'Which means…?'

'The more lights the merrier!'

He mutters something un-festive under his breath and Rosie gasps.

'Uncle Gabe! You're gonna be on Santa's naughty list!'

Everyone chuckles save for Avery. 'Erm, honey…?'

We all still. Turn to look at her. One hand is cupping her bump, the other is outstretched, holding the steaming mug.

'I think the lights are going to have to wait.'

'Well, thank the Lord for… Wait! What are you saying?'

Terry grabs the mug from her hand as Margot reaches around her.

'I'm saying, I think your child has other plans for their father tonight…'

* * * * *

COMING SOON!

We really hope you enjoyed reading this book.
If you're looking for more romance
be sure to head to the shops when
new books are available on

Thursday 7th December

MILLS & BOON

MILLS & BOON®

Coming next month

HOW TO WIN A PRINCE
Juliette Hyland

'Brie,' he started over. 'We have guests we need to see to. Expectations to meet.'

'Expectations.'

She propped her hands on her knees. In another time or place, they might have been sitting in the schoolyard waiting for their turn on the tennis or basketball court. Instead, they were in fancy clothes on the floor of his father's office—a room his brother still refused to convert to his.

'How can you possibly think of expectations? We don't even know each other. What, we just go out and role-play happily-ever-after?'

Role-playing was the name of the game. Hell, he'd expected his bride to be so excited. That way people might not notice his own discomfort. Instead, he was trying to convince her to go along with the day's duty.

'We have our whole lives to get to know one another.' Not exactly comforting but true.

'Our whole lives!' Brie stood, her dress swooshing with the quick movement. She walked past him and started pacing. 'Our whole lives, Your Royal Highness—'

'Alessio,' he interrupted as he stood. 'It is only right that you call me by my first name, too. At least in private.'

'In private. This can't be happening.'

He'd felt the same many times. Yet it didn't change what had to be done. 'But it is.'

'I don't want to marry you.' Brie planted her feet, preparing for battle.

This was not in the day's script. His mind raced; what was he supposed to say to that? The rebel buried in his soul shouted with joy before he reminded himself to keep calm. Duty was his life now.

Alessio sucked in a deep breath. That bought him seconds but didn't stop the pounding of his heartbeat in his ears. He'd spent a year figuring out how to make his father's goal a reality—a royal wedding for the country to rally around. Then another year prepping for today. It couldn't unravel. It simply couldn't.

There was no other plan. If this imploded today, Celiana's name would be in papers globally for days, maybe weeks.

For all the wrong reasons.

He could already see the headline: Princess Lottery Bust!

The success Celiana had gained would evaporate overnight. And coming home after his father's stroke, taking up the mantle of duty he'd sworn off, being the face of Celiana's resurgence…it would all have been for nothing. That couldn't happen.

'If you didn't want to be a princess, why was your name in the lottery?'

Continue reading
HOW TO WIN A PRINCE
Juliette Hyland

Available next month
www.millsandboon.co.uk

OUT NOW!

LET'S TALK

Romance

For exclusive extracts, competitions
and special offers, find us online:

f MillsandBoon

🐦 @MillsandBoon

📷 @MillsandBoonUK

♪ @MillsandBoonUK

Get in touch on 01413 063 232